9/14

Autumn Odyssey

Autumn Odyssey

A Novel

by

Thomas Wells

ISBN –9781497520066

ISBN –1497520061

1. Travel in Europe – fiction. 2. Prague and Brno – fiction. 3. Paris – fiction. 4. Venice – fiction. 5. Rome – fiction. 6. Athens - fiction I. Title.

Published in the United States by CreateSpace a division of Amazon.com.

ONE

I was sitting on the low wall next to the Saint's statue at Wenceslas Square in Prague, admiring the beautiful old city and quietly daydreaming when a woman nearby spoke. "Excuse me sir, could you tell me the time?" Her excellent English was heavily accented with German and I looked at my watch and answered, "Two-thirty." I could have turned away and thought nothing more about the incident, but I hadn't. I kept studying her longer than I knew I should, then wondering why I did. After all, she was no raving beauty and here I was alone in a strange city in a foreign country where I didn't know anyone. And like a typical American I didn't even know the language, either.

I looked again at the stately old buildings of honey-toned stone that sat so solidly on the Square as if they belonged there, looking much like little old ladies playing a game of bridge, each precisely knowing its place, while they looked skeptically at the new steel and glass structures that didn't quite seem to fit in as if they were some new young upstarts interrupting their game. But undeterred, the newcomers seemed to announce themselves proudly: We are part of the *new* Prague. The Prague where thankfully Stalin's communists are gone at last. Hurray!

Looking closely at the German woman I was surprised when my heart did one of its funny little skip a cardiologist had once told me was a quick double beat and not skipping a beat like it felt, and that it was nothing to worry about. But why should it do that when I was looking at this woman? And for some reason I didn't fully understand, I immediately sensed that this German woman was the kind of person I might like to get to know. Now, what in the world made me think something like that?

Later I could never explain to myself why I hadn't simply told her the time and turned away and forgotten the whole thing. And how did she know I could speak English? Probably my American clothes. But for the rest of my life I could recall her exact words and how she looked on what turned out to be that first special day.

Just at that moment while I continued looking at her but trying not to be too obvious about it, and hoping she wouldn't take offense if she did see me, the relative quiet of the busy square was disturbed by a group of young Americans; university students by the looks of them. Laden with their ubiquitous backpacks they came pushing and shoving through the crowd that was coming up the exit ramp from the Prague Metro's *Muzeum* stop, their logo sweatshirts proudly announcing their universities: Harvard, Yale, Brown, Virginia, Stanford. They were all busily talking and laughing at the same time in the loud, raucous way that's so typical of American young people. And even though I was irritated at their disturbing behavior, I couldn't help but envy their youthful exuberance and the intensity of their razor-edged enthusiasm for life.

For some reason I felt I ought to apologize for them, and I stole another quick glance at woman with the German accent, slightly embarrassed by the young Americans' disruptive behavior. I could see that she, too, was watching them closely, but at least not critically. In fact, she appeared to be slightly amused by them. But still, I wondered what could she be thinking of them and their behavior? And of me as well, my accent clearly identifying me as an American.

"Please forgive my young countrymen," I managed to say with a half-hearted chuckle. "They really do make quite a spectacle of themselves sometimes. And, of course, it's most usually in public."

"I suppose it must be part of their American frontier spirit. Vibrant, adventurous, afraid of nothing," she replied without rancor, her interest already aroused by the obvious attention of this handsome if not such a young American man. Yes, he really is quite handsome, she thought, casting another quick glance his way. Tall and slim and not too old. Possibly just a little older than my forty-eight years. No, not really too old at all. And she noted with an approving smile, he did not even have the beginning of a belly like so many men his age – especially the Americans. And he is ruggedly handsome in that sexy way some older men have; their looks and self-confidence having matured later but at the same time. Not at all like that overly aggressive Englishmen last night in the beer

5

garden, his hands reaching out to touch my arms, my shoulders as if he had known me for ages.

She felt herself flushing even though she was almost sure he hadn't seen her quick appraisal of him. But probably, she thought, glancing at his face again, my eyes are giving me away like they always do. And she had to admit she liked the way this American was smiling at her answer about the students, and she noticed immediately that his rather piercing green eyes were almost the same color as her own. And better yet, she sensed an element of sincerity in those eyes that was somehow very comforting as if he intended her no harm; more like a pleasant greeting in passing. A strange man in this foreign country who wished only to be nice to her; to just say hello and be gone. His smile was pleasant and friendly and not at all aggressive. His dark brown hair was flecked with silver at his temples and it was slightly long, but not in a greasy, unkempt hippie sort of way. And his high cheekbones gave him a slightly Oriental look. Or could it be part American Indian?

Her thoughts were interrupted by the laughter of the young Americans again, their voices blending with all the new sounds of the city of Prague that was once more on the move, this ancient city that was happily soaring into its newly resurrected freedom from tyranny.

"Maybe," I answered, amused at her reference to the American frontier. "But I doubt if any of them has any knowledge of the frontier other than what they might have seen in a Clint Eastwood film. And I do wish they would do it a little more quietly." We both laughed and I was glad I hadn't said more as I sometimes do.

"Excuse me Miss, my name is Richard Rouse," I said, stumbling a little, trying to decide if I should offer her my hand. Then I wondered why did I think I should introduce myself?

"And my name is Helga Wintermantle and I am very pleased to meet you Herr Richard Rouse." Her precise pronunciation of English words had already intrigued me.

6

"That's an odd, excuse me, ah, unusual name. Wintermantle was it?"

"Ja, it's German for winter coat," she replied, pronouncing the W like a V, an ingrained German speech pattern she was never able to overcome.

"And what do you do Miss Wintermantle," I asked, still struggling with the unusual name. "Is it Frau or Fraulein Wintermantle?" I tried to stop but I knew it was already too late embarrassing myself by asking what must surely have seemed an improper question. Asking if she were married or single.

"What is it I do? Why I live, that's what I do. I live every day to the fullest with what the French call the *joie de vivre*. The joy of living it means. However," she paused, looking closely at me as if trying to gauge my intent, then added with a mischievous smile, "I think you Americans mean something different when you ask someone what is it they do, Ja?"

"Ja, ah yes, I'm sorry. I didn't mean to be impertinent. And, of course, you are quite right about us Americans. We usually ask that question to find out what kind of work a person does. To categorize them, I think." I paused hoping she would say something to ease my embarrassment at what surely had to have been very improper questions about her marital status and what she did for a living. But she answered nothing, perhaps deciding to let me squirm a little.

.   "I suppose it seems rather rude to Europeans. But it's our way of finding out what status a person has. We very proudly claim to have no class system in our country, but this is only a thinly disguised way of finding out the same thing. Usually based on a person's occupation which, of course, translates into income."

"Ah, yes, the American preoccupation with money. I thought as much."

"I'm afraid you're right," I said slightly embarrassed at her all too accurate assessment of my comment about money. "And some might even call it an obsession," I apologized, trying not to sound offended or pretentious.

"Yes, I thought work or status was what you might have meant. We meet so many Americans over here. And, of course, we see your films. So we know of your interest in how much money a person makes."

"I am sorry. And I do apologize on behalf of my countrymen and our sometimes rather abrupt, if not crude way of gaining information." And rising, I made a slight bow while trying to keep a smile on my face and hoping I was not making a complete fool of myself.

"And I accept your apology on behalf of all Europeans," she said as she stood and very gravely gave a little girl-like curtsey. Then we both laughed at our silly behavior and I think we each felt a little tension slip away. And I was surprised how quickly my feeling of embarrassment had faded, and I realized how glad I was.

TWO

"And now for what, as you say, it is that I do?" she continued with another infectious grin, "I teach German in a small private language school here in Prague. It's just off Old Town Square on Celetna Street."

"That's quite a coincidence. I'm a language teacher myself. I teach English as a foreign language at Masarykova University in the city of Brno."

"So, if you teach at a university you must be ein professor, Ja?"

"Ja, ah, yes, I'm a professor with a teaching fellowship on leave from the English department at Tulane University in New Orleans. New Orleans is in the state of Louisiana."

"Ja, on the Mississippi River near the delta. We do study American geography in our European schools," she said with a teasing grin.

As the usual tension that comes with first meeting someone slowly began to ease, our conversation became a pleasant, rather low key exchanging of information about work and home and the other kinds of trivial topics two people use when just getting acquainted. And looking closely at her I was beginning to sense that something might be astir here, but certainly not saying or hardly even thinking anything yet. Certainly not yet. But I was already a little interested and I wished I could know what she was thinking.

"And where is your home?" I asked. "I mean, when you are not here in Prague."

"I live in Heidelberg, Germany," she said, "with my father when I am not teaching in Prague"

"Ah, yes, Heidelberg," I said, smiling at a memory.

"Have you been there?"

"Yes, I taught in Heidelberg for an American university on our military bases a few years ago."

"That is a coincidence – that we both know Heidelberg."

Abruptly, for some reason I wasn't quite sure I understood, an unexpectedly warm sensation stirred inside my chest, and I felt a strong urge to know if she was married. Since she hadn't answered when I asked before and I couldn't see a ring on her left hand, I decided to take a chance and asked, trying to sound more nonchalant than I actually felt, "And your husband? Does he live in Prague with you when you teach here?" The question sounded awkward and confused and I immediately wished I hadn't asked, at least not that way.

"You remember, I didn't answer Frau or Fraulein when you asked earlier. But I am not married so it is Fraulein Helga Wintermantle," she said with her faint, slightly mysterious smile.

Now, why did I think it was important that I know if she was married? But maybe I already knew. Or at least I hoped I knew.

THREE

Her answer about not being married gave me a surprisingly pleasant feeling and I wondered about it thinking, what in the world had come over me?   And confused though I was, I immediately realized I was glad she was not married, but I was still not quite sure why other than the usual male on the prowl thing.   Male on the prowl?   That's not really me.   Why did I think that?   I guess it's because we men just automatically evaluate women we have just met as . . .   As what?   A potential mate?   No, not that.   Not exactly.   Not this quickly.   A prospective date?   Yes, maybe.   Sex even?   Yea, I know lots of guys who think that way.   'Just checking 'em out for future reference,' my college roommate used to say.

I remembered trying, without much success, to explain to two young women teachers – one French and one Dutch – who lived in the single professor's house where I lived in Brno about how men are by nature visually attracted to women.   Apparently no one had ever explained that to them.   Makes one wonder about sex education, doesn't it?   But a male on the prowl?   That's not like me?   Not now.   Not at this age.   And not even when I was much younger.   Was I ever?   But on the other hand, just because I'm fifty-five doesn't mean I'm dead from the waist down.   Not by a long shot!   I still like to look.   And fantasize a little, too.

And looking more closely at her but still trying not to be too obvious about it, I realized she was prettier than I had first thought.   Although she appeared to be somewhat close to my age, there was a surprisingly youthful look about her and her charming smile made her look even younger.   She had a kind of fresh, wind-blown, adventurous look I've always liked in a woman.

Just then a balmy April breeze whispered pleasantly across my face, softly insistent and comforting and smelling of fresh flowers and I smiled, but I wasn't quite sure why.   Then I had another unusual thought.   I liked the feeling I had when I found myself smiling at this woman. Now, wasn't that an odd way to think about it? Enjoying smiling at someone? But then why not?

I see he is assessing my looks again, but this time he's not being very subtle about it, she thought with a slight smile. I hope he likes what he sees. But why should I care what he thinks about how I look? But strangely enough I do. Maybe the two things go together; his assessing my looks and my caring what he thinks of me. And why this interest in my marital status? As if I didn't know, or at least suspect. After all, I'm not a naïve teenager.

But then she found she really was curious about why he had asked, perhaps hoping to discover his intent. And deciding that maybe it would be better to take the direct approach, she asked point blank, "And you, Herr Professor Richard Rouse? Are you married?"

"No, not married. Divorced. A long time ago."

Now what could this mean? Another divorced American man who thinks all European women are easy marks? She considered a minute longer, looking so intently at him he began to squirm a little, apparently uncomfortable under her gaze. I wonder about his interest? I thought older men, especially the Americans I have read about and seen in films like the younger . . . What is that American word? Bimbos, I think it is. I am certainly not in that class and I'm sure I don't look the part, either. To be a bimbo I think one must be much younger and have a marvelous figure with large breasts and a very small brain.

But no, on second thought I don't think I shall worry about his intentions just yet. There's something about his eyes I like. I think there is kindness in those eyes. And he is certainly acting like a gentleman. Perhaps I should just wait a little longer and see. After all what could it hurt? Anyway, I'll probably never see him again.

But then her imagination unexpectedly took wings and she could vaguely see two people standing very close facing each other. But it was as if it were seen from behind a gauzy curtain. Now what could that mean? Who are they? And what are they doing? Or about to do? But just when she thought she might see who they were the fantasy evaporated, leaving her with only the mystery to wonder about.

They talked on, their conversation casually unhurried, and Richard found himself more and more intrigued by this unusual woman. But he couldn't quite put his finger on what that unusual quality was. And like a challenge he wasn't sure he understood he found himself wanting to explore it further.

She was, to my typically male eye, not overly pretty. Well, maybe a little bit pretty but . . . Then she's what? Cute? No, that's not it. Little girls are cute. She's more like . . . Oh, I don't know what. Good looking? Yea, but that sounds so mundane. Then what is it? Why do we men put so much emphasis on looks; struggling and grasping for definitions sometimes better left unexplored? Damn testosterone. But then what in the world would we ever be without it? And what it can lead to.

But right now, here on this old Square I was definitely thinking of the present as I stood there still doing the usual male appraisal thing. She's kinda tall and lanky. Seems to be almost as tall as my six foot one. Looks to be what, maybe five eleven? I know lots of men are intimidated by tall women. I guess it could be one of those equality things that are so current today that many men don't like because it threatens their fragile egos, and their, sometimes raging insecurities. But I have never felt threatened by that. In fact, I immediately liked her being tall. Liked being eye to eye when you kiss someone. Kiss? Now, why in the world am I thinking about kissing? But I looked closely at her lips anyway and found myself imagining what it would be like to kiss them and I wondered how they would taste. What an odd thought. Taste?

And being a man, of course I wanted to look at her figure, but she was wearing some kind of very long, rather drab coat. A kind of washed out green that looked like the color of over-cooked asparagus. So all I could see was her face. It was a pleasant face, warm and open and completely without guile as if she had no need for secrets. However, that turned out to be the best thing that could have happened – seeing only her face without the distraction of any of the other physical stuff. She had beautiful red hair and like Charlie Brown in the comics, I have always been attracted to red haired women. Her eyes were green just like mine and a few freckles were scattered across the bridge of her nose. It was a rather cute nose too, and it crinkled in a funny way when she laughed that seemed to make the freckles dance. And her laugh. Even her laugh bubbled with personality like her eyes and that freckled nose. Just then and quite unexpectedly a warm, pleasant thought occurred to me. Some lucky man could easily get used to those eyes and that nice smile.

I thought again about not being able to see her figure because of that long coat, but then her bright eyes and cheerful smile made me forget everything else. Well, not forget entirely. But maybe we should just say wait a little while longer and see? And what could be the harm in waiting? Might be nice. The poets have always said the eyes are the windows to the soul. And hers immediately seemed to allow a glimpse into the very special person that was deep inside. But when I thought about her being nearly my age and still single, I wondered if there might also be a lonely person behind that smile that longed to be set free?

I knew instantly with some kind of surprising insight that this woman must surely have a most wonderfully pleasant personality. I didn't know why I thought that, but I could feel it. Felt it deep inside myself like a warm, insistent hand beckoning, calling out to be understood. It was obviously more than just her being pleasant or witty or some of the other traits of a nice personality. Looking at her smile again, it was as if she radiated a kind of cheerfulness that was contagious, and I could already feel myself beginning to catch whatever it was. And there certainly didn't seem to be anything superficial or shallow about her. Most definitely no superficial.

Now why did I think superficial? She was certainly not anything like Jennifer Smartley my colleague in the English department at Tulane. Personality? Jennifer?

14

Those two words just don't go together at all. Jennifer was as hard as nails and often downright caustic with people. And she had absolutely no patience with those she considered her intellectual inferiors, and that seems to include most everyone. Personality? No, not Jennifer. But my God what a body! Which she could use very effectively, I remembered!

.

My thoughts returned to the German woman and what I realized was quickly becoming a special moment here on this old Square that was itself vibrant with the energy of the remarkable new changes everywhere. Maybe there's some kind of symbolism in that. New changes like my meeting her? And that personality of hers certainly seems to fit the definition for vibrant.

There was something profoundly pleasant about this calm, shyly smiling woman that was almost magnetic, and I knew immediately I wanted to get to know her. How could something like that happen? After a ten minute conversation? After all, I'm no starry-eyed teenager. I know my way around women. Or at least I thought I did. I do know I have always been cautious with women, especially meeting them for the first time. But somehow this time seems to be remarkably different, and I'm not quite sure why excerpt that I find myself liking it very much. And, of course, that made me want to find out more about her. Maybe lots more.

I think it was her smile that was so marvelously innocent that first attracted me. Not a little girl innocence, but something excitingly different from other women I have known that made me want to get to know her. There was something mysterious, maybe even mystic behind that smile. But at the same time there was an honest openness about the things she said that intrigued me even more. And there was also a hint of something warmly sensual about her that attracted me as well. Oops, there goes that testosterone, again.

I could feel myself beginning to get very interested in this woman, and even at this first meeting my stomach wanted to get into some sort of nervous flutter I didn't fully understand. Those sorts of things only happened in old Doris Day movies, didn't they; looking moon-struck at some woman you've just met? Of course, that's it. Just fiction like in the movies. But still I'm beginning to think . . . To think maybe I could . . .

Finally, making what I hoped would prove to be a good decision, I stood and turned to her and asked in what I thought might be at least a poor imitation of European formality, "Fraulein Wintermantle," I began hesitantly. "If you are not otherwise engaged this evening would you do me the honor of having dinner with me tonight?" I paused, waiting, my heart pounding.

"Ja, Herr Professor Rouse. It would be mein pleasure."

I relaxed as we both laughed at her partly German answer, and a long forgotten feeling tugged at my memory. I felt relieved like a teenage boy who, having just asked for a first date, had heard the wished for *yes* answer. And I suddenly discovered I had been holding my breath.

Just then a small cloud moved away from the sun and the bright April sunshine came sparkling off the saint's standard with its little flag making a warm glow they both felt. And each of them smiled at the same time without quite knowing why.

FOUR

Later on that first day when we had just met and I had invited the German woman to dinner, I came again to the Saint's statue in the last fading light of a golden sunset that was even now quietly softening the already beautiful old Square. The ceaseless hum of afternoon traffic with taxis honking for recognition was slowly fading like a wished for blessing at last granted.

I had bought a small nosegay of flowers from a wrinkled old lady street vendor whose faded blue dress had seen more washings than she could remember, and whose cotton hose were rolled down below her knees. When I had stopped and looked at her flowers obviously undecided, she said something to me in Czech as she gestured at the violets and she smiled a broad, gap-toothed smile. I smiled back when I paid her for the flowers and for what I found myself hoping had been some kind of romantic encouragement for the coming evening that lay behind her friendly grin.

Helga was sitting on the wall by the statue patiently waiting, an expectant look on her face. As I approached I felt an exciting little catch in my heart when I first caught sight of her. And when she saw me coming she smiled and said a little too loudly as if trying to cover up her excitement at seeing me, "Ah, there you are. I waited here."

There was something uniquely sincere about her simple greeting that was warmly pleasant although her face held a vague look of apprehension as if she had half expected me not to appear. But now she was clearly relieved that I was there and her bright smile told me so. And so was I relieved.

I caught a glimpse of a pretty dress with large, gaily printed flowers under that green coat, and I was glad I had changed to chinos and my navy blue blazer with my orange and blue University of Virginia tie.

Quite stylish, she thought with a pleased smile, looking closely at him and admiring his clothes. I see he dressed for our dinner. I think that was a nice thing for him to do.

17

When I handed her the violets she stood and smiled and murmured her thanks as she buried her nose in them.   Then she looked up smiling at me with tiny bits of pollen on her nose.   And when she held them against her chest she moved quite close to me still smiling shyly and looking into my eyes, and I felt that funny little catch in my chest again.

I offered her my arm and guided her between the large concrete planters in the center of Wenceslas Square that were overflowing with a profusion of bight spring flowers. I smiled, thinking that the flowers seemed to be sending a warm, evocative perfume across the Square, perhaps sending a message promising pleasant things to come.   Who knows, maybe this very evening?

Before we crossed over to Krakovaska Street away from the Square, Helga stopped at one of the planters for a moment to admire these other flowers, her fingers lightly stroking their petals and then smelling their perfume on her fingertips.   She smiled shyly and said, "These are nice, too."

'Yes, like you,' I mumbled under my breath and then wondered, why did I think that?   And did she hear me?   I had almost said it out loud.

But she was almost sure she had heard what he said and she was pleased.

When we started up the street we approached a KFC on the corner where the air was heavy with the delightful aroma of fried chicken.   "Thank heavens," Helga said with a sigh of relief as we passed on by.   "For a minute I thought that was where we were going to dine."

"Heavens no," I laughed at her suggestion.   "I make it a point when in Europe never to eat American food.   And most certainly not fast food, although their chicken is very good."

As if by mutual agreement we casually strolled up the street, and trying not to be too obvious about it I allowed myself a quick, admiring glance at her legs.   Nice, I thought.   And I'll bet the rest of her is nice, too.   Now why did I think that?

As we walked along I was surprised how quickly it felt as if we were two old friends out for a walk. Or better yet, a special couple on our way for an evening dining out, unhurriedly window-shopping along the way. And I was surprised again when I realized how it already didn't feel as if I had just met her. That feeling puzzled me a little, but then it pleased me, too. There was a pleasant freshness to this feeling and an unexpected newness which puzzled me; but it was a comfortable feeling, and I liked how it felt quietly unhurried.

While we strolled, I was busily trying to deal with this warm new feeling inside myself and wondering about it although I had to admit I was beginning to enjoy it. And wondering, too, what she might be feeling. And wishing I knew.

Each of them was busy with their own thoughts that were hesitantly beginning to reach out toward some as yet unnamed something. Richard especially, imagined the feeling was very much like a cloud slowly parting to reveal a beautiful scene; a feeling that was pleasantly warm and not at all disconcerting, but was still ambiguous and, of course, still cautious. Then he was surprised by a new thought. The most amazing thing about this evening is that I can already feel my usual caution with women I have just met quickly fading, almost as if it were melting in the presence of some vaguely warm source.

And the feeling each of them had in different measure, and unknown to the other, was a peculiar mixture of a warm emotional feeling for their being together, and a kind of adolescent excitement that comes with being on a first date. And he was suddenly reminded of what the American entertainer Jackie Gleason would have said in a situation like this, 'How sweet it is!'

There were also subtle attempts at wanting to be more mature about being together, and their not being entirely successful, especially on Richard's part when he kept remembering long-ago teenage dates. And they each smiled secretly at their new feelings, unaware that the other was also smiling.

The warm, comfortable feeling Richard felt as he walked slowly along beside her made him abruptly think how unlike this was from walking along the Riverwalk in New Orleans with his date Professor Jennifer Smartley, and his not being at all pleased with what he thought were her unnecessary, overly critical, even caustic comments about things she didn't like: in shop windows, people's clothes, teenagers' behavior, all sorts of things as if each needed her personal assessment. He often wondered if that gorgeous woman, Jennifer, had ever been happy. And what kind of childhood could she have had that made her so abrasive?

And thinking about Jennifer and the Riverwalk, I realized I was subconsciously comparing her to Helga Wintermantle whom I realized could never be as stunningly beautiful as Jennifer. But then I was startled by another new, wonderfully pleasant thought when I glanced at Helga. Right now, here in Prague at this very moment, I find myself feeling very happy. And I'm glad I have that feeling when I am with this woman.

When we reached the restaurant I opened the door for her. "After you madam, ah, I mean Frau Wintermantle. No, no. Wait, wait. I - mean - Fraulein - Wintermantle," I said slowly, deliberately emphasizing each word, and finally saying the form of address and her name correctly. She laughed, her eyes sparkling mischievously, "Perhaps you will learn to get it correct sometime soon, mein professor."

I liked the feeling it gave me when she said, sometime soon. Was she already thinking about future dates? And I remember as a teenage boy building up all kinds of expectations from something a date had said. Often something entirely innocent and usually with more than one meaning. But surely this woman wouldn't have said that about 'sometime soon' if she didn't have something in mind. And should I want there to be another sometime soon? Isn't that rushing things a little? Maybe I'm reading too much into what she says? But no, I really don't think so. And I found myself still not quite sure why, but I was beginning to hope not. And I've made up my mind not to let myself think a single negative thought about this woman. Not now. Not tonight. Not this unusual woman.

Standing just inside the restaurant door and hoping to see a vacant table, I glanced at her smiling face and I felt that funny little skip in my heart again and I thought, what in the world is going on with me?   Surely I'm not having a heart attack?   If I was I'd be dead by now.

The restaurant was crowded and very busy, but it still managed to have the kind of warm friendly atmosphere I remembered from having been there before. The air was heavy with the smell of roasting meat and the tangy, slightly musty smell of beer, and a few not so recently washed old men's bodies.

FIVE

Just then I saw proprietor approaching with a huge grin on his face, "Ah, professor Rouse, you honor establishment again," the proprietor Ivo called to him in his best broken English, the absence of articles in the Czech language making his limited English sound even more broken. Nudging his buxom wife who was busily drawing large mugs of beer, he asked, "And who is lovely young woman you have bring to brighten our evening?"

"This is Fra . . . Fra . . . ah, this is Miss Helga Wintermantle."

"And she is?" the proprietor asked playfully, as he enjoyed seeing Richard squirm a little. He and Richard had become good friends over the past year and each enjoyed a bit of teasing.

"She's . . . ah . . . We just, ah . . . We just met on the Square."

"Ah, Saint's Square is magic place, yes?" Seeing the violets in Helga's hand he lowered his voice and whispered to Richard with a knowing wink, "Good place for romance, I think."

Richard, trying to hide his embarrassment, quickly introduced Helga and she shook the man's beer soaked hand as she smiled disarmingly.

When they were seated, she asked, "Richard, you must come here often. They seem to know you, Ja?"

"Ja, ah, yes, they do, I mean, I do. Every time I come to Prague on a day trip or overnight I like to eat here. As you saw it's just one block off the Square but the prices here are about half of what one would have to pay at the touristy places on Wenceslas Square. And the food is much better and with larger portions, too. So, on a teacher's salary, ah . . . Well, I think you understand."

"I thought all American professors had very large salaries?"

"No, not so large. But here in this country I am on a Czech professor's salary. A visiting professor, I might add. And," he paused, thinking about something he found very odd, "I still can't get used to their paying in cash every two weeks. I keep thinking of coal miners somewhere lining up to receive their pay packets."

"How do your American universities pay?"

"They pay by check once a month. And if one wishes the check can be directly deposited into your bank account. You need never even see it."

She frowned at what she thought was an odd way of doing things.

With the menus in English that he had requested, Helga ordered Wiener schnitzel and Richard chose his favorite roast duck with mushrooms and roasted potatoes.

The tantalizing aromas coming from the kitchen near their table served to heighten their enjoyment of their own meals, and Helga quietly started a game of, What's That Dish? Each of them tried to guess what the waiters were serving as the young men hurried out the kitchen, and they laughed when they each guessed something different and both were wrong. And Richard added jokingly, "Maybe I should go to each table to see which one of us has guessed correctly?"

Helga, joining in with the joke added, "No, wait until the people leave and go look at the scraps left on their plates. You should be able to tell by the bones, especially if they had fish." They both laughed again and smiled at each other, and each of them was surprised by another unexpectedly warm feeling.

They ate slowly, savoring their food and this new experience of being together, and Richard found himself unexpectedly hoping the meal would last longer. He even toyed with the idea of ordering dessert which was something he had never done at other times when he had eaten there alone.

When they had finished eating and were having a second glass of the wonderful Czech beer, a group of unruly people at a large nearby table was becoming increasingly loud and boisterous. They began banging their mugs on the wooden table shouting in German, 'Bier hier! Bier hier!' Apparently demanding to be served more beer.

"Now it's my turn to apologize for my countrymen," Helga said, frowning at the rowdy Germans. She was acutely aware that their behavior was embarrassing her in front of this nice American whom she already realized she wanted to impress, hoping perhaps to get to know him better. "They are German tourists who come to Prague because they find many bargains here. But that is their beer garden behavior, I think. Not very appropriate for a nice family restaurant like this."

"Then I suppose this makes us even," I suggested. "I had to apologize for the young American students. Now you have to apologize for your fellow Germans. Maybe we should make a fresh start."

She nodded, flashing her bright smile. "Ja, I think a fresh start would be nice." Very nice indeed, she thought, looking at his handsome face.

That incredible smile! I really like looking at her–at that smile. And hearing her perfect English with that neat German accent. What in the world is going on here? I'd better watch myself I could get used to this. I'm not exactly sure what I meant when I said maybe we should make a fresh start. I know it's just an expression, but she really picked up on it right away. But still, I do think I'd like to make, ah . . . What would a fresh start mean, anyway? And why did I get that strange tingling feeling when she agreed? I don't know exactly what's happening to me, but whatever it is I'm beginning to enjoy it. She's really very nice to be with.

Whoa, now. Just hold on a minute, Dick, he cautioned himself. You better look before you leap. I mean, you don't really have any idea what's going on here, now do you? And why am I thinking in clichés? Look before you leap? Yea, I know. Pretty weird, huh? But really I do like this feeling.

24

SIX

Walking down Wenceslas toward Old Town Square where she directed him toward her lodgings, he couldn't help thinking about what he would do when they reached her door. Should I try to kiss her? Shake her hand? Surely not shake her hand! But what then? Did other guys think about things like this? I remember as a teenager every time I took a girl home I went through this same thing. Should I try to kiss her? Especially if it was the first date? But what if she says no? That'd be a serious putdown, wouldn't it? Maybe no more dates? What a gut-wrenching decision about something so simple. But he remembered that in those confusing teenage years nothing seemed simple. And here I am thinking about it like a teenager again.

I've read about what girls and women, too, say about the dating ritual, sometimes called the dating game. But I guess the women do have a point, sitting there waiting by the phone hoping to be asked out, never knowing for sure until the phone rings. And what if it's the wrong guy? Damn, I never thought about that. But at least they don't have to stand there with the phone in their hand feeling like some kind of a dummy like we guys do. Waiting for, even expecting excuses. Or worse yet, not very subtle rejection? 'I'm Sorry, I've have to wash my hair Friday night.' Oh, come on give me a break, will you? What a crappy excuse.

I don't suppose it's like that these days. More likely the woman would be calling the man. But at my age I guess I'm still a little old fashioned. And in a way I'm glad. I like the man doing the asking, behaving like a gentleman opening doors, helping her to be seated, getting her wrap, all that sort of stuff. And I can't help thinking that women today still would appreciate that kind of thoughtful, attentive consideration.

But I wouldn't be offended if a woman asked me out one of these days; especially this woman. When I think about it that would be a very nice compliment. Out of the hundreds of guys she knows she would be asking me. I wonder if women ever think about it that way when they are asked out. Probably not. But then what do I know?

But the kissing dilemma remains. Even if she wants me to kiss her, how am I supposed to know? I'm not a mind reader. And if she does, then what? Even at fifty-five I'm still not sure I know what to do. And what's the European thing to do? Or more importantly, what's the Czech thing to do. Hey, wait a minute she's not Czech, she's German. Maybe that's different, too. Man, I really am confusing things.

I really don't want to mess this up. I think I'm beginning to like this woman and I certainly don't want to seem too aggressive. But then not being assertive enough can be just as bad, maybe even worse. I sure don't want to come across like some sort of wimp. And I certainly don't want to mess this up with some hormone thing and act too aggressive. But we guys are so hormone-driven that I think not kissing her would seem like some kind of masculine failure on my part. And believe me I'm not too old for one of those hormone things!

I think our ages, hers and mine, actually makes it more awkward because each of us probably assumes the other one knows everything about love and romance and stuff like that. Like by now we're supposed to be so sophisticated and worldly. Oops, did I just say love? Better watch yourself, Dick.

But what if I tried to kiss her and she said something like, 'Why don't you act your age? You are too old for that sort of thing.' Then what would I do? I guess I'd look for a rock to crawl under and die of embarrassment. But she doesn't seem to be that kind of person. And I really don't think she is. Surely not? At least I hope not. Can a person ever be too old for a kiss; too old to appreciate an outward sign of someone liking them? How could anyone object to that? I really don't think she'd be like that. No, I really don't.

A few minutes later when they approached her lodgings on Jakubska Street, Richard stopped and hesitantly took her hand. And hoping to postpone the kissing decision a bit longer, he said hesitantly, "My train for Brno leaves tomorrow afternoon at four-ten. Would you have lunch with me before I leave?"

"But of course. I was hoping you might suggest something like that," she said, her heart racing a little.

Now, why was her, 'But of course,' so much nicer than a simple yes? And she said she had been 'hoping I might suggest something like that?' It's absolutely amazing how a few well-chosen words can make a simple answer seem so much nicer; so much more complimentary as if it meant something special to her. But I don't think her words were well-chosen so much as they just seemed to be her naturally pleasant way of answering my invitation; a completely unaffected expression that showed the kind of person she is. An answer like that makes it sound so much more sincere and . . . and encouraging. More heartfelt. Yea, that's it. Like she sincerely means it. Something like that can really make a guy feel encouraged. Like he's somebody special. A man could easily get drunk on expressions like that. And I'm already amazed at the things this woman has said that sound so simple, and yet are so laden with feelings. Like her, 'but of course,' rather than a commonplace, yes.

"Shall I meet you let's say about twelve o'clock tomorrow?" I finally managed to ask.

"That would be fine. But where?"

"Why not at the Wenceslas statue again? For good luck?"

"So you think we should have good luck do you?" she said with a mysterious smile. "But yes," she added quickly, "I think that would be very nice. I like your idea. I will be there."

There's another one of those really nice, simple but very special answers. She could have just said yes which would have been fine. But her 'yes, that would be very nice,' was so much more pleasant and sincere because it seemed to go straight to the point, sounding almost ordinary until you have time to think about it. And then you realize her words had just a little something extra that made them remarkably different. Something

27

that seems to come straight from the heart that made it a world away from ordinary; special because the words were so completely unaffected. Completely spontaneous, and yes, even enthusiastic. That's the part I like – her being enthusiastic. There seems to be no pretense about this woman. And that's what I'm already beginning to like about her. She seems so unaffected, so natural. And enthusiastic about being with me. Now, that's a great feeling! I wonder if women ever consider how the things they say can make guy feel?

When have I ever had a woman act enthusiastic about being with me? Can't remember. Must have been a long time ago. Well, there was that cheerleader at East Carolina University years ago, but I'm not sure that counts. She wound up marrying my roommate, Charlie.

I looked again at Helga's pleasant face smiling at me expectantly as if waiting for me to say or do something more. Still I hesitated, but I was not quite sure why. What was I supposed to do now? What is she waiting for? Is there some European thing I'm supposed to say or do now? I once saw a movie where an Italian man said *permiscion* every time he wanted to kiss Ava Gardner. I think he was asking her permission for a kiss. Is that what I'm supposed to do now? But this isn't Italy. Now what'll I do? Surely asking her permission would sound ridiculous.

She paused a moment longer watching him closely, her eyes locked on his as she seemed to be thinking very seriously about something and was obviously waiting. And then, solving his dilemma for him, she said with a smile, "Aren't you going to kiss me goodnight?"

"I would like to," I said, slightly taken aback, "but I was afraid you might think me an overly aggressive American since this is only our first date."

She liked the warm feeling his looking straight into her eyes gave her, and she smiled at him, liking his answer. Did his saying 'only our first date' imply there might be more to come? That would be nice to think about.

28

"But in your American films the man always kisses the girl on the first date. Often quite passionately."

"Perhaps we are too forward?"

"Perhaps. But then maybe . . .

There was another of those awkward pauses filled with promise. Or could it a warning not to . . . Not to do what? Come on Dick, lighten up. Don't try to analyze it, just go with what's happening. After all, she all but suggested you kiss her.

I looked into her beautiful green eyes, and making my decision, I put my hands on her shoulders and gently pulled her close and I kissed her lightly on the lips. I was pleasantly surprised at how soft her lips were and that they were actually sweet tasting. But then I felt my kiss wanting to turn into something more until I knew I had better stop. Well, there goes that hormone thing, again. That and her asking me about a kiss. What a

nice charming way to make a guy feel wanted. I liked her bit of assertiveness, asking if I was going to kiss her. And what's equally important is that her little assertive gesture didn't push her into some different kind of aggressive category. Not at all. It was really nice. You could almost say ladylike. My God, my heart's thumping again.

"Goodnight Helga Wintermantle," I said, a little more breathlessly that I had intended. "It has been a most delightful evening and I look forward to our lunch tomorrow."

I stood waiting on the sidewalk until she reached her front door and began fumbling for her key. As she stood there with a gentle evening breeze ruffling her hair, I imagined that the overhead light was spotlighting her smiling face in a kind of elegant portrait. She looked back and gave me a smile and a little wave. After she opened the door she gave another wave and disappeared inside.

I thought about the kiss and liking how tall she was and that we were almost eye to eye when we kissed like I had thought earlier.   And licking my lips I tried to recall how sweet her lips had tasted.   That was really something.

Minutes later I found myself skipping down the cobbled sidewalk like a young kid, thinking how my large adult frame must have looked so out of place with my childish behavior.   And I didn't care.   I was that pleased at how well the evening had gone.

SEVEN

In her room Helga lay on her bed and thought about their evening together, and especially the goodnight kiss. That was very nice, she thought. He is a good kisser. Not sloppy or aggressive like some men. He was rather hesitant, I think. Is he really that shy or was he just being a gentleman? Either way he's nice, and I think I would like to see more of him. I especially liked feeling his arms around me. Not crushing in some absurd macho way, but warm and comforting like a . . . I am not exactly sure what it felt like, but it was very pleasant and it felt very comforting. And non-threatening. It was very nice and very special, I think.

A few minutes later her roommate Monika Schmitt came in and immediately noticed the mysterious smile on Helga's face.

"I have just met a man," she said before Monika could ask, knowing how easily Monika could read her face – almost like reading her mind.

"Oh?" Monika said in that noncommittal but questioning way of hers that always seemed to get her friends to share their deepest secrets with her, but helped keep hers to herself.

"Yes, he's an American and he is nice. Seems nice, anyway," she added trying not to sound overly enthusiastic.

"So, tell me about him, Helga. You sound excited."

"I think I am. I mean, I know I am. Excited, that is. But after all, I just met him today and he seems very nice," she repeated.

"That's nice," Monika said, repeating Helga's appraisal of this unknown American that made them both laugh.

"It was just a chance meeting at Wenceslas Square. All I know is that his name is

Richard Rouse.   And he's an American."

"You already said that," Monika chided nicely.

"And he is a professor at Masarykova University in Brno."

"Do you think you will see him again?"

Helga thought for a minute.   "We are having lunch tomorrow before he takes the train back to Brno," she said with a small sigh.

"Oh?" Monika said with another of her knowing looks.

EIGHT

Later that night after seeing Helga home, Richard sat on the side of the bed in his hotel room thinking about what he now realized had turned out to have been a very special first date with that unusual German woman. He was surprised at how he kept thinking of her as unusual. But the word just seemed to fit perfectly as if it had been invented to describe her and no one else. And she most surely was that – unusual.

But unusual can also have a negative connotation. He remembered old lady Ramsey in his hometown everyone described as unusual. But she was a cranky, ill-mannered, gossipy kind of unusual. But this German woman, this Helga Wintermantle, was unusual in a nice sort of way; in a special sort of way he had already decided. He smiled when he remembered her name. Even the last name was unusual. Wintermantle? Winter coat? What an odd name. But somehow it seemed to fit her in a warm, comfortable sort of way. Like a coat? he chuckled. And her smile, her laugh, her bubbly personality made her unusual in such a nice way. Bubbly personality? It's been a long time since I've heard that expression, or used it myself. But it fits her. Fits her perfectly. "Bubbly personality," he said aloud, liking the feel of the words on his tongue.

Trying to remember every detail of their date, he ran his fingertips over his lips, remembering how soft and sweet her kiss had been. He couldn't remember when he had ever thought a woman's lips were that soft and actually sweet tasting except maybe for Mary Alice, his wonderful high school sweetheart ages ago. And the kiss tonight was that same way. Almost like a loving kiss.

Come on now, loving? Get real, Dick. Well, there certainly seemed to have been a great deal of feeling that went into it. He smiled and touched his lips again, almost kissing his fingers as if testing, and he thought again about their date, playing it over in his mind, trying to remember every detail, how everything seemed to have gone so well. Actually it had been just about perfect. There had been virtually no awkwardness and certainly no playing of the vicious little mind-games as so often happens. It had been, he thought, playing the evening over in his mind again and again, extraordinarily nice in its simplicity. I think that was what impressed me the most about her. Her quiet, unaffected simplicity. But calling it simplicity is misleading because it was an elegant kind of simplicity and not really simple at all. I guess you'd call it straightforwardness. I think this woman has a great deal of character.

But then thinking about the date, his mind turned unwillingly to his first date with Jennifer Smartley, and he marveled at how different this first date tonight had been from his first date with Jennifer. He had just joined the faculty at Tulane University when one day Jennifer came by his office and introduced herself. He had seen her in the hall and the department office a few times, but up close he was even more awed by how beautiful she was. After a few minutes of conversation he was surprised when she asked him, "Why don't we go out to dinner Saturday evening, okay?"

I must be more old-fashioned than I realized. I thought it was the guy who was supposed to do the asking. Must be one of these new feminist things. And the way she said it didn't leave any room for him to decline.

"I'll pick you up at seven," Jennifer said.

"Well, yeah," he stammered, still shocked at her aggressiveness. "Do you know where I'm living?"

"Of course. I've already checked."

The Court of the Two Sisters restaurant was at its best. The September night held a pleasantly hopeful feeling as it was just beginning to cool off after a sultry day. The moon was almost full and the palms swayed in a light breeze. After they were seated at one of the outdoor tables in the courtyard Jennifer glanced at her menu and then handed it back to the waiter and proceeded to order for them both. "I hope you don't mind my ordering," she said matter-of-factly as if that was her usual routine on a date. "I come here

34

quite often. I think you'll like what I ordered."

He did like it, but still . . .

After dinner she said, "I feel rather tired tonight. How about if we make it an early evening and just go back to my place for a glass of wine?"

Later, in her small but elegantly furnished apartment after one glass of wine, she said, "Don't you think we might be more comfortable in the other room?"

Richard was pretty sure the only other room was the bedroom unless she meant the tiny kitchen, and he had an idea that was not what she had in mind as he cautiously nodded yes. Standing next to her bed Jennifer put her arms around his neck pressing her breasts firmly against his chest. "You're a very handsome guy, Richard. I think you and I are going to get along just fine," she said as she began unbuttoning his shirt.

What followed was the most aggressive, the most domineering session of sex he had ever experienced. She told him how to take off his clothes and where to stack them neatly on a nearby chair. She even told him in great detail what position she wanted him to get in and finally, exactly how he was to perform.

"I hope I didn't shock you too much," she said afterwards. "I guess you could say I have this thing about control. You didn't mind, did you?"

How the hell do I answer that?

He hurriedly dressed, hoping he was not showing undue haste and he left as quickly as he thought appropriate, feeling almost as if he had been used like a prostitute. He wondered if maybe he should have looked to see if she had left any money for him on the dresser. It was very much like being a slab of beef on a hook. I hope at least I was USDA Prime he tried to joke with himself. He grimaced, wondering if she cut notches on her bedpost like an old West gunfighter.

They dated occasionally after that but it was always at Jennifer's invitation and under her conditions. Each time he was amazed, no, appalled would be a better word, at her aggressiveness. But it was hard to ignore that gorgeous body.

NINE

The next day Richard met the German woman, Helga Wintermantle again at the statue on Wenceslas Square, and together they strolled down the street talking quietly as they looked for a place for lunch, eventually stopping at an outdoor terrace in front of the Hotel Ibis. A dozen or more small tables lined the terrace, each covered with a blue and white checked cloth. Their table was next to one of several large planters that were overflowing with the bright spring colors of impatiens mingled with petunias. The setting seemed perfect for the kind of quiet, leisurely lunch they were both hoping they would have.

They talked quietly while they waited for the waiter to bring menus, and Richard found himself thinking more and more that he did indeed want to get to know this unusual woman better. Who knows, maybe a lot better? There's that word unusual again. What could that mean? Something good, I hope. Surely it means something good.

He glanced at Helga as she was busily examining the nearby flowers, and in a twinkling of an eye he was borne away on the wings of a fantasy, flying to some romantic place with blue water and trees laden with small green things. He thought maybe they were olives but he couldn't be sure. And best of all, there was a woman with him and she seemed to be on her knees planting some very small flowers, but he wasn't quite sure who she was. But no, after another moment's thought he was almost sure he knew who she was. Then he realized he had pulled her to her feet and had his arms were around her holding her very close and she was smiling. And he tried to change the fantasy so that it would be her, but then it faded when the waiter appeared.

"I've always wanted to see some of those romantic Greek islands," Richard said thinking about the fantasy and pushing their conversation into new, uncharted waters. "I have heard so much about them. How beautiful they are."

"Romantic?" she said teasing, but there had been a slight hesitation in her voice.

"Yes, you know, the kind of quiet peaceful atmosphere that's so, so comfortable and pleasant," he faltered, finishing lamely. Why did I avoid repeating the word romantic? What could that be about? Trying to be a little careful, I guess. But he knew he would definitely like to get to know her better, and he watched her face while a faint, mysterious smile played on her lips.

"And I, too," she said, hoping she was not being too aggressive, "have always wanted to go there." But then to soften her suggestion which she thought might have seemed a little too forward, she added, "Many German tourists like to go there."

Nearby two young American girls were struggling with the Czech menu while from inside the hotel lobby the strains of a Chopin Concerto floated softly in the air. The warm, soothing music contrasted with the haughty demeanor of the waiter who stood glaring at the girls as if they had made some grievous error by not knowing his language. And it was clear he had no intentions of helping them.

He must have learned to be a waiter in Paris, Richard thought, recalling similar experiences there. Even though he spoke a fair amount of French, Paris waiters all seemed to act that same way. They really are a haughty lot. A French friend had once told him that they even treat other Frenchmen that same way.

"May I help you?" he asked the girls.

"Oh, thank heavens," one of the girls gushed. "An American! Do you speak Czech?"

"Only a little, what did you want to order?"

"Just some tea," the two answered together.

"Just say *chaiz,*" he replied with the native pronunciation. One of the girls wrote it on a napkin when he spelled it for her and she practiced saying it. "It's like saying the word size but beginning with CH," she said with a grateful smile, thinking how pleased she was with herself.

"You've got it," he complimented the girl, thinking to make her feel like she had accomplished something. "And always say *prosim* pronounced like pro-seem, which means please," he said, pronouncing it phonetically for them. "Everywhere you go in Europe people really appreciate it if you at least learn to say please and thank you in their language. It's the least we Americans and Brits can do since most everyone over here now speaks English. And by the way," he said with a smile, "you had better learn how to ask where is the toilet in every language." They all laughed although they knew the suggestion was a valid one.

"That was most kind of you, Richard Rouse," Helga said with another of her bright smiles. "To help those young girls like that. I think you are a kind-hearted man; a rarity these days, I think. Is rarity a correct English word?"

"Yes, it is. And I thank you Fraulein – Helga – Wintermantle," I said very slowly, enunciating each word carefully. After a pause adding, "I think I finally got it right again, didn't I?"

She clapped her hands gleefully, "Ja, mein professor, you got it right again. *Das vast sehr gut (*that was very good). Soon you will be speaking perfect German like a native" she said, laughing heartedly at her own joke.

Then she looked closely at him and smiled her gratitude, again liking the warm sense of security his comment about her name made her feel. And she found herself hoping there might be more, maybe many more occasions like this. But who could say for sure about a thing like that? And was it a mistake for one to wish for such a thing so soon? But why not? Surely it wouldn't hurt, she whispered to herself. The wishing, I mean. When we are together I feel something inside myself that I like very much. There is such a nice warm, comforting feeling here when I look at him and when I am with him, she thought, hardly aware she was gently touching her chest over her heart. And it is a very good feeling. Is it wrong for me to be feeling this way so soon? Maybe I shouldn't, but the way he smiles at me I think maybe he, too, has the same feeling.   Who knows?   But I do hope so.   Already I hope so.

At three-forty five that afternoon Richard was sitting on a bench at the Prague main railway station waiting for his train back to Brno when he looked up, surprised to see Helga approaching.

"I thought I would . . .   Now, what is that American expression I hear in your films?   See you off, I think it is?"

"Yes, that's it.   And what a pleasant surprise it is to see you here.   I didn't think I would see you again after lunch."   He paused thinking for a moment, would it be all right to say something else that was on his mind?   But if I'm thinking it, why not go on and say it?   "However, I do hope to see you again sometime soon.   Perhaps when I come to Prague next time?"

"Or I might come to Brno some time," she said smiling brightly.   He noticed she didn't make it a question, and his imagination unexpectedly took wings again.   Now what could she mean by that?   Come visit me?   That would be nice.

"If that would be all right?" she added, hoping to lessen her aggressiveness a little.

"Of course, it would be fine" I answered happily.

Just as I was about to step onto the train she reached for my hand and hesitantly pulled me into her arms.   And her lips were softer and even sweeter than I remembered from last night.

As the train pulled away I looked out the window at Helga cheerfully waving goodbye.   Her bright smile was so real and unaffected and I thought about her virtually inviting herself to Brno, and I was pleased, and not at all shocked.   On the contrary, I was surprised at how much it pleased me.   I couldn't say exactly why, but I really was very pleased.

I've always said I don't like aggressive women. Like that Jennifer Smartley. But I do like assertive women. Women who know who and what they are and have a mind of their own and say what they think. And I think I've found myself a winner! Or did she find me? But then what does it matter who found whom?

And now I don't think there's much doubt about where I'll be next weekend.

TEN

Later that evening back in Brno, Richard was sitting on the side of his bed in the *Lektorsky dum* (the visiting professors' house) thinking about the weekend and having an earnest conversation with himself. He was talking out loud, as if hearing what he was saying might help him understand what had happened the past two days.

"What happened back there in Prague? This weekend? Just last night, I mean? Was it a dream or did I just meet the most unusual woman I have ever known? Unusual? Did I say unusual again? But no, it was far more than that. Much more than just unusual."

Well, what then? a sly little voice inside his head said.

"I'm not sure I know how to describe it, but it certainly was something special. Something quite, ah . . . It was like . . . Like . . ."

What are you trying to say? Remarkable?

"Yea, I guess that's it. It really was remarkable."

Oh, yea?

"Now wait a minute, I'd better think about this carefully. What's that old saying? It's always best to look before you leap? And why am I thinking about leaping? Metaphorically, of course. Would that mean jumping into something unknown with this woman? After all, she's not even very good looking. Sort of tall and lanky. Well, maybe a little bit good looking in an understated kind of way, but she's . . . she's so . . ."

She's so, what?

"I don't know. Just special in a funny sort of way."

A funny sort of way? That's a strange way to put it. What's that mean?

42

"I'm not sure. But it feels like she's . . . Like she's something special. Yea, that's it. Something really special."

Now just hold on a minute. You're already getting carried away. You know how you are. You just said she's not even all that good looking.

"Yea, but looks aren't everything."

Oh, yea? Since when?

"What the hell am I saying? She's the most interesting woman I've met in . . . in twenty years."

Yea, yea, yea, that may be. But you don't even know what's inside that awful green coat, do you? Bet you wish she had taken it off, huh? You better think about what you're saying, Dickie boy.

Trying to get a firm grip on himself, he thought again about the green coat and not being able to see her figure.

"Thank goodness I've finally reached the age where a woman's looks are not the most important thing to me. Still important, yes. Very important. But not the only thing. Not like when we guys were so painfully young with our out of control hormones, and all we could think about was boobs and buns and nice legs with maybe pretty hair thrown in for good measure."

Come on, Dick, act your age. You're thinking like a teenager, again.

"Yea, I know. But it does feel kinda nice in a way funny sort of way." After a moment's reflection he thought: "Why do I always have to act my age? Why can't I act like a lovesick teenager if I want to?"

You? A lovesick teenager? Come on, now.

"Okay, okay. I get your point. But still, she's so, so . . . unusual," he said with a

43

sigh. "Act my age? I remember one time when Jennifer Smartley told me to act my age on the Riverwalk when I was pissed about something and I was complaining rather loudly about it. And I wanted to tell her, 'Go to hell, will you! You're not my mother. You can't tell me what to do.' But I didn't say that. And maybe not speaking my mind at times like that is why I've wound up where I am today."

Okay then, where is that?

"Fifty-five, single and alone. That's where I am, dammit. Through no fault of my own, I might add."

Oh, come on now, get real will you? You know your being single and alone are just as much your fault as any of the women you've ever known. Maybe even more your fault if the truth were known.

"Getting a little personal, aren't we?"

Well, you asked for it.

"So, what am I supposed to do now? Sit here on my butt and let the opportunity with this German woman pass me by? I don't know, but it sure would be safe. "

Opportunity? Safe? Damn, you're starting to sound like some kind of stockbroker. For God sake she's not the first woman you've ever met and taken out to dinner. What's the big deal?

"That's just it, I don't know. But there certainly is something, that's for sure. She's so different. I do know I really like the feeling I get when I'm with her."

Feeling? What kind of feeling is that?

"That's the problem. I'm not even sure what kind of feeling it is. It just kinda makes me feel funny inside."

Funny? You already said that.

44

"Yea, funny. But a nice kind of funny. You know, sort of a warm glow like something nice is happening."

You know you're beginning to sound like a high school sophomore again, don't you? I suppose you remember that time you finally got up the nerve to ask Barbara Rowe, the girl next door, to go to the dance with you after the football game, right? And you saw her teasing her little brother and dancing around on her back porch that afternoon as if she was really excited about the coming evening – excited about going out with you.

"Yea! Going out with me! That was it. Isn't it amazing how something that simple can be such a boost to a guy's ego? At the time it just blew my mind she was that excited about going out with me. Later after the dance, I drove my dad's car down to the river and we sat in the moonlight until I finally got up the nerve to kiss her. And I was surprised how aggressively she kissed me back. And I liked it. Liked it very much. And now I'm just as surprised and pleased that it felt that same way last night when Helga Wintermantle asked, 'Aren't you going to kiss me goodnight?' What a nice feeling that was."

You really liked that, didn't you?

"Damn right I did. I really liked that feeling way back then with that high school girl. And now I think I'm starting to feel that same way again."

Oh, boy, here we go again.

ELEVEN

Back in Prague the next Friday afternoon Richard, his heart aflutter, realized how much he wanted to see the German woman again; that unusual Helga Wintermantle. During the week he had practiced saying her name to himself, making sure he got it just right, and hoping he would have another opportunity to use it.   Yea, that'd really be great.

When he jumped off the train and began hurrying through the station, he suddenly stopped, struck by an awful thought.   How am I going to find her?   Maybe I should go to her lodgings.   But that would be rather presumptuous, wouldn't it?   And besides, I'm not even sure I remember which street she lived on.   But if not that, what then?   I could go to her language school but I'm not sure where that is either.   She mentioned the name of some street last weekend but I've already forgotten that one, too.   I was too interested in other things – like thinking about Fraulein Helga Wintermantle.   And because I missed the three-thirty train this afternoon I'm sure her school will already be closed even if I knew where it was.   I guess I was too busy last weekend enjoying that smile and looking at her legs.   I wish I could have seen more.   Damn green coat.

Suddenly desperate to figure out how to find her, his heart unexpectedly racing, he was beginning to panic when he remembered the telephone.   Of course, the telephone! How stupid of me!   When he had been buying his train ticket this afternoon he had seen the small scrap of pink paper carefully tucked away in the corner of his wallet.   Thank goodness I asked for her phone number last weekend just before my train pulled out.

The phone rang and rang while he fidgeted, his heart seeming to try to keep time with the steady, rhythmic ringing.   Just as he was about to hang up in defeat a woman answered, her German accented voice declaring it must be Helga and his breath caught in his throat.   He'd found her!   But she identified herself as Helga's roommate Monika Schmitt.

"May I speak to Helga Wintermantle, please?"

"Who is this?"

"I'm Richard Rouse, the American professor she met last weekend."

"Ah, yes, of course. But Helga is not here."

When the American identified himself, Monika paused for a moment, undecided. Maybe she should help her friend Helga who had been so excited last weekend, and she decided to add, "She has gone to Wenceslas Square."

Taking a chance, but knowing I shouldn't, but I asked anyway, "Did she say why she was going to Wenceslas Square"

Monika paused a moment, then decided, why not? "She said she was to meet someone."

"To meet someone?" I croaked, unable to hide the disappointment in my voice.

"Someone special, she said. She sounded very mysterious." Monika decided she probably should say no more. Could this be a different American?

My heart sank and I forgot to thank the roommate when I hung up. Oh, no, how could this happen!

Monika was still holding the phone thinking about what she had told him, I hope I didn't interfere with her plans. I guess I could have told him more but I think that should be up to Helga.

A cloud of doubt began to settle around Richard's shoulders, enveloping him like an unpleasantly cold mist. He thought about sitting down for a minute and trying to think what to do but there was nowhere to sit near the pay phone. Just he and an old Czech man nearby who was staring at him oddly.

I wanted desperately to ask this Monika person who Helga was meeting, but I didn't dare. Suppose I asked who it was and the roommate gave a name. Or even worse, what if later the roommate told Helga about my call and the two of them laughed at my adolescent eagerness? Oh, no, how could this happen? And why did it suddenly seem to matter so much? Why should it matter at all that she was meeting someone? After all, I've only met the woman once. No, twice. I forgot about the dinner last Friday night. It doesn't really matter if she is meeting someone, does it? Of course it does! Dammit, I already like this woman. No, wait it was three times, I forgot about the lunch. No, it was four. She came to the train station to say goodbye.

But who could she be meeting? What if it's someone she'd known before and suddenly he's come back into her life? Recaptured her affection as if he had never been away. But when could this terrible thing have happened? Just this past week? And why did it have to be a man? It could be a woman friend I thought, trying to force myself to be upbeat. Sure, probably just a girlfriend from school. But no, the roommate's voice had conveyed a different meaning in a decidedly different tone as if Helga had shared a romantic secret with her. And where does that leave me? Striking out? Out before even reaching first base or what? I can't even think of an appropriate baseball analogy. Left standing there looking foolish with egg on my face? Damn! What do I do now?

I was tempted not to go. But I knew I had to go to the Square – had to see for myself if she really was there and with someone.

As I hurried past the Hotel Savoy I recalled how last year the nice young man at the desk had helped me get a call through to VISA in America to report my stolen credit card. Although I have always considered myself a savvy international traveler, I had been completely fooled by the group of three pickpockets who, to distract me, pretended to be laughingly drunk as they bumped up against me when the subway started with a jerk. I never even felt a hand in my pocket. Thank heavens it had been a BankofAmerica Visa card with my photograph on it. Probably that's why it had never been used. I suppose the pickpocket and I didn't look at all alike.

Rushing headlong on the crowded sidewalks I found myself walking fast, pushing through the crowds, oblivious to hard looks and muttered comments, then running the last few blocks toward Wenceslas Square all the while trying to imagine her there alone, but failing. I finally managed to make myself slow down thinking, why am I hurrying? Would rushing to the Square make me seem even more adolescent? I had to fight the temptation to turn around and go back the way I'd come, the fear of being disappointed at what or who I might find with her threatening to overwhelm me. But then again I would die of curiosity if I didn't go. What else could I do?

My heart was pounding out a strange, unhappy tune. What if she isn't there at all? Or worse yet, what if she's sitting there with some guy? Then what should I do? Walk right on past? Pretend I didn't see her? Surely that would be too obvious. It might be better not to go at all. Maybe not knowing she is or isn't there with someone would be easier.

He stopped, thinking again about turning back. But no, not really, I can't do that. That would just create more doubt, more mystery. My mind would be in a muddle for days. And after all, the roommate had said that was where she would be. And to meet someone special she'd added. As if I weren't already nervous enough.

He started again, hurrying in the direction of the Square intent on exactly what he wasn't sure, but hurrying nonetheless.

In my panicky hurrying I had momentarily forgotten how much the intensity of this new feeling about this Helga person surprised me with its hint of promise. But then it came rushing back with an unexpected bitter sweetness, teasing me, shaking my resolve, making my knees weak so that I had to slow down. And the gloomy vision of someone else being there was fighting with my excitement when I remembered last weekend and the kiss. Yes, that's it! Focus on the kiss. Like the battle cry for Texas independence. Remember the Alamo! Only this time, Remember the Kiss! Remember the Kiss!

Please don't let anyone else be there, I kept muttering as I tried not to hurry. But then I was running again, unable to stop myself.   Please don't let anyone else be there!

And suddenly there she was sitting near the Saint Wenceslas' statue.   Alone! And I thought for a minute my heart had stopped.

And Helga felt her heart leap when she saw him coming, pushing through the crowd of young people gathered around the Saint's statue.   He was dressed in jeans and an Oxford cloth shirts rolled up to his elbows and he had a sweater tied around his neck.   She immediately thought that his hard lean body made him look like an overgrown teenager. And she was surprised that she wanted to touch him.   He had come!   Come to find her!

"Ah, there you are," she said, trying to speak calmly as he hurried up completely out of breath.   It was as if she had been expecting me that very minute.   "I was hoping you might return.   And so you have.   I waited here."

She had been waiting for me!

Her simple, direct words found some deep hitherto untouched corner of my heart, making me dizzy with excitement and pleasure.   Her calm comments were so unpretentious and so completely without guile I could hardly believe my ears.   How could a woman say something so calmly that sounded that simple and yet make it sound unbelievably intense?   And in that simple intensity there was a hint of the complexity of her personality I was just beginning to grasp.   And I knew I wanted to understand it better. Probably much better.   Oh, yes.

"I was hoping you might return," she said repeated softly.   "I waited here."

Someone could write a book about those words, Richard thought.   Or at least a poem.

I marveled again at how any woman could be like this.   So many young people today seem to be intent on playing mindless little games at being coy, hard-to-get.   A kind of, *See if You Can Guess What I'm Thinking* game.   And you knew you were finished if

50

you guessed wrong. And guys play it too, not just the girls.

But not this unusual woman. She's so . . . so . . . Oh, my God, I can't believe it! She had waited here. Waited for me! She seems to be so . . . I had to stop myself. I couldn't catch my breath. Had she really said, 'I was hoping you might return?' Yes, she had! She really had! And when she said it my insides turned to jelly. No, more like Jell-O, all aquiver. And then she'd said 'I waited here' like waiting for me had been something very important.

And as I stood there like an ill-at-ease schoolboy I could feel my face flushed with excitement. Or was it embarrassment? Or exertion from running? No, I think it was excitement. Yes, I'm sure it was excitement! Excitement over finding her here waiting. Waiting for me! Can you believe it!

She couldn't possibly hear the pounding of my heart, could she? But if she could I'd have to say it was from running. But then running to find her was just as adolescent wasn't it? She couldn't really hear my heart, could she? But now, looking at her smiling face I didn't care if she could, adolescent or not. I was still so nervous my tenuous grip on reality tried to say no, she couldn't hear it, but I wasn't sure. And why was I thinking like this and feeling this way? Feeling giddy? When have I ever heard that word used lately? Giddy? But it fits. Yes, it surely must be from the excitement of finding her here alone. Excitement? My God, yes! Giddy with excitement!

Go slow, Dick! *Just slow down, now!* Oh, shut up, I warned that voice inside my head. Just leave me alone to enjoy this. Oh, my God, I still can't believe it! She had been waiting for me. Expecting me! She'd said, 'I waited here.' I don't think I will ever forget those words.

"I had to come," I mumbled still out of breath. "I mean I thought . . . that is, I hoped you'd be . . . maybe you'd be . . ." My God, I'm babbling like an idiot and I can't stop myself. What's she going to think? That I'm some sort of a wimp? Certainly not that. Oh, Lord, I hope not.

Come on Dick get hold of yourself. After all she's only a woman.

Yea, I know, but she's . . . she's so . . . so special, so unusual.

Yea, you already said that – about twelve times.

Just then she smiled that magical smile at me again and tentatively reached out and took my hand and said, "Sit with me?" And her warm hand in mine told me everything was going to be okay. And when I looked down at her hand I could see the pulse pounding in her wrist, and I thought I could feel *her* anxiety, *her* worry, and *her* delight. Her delight? Oh, yes. I think she's as delighted as I am. I can see it. I can feel it. It was definitely delight that showed on her pretty smiling face. I'm sure of it. Smiling at me. Oh, my God, smiling at me like that! At me! Just me! There's no way I can find words to explain the wonder of this moment. The intensity of what I'm feeling is threatening to consume me – and I love it!

When I sat next to her she was still holding my hand and I tentatively reached out and touched her face with my fingertips, and when she smiled at my touch all my worries vanished. Just then the sun spangled the old Square in a blaze of glory, and I knew I had never known sunlight to be so vibrant with such amazing clarity, illuminating everything in its path with a golden glow. And the thought came to me that if only I could make this moment stand still I think I might. Gladly. And the intense bittersweet pleasure of that moment was more than I thought I could bear. But I did bear it and wished for more. Maybe a lot more.

TWELVE

As they walked away from Wenceslas toward Old Town Square, the suave, sophisticated Richard Rouse, man of the world, breaker of more than one woman's heart, timidly reached for her hand, cautiously glancing at her for her reaction. And she, still trying to calm her own pounding heart, looked up at him and smiled shyly like a very young schoolgirl. Then feeling him squeeze her hand, she smiled at him again with more confidence.

The warm sunlight filtering through the plane trees along Wenceslas dappled the sidewalk with shifting patterns of excitement and promise. Promise? Well, maybe, I thought. Yes, please, why not promise? Maybe promises? I'm sure I would like that.

While we strolled, I gradually forced myself to calm down and enjoy the walk and the sensuous pleasure I could feel radiating from her closeness, and the delightful sights and sounds and smells of the city, but never letting go of her warm hand. I could smell the earthy, age-old aroma of freshly baked bread beckoning from inside a small neighborhood bakery, while quietly nodding flowers on the sidewalk in front of a florist shop happily shared their subtle fragrances with us as we passed. And as always, there was the tantalizing aroma of sausages cooking on a street vendor's stand where Helga spoke to the old man who smiled at her, clearly showing that they knew each other.

As we strolled my heart was finally beginning to calm down, and I found myself fantasizing that we were on a shopping trip together, collecting food for our supper in some imaginary place in the countryside. Maybe a cottage on a remote Greek island like the one we had talked about last weekend. And quietly studying her features, I smiled at the images and the pleasant vision they evoked. And of course I knew she would be there in the fantasy.

Abruptly I looked around at the beautiful old city, realizing I was enjoying the sights and smells of everything as if I had never known them before; thinking vaguely it was as if I had never been to Prague. It's like I'm seeing this wonderful old city anew because I'm with her and neither of us has ever been here before, and we're discovering it for the first time together. Together? I like that word. Has a nice sound to it. Together? I smiled thinking: It's almost as if the air is fresher, the streets cleaner, and more people seem to be smiling. Smiling at us I imagined, and I found myself smiling at complete strangers.

Once, standing close to her when we had stopped waiting for traffic on a busy cross street, I caught the unmistakable perfume of her hair that smelled of lilacs in bloom. And I was immediately enveloped in a soothing feeling as if I were standing in a beautiful meadow among acres of flowers. And I was disappointed when the light changed and she pulled on my hand and we began walking again.

"Where are we headed?" I asked as we passed elegant shops already filled with American clothes and Italian shoes, showing off the rapidly encroaching abundance of Western life and making a mockery of the drab, utilitarian bleakness of communism.

"I thought you might like to go to Old Town Square and see the clock."

"Yes, that would be nice," I answered, but my thinking was miles away from old clocks. It was already beginning to fill my mind with what I hoped were not impossible dreams; dreams that insisted on becoming clearer moment by moment as they edged ever closer, and I warned myself to slow down, but without success. Even though the dreams startled me with their surprising vividness, I welcomed them like reading a good book and wanting to hurry on to the next chapter.

Glancing at her in an unguarded moment when she stopped to look at some shoes in a shop window, I found myself wondering what could she be thinking. I hope she's thinking about . . . I don't know exactly. What do I want her to be thinking? If someone were to ask her at this very moment what had she been thinking, what would she say? I hoped it would be about more than shoes she had seen and liked. Would it be about me? I hope so. I really do hope so. But only if it was something good. I chuckled under my breath thinking again about our preparing supper together in a cottage on a Greek island.

"Why did you laugh just now?" she asked.

"I was thanking something funny."

"What was it about?"

"Just something about myself. And a Greek island," I added after a moment trying to make light of it, but still hoping she would remember our comments last weekend about Greek islands.

"Oh? Thinking about a romantic Greek island again?" she said with a mischievous twinkle in her eye.

She had remembered! And she had remembered the romantic part. What would she say if she had known what I was really thinking? But she couldn't read my mind, could she? And thinking about the romantic vision I had just had, I almost wished she could.

Standing at the rear of the crowd at Old Town Square, she timidly reached for my hand as we watched the three tourists groups whose guides held aloft their ever-present umbrellas like flags calling for their charges to 'rally round the flag boys.' And girls, too, especially since most of the tourists were older women in sensible shoes.

THIRTEEN

Several hundred people, all anxious to see the promised show, crowded close to the ancient astrological clock, their upturned faces alive with excitement as they waited for the hour to strike with its dancing figures. And a few moments later it did. She had timed it just right I thought, and I gave her hand a squeeze for thanks.

"I think the way the skeleton jiggles about is very funny," Helga said, laughing and pointing. "Don't you?"

"Yes, he reminds me of my older brother who is very thin."

"I hope not that thin," she said. And when we both laughed I realized quite unexpectedly how our laughter together had begun to resonate like . . . like what? A song? A poem? A melody? That's kinda silly, isn't it? But whatever it is, I still liked the sound of her laugh. And especially our laughter together because that meant my heart was beginning to feel happy, hopefully along with hers.

Later, on a narrow street with those quaint little shops on either side, we stopped to get away from the jostling crowds for a few minutes. We looked at the puppets in a shop window, pointing to the comical ones and laughing together again. "That one with the odd nose looks just like my grandmother who has a very crooked nose," Helga said pointing, and we both laughed uproariously at the image we both saw, but then we tried to stifle our laughter in our hands.

"There's one that looks like that skeleton in the clock," I said. "They must be brothers." And we laughed even louder. When people began looking at us strangely we laughed again, trying unsuccessfully to stifle our laughter, our hearts slowly relaxing and becoming carefree like small children just freed from school for an unexpected holiday eager to enjoy the newness of this strange as yet unnamed thing that each of us was beginning to feel. And like happy, excited children anticipating a special treat they hoped was coming, we wondered what it could be? When would it come? And how would it feel?   Would we like it?   And quite unknown to the other they each smiled inwardly and hoped so.

As we resumed our slow stroll along the cobbled street we talked very little, simply enjoying the sights and sounds and the pleasant walk and our being with each other, our hands still warmly entwined, and I was reminded of a woman I had met in one of those wonderful jazz places when I had first moved to New Orleans.   I swear that woman could talk the ears off a brass monkey.   I sure was glad to get away from her.   But this woman, this Helga Wintermantle – I like saying her name to myself – is not at all like that.   This is the only woman I have ever been with anywhere that I feel perfectly comfortable not having to talk every minute.   The thought surprised me, and I felt that same pleasantly warm sensation in my chest again when I gently squeezed her hand.   What a difference! This is really nice!   Everything about this is very nice.   And we continued strolling along the street, each of us enjoying the pleasantly companionable quiet.

At first seeing his serious expression Helga gave him a quizzical look, but then she smiled and squeezed his hand in reply to his touch as if she, too, were feeling something very special.

The sparkling newness of their feelings caught them both by surprise again and again, easily taking their breath away but easing their doubts, too.   It was a new feeling that was still an unknown, perhaps even unknowable.   But no, that couldn't be.   Not this new thing that was already beginning to pulse with a life of its own, clambering for their attention, already whispering softly in their ears demanding to be heard.   Both of them, Richard especially, heard the whispers and wondered could this really be?   Could this really be happening to me?   To us?   This easily?   Already feeling this special?   This soon?   Even the pigeons that cluttered around their feet seemed to sense their pleasure and smiled funny little pigeon smiles.

Well, didn't you expect it to be this nice? that voice said in his ear.

No, not at first.   And certainly not this quickly.   Not like this.   This soon?

57

Come on now, I tried to restrain my thinking. Even those mushy old romance movies weren't like this – everything happening so quickly. I don't know, but I think I'm already hoping so. Yea, I guess that's it. But even at that it's still surprising. It feels so . . . Oh, I don't know how to put it into words. So comforting, calming even? But that sounds so mundane. But at the same time it's an exciting, almost a raging feeling that's reaching out for something. But it's a good kind of exciting feeling. Yea, I guess that's it. It's so . . . so . . .

So what? Nice?

No, it's more than nice. Already this is much more than just nice.

And he was taken by surprise realizing that from the very beginning how much he had hoped it would be this way with this unusual woman.

FOURTEEN

After having a sausage for lunch at one of the numerous street vendor's stands, Helga suggested as she wiped the grease from her fingers with a paper napkin, "I think I must show you the Mala Strana."

Richard, who had been there several times, nevertheless asked innocently, "What is that?" *I don't think I should tell her I have already been there and disappoint her. Probably best not to. No, don't disappoint this special woman. Now, why do I keep thinking things like that? Unusual woman. And now, this special woman? Well, sure, but that's exactly what she is. Special? Yes, at least to me. My heavens, yes!* And he felt a warm, pleasant shudder run through his body.

"It's called the Little Quarter across the Vltava River on a hill where the president lives. And there is Prague Castle and many government buildings and St Vitus Cathedral. He's the Czech's patron saint. We can take the tram up and walk back down. There will be many steps but it is all downhill."

"Take the tram? Oh, yea, I've seen them going by. But we call them streetcars in New Orleans."

"Yes, I know. I have read the Tennessee Williams play, *Streetcar Named Desire.*"

"You never cease to amaze me. You know American geography and now American literature. What next?"

"And I read it in English, too." She smiled sweetly and said nothing more thinking that leaving just a hint of mystery would be all right. Maybe just to let him wonder about some things a little longer. But not too long. No, not too long at all. And she smiled thoughtfully, thinking it would be nice to see what else he might say to her. And like the curtain opening on a play, she was anxious to see what came next.

They sat close together on the small wooden seat as the tram clattered happily up the hill to Prague Castle, and once more Richard found that his heart seemed to be pounding with that same exciting rhythm, keeping time with the clacking of the tram's wheels. My God, I really do like this feeling. Whatever it is.

Come on now, Dick, the voice reminded him.

Yea, yea, I know, calm down. Okay, I know I should wait a little longer to see what happens. After all, what's the hurry?

But looking at her again he found himself thinking, I'm not sure how long I want to wait. How long I can make myself wait?

FIFTEEN

After they had walked through the president's rose garden where a guard had allowed them to take a few pictures, and to please him they had taken his picture, too, they were strolling past the two fancy dressed guards at the entrance gate to Prague Castle when Richard nudged Helga and whispered, "Did you see that young guard? Standing there so stiff and rigid at attention never moving a muscle. But I noticed his eyes were following a very pretty girl as she walked by.

"Well, yes," Helga smiled and quoted: "In springtime a young man's fancy turns lightly to thoughts of love."

. "Yes, and in America we have a joke. In springtime a young man's fancy turns lightly to thoughts of what a young girl has been thinking about all winter."

"This is very true," she said laughing. And taking his hand she found herself hoping maybe it could be true. Could this really be happening? This soon? But who knows? And she had to remind herself not to forget what the grandmother with the crooked nose always said about not counting your chickens before they hatch. But still, I already think I would like for something to happen. And surely there is no prescribed period of time one must wait for love. Love? Did I say love? I suppose one should just let it happen in its own good time. But somehow I have this unexpected urge to hurry. Why is that? Maybe at my age I want to – now, what is that expression I hear Americans say – just get on with it! My heart already says that maybe it would be all right. I do hope so. Maybe it could even be quite delightful, and she smiled an even deeper inner smile. Yes, it definitely would be more than just nice. But I suppose I should still be a little cautious.

As they walked down the hundreds of steps away from Prague Castle toward the river, Helga pointed to a small house and explained, "That house is where the famous Czech writer Franz Kafka was supposed to have lived. But I have heard," she continued,

61

"there are thirty-four houses in Prague where he supposedly lived. Either his family moved every year, or more likely, I suspect some of those places are the invention of unscrupulous tour guides."

Later, approaching the Charles Bridge over the broad Vltava River, Helga paused at the old tower and pointed to one of the many statues that lined each side of the bridge. "There is the statue of St. Vitus, the Czech's patron saint," she said as she walked over and rubbed the head that was already bright and shiny from thousands of hands. "Come, you must rub his head, too. For good luck."

"Oh, do we need good luck?"

"Yes, I very much hope so," she said with a bright smile. "But perhaps we should just make our own luck."

Now what could she mean by that? Something good, I hope. But I walked over and rubbed the shiny head anyway. Why take chances?

Those mysterious comments she makes every now and then, like making our own luck, really are intriguing and I like that they never seem to be overly cautious or threatening. Actually, they are just the opposite. They sound encouraging. And I'm already learning to take at face value the things she says. Like needing good luck or making our own. This woman says exactly what she thinks and feels, and I find that really remarkable. And I like it.

Further along the bridge we stopped to watch one of the many puppeteers performing on the bridge. His silly looking puppet wore a cowboy hat and boots and he had a long crooked nose, and he was happily dancing as a small crowd gathered while the puppeteer played rock and roll music on his tape player.

"Maybe he's grandmother's brother," Helga said laughing as she pointed at the puppet's nose.

Standing behind her as we watched the puppet, my hands lightly on her shoulders, I looked at the bridge and the Prague skyline and then back at Helga as she reached back for my hand and I was seized with a sudden shudder. But it wasn't a fearful shudder. It was a decidedly happy shudder as if I had suddenly remembered something very pleasant like the kiss last weekend. And in my imagination I could picture her on a swing like in one of those TV soap commercials, swinging very high and flashing her bright smile.

And his heart sang with happy music only he could hear.

But just then a small moment of doubt gnawed at the edge of his consciousness. Was he really ready for this? For even the slightest hint of commitment. Commitment? Who's talking about commitment? Am I rushing into something here? Into what can only be a momentous change?

Whoa boy, better slow down. After all those years of being alone, the voice whispered in his ear.

Just then a slight tingle stirred inside him again as Helga shifted her weight, her body brushing against his, her hips warm and exciting as they pressed against him, and he found himself thinking very earnestly, I don't want this to end. No, I really don't. After another long thoughtful pause he whispered to himself, I don't want to rush into anything, but I really don't want this to end. I know I don't. I already know I want to see what's coming next.

At the end of the bridge we turned right and walked through an arcade of shops and out onto a sidewalk overlooking the river. I could smell the sweet musky odor of the tumbling water as we sat on a bench and watched the river as it rushed over a weir, hurrying on to . . . To where? Like our lives, he thought abruptly. Like everyone's life. Going on to what? To who knows where? But isn't taking a chance on something going somewhere better than doing nothing? And I found myself whispering a silent prayer hoping that we would . . . Now, what did I hope? But I was pretty sure I already knew.

Just then the most startling revelation of the day dawned on me. I've been enjoying being with her so much today I hadn't even noticed she was not wearing that long green coat. And even then I gave only a quick approving glance at her rather nice figure, so captivated was I just by being with her.

SIXTEEN

The one hall phone in the Lektorsky dum rang incessantly, demanding attention until Matthew Smithson came out of his room and down the steep stone steps to answer it. Matthew, the young Englishman who seemed to have been around forever, knocked on Richard's door and shouted, "Phone for you, Dick. Sounds like a young lady. Is this what you have been up to recently, you old dog?" he teased when Richard opened his door. "Going to Prague every weekend?"

"Oh, go away, you bloody Englishman," Richard laughed. "And, by the way, this old dog is learning some new tricks, thank you very much," he added, trying to make his grin as mysterious as possible as he took the phone hoping it was Helga. But who else could it be? Surely not that old woman in the University library who seemed to have taken a liking to him? He'd only tried to be nice to her, but he was afraid she may have mistaken his attention for flirting.

"Hey, bring her to the party Saturday night," Matthew called with a parting shout. "But you have to find her a strange hat, you know."

His heart racing, Richard picked up the phone surprised at how much he was hoping to hear Helga's voice, and not knowing exactly why he thought it might be her. But it was her and he grinned foolishly then looked around self-consciously to see if anyone had noticed. But then he realized he didn't care and he grinned again.

"Richard, I think I would like to come see you this Saturday. I have never been to Brno. Would that be all right?" I hope he will not think I am being too forward, she worried.

Would that be all right? Richard thought, repeating her question to himself. It would be wonderful. She must really be interested. Wanting to see me again this soon, and on my own turf at that. And he remembered her virtually inviting herself to Brno that first weekend when she came to the Prague railway station to tell him goodbye.

65

"That would be wonderful," I said trying not to sound too anxious even as my heart insisted on having another of its funny little skips. "When do you think you'll arrive?"

"The railway schedule says a train will arrive in Brno at thirteen hundred hours. That's one o'clock in the afternoon the way you Americans tell time. Will that be all right?" she repeated a little more excitedly than she intended.

"There's a train at five a.m. Why can't you take that one?" he teased.

"Now you are being silly, Richard," she laughed. "But I would very much like to see Brno. And you. I will be there at one o'clock. Will you meet me at the station?"

"Of course I'll be there," he added emphatically already seeing the scene in his mind. He, rushing across the station platform grinning from ear to ear and seizing her in an enormous hug. And she, falling into his arms in sweet and complete surrender. Sounds like a grade B movie. Why is it when we dream of things we want to happen they always seem to work so perfectly? But in reality they seldom ever work out that same way. Well, at least not often enough.

For the next two days he was in a kind of daze. Even his advanced Business English class noticed right away and his favorite student Vitezslava Hodova asked if he was okay. "Yes, of course. It's just that I'm having a visitor Saturday and . . ." I stopped, suddenly aware I was about to tell my students something very personal. But this was something so special I didn't want them to know about it; didn't want to share this new, wonderful discovery with them. Discovery? What a strange way to think about it? But yes, that's exactly what it was. A miraculous discovery. Or had she discovered me?

I was slowly drawn into a vision of being with Helga in some far away romantic place like before, only this time it was even better. And in this vision we were laughing together and gazing into each other's eyes. And her lips were moving as if she were telling me something very important, and I was smiling happily back at her. I wished I could know for sure what it was she was saying, but it was enough that she was talking excitedly to me. And best of all she was smiling a shy, encouraging smile.

Returning to the reality of the classroom where his students sat waiting, their faces showing their confusion over his dazed look and the prolonged silence, he was remembering how he had become good friends with Vitezslava and her family and had often been invited to their home. And each time her mother and grandmother had prepared a wonderful Czech dinner. When he had first visited in their home he had been surprised to see all their shoes lined up in the hall near the front door, and Richard had dutifully slipped off his shoes, hoping there were no holes in his socks.

On a recent occasion they had had wine and cheese in their garden under an apple tree, and he remembered it had been springtime and pink apple blossoms kept falling in his wine glass. He found himself thinking again about his affection for their family and what future he could envision with Helga, and he whispered to himself, 'I think I would like to stay in this country longer.' And thinking about Helga again, he added, 'Maybe a lot longer.'

It was Saturday just past noon when he came to the Brno main railway station, knowing he was much too early. And he stood anxiously waiting on the platform, looking at his watch every five minutes. When the train finally arrived Helga stepped off and she stood looking around at the bustling crowd. When she spied him standing nearby she gave a little wave and rushed into his arms, all thoughts of restrained ladylike behavior forgotten. And their long, lingering kiss was much better than that first time. And even better than the ones just last weekend, too.

They took tram Number 3 to the end of the line, holding hands and laughing at the silly things they said to each other as they tried to cover up any lingering nervousness about being together. But already that tense, uncertain feeling that comes with starting a new relationship was fading, and a calmer more comfortable feeling had begun to replace it, although his heart continued to have that strange skipping each time he first saw her. But

67

that fluttering had begun to be a pleasant feeling as if it were a sign that good things were coming. And she, too, was giving off what he thought were unmistakable signals that she was thinking very much the same way. Maybe even more so than he, although he couldn't be sure. Probably best not to try to guess a woman's feelings. Most men who do are usually wrong and they wind up getting into trouble.

While she was looking out the tram window at some of the unfamiliar Brno sights Richard was closely studying her face and trying to recall when he had ever felt this excited about being with a woman. Any woman. Certainly not with his wife Mary even before they were married. And even less so afterwards. What a disaster that had been! And he had most definitely never felt this way about Jennifer Smartley. Jennifer with her perfect body was about sex – nothing else, just sex. He sometimes found himself thinking that the opinionated, abrasive Jennifer could have easily been a Nazi storm trooper, or whatever the female equivalent might have been in those days.

At the end of the tram line they got off and walked the four blocks to the Lektorsky dum while he gave her a running commentary on some of the sights in the neighborhood and some of the people in it. But his nervousness at having her on his home turf kept him on edge and he found himself repeating things like twice pointing out the shop where he usually bought his breakfast rolls.

When he opened the front door to the Lektorsky dum they almost collided with Matthew Smithson who was on his way out. After a quick introduction by Richard and a thoroughly appraising look at Helga by Matthew, Richard hurried her to his room, but not before Matthew could shout, "Don't forget, she has to have a strange hat tonight, you old dog!"

"So this is where you live?" Helga commented as he showed her his corner room. "But there is only one bed," she said with an impish smile eyeing the one very small single bed.

"Yea, but we could . . . ah, I mean couldn't we just, ah . . . I could get the

68

maintenance man to move another . . . ah," he stammered. Regaining his composure he reluctantly pointed to the yellow house across the street, "I have asked the lady in that house if you could have a room over there for tonight. She rents rooms and I'm sure she speaks German. Many of the older folks here learned it during the Nazi occupation in the nineteen-thirties and forties.

"You said something about a party tonight," she asked. "And that I must have a hat?"

"Yes. You just met Matthew Smithson few minutes ago. He's quite the party man and he's giving a party tonight in our basement all-purpose room, and in order to attend everyone must wear a strange hat. It's called, needless to say, Matthew's Strange Hat Party."

"It sounds like it might be fun."

"The stranger your hat the better. And by the way, you should feel right at home. There are five young German language teachers living here."

"But I must have a strange hat."

"Don't worry. We'll get you one when we go out later this afternoon. You said you have never been to Brno so I want to show you the sights."

69

SEVENTEEN

Later on the tram ride to the center of old Brno he pointed out the opera house where he told her that Thomas Edison had personally designed the lighting. And he said it was on Malinouskeho Square which was named for the Russian general who had liberated Brno in 1945. A few minutes later they stood in a very large public with people bustling everywhere and Richard was explaining: "After the country of Czechoslovakia was created in 1919 by the Treaty of Versailles, this square was named *Namesti Svobody,* which means Freedom Square. Then after the Germans invaded in 1938 it was called Hitler Square; when the Communist took over in 1948 they renamed it Workers' Square; and now, with the end of communism, it is once again Freedom Square."

"How very interesting. But doesn't Brno have a Romance Square or better yet, a Lovers' Square?" she asked with another of her impish smiles that made the freckles on her nose do a particularly devilish little dance as if they were joining in teasing him. But then she was embarrassed and blushed, thinking maybe her comment might have been a little too risqué.

"I don't think so but maybe we could find one, or make our own," Richard said without thinking. But then it was his turn to blush as he stammered, "Or something. Or we could . . . ah, that is, couldn't we just . . . I mean we could . . ." Then he blushed again thinking how he was acting like an immature schoolboy. I have never acted this way with a woman since when I was fourteen and had a crush on Ms. Williams the Home Economics teacher, and he still remembered how nicely she had turned down his juvenile overtures.

Helga smiled again but said nothing more, her eyes twinkling as she suppressed a giggle, perversely enjoying his discomfort. But then she took his hand and squeezed it so he would know everything was okay.

Later he took her to his favorite coffee shop under the shadow of the St. Peter and

St. Paul Cathedral. The name of the café was *Kavarna u Kapuchinu* (coffee and cappuccino) and the waiters and the cashier all knew him well from his regular visits, and they crowded around to meet Helga, each one in turn practicing their English or German. They all seemed very pleased with Richard's apparent good fortune at finding such a nice woman friend. And several of them cast sly winks at him and patted him on the shoulder, especially Pavel his favorite waiter who had also become a friend. And Richard grinned happily at each of them.

Walking down the street away from the café Richard pointed out the Italian restaurant where he often came on Sunday mornings for a mushroom omelet breakfast. "But now it seems I'm going to be spending all my Sundays in Prague," he said, embarrassing himself at what he thought might have seemed a presumptuous comment.

But Helga said nothing only smiling broadly.

As they walked past the many quaint little shops and restaurants, the sidewalks busy with shoppers, he asked, "Helga, have you noticed the mothers and teenage daughters walking along the streets here holding hands and talking and smiling at each other? Mothers and daughters actually smiling and talking to one another? Not at all like American hormone-driven, pouting teenage girls who seem to think that to talk to their mothers or, God forbid smile at them, would be some kind of surrender of their new-found independence. That they would be immediately thrown out of their high school cliques and denied admittance to any other. Banished forever to an unspeakable life of having to act like reasonable, pleasant, caring young women. And American boys are just as bad but in a different more macho way."

"Richard, I think you are too hard on American teenagers."

"You think so, do you? Wait until you see some of them in New York or New Orleans."

"Oh? Am I going to those places?"

71

Richard wanted to change the subject and he mumbled something about the weather, but then he thought again about how nice it would be to have her over there in New Orleans with him.   And suddenly in his mind's eye he could see the two of them very clearly strolling down Bourbon Street holding hands while the sounds of jazz drifted out open doors.

Back in the center of the city on a side street they found a second-hand shop run by an old man with no teeth but a big smile, and after a lot of browsing Richard found and bought a New York Yankees baseball cap for Helga.   "Now you can go to Matthew's Strange Hat Party."

"Should we eat dinner somewhere nearby tonight?" she asked.

"Probably not.   There will be lots of snacks at Matthew's party.   And lots and lots of wine."

EIGHTEEN

Of course Helga fit in perfectly at Matthew's Strange Hat Party. Everyone wore unusual hats, the more outrageous the better. The two French girls had made their own and they looked particularly ridiculous which, after all, was the whole idea. Richard's hat was a rather conservative beret he had bought in Paris a few years ago.

And Helga, wearing her New York Yankees baseball cap, met all the foreign language teachers: the French, the Spanish, and the Belgium, the Macedonian and Italian, the Greek and Polish, and Turkish teachers. And, of course, she talked at length with the five German teachers, including Winfred who was young and very handsome and with whom she seemed to be enjoying a particularly animated conversation. And Richard was jealous.

And although Helga recognized that Winfred was handsome and a little sexy, a prize most any woman would love to have, she realized he was young and inexperienced. But most of all, there was no way he could measure up to Richard. Not to *her Richard*, as she had begun to allow herself to think of him. But carefully, very carefully. And never saying it out loud.

Looking for some excuse to get her away from Winfred, he abruptly interrupted their conversation and said, "I wanted to show you something very interesting over there."

"Did you think I might be interested in him?" she asked, slightly annoyed at his pulling her away from Winfred. But then she bit her lip, stopping herself from adding, 'Surely you don't think I would prefer him over you. Winfred is simply an unfinished older boy. Compared to you, Richard Rouse, he is a mere child.' She knew that was what her heart already wanted her to say to him, but maybe it was still too soon.

"Do you see those two young men over there who are talking so earnestly," Richard asked, unaware of her turmoil. "They are both Polish, but in the kind of international community we have here at the Lektorsky dum, English is the common language. They

73

both had been here nearly a month when one of them said some Polish word one day and the other asked incredulously, 'Are you Polish?' Neither had any idea the other one was Polish as they had been speaking only English for so long. And they have been talking Polish nonstop ever since."

Much later, after getting two more glasses of wine he looked around for Helga and saw that she was talking to Matthew. Just as he approached, Matthew was called away by someone who wanted him to open more wine, and she asked, "Matthew is an interesting man, isn't? Do you know much about him? He is always laughing and joking, but I think he has sad eyes."

"Yes, I think you're right. And very observant."

"Tell me about him," she encouraged.

"As you know, he's British. He has been here in Brno teaching at the Technical College for more than nine years while most visiting teachers only stay two years. The story, as I heard it, is that he was madly in love with a beautiful young girl in England and she jilted him and ran away with Matthew's best friend. And Matthew, heartbroken, fled over here trying to forget."

"What an awful thing for him. He's such a nice, pleasant person."

"Yes," Richard agreed. "And I expect, as do others, that his cheerful, easy-going façade is a cover-up for a badly broken heart."

"I think you may be right. Behind his smile his eyes are very sad. I think I should talk to him again. Cheer him up, perhaps?"

"I think that would be very nice of you."

He watched as Helga walked away in search of Matthew with her long-legged stride, her hips undulating in a wonderfully sensuous way. And even with the dozen or more young men there, he thought he already knew her well enough to know that her walk was not for their benefit, but was entirely unconscious on her part which, of course, made it all the more provocative.

The party lasted on into the small hours of the morning, but at three a.m. Helga finally suggested maybe they should leave.

NINETEEN

The following morning Helga knocked on Richard's door very early, and when he finally stumbled to open it she said, "Richard, Frau Pindurova asked if I would like to invite you to come over and have *fruhstuck* with us. That's German for breakfast."

Richard, holding his head in both hands groaned loudly, still barely awake from a groggy, wine-heavy sleep. And remembering the previous evening and he asked hesitantly, "Will she have lots of coffee?"

"Yes."

"And do you have some aspirin?" When she nodded yes, he agreed. "Okay, I'll come then."

The typically Czech breakfast consisted only of rolls and jam and coffee. But for the now fully awake Richard eating with Helga so early in the morning was more like a feast fit for a king, and even his headache couldn't dull his pleasure. It was not at all like the fantasized meal together in a Greek cottage. But maybe that was still to come.

His heart continued to have that funny little skip whenever he first saw her, and he was sure something serious was happening, but not a heart attack like he had thought once before. Couldn't be a heart attack, I'd be dead by now. But what it was he couldn't say for sure. But he was beginning to have a very strong suspicion.

Later that afternoon he suggested she might like to go for a walk before it was time for her to get the train back to Prague. They crossed the broad avenue near the Lektorsky dum and climbed a winding path through a wooded park on a nearby hill until they came upon a quaint little beer garden near the top that he knew about.

They sat at an outdoor table drinking beer and watching young children at play nearby, and he was reminded how ridiculously puritanical American attitudes were toward drinking and other pleasant things like sex. No American bar would allow children to play there or even nearby, although Joe Six-Pack drank beer all night with his children playing right there on the living room floor in front of him.

But his mind was on much more important things, wrestling with how to say what he found myself wanting to tell her. And he kept going over and over it in his mind like rehearsing a speech, which is exactly what it was. But maybe it's too soon? After all, we've only just met. How can I be sure? And I certainly don't want it to sound like a rehearsed speech. Will she think I'm a real jerk blurting out something about love this soon?

Love? Am I even sure? But yes, I think I am. Sure that is. Is one ever really sure about a thing like that? Love? Yes, I think that's what I'm feeling. I mean, I know it is – I think. But still it's kinda scary. And although this park-like setting is pleasantly comfortable this doesn't seem like the right kind of place to say what I've been thinking, what I'm feeling. And I keep hesitating, trying to decide. There should be a full moon shimmering on a beautiful indigo lake with violins softly playing as I hold her close and whisper loving things in her ear. Certainly not this place where all the adults are enjoying their afternoon beers amid boisterous, laughing conversations and where rambunctious children are playing nearby as little boys chase screaming, delighted little girls.

Go on, I tell myself. Plunge right in. Press on, I think is what the British say. What's it going to hurt? Mustering up all my courage and still trying to calm my racing heart, I hesitantly began, "Helga, I know we haven't known each other very long, but I'm beginning to feel . . . Ah, that is, I like you very much and I think I'm . . . I'm . . ." I stumbled, forgetting the eloquent words I had practiced as my voice trailed off, and in the awkwardness of the moment I sloshed beer on the front of my shirt.

"Richard," she said, smiling as she mopped his shirtfront with a napkin. "I, too, am beginning to feel something very special. But how shall I say it? What name can I give to it? When I am with you there seems to be something quite warm and pleasant inside here." She lightly touched her chest over her heart like she had done once before. But then she stopped, thinking again that maybe she had gone too far.

Richard's spirit soared into the sky like a young eagle just learning to fly, awkward but confident, and he wanted to shout, 'Yea, that's how I feel, too!' But he didn't, but it was all he could do to restrain himself. But he did allow himself a broad grin just as a little girl came screaming by with two little boys chasing her making strange animal noises and grinning their best monster faces.

At the station waiting for the train that would take her back to Prague late Sunday afternoon, without a cue of any kind, they simultaneously moved into each other's arms. "I'm going to miss you, Helga Wintermantle."

"I will miss you, too. You will come to Prague next weekend, Ja?"

"I'm going to start spending all my Czech salary on train fares," he said, trying to make a joke, but his voice broke with a squeaky sound, making him sound like a teenage boy. "Yes, I'll be there. Wild horses couldn't keep me away."

"Goodbye, Richard," she said, smiling when he pulled her into a closer embrace, pressing their bodies tightly together when they kissed. This time the kiss was much more intense than their first tentative kiss. Already it was a little passionate, and Richard smiled a goofy self-satisfied smile.

"Goodbye, my dear, sweet Helga. I'll see you next Friday afternoon. I promise."

TWENTY

Helga stared out the window of the fast-moving train, her mind a jumble of confused thoughts. What was he trying to say back there at that little beer garden? What did he want to say to me? Yes, he had said, 'I like you very much and I think I am . . .' but then he stopped. I think I can guess what it was he wanted to say. And I'm sure my answer would have pleased him. Why didn't he finish? A woman could die waiting, wishing for the rest of that sentence. It seemed as if he was trying to express some very serious thought, but then why did he stop? Maybe it was spilling his beer and the screaming children. Or was he still not sure of his feelings? Perhaps he doesn't yet feel what I thought he was trying to say. But if not, why did he begin? I do hope it was what I think he wanted to say. And when he finally does say it – she allowed herself a small prayer – I know what my answer will be. It will be an answer that will please him. Of that I am already very sure.

Why didn't I say more? But isn't it the man who always expresses his love first? My friends have all said so and I see it in films. The man always says it first. Love? Why do I think he was about say something about love? Was that what he was going to say? I love you? Does he really love me? Are we even sure about our own feelings yet? Perhaps it's too soon? But I hope not. Already I very much hope it is not too soon.

When she tied to think of something positive, she immediately remembered he had said, 'Helga, I like you very much and I think I'm . . .' but then he stopped. But isn't saying 'falling in love with you' what should come next? If he would say that I think I might say it back to him.   No, I am sure I would say it to him. I know I am beginning to feel the same thing very strongly. Love? Oh, yes, I do hope so!

Would it be so terrible if the woman said it first? But no, I think I should not have said it. I must wait and see. But the waiting will be difficult and painful, excruciating even. I don't like the feeling of hanging there twisting in the wind.

As the train passed through a small village she could see lights shining through stained glass windows in a pretty little church on a hilltop. Could this be my chance? she thought, looking again at the church. Perhaps my last chance for a marriage like my sister Eska with her two angelic children. Do I dare hope? I know I feel very strongly about Richard. But why am I thinking about love and marriage after only three, or is it four dates? But how many does it take? I do know I must not rush him or myself. Even if it is the last chance I will ever have I must not rush, she whispered so emphatically to herself the woman seated next to her gave her a questioning look. Even at my age I must not let myself become desperate. I still must be sure. But I hope. I do so very much hope it will be with him.

He is such a handsome, wonderful man. And he treats me so very nicely. Would it work? A marriage with him? After all he is an American. But why should that make any difference? He is a man and I am a woman. Is that not what it takes?

She had no answer to this multitude of questions, remembering only the pounding of her heart whenever she saw him, whenever the mere thought of him made her heart race. And closing her eyes, she could still feel his lips on hers.

TWENTY-ONE

Jumping off the train in the Prague railway station early Saturday morning, Richard began running without even thinking about what he was doing. He had called Helga last night explaining he had to remain in Brno to attend a departmental function at the chairman's home. One he said he had rather miss but probably shouldn't. She said she understood, but he could hear the palpable disappointment in her voice.

But now he was here, he thought with a broad grin as he rushed toward Wenceslas Square smiling and mumbling to himself like a crazy man, and people were staring at him, even getting out of his way as if he really were crazy.

He didn't even think about phoning her, his confidence in her being there already assured. Or at least he hoped so. Come on now, don't start thinking negatively. Yes, she'll be there. Of course she will! And he tried without success to slow down.

After Helga's visit last weekend in Brno, and what they had almost said to each other at that little hilltop beer garden, he was even more excited about seeing her now. What would this lead to? Is it really what I think it is? Oh, God, I hope so, I really do. This could mean . . . It could actually be . . . Whoa, it might be bad luck to say it out loud. Or even think the words. Better not. At least not yet. But I just know it is. Bound to be.

Before she left Brno last Sunday afternoon we had agreed to make Saint Wenceslas's statue in Prague our regular meeting place, because I think we both associated it with our first meeting there, and what that seems to be leading to. Like this large, growing feeling I have here in the center of my chest. He tapped himself over his heart to reassure himself the feeling was still there, and grinning foolishly he ignored people's stares, even though he knew he had been talking out loud. And he kept touching his chest. Crazy, maybe? Crazy like a fox, I hope.

One man in the crowd told his wife, "I think he's crazy. He may have escaped from an asylum. Maybe I should call the police." His wife smiled at her foolish husband. "No, don't do that. Look at his face. I think he's hurrying to meet someone special. He's probably just in love."

Richard thought again about their agreement to have a special meeting place all their own; a secret known only to the two of them. And he was sure that Wenceslas Square had already become their special meeting place even before they mentioned it last weekend.

I love the uniqueness of it and the symbolism it holds for me. And for us both. And now it seems we are about to make it permanent. Permanent? That's a scary kind of word, isn't it? But I think that's okay. And who knows, maybe we're headed for permanence? That in itself has the makings of a commitment of sorts, doesn't it? Commitment? Scary word. But God, I sure hope so. I think I'm ready for it.

He arrived at the Square still hurrying and out of breath, but trying hard not to seem so. And she was sitting there, calmly smiling her wonderful smile at him.

"Ah, there you are," she said as casually as if I had been gone no more than five minutes. It had become her usual greeting there, and the sound of it thrilled me every time I heard it, giving me yet another feeling of her uniqueness and, hopefully, our uniqueness together. She just saying that simple greeting made me feel as if something inside me was about to burst it pleased me so much, and I guessed she never said it . . . No, I'm sure she never said it to anyone else. Not like that! And her flushed face betrayed her own pounding heart. "I waited here," she managed to mumble slowly her voice gaining strength with each word.

"Yes, here I am, Helga." I paused momentarily, thinking would it be okay if I said something more? Sure, why not? "Yes, here I am; here for you, Helga."

"What a nice thing for you to say, Richard," she said smiling. I loved watching her smile make those freckles jump around.

The simplicity of her comments had always startled me until I had a moment to reflect on their meaning and their quiet intensity. How could anyone put so much feeling and sensitivity into such a few simple words, and yet make them sound like the most beautiful poetry in the world? Then I thought dumbfounded with amazement and still trying to catch my breath, those incredible words were directed only at me. Just me!

"And Helga, I have a thousand more things I want to say to you. All of them nice things, I promise. I already know I could never think or say an unkind thing to you or about you."

She smiled radiantly, very pleased. "Thank you for that, Richard, and I like saying nice things to you, too," she said with a smile that was cautiously peeking out from behind the confidence of a woman falling in love.

Looking at her enchanting smile I remembered that last weekend in Brno I had laughingly told her, "I think I'll call you Mona Lisa."

"Why is that?" she had asked.

"For your mysterious smile."

"You mean I look like a slightly overweight Italian woman?" she teased.

"No, I didn't mean it like that."

"And I shall call you David. Like the statue in Florence."

"Oh, sure, and with no clothes on, right?"

"But, of course. And you *are* quite handsome like King David. And like the statue, with no clothes maybe it would be even better." Then she blushed furiously at how risqué her words had sounded. And Richard blushed, too, but still liking what she had said. Then they both laughed at the mental image they each saw, Richard more clearly embarrassed than she.

TWENTY-TWO

All day Saturday they wandered the back streets of Prague, saying very little, each sensing they were anxiously waiting for nightfall, and nervously anticipating what the coming evening might bring; each silently wishing for what they hoped it would bring.

Hand in hand they strolled quietly, seeing streets and whole neighborhoods Richard didn't even know existed, peeking into shops and looking in used book stalls. Helga found and bought a favorite childhood story written in German. And they walked through the old Jewish cemetery with its crazy quilt of leaning gravestones that were only now being repaired and lovingly cared for after the Nazi vandalism, the atheist communist having had no interest in restoring them.

They had a sausage for lunch at the same street vendor's stand, the one where Helga had smiled at the old man before. "His name is Ivo," she explained quietly as they ate enjoying the enticing aroma of the food and the experience together, "I eat lunch here with him quite often. He is such a lovely man, and I have learned about his family. His wife is an invalid and she must stay at home cared for by a not very pleasant neighbor woman. He is devoted to her, but of course he must come here every day to work."

They ate standing up at a high table under the shade of a plane tree that sent large leaf-shadows flitting over our sausages that kept threatening to roll off their paper trays while they tried to eat and talk and watch the busy street scene all at the same time. I thought about her story of the old sausage vendor and his wife, and I remembered that old familiar prayer. *There but for the grace of God go I.* We should always be thankful. Every day. And I looked at Helga and thought, yes, thankful every day for all kinds of blessings.

Afterwards they wandered the streets again, wiping their greasy finger with paper napkins, each of them thinking about the coming night and trying not to make plans. Especially Richard. Don't plan it, he kept telling himself, just let it happen. Whatever *it* turns out to be. He cast a sidelong glance at Helga, thinking that whatever happens this night or any other night would be fine with him. This is one incredible woman. He realized abruptly that 'incredible' had replaced 'unusual.'

In a shady corner of the quiet old Jewish cemetery he had pulled her into his arms and kissed her tenderly. "What was that for?" she asked with a smile, even though she knew a loving kiss should never require an explanation.

"Just because," he said with a mysterious smile of his own.

"Because why?"

"Because I . . . I guess you'll just have to wait and see, won't you?"

She thought for a moment about what he could mean and started to ask again, but thought better of it. Just wait and see what happens like he says, she cautioned herself. It's probably best not to try and guess and then be disappointed if I'm wrong. But by the look on his face I think I know what he means. I do hope so very much that I am right.

"Do you think that it could be some kind of sacrilege," she said, breaking their silence after a thoughtful pause and looking around at all the old grave markers, "for us to be kissing here in this cemetery?"

"No, I don't see why. The Jewish people I've known are just as warm and loving as anyone else."

"Good. I would like to think of them looking down at us from the Jewish heaven and smiling."

"What a nice thought, Helga."

TWENTY-THREE

They had dinner that evening at another of Richard's favorite out-of-the-way Prague restaurants not far from Old Town Square. The *Sign of the Spider* was a warm, pleasant place that announced itself with a small cast iron rendering of a spider web over the front door. He told her the food was excellent, the staff helpful and friendly, and it was on Celetna Street not far from her language school. And he promised they would have lunch there often in the future and that on sunny days they could eat on the back terrace and enjoy the warm sunshine. Maybe next weekend he thought, already making plans. And he ordered his favorite mushroom soup for them both. "You could have whatever you like, of course," he explained hurriedly. "But I wanted you to try their mushroom soup. It's my favorite and I always have it when I come here. Usually for lunch."

"It's delicious," she said. "And with this wonderful brown bread it's just enough. How thoughtful of you to order it for me." Once again he thought about the wonderful simplicity of the things she said that were so overlaid with such warm, heartfelt feelings. This woman is becoming dangerously perfect. Could anyone possibly be *dangerously perfect*? I don't know, but I'm beginning to think she is just exactly that, but in a most wonderful way.

Later they were sitting at an outdoor café table on Old Town Square having a glass of wine and enjoying the last glimmering of twilight while they listened as a lone violinist played near the statue of the martyred religious reformer, Jan Hus. The violinist, an old man with long gray hair was smiling his gratitude at each coin that was tossed into the open violin case at his feet. After a few minutes thought Richard asked Helga how to say a song title in Czech, then walked over to the man and asked him to play *Autumn Leaves*, his favorite song. The old man played with such feelings that tears came into Richard's eyes, and he saw that Helga was smiling at him and there were tears in her eyes as well. And he smiled happily, knowing that neither of them had any reason to be embarrassed by their sentimental tears.

86

Later Helga excused herself and went to find a payphone, saying she had to make a call. She returned a few minutes later with a disappointed look on her face. She put her arm through his, their shoulders lightly touching, and leaning very close, she whispered, "I would like to invite you back to my flat for a drink or something this evening but my roommate Monika will be there."

"Maybe I should go ask her to leave?" I tried to make a joke, but my nervous laugh probably gave me away. "Should we go someplace else?"

"Do you have to leave tomorrow?" she asked.

"Yes," I replied, the intensity of my disappointment like an unpleasant taste in my mouth. I could sense she had something special in mind, and I hoped I knew what it was, but I didn't ask; wouldn't dare say anything that might break the spell of this magic moment. "But I suppose I could take a later train," I suggested. "Maybe even Monday morning. I don't have any classes until after lunch on Monday."

"Ja, I would like that. Like it very much."

TWENTY-FOUR

Thinking about what might be coming soon I reached for her hand, remembering the words of the song the old violinist had played for us. If only I could say it the right way like in that song. *But I love you most of all, my darling, when autumn leaves start to fall.* I know exactly what I want to say to her. There is no longer any hesitation, of that I'm sure. I almost said it last weekend at that hilltop beer garden in Brno. And now that I'm all keyed up to say it tonight, I have to wait until tomorrow. Damn, and double damn.

Richard was thoughtful for a moment, listening as the old violinist played a different tune. He looked at Helga with a warm, satisfied smile. He knew he had always been confident with women. That is, after he had finally matured emotionally. About age thirty or so. He had always known just the right things to say, how to be cool or passionate as circumstances dictated, and he was never at a loss for words or how to act with a woman. Well sure, there were those awful teenage years filled with zits and the sometimes unbearable uncertainty with girls. But thankfully those years were long past. Now, emotionally mature at last, he never hesitated to ask a woman to go out with him or to say exactly what he thought. And if there was an occasional 'no' answer to his date request he would always say very nicely: 'That's quite all right. Your loss, though.'

Now, I think an honest expression of feelings is the right way, the only way to be with a woman. And that is definitely the way I intend to act with her, he thought, looking at Helga with another warm smile. I have finally learned to let my feelings speak for themselves and not hide behind uncertainty or machismo. Lord, no, I have never been macho. I think that kind of behavior is probably more demeaning to the man than it is to the woman. I have always wondered what could a woman think of a man who belittles himself like that, although he thinks he's impressing her. Maybe some women like it. Who knows?

No, it's time I let my true feelings show with this unique woman. This whole thing with her is already far too special for me to indulge in any kind of egotistical, self-serving macho thing. I know I've never been like that. No matter what happens with us, I want to be honest and straightforward with her, and always the gentleman. I already know I don't ever want to do or say anything that would hurt her or even confuse her. I can already feel what a wonderfully unique person she is, and I think she deserves that much. And a lot more, too. In fact, I think I have just made a momentous decision. No, it's more like a discovery. This woman is simply too good to be true! But if this is a dream, please dear God don't let me wake up.

I have always prided myself with treating a woman like a lady – any woman. My philosophy has always been if they are not ladies then let them prove it or disprove it as the case may be. It shouldn't be up to me to make that judgment. But with this woman, this incredibly wonderful Helga Wintermantle, there is simply no question about it. She is surely a lady of the finest character, of that I'm sure.

"My roommate will not be there tomorrow evening," Helga whispered, leaning a closer, her lips gently touching my ear, dragging me back into the present. "She is going to be with her family for an overnight visit."

"Maybe I could take that early Monday morning train."

"Ja, that would be nice."

He reluctantly found a room in an inexpensive hotel on a nearby side street a Czech friend had once recommended, and he slept very little, thinking about tomorrow, and especially tomorrow night.

All the next day they waited impatiently for the roommate Monika to leave while they explored Prague again like a couple of children on holiday, laughing and chattering to hide their nervousness. They bought ice cream cones from a street vendor who, even though the day was warm, wore an old brown coat with patches on the elbows, but he made up for its drabness with a flower in his lapel. And he smiled at them, sensing they were lovers and he gave Helga an extra scoop with a secret wink. And when she quickly kissed him on the cheek he grinned hugely. They walked on, smiling at each other and licking their ice cream cones and trying not to think about the coming night. But then they were happily laughing again when Richard managed to drip ice cream on his shirt.

As the day wore on they became increasingly quiet and thoughtful as if they both realized something momentous was close at hand. And they each hoped so even though they were still careful not to make plans. Don't plan it, Richard kept warning himself. Just let it happen. Whatever *it* is.

The evening finally came on in a soft glow, touching housetops and café umbrellas on Old Town Square with the pink and peach that dreams are made of. They had a light supper at another small café near her flat, neither of them eating very much, the tension and anticipation clearly showing on their faces.

TWENTY-FIVE

As darkness finally fell and Helga was sure the roommate had had ample time to be gone, she and Richard returned to the apartment she shared with Monika. It was on Jakùbska Street just around the corner from the city's ancient Powder Gate, that huge old stone tower that had loomed high and benign over the city for hundreds of years. And even though the old house where she lived had been divided into apartments, it still managed to retain much of the charm from its distant past, and without quite knowing why, he was glad it was like that and he smiled while Helga nervously fumbled with her key.

After he was seated on the couch Helga went to the tiny kitchen and brought out a chilled bottle of that wonderful Czech white wine Oblast Mikulovska which had always been his favorite. But after hardly touching their wine and a few awkward attempts at conversation, they were sitting very close to each other on the sofa, and they finally lapsed into an awkward silence, each trying to hide their nervousness. Helga snuggled closer, her lips touching his neck, breathing in the pungent, very masculine smell of his Old Spice aftershave.

I knew the moment was here at last, and I reached out and gently touched her cheek with my fingertips and my lips found hers, and I was pleasantly surprised when her tongue began a softly insistent exploration. I returned the kiss with more feeling and gently touched her breast, all hesitation and nervousness gone. When I touched her Helga's breath caught in a sharp gasp and she said smiling, "Richard, I want you to know that I am not what they call in the films a loose woman, but I think something very wonderful is happening to us, Ja?"

"Ja, Ja, ah, yea, yea. I mean yes, yes!" How could anyone get so flustered trying to say yes? "I mean yes, I feel something, too. Very much so. A loose woman? I could never think anything like that about you. I know you are and always will be a lady."

"Thank you for that," she murmured softly.

I hesitated again, not from indecision, but trying to think of what I wanted to say and how best to say it. To make sure I said it exactly right. Not practicing it like at the Brno hilltop beer garden speech, but almost.

Taking a deep breath and trying hard not to stumble I said, "Helga, I already know I am falling in love with you and I . . ." Before I could finish she smiled the most profoundly loving smile any man could ever hope to see. And it felt as if my words and her smile had enveloped the two of us in what seemed like an unbelievably soft, rose-colored cloud that was incredibly warm and comforting.

She said nothing, but I could sense the depth of her reaction, her body trembling slightly, her arms tightening around my neck. And no thought of rejection or disappointment dared enter my mind. I was alive with the splendor of the moment, completely consumed by the bright fire of it.

Still she said nothing but her radiant smile was speaking volumes. I had stopped, surprised and pleased at her reaction waiting for her to say something. Then it dawned on me she was waiting to see if I had more to say, that she wanted me to finish and so I hurried on. "I don't want us to do anything that would make either of us feel rushed or sordid. This feeling I have for you inside me is so wonderful," I said, touching my chest over my heart, "I don't want anything to spoil it. Or cheapen it. I already know I could never do anything cheap or degrading with you."

Finally she spoke. "I am feeling the same way about you, Richard. And I know I am falling in love with you, too. It is the most wonderful feeling I have ever known. And I know we could never do anything cheap or degrading with each other. And I already know that being with you has become the most important thing in my life."

"And does that please you?"

"Oh, yes, Richard! A thousand times yes! More than I could have ever wished for! Could have ever dreamed of in my wildest imagination. Everything between us has become so special so quickly, and I am very glad. I feel so safe, so loved and loving with you. I have waited for you all my life, Richard," she said very quietly but with such intensity that it amazed me and completely defied description. And my eyes burned with tears at the wonder of her words.

"And if you would like," she said quietly after a pause but still very intensely, "Do you think we could, ah . . ." Her voice trailed off with another shy smile and she looked toward the bedroom door.

"Yes, I would like very much to take you in there and make love with you. But only if you are very sure." I gently touched her breast again waiting for her answer.

"Ja, I am sure," she said with another gasp. "Very sure. Oh, yes, very sure!"

"But Helga, my dear, because of the way I already feel about you I want to make sure that if we go in your bedroom, what we are about to do in there is to make love, not just have sex. I really want us to think of it that way."

"Richard, you amaze me. I have never known a man like you. With your sensitivity. Of course you are strong and masculine and I love that about you. But your sensitivity toward me and the way you treat me are the things that make you such an incredibly wonderful man. And yes, I feel the very same way about it as you. I think making love is such a wonderful way to think of it. And to say it. And because we have now said we love each other, we truly will be making love."

Later in her bedroom I gasped aloud when she removed her dress and underclothes. Her plain clothes and that long drab green coat had hidden a marvelous body.

"Is something wrong?"

"Heavens no! Helga, you're beautiful! What a gorgeous body!"

She smiled shyly at the compliment.

When she lay down beside me I tenderly touched her breasts, and never having had children, they stood out beautifully high and firm and even a little haughty like those of a much younger woman and I reveled in the exquisite beauty of them. When I gently tasted each nipple she moaned softly. I caressed her delightfully flat belly as my lips brushed her beautiful red pubic hair, then a thigh, and then most tenderly of all, back to her face. Her skin was firm and supple and warm under my fingers. "I can't believe what you've been hiding behind that green coat. Excuse me, I didn't mean to criticize your clothes but . . ."

"I guess I have always worn it as a defense against men's eyes. I suppose I didn't want them to see me as I really am. At forty-eight I was afraid my figure wouldn't measure up to their expectations."

"Helga my darling, you have already far exceeded my expectations. And I don't just mean your beautiful body."

She never wore the green coat again.

"You are quite beautiful yourself, Richard Rouse," she said as she helped me out of my clothes.

When I laughingly mumbled something about "Men aren't supposed to be beautiful," she put her arms around my neck pulling me closer and she whispered in my ear, "But you are to me." Snuggling in the crook of my arm, her hand gently caressed my chest hairs and my growing arousal.

From Richard's point of view and he hoped hers as well, what happened next was the absolutely perfect way for their lovemaking to begin. Instead of launching immediately into vigorous, sweaty, hormone-crazed sex like some overwrought teenagers, they lay very close together, wonderfully naked, their bodies lightly touching, gently kissing and stroking one another. Richard marveled at the soft, supple coolness of her skin while she nuzzled against him, running her fingers through his chest hair again and ruffling the thick masculine hair on his arm.

94

Very slowly I raised myself on one elbow and kissed her breasts again, a little more enthusiastically this time. "Yes, yes, please," she managed to gasp. "Please do it some more!"

When I entered her I felt a rush of the most incredible pleasure I had ever experienced. And Helga gasped at her own amazing feelings at the same instant, transported to a level of love and pleasure she had never known, had never expected to know. And our rhythmic lovemaking seemed to weld our two bodies into one exquisitely pleasurable whole, and it pulled us upward into a realm of indescribable joy and love.

Afterwards, spent and happy, we lay quietly together still touching, our bodies glistening with a thin sheen of sweat when she whispered with her lips close to my ear, "I wouldn't mind if this went on forever."

"Yes, me, too."

"I have waited all my life," she whispered very quietly, "for someone wonderful to come along, knowing it would probably never happen. And the older I got the more it seemed it was destined never to happen and I had accepted that. I didn't like it, but I accepted it. And now here you are more wonderful than any man I could have possibly imagined. I could never have dreamed of finding a man like you when I was twenty-one or thirty or anytime in my entire life. And now here you are in my arms where I hope you will always stay."

"This is where I want to stay, Helga Wintermantle. With you, always. I do love you more than mere words could ever say."

"And if I were a world famous artist," she murmured very softly, "I could not paint a picture of you that would do you justice. Never in my wildest imagination could I have dreamed a dream that would get you closer to my heart. That would get you inside of me. Into my very soul, filling me with love."

Richard was so awed by her declaration of love that tears came to his eyes and he was having trouble catching his breath. The intensity of her words left him completely speechless. He could only cling tightly to her as if to let go would be to lose her forever.

As he lay holding her close the wonderful simplicity of her love for him breathed a sweet caress on his brow as soft and as tender as a mother's lips on her child's face. And he knew a kind of contentment he had never known before, its depth and power and the newness of it taking his breath away again. He was so immensely happy he couldn't speak. And he tried unsuccessfully to hide the tears of joy that rolled down his cheeks.

"Why did you want to call it lovemaking," Helga asked quietly, noticing his tears, but saying nothing, only gently brushing them away with her fingertips.

"Because that was what I was trying to tell you in Brno at that little beer garden. I was already trying to find the words to tell you that I love you. And what we did here tonight was truly an act of love. We were expressing our love for each other in that most unique way. I want us always to remember it that way. I think I knew I loved you from the first time we met, but I hesitated wanting to be sure. Wanting at least to have time to think, to hope that you might love me, too"

"Oh, it took me much longer to realize I was falling in love with you," she said laughing. "It was at least the next day."

They pulled into each other's arms again in a hard, fierce embrace laughing and crying a little, then relaxing in a slow, tender kiss that spoke more eloquently than either of their words could have.

Richard lay very still holding her close and looking at the ceiling as if trying to find an answer there to a question so profound it startled him. Where has this new, bursting love for this woman come from? This love that has lodged itself some place in the very center of his being – in his heart. I have seen paradise tonight and I can hear its insistent voice calls my name even now while I lie here beside her. Her soft, warm breathing touches my cheek, melting my heart even more.

TWENTY-SIX

Early the next morning they were sitting on a bench at the railway station waiting for his train to leave for Brno when Richard said, "You know, I've been thinking. Summer's coming soon and classes will end and we could spend a lot more time seeing each other. Perhaps take a trip together?"

"A trip? That would be nice. I would like that very much."

He felt his heart make that now familiar skip at her answer, and he hoped he was making what would be a good decision; a decision that could and probably would change the course of his life, and their lives together. "I've had this idea floating around in my head for a long time. Buy an old used car and travel around Europe. See everything: France, Italy, Greece, and especially the Greek Islands. And oh, yes, maybe Germany, too."

"Ja, most definitely Germany. You can meet my father."

"Oh, yes, of course. I hadn't thought of that," he lied with a sly inner smile. He had already been planning to surprise her with a trip to Heidelberg. "That'd be nice, too," he continued. "Maybe we could spend the entire summer just driving around seeing things, especially quaint, out of the way places. And certainly quiet, romantic places."

"Oh, Ja, most definitely romantic places. That sounds wonderful. Am I invited?"

Richard took her two hands in his, kissing her fingertips, "I wouldn't go without you."

After seeing him off on the train for Brno Helga returned to her flat, her mind in a daze replaying every moment of their evening together. They had spent the entire night in each other's arms, their bodies entwined, sleeping very little, enjoying every minute of the night. She tried to remember every word of his pledge of undying love, to memorize his every move, his every touch as they had made love, to firmly plant each memory in her

97

mind so she could pull them out whenever he was not near and play them over and over like some exquisite music – a symphony to their newfound love.

As she prepared to take a shower and dress for work, her thoughts turned again and again to Richard and her now even more intense feelings for him. She stood next to the bed, her clothes in a jumble around her feet, her hands gently brushing her breasts and her belly, and she smiled thoughtfully, remembering he had said she had a beautiful body. I never thought so, but I am glad it pleases him. And stroking her breasts again and lightly touching her pubic hair she said aloud very quietly, "And it's all his. Forever."

But then some unwelcome memories intruded. She remembered several occasions when other men had interested her. A few had even excited her. But much too often she had been unsure of herself, certain that her looks were not adequate. And that uncertainty had created a trap into which her insecurity pulled her, sometimes hesitantly, resisting mightily, into a depressing fatalism.

And each time she wondered what the men saw in her, what they really wanted from her. Sex, of course, was the most common factor of that she was quite sure, and she had submitted a few times. Her use of the word submitted disturbed her. It conjured up a picture of a cow placidly chewing her cud while the breeding bull was atop her.

And what was worse, there had never been any expressions of love from the men, no blinding flashes of breath-taking romance. Hardly any passion at all. It had been all too mechanical and she recalled again the bored expression of the cow. I wonder did I look like that when I was doing *it* with one of those men?

Sometimes she even found herself wishing that maybe her heart would be broken. At least that would be something to remember; some piercing, devastating feeling of love, lost though it might be. But even that had not happened.

But now, having Richard's love to enfold her, to keep her safe and warm, suddenly all those memories of past experiences just vanished. And she felt as if she were standing alone facing a vast ocean and being completely unafraid, facing the most incredible reality of her life with only wonderful moments and uncounted memories ahead just waiting to be stored away.

Of course she was not a virgin, but what they had done last night made her think that must be what a woman felt when her first time happened perfectly. Everything he did, everything they did to each other had the feeling of sublime perfection. And most importantly, this marvelous man wonderful beyond belief, loved her! Adored her! And what was most wonderful of all was that she was so sure of his love for her it made her tremble with joy just to think about it. And her love for him even now was swelling her heart near to bursting, knowing no bounds. There were no possible limits. As far as her eye could see there were only days and months and years of incredible love ahead with him.

That morning on the train back to Brno Richard was replaying every moment of their evening together just as Helga had been doing. And remembering their incredible night of lovemaking, he kept saying over and over in his mind: This is simply too good to be true. *Too – Good – To – Be – True.* He repeated the words separately and carefully as if each deserved a garland of roses or something even more romantic and wonderful. What it would be, he couldn't imagine, but surely there had to be something to describe their evening together and the new, incredible love he felt for her.

TWENTY-SEVEN

Their trip that summer was an incredible journey into the spectacular wonders of Europe seen entirely anew through the eyes of the two lovers. It had been a never-ending discovery of love and fulfillment that seemed to grow daily and it left them both amazed and breathless with wonder. They made a quick trip to Heidelberg where he met her father, then back to Prague as if touching home base before starting out on their wonderful adventure. They visited Brno where Richard had been teaching and then city after marvelous city: Paris, Venice, Nice, Rome, Athens and many others, especially countless small towns and villages, each seeming more quaint and romantic than the last. And finally like a vision realized at last, there was their dreamed of romantic Greek island that was even more idyllic than either of them could have possibly imagined.

At a sidewalk café in Paris one evening only a week into their incredible trip, they were sipping wine and watching people strolling by on the Champs Elysees when Richard, seeing yet another dream, asked, "Helga, when we finish our auto trip would you come back to America with me? To New Orleans?"

"For a visit?"

"No. To live together."

Her heart pounded from the sheer joy of hearing it. Could this be true? That he wanted her to live with him in what she imagined was the magical city of New Orleans?

Later that evening while they were sipping wine at another Paris café, she knew she wanted to hear more about this marvelous idea. Wanted to hear about all the things they would do and how they would live. Yes, he had said live together, but she wanted to hear more; longed to hear details of how their lives together would be over there. And where in the magical city of New Orleans would they live? What would she do with her time?

100

Could she find work? What would their days and nights be like? Well, the nights, she thought with a smile, would mostly be filled with love and lovemaking. Deep, passionate love as they enjoyed each other's bodies. But also, there would be warm, quiet moments of romantic love as gentle as a soft spring rain.

But thinking about it again, she hesitated asking so many questions, fearful of pushing him too much. But still, she yearned to know how they would live. Surely they would live as . . . as a man and woman should? What else?

She finally ventured what she realized was a very important question. "Where would we live in New Orleans?" she asked quietly as if afraid to pursue the subject, afraid she might burst the bubble of her dream.

"I have a house on Pine Street not far from Tulane University. You'll love it."

"Yes, I'm sure I will." She hesitated, uncertain if she should ask more. "And how will we live?"

Richard, unsure of what she was driving at asked, "What do you mean?"

"Will we have, ah, enough for the two of us to live together?" She made herself resist saying, 'have enough money to live on?'

"Of course," he replied, thinking he knew what she meant, but missing the true intent of her question. "I have a fairly nice salary at the University. And I own the house on Pine Street with no mortgage." He paused, still slightly mystified by her question. "Does that answer your question?"

Helga, cautious about pursuing the question of their living arrangements any further, nodded slightly and decided to say nothing more. But she still wondered just exactly what would be their personal relationship when they were to live there together. That was the question uppermost in her mind and the one she most wanted to hear answered.

TWENTY-EIGHT

"Well, here it is, darling. Our little love nest on Pine Street," Richard announced as he opened the taxi door for her.

"It's adorable," she said as she stood looking at the typical small New Orleans shotgun bungalow tucked quietly behind several large azalea bushes and one tall looming banana tree. "I'm sure I will be very happy here. With you."

Yes, always with me, my darling, I thought. Forever. How could it ever be any other way? Looking at her and then back at the house again I could feel that familiar skip in my heart when I thought about our living here together. And my imagination pulled up one loving scene after another of our lives here in what suddenly seemed to have become an enchanted cottage, each scene happier than the last as they flashed through my mind like a fast-moving kaleidoscope.

When we had flown into New York's JFK Helga was so excited she was hopping about like a little girl. "Richard, look! Look at all the airplanes parked everywhere. I have never seen so many!"

Every few minutes there was something new. "Look," she whispered, grabbing his arm, "there goes an Indian man with a turban and his wife in that sari thing. And look how she walks behind him. She really does! Can you imagine? And there goes a real live cowboy! With boots and cowboy hat and everything. Richard, look!"

Her excitement and childlike wonder at everything she saw and heard was so refreshingly innocent. And I loved it. Oh, my God, how I do love her! I think it's finally dawning on me, my falling in love with this incredible woman. And to make it even more incredible she falling in love with me! What's that Bible verse that keeps popping into my head? Twenty-third Psalm, I think. My cup runneth over. It surely does! How could I have been so lucky? I still keep wondering where did she come from? How could she have just appeared in my life like that? Sitting there by the statue on Wenceslas Square as if just waiting for me? Unbelievable! And she's mine! All mine! Well, not mine like a possession, of course, but . . . but . . . we belong together as surely as any two people ever did. I have never felt so positive about anything in my entire life. Never!

"So many people and everyone speaking English," she had joked in the arrival hall. "And everyone seems to be in such a hurry, scurrying here and there like so many frightened mice. They all seem to be marching along like toy windup robots. But very fast robots. And Richard, did you notice when we were on the elevator as crowded as it was no one seemed to be touching. Perhaps someone had a bad disease?"

"No, that's just the way life is here in New York. I call it New York-itis like it was a contagious disease."

"But no one spoke to anyone else, either. Why is that?"

"Again, that's just New York for you. Everyone is always in a hurry. There are simply too many people. It's the curse of big cities everywhere. People weave their lives into insulated cocoons to protect themselves from the rigors of their stressful lives. It's one of the ways they are able to maintain their sanity. And yet they all seem to love living here."

"But it's not like that in Heidelberg," she paused, thinking, "and not in Prague either, I think."

"You are quite right, my love. Those cities are much smaller and the pace of living is slower, much more calm and easygoing. The different pace of life is one of the things I like most about Europe. I tell my friends back here at home that the Europeans really know how to live. After all, they've had more than two thousand years to develop their culture. What you are seeing here is an unfortunate symptom of the hectic, stressful way of life in America. I sometimes think of Americans like dogs chasing their tails around and around in a circle fast and furious, but getting nowhere. But always in a hurry to get there. Our country is hardly more than two hundred years old, a mere infant in comparison to the sophistication of European culture. We certainly still have a great deal to learn. If we can only manage to do so without rushing ourselves headlong into early graves."

When we had been in the New Orleans house only a few days, we were sitting in lawn chairs on the back patio one afternoon when Helga commented, "I really do like your house Richard."

"It's our house now, my love. I want you to always remember that. It's *our* house. Yours and mine together. Forever. That I promise you."

She got up and slowly walked over to the banana tree, aware she was still a stranger in this country she thought she knew but now realized she didn't know at all, still trying to become accustomed to the people, the intense heat and humidity. And she remembered the cool, comforting breezes of autumn in Prague and Heidelberg with a wistful smile. She looked at the tree's huge leaves and unusual withered blossom and asked, "What kind of tree is this, Richard? Or is it a large bush?"

"It's a banana tree. Don't you see the bananas that are just beginning to ripen that are hanging down from that odd looking stalk? They grow all over New Orleans. And oranges also grow a little further south from here in towns like Venice near the mouth of the river."

"Not the Venice where I got lost?" she asked with a chuckle.

"No. This one is Venice, Louisiana."

"I have only seen bananas in fresh food markets. I cannot imagine growing them in your own garden. I must write to my father and tell him about it."

"It's our house and our garden now, darling," I repeated. "I hope you understand that everything I have is yours now. Everything! Especially my heart and my love for you. And I am still amazed at how much a part of my life you have become, and so quickly."

"Have I been too aggressive?"

"No, of course not. What I'm trying to say, rather badly I'm afraid, is that my love for you has very quickly become like an all-consuming, unquenchable fire within me. I've waited all my life for you to come along and now that you are here with me I guess I'm in a hurry to enjoy you all the time; to spend every moment of the day with you. I simply cannot get enough of you, Helga my love. I don't want to miss a single minute with you."

"Yes, my darling, and I thank you for that my dear sweet Richard. And I too, have waited a lifetime. But now I realize all the waiting was worth it. Yes, a thousand times over," she said with a bright smile.

But then her smile slowly faded as she looked toward the unfamiliar trees in Audubon Park that bordered their back yard. Trees that seemed to be marching forever in the same place, and once again she had that same nagging thought that always seemed to be lurking in the back of her mind. What will we become? In the future? Will we ever marry? Have children? What could my future hold with this incredibly wonderful man? And why the issue of children? But she already knew the answer to that as her mind slipped comfortably back to the memory of her sister Eska and her two wonderful children. I have always wanted children. It would be so nice to have a few of my own. Our own, she corrected herself, looking at him. But what would Richard say? Is he too old? But no, men are never too old. Didn't that American senator father a child at the age of ninety?

However, I know I am quickly getting too old. What is it they call it? A

105

woman's biological clock? Yes, that's what I've heard it called. And I know mine is running; hurriedly, desperately running ahead of me, and I'm powerless to stop it. I have heard it said that it becomes more dangerous for a woman to have a child at my age. Is forty-eight too old? Maybe. But I would risk it if Richard were the father. Oh, yes, I would.

A week later they were sitting on their back patio again, thankful for the huge old oak trees at the edge of Audubon Park that shaded their yard. The slightly cool air promised a tantalizing hint of coming autumn, but it was not there yet.

Their talk was vague and random with long pauses when each of them wandered off into their own private dreams. Helga's always seemed to turn to visions of marriage and children. What am I doing in this hot, humid place so far from home? Glancing at Richard she thought once again and this man I love so much, why does he resist marriage? At least we could talk about it. But every time we even get close to the subject he veers off onto another topic almost as if he is desperate to avoid the subject. And I am left hanging hopelessly alone with my private thoughts and my increasing uncertainty.

TWENTY-NINE

In spite of Richard having to go back to work at the beginning of the fall semester, the next few weeks flew by in a dizzying blur of excitement and new experiences. For Helga getting to know some of the wonders of New Orleans was like a dream come true in a strange new fairyland that never closed. And Richard found himself seeing and feeling every experience differently through Helga's eyes as if he had never lived in New Orleans. The exuberance of her childlike wonder at everything she saw made his heart leap for joy.

"Richard I love Bourbon Street! One can almost taste the excitement in the air," she laughed as they strolled along that exciting street one evening.

"And smell it, too," he joked, thinking about the young tourists and university students who, having had too much to drink, always seemed to manage to throw up on the sidewalk, missing the gutter entirely.

"And the people! So many people! And everyone seems to be in such a holiday mood, laughing and cheerful and, I suspect, a little drunk, too" she said as they were herded along with the constantly moving crowd. "At least they are not in such a hurry like in New York."

Little old ladies, always seeming to be in pairs, were pushed relentlessly along by the crowd as they desperately clutched their purses tightly against their chests with both hands. There had certainly never been anything like this in Waterloo, Iowa.

"Yes, everyone does seem to be in a holiday mood," he agreed, "and as you said, many of them are quite drunk, I'm sure." He smiled at her and gripped her hand tightly as they walked along this the most incredible street in America. "It's like this every night, but especially on weekends. And wait for Mardi gras this spring. You simply will not believe it." She smiled happily at the thought of another new adventure that was surely coming, and she gave his arm an affectionate squeeze. And he found himself loving her touch more than ever as she held tightly onto his arm while they were being pushed roughly along with the crowd. Once more he knew he could never get enough of her touch or that incredible smile that always seemed to light up her face at special moments like this.

Late one afternoon in the French Quarter they passed a street sign next to Saint Louis Cathedral that said Pirate Alley. "May we go there," she asked. "I would like to see where the pirates live."

"There are no pirates there, my darling. That's just the name of a short, dark alley where the winos go to pee."

"Then please don't leave me here, Richard or I shall be lost forever in this wonderful city. And I could not endure it with only pirate pee everywhere and no way to find you."

"Not to fear, my darling. Now that I have found you, I'm not about to let you go. Ever!"

Later that same evening as they were waiting on Carondelet Street for the streetcar to come and take them back to St Charles and Pine Street, a man's voice seemed to be coming from inside a trash container. Several other people standing nearby waiting for the streetcar were also mystified, whispering to each other, trying to imagine how this could be. Someone said they thought a drunk had managed to squeeze himself into the trash container. Others, looking suspiciously at one another, whispered that someone in the group must be a ventriloquist. When Helga asked Richard about it, he answered matter-of-factly, "That's just New Orleans for you. You never know what you'll see next. Or hear," he chuckled.

Helga particularly enjoyed Saturday nights at the Maison Bourbon jazz club where the music was free but every drink cost ten dollars no matter what you ordered, even if it was only a bottle of water. Helga, who loved wine, nevertheless always ordered a Coke. When Richard asked her about it one Saturday night she replied, "I am so high on my joy for being in this remarkable place and my love for you I don't need alcohol." And he grinned crazily to himself, completely amazed at how lucky he was to have found such an unbelievably wonderful woman.   And his heart happily marched right along with the band when they played: *When the Saints Go Marching In.*

One afternoon across the street from the Café du Monde the mime with his white painted face intrigued her and she loved watching his antics.   And she could never quite figure out the young people who moved and stopped with jerky motions that made them look like robots.   One day, determined to see how they did it, she stood within inches of one guy, staring intently at his face.   "Richard, is this a real person?"

"Kiss him and see."

She did so kissing him on the cheek and after a moment the robot calmly winked back at her, and she clapped her hands and exploded in joyous laughter.

THIRTY

Sometimes she would surprise him with a small picnic lunch on one of the benches by the fountain at the St Charles Avenue entrance to Audubon Park just across from the University. And in his haste to meet her, Richard would sometimes cut short his favorite advanced class on British Poets and hurry across the street, ignoring clanging streetcar bells in his eagerness to get there; to be with her once more, as if having seen her at breakfast that morning had been ages ago.

Whenever they sat on one of the hard metal benches to eat their picnic lunch he was often reminded of how many times in the past he had eaten there alone, enjoying the relative quiet and the flowers and the splashing fountain, but always vaguely sad at being alone in this wonderful setting in such an incredible city. But now being with her in that same place made everything perfect, and the wonder of it took his breath away each time, adding to his never-ending amazement at his love for her.

Whenever Helga brought a picnic lunch she would have a real baguette from a little French bakery she had found, and she always made sure to bring his favorite Brie cheese and some fruit and a little wine. Even while they were busily eating, they would smile foolishly at each other and giggle like teenagers. And whenever Richard would fondle her legs while they were eating, Helga would smile to herself and welcomed his attention, knowing it was a sign he was ready to have sex again when he couldn't keep his hands off of her even in public. And she longed for the coming night and the incredible pleasure she knew they each would give to the other.

Sometimes he would glance at her happily munching her apple or a pear and a lump would rise in his throat, and tears would form in his eyes thinking how much he loved her. And each time when Helga noticed his tears, like the night when they first had sex and proclaimed their love for each other, she understood and was struck again by the depth of feelings in this wonderfully sensitive man.

110

For older folks they made love quite frequently, and always it was with breathtaking passion with each of them intent on giving pleasure to the other with never a thought of payback, and fiercely loving every minute of it. And each time it was with an overpowering sense of love and commitment and the profound wonder at having found such an exquisite, unbelievable love so late in life. And Richard's heart would take wings and soar into indescribable heights of delight, his physical climax mingling with his extraordinary love for her as it took his breath away every time.

Afterwards, always smiling happily at each other while they lay close together, their separate bodies still spiritually one, they would renew their vow that they would never just have sex but, rather, it would always be making love. Yes, yes, he thought. With this incredible woman it's so absolutely wonderful I can hardly believe it! And thus it had always been with their lovemaking; each giving completely of themselves and each receiving double or more in return. And always wanting to give more. Some nights Helga was completely overwhelmed by the sheer joy of their love for each other that it made her physical pleasure so much more intense it took her breath away, again and again.

THIRTY-ONE

Helga had hoped to be able to teach some German classes at the University. After all she had an excellent command of English and had experience teaching German as a foreign language. But without an advanced degree she was not qualified. Old Professor Frau Meir, a friend of Richard's, often asked Helga to talk to her classes so her students could hear German spoken by another native speaker other than herself.

One day Helga was telling the students how a person could never have full command a foreign language until they had learned to think in that language when a pretty young girl asked, "Fraulein Wintermantle, English is a foreign language for you. Do you always think in English?" And Helga, not really thinking about what she was saying answered, "Ja, most of the time I do. But sometimes when we are making love, I think in German how good it feels." The entire class laughed uproariously, but she sensed their understanding and laughed along with them. Only old Frau Meir seemed to be embarrassed.

Soon after their arrival in New Orleans there came a time for her to meet some of Richard's colleagues. When he had first taken her to the department office the secretary, Mona Herbert, loved her from the start, especially when Helga immediately used the correct pronunciation of Mona's French Cajun name. "Just say a-bear," Mona had coached and Helga, with her excellent knowledge of French, got the name right the very first time. And later, while Helga was casting her spell over Bob Worley, the department chairman, Mona whispered to Richard, "Where in the world did you find her? She is absolutely adorable. I love her already."

"Yes, and so do I," he said quite seriously.

A few days later when he introduced her at a faculty meeting other members of the department also enjoyed meeting her, and all of them were impressed by her excellent command of English and her cheerful, vibrant personality. Especially the men. But, of course Jennifer Smartley was conspicuous by her absence.

Richard had already noticed that whenever Helga walked into a room everyone seemed to perk up a little, even the women. And it seemed strange to him that with such a wonderful personality the women didn't seem to feel threatened by her. Maybe it was because she wasn't beautiful like Jennifer. But if the women had only known what lay behind that not so beautiful exterior, they would have seen an inner beauty and a personality that would have made each of them insanely jealous. But they did get a glimpse of it through her infectious smile and sparkling eyes.

But then there was Jennifer Smartley. And everyone knew what lay behind her beautiful exterior. Shallowness and nothing more. Some of her students snickered behind her back and called her Miss Ice Cubes.

Later that same evening after she had visited the department faculty meeting, they were preparing dinner together in the Pine Street house when Helga asked, "Did you notice how the men in your department acted with me today? I didn't understand. Why did they seem so interested in me?"

"Because, you adorably silly woman," he said laughing, "you are a novelty and they were enjoying your newness. But more importantly, you still don't understand that your wonderful personality is so pleasant and cheerful the men were completely captivated by you. As am I," he added happily with a quick kiss, "you delicious thing."

"But I am not pretty. I thought all American men liked only pretty women."

"But you are pretty," he added diplomatically. "Certainly all men like to look at pretty women and that definitely includes me. Especially those gorgeous young things in my classes with their perfect figures and the Miss Clairol hair. But men like to be with, enjoy the company of, and marry women with character and personality like you."

Helga's breath caught in her throat, her mind immediately in a whirl. Why did he say marry? Was he thinking about it? Or was that just an expression? I hope maybe he is beginning to think about it.   Oh, yes, please!

Richard paused a moment trying to remember something from the past.   "Helga, my love, like I told you one time in Europe, in the French city of Nice, I think it was, you may not be prettiest woman in the world, but you are beautiful.   Your beauty comes from a personality that shines through your face from deep inside you, from the very center of your being.   It radiates the very essence of who and what you are.   And I am sure all those men this afternoon sensed that immediately.   And I think you are so very, very lucky because that kind of beauty will never fade.   It will never grow old."

She threw her arms around him hugging him fiercely as she felt a warm shudder run through her body at hearing such a wonderful compliment from this special man.

One day for lunch he took her to the quick lunch counter in the basement of Richardson Hall at the University.   When he handed her a bowl of Jambalaya she cried out in a terrified voice, "Richard, there is some kind of giant bug in my soup!   It has big legs and claws."

"No, that's just a crab.   You are supposed to eat it."

When she dutifully crunched on a piece and made a strange face, he said, "No, silly, you're supposed to eat the meat inside the shell."

"I will never learn about all these American things," she said with a half-hearted pout.

But the thing that quickly became Helga's absolute favorite was to have café au lait and beignets on Sunday mornings at the Café du Monde in the French Quarter.   They would sit for hours under the awning, drinking coffee and talking about everything and nothing and watching people go by.   Sometimes when a couple who were obviously lovers would stroll by arm in arm Richard and Helga would smile slyly at each other

114

thinking, 'We know a secret. We love one another more than any of you other people.' And they would grin and look at each other knowing instinctively what the other was thinking, and they would have to suppress a giggle, but still knowing it was true.

The ornate wrought iron balconies that overhung many of the streets in the French Quarter fascinated her, and in a shop one afternoon she saw a print of Royal Street that showed the wrought iron perfectly and she had to have it. "I shall hang it in our house next to my picture of Heidelberg." She had brought the picture of her home city with her hopefully as an antidote to homesickness. And on occasion when she was alone in the house she would find herself looking at the picture for a long time and dreaming. But she was never quite sure where the dreams fit in her future.

Once, soon after their arrival in the city they were having a delightful lunch at an outside table at the Café La Madeline where St. Charles Avenue turns into Carrollton Avenue when Helga asked excitedly, "Richard, what is that?" she said pointing to something moving through the treetops south of St. Charles Avenue.

"That's an oceangoing ship headed up the river to Shreveport."

"But how can it be in the trees?"

"It's not really in the trees, it just looks that way. It's in the Mississippi River. But the levees in this area make the river so high it looks like the ships are, as you said, in the trees. You remember that New Orleans is below sea level so there have to be levees to hold back the river."

"Yes, and you showed me how the graves in the cemeteries are above ground so the dead will not float away after a heavy rain. And I thought it was very clever how many of the ornate mausoleums are built to resemble little churches."

Life seemed to be perfect for the two lovers. Endless days of summer, the French Quarter with its old world charms, strange new food and experiences for Helga, and their perfect lives together loving each other in the little house on Pine Street.

115

But there began to be a downside to this idyllic life of endless love and new adventures. Helga was having more than a little trouble adjusting to New Orleans, and other more subtle problems were beginning to make themselves felt.

THIRTY-TWO

"Richard, I can't understand these Southerners when they talk. It sounds as if they all have mush in their mouths or something. The man in the butcher shop always says to me, 'How ya'll doin' dis mawnin,' darlin'?'"

"I really don't think it's all that bad. It just takes some getting used to," he had told her on more than one occasion.

"I just wish I could hear some German spoken once in a while."

"I'm sorry, but that's not very likely to happen, is it? Unless you run into a group of German tourists. But you do enjoy Frau Meir's class, don't you?"

"Yes, but they all sound like young Americans trying to speak German."

At her request he had bought her a bicycle, and a few weeks later he asked one day, "Helga, why do you like to ride your bicycle so much?"

"It's so that when I am riding alone I can think in German," she had said a little sadly.

He chuckled but decided it might be best to say nothing more.

Richard knew he should try to be more supportive, but with a new semester beginning and trying to work on his book about modern British poets, he didn't feel he had time to 'wet nurse' Helga as he sometimes found himself thinking of it. He loved her dearly but he knew that occasionally he allowed his patience to wear a little thin. And when he did he would become angry with himself when he felt it happening. Then he'd chasten himself for being unfeeling and would do things to make up for it, thus finding himself running hot and cold far too often.

Sometimes when she knew she was complaining too much she would say, "Just ignore me, I'm just being a silly woman." However he sensed her heart really wasn't in what she was saying and it worried him.   Could there be something wrong I don't know about?   Have I done something to upset her?   Something I should have seen but hadn't?   And why can't I be more supportive?

He tried to imagine what it would have been like if the tables had been turned and they lived in Germany and his not speaking German.   Of course almost everyone over there now spoke English.

And lately she had begun having frequent headaches and some other vaguely uncomfortable feelings.   But when he asked, she downplayed them as, 'Just some female thing.   You mustn't worry about me, I'm fine.'   But she had quietly visited a Dr. Rashmani, a noted internist at the Tulane Medical Center, and had received some disquieting news she chose not share.

But it was what happened at the department Mardi Gas party that he later realized must have been the so-called straw that broke the camel's back.

"Hurry and get dressed, Helga.   The party starts at seven-thirty and we still have to catch a streetcar to Oak Street and then walk the three blocks to Bob's house."

"Do I look all right?" she said turning in a complete circle to look at her dress in the full-length mirror.   "I am very nervous about meeting more of your colleagues.   And this time with their wives."   She emphasized the word wives more than she had intended but her meaning was clear.   And he duly noted it and it worried him.

"You look fine."   When he caught the dubious look in her eye he quickly added, "Quite beautiful, really.   I love that new dress on you.   Or off of you maybe later," he added slyly, trying to lighten her mood.   But Helga seemed either to have missed or ignored his meaning.

118

By the time they arrived at Bob Worley's beautiful house on Oak Street the party was well under way. Richard introduced Helga to a few other faculty members she had not previously met, most of them with their wives. But he felt awkward and uncomfortable introducing her as 'my partner, Miss Helga Wintermantle.' Each time he introduced her that way he could see the disappointment in her eyes and he felt a shudder of guilt. He couldn't introduce her as 'my companion.' No, certainly not that. Rich little old ladies had companions. But he couldn't think of any other way to introduce her and he finally settled on 'my friend.' But that wasn't very satisfactory either.

Bob Worley, the department chairman, took Helga in tow and began to introduce her to several other people, many of whom she assumed were faculty wives as she struggled to remember their names. Richard watched closely, trying to gauge her reactions to the others, especially the women. Helga was more than holding her own and she seemed to have some of the younger wives completely mesmerized with her charm and that delightful accent. When he finally found them at the punch bowls he took her arm so Bob could get back to his wife Emily.

"Richard, why do they have two punch bowls?" she asked.

"That's one of Paul Donnell's little jokes. He says one is regular and the other is high test." But then he had to explain to her about spiked punch and gasoline octane ratings.

"Who is that tall woman standing over in the corner?" she asked.

"You mean the one with all the men gathered around her?"

"Yes, that very beautiful one in that gorgeous red dress."

.

"That's Jennifer Smartley."

"Is she someone's wife?"

"No, no. That's Professor Jennifer Smartley. She teaches Modern American literature."

"Richard, why does she keep looking at me? And at you?"

Richard frowned and answered weakly, "I knew I'd have to tell you sooner or later. Jennifer and I once had a brief affair. It didn't last long," he said, trying to minimize the affair, but he knew he was blushing.

"After you met me?"

"No, of course not. The year before that. It ended before I ever came to the Czech Republic. Long before I knew you."

Helga looked thoughtfully at the tall, beautiful woman with men gathered around her like drones around a queen bee. The skin-tight red sequined dress Jennifer was wearing stopped well above her knees and it was cut so low her ample cleavage left little to the imagination.

"When Bob was introducing me to people she turned away when I offered my hand and looked at me as if she had a bad taste in her mouth, and she said something to the man she was talking with as we walked by."

"What did she say?"

"I am not sure. It was in English, of course, but I couldn't understand what she said. I think she said something about a door."

He wondered why would Jennifer say something about a door? And he began to think about homonyms. Now what's another word that sounds like door? Bore? Store? More? Shore? Poor?

But Bob Worley had heard exactly what Jennifer said as they walked by and it was certainly not about a door. He had hurried Helga quickly on past, but he had heard very plainly when Jennifer said, "So that's the little German whore he brought back with him, is it? Where in the world do you think he found her? In some Frankfurt brothel? Kinda mousy looking, don't you think?"

"Really, Jennifer," the transplanted Englishman standing with her said, "That's a little over the top, don't you think?"

"Oh, hell, Henry, grow up. That's the competition."

Later when Helga was temporarily alone by the punch bowls, Jennifer expertly guided another woman that way until they were standing very close by as Jennifer pretended to refill her cup. "Did you know," she said in her loudest, most unpleasant voice, "In Germany they don't even shave their underarms or their legs. I wonder if she even shaves 'down there'? Probably doesn't need to. I doubt she would ever wear a bikini. Sure doesn't have the figure for it, does she? After all, she looks ancient. How old would you say she is, fifty maybe? No, more like sixty, wouldn't you think?"

This time Helga understood exactly what had been said. And as it was obvious that the comments were aimed at her, she quickly moved away but managed to suppress the desire to run from the room.

Richard, always suspicious of Jennifer, had been watching Helga and the other two women closely, and he sensed something was wrong and he hurried to her side.

"Can we leave now, Richard? I am very . . . really very . . ." she stopped as she brushed a tear from her cheek. "I really would like to leave now. I don't feel very well."

"Of course darling."

However, Jennifer managed to get in one last vicious dig. While Richard went to get their coats, Jennifer said to someone standing nearby in an inordinately loud stage whisper, "Well, I was certainly glad to have met that little German plaything Richard brought back here to play with. I wonder if she's any good in . . . you know? In bed?"

The next day Richard was in the department office when Bob Worley asked him to come in his office. "Close the door, Dick."

Richard thought that was unusual as Bob had always maintained an open door policy, so a closed door meant something private and very probably serious.

"What's up, Bob?"

"I noticed that you and Helga left the party rather abruptly last night."

"Yes, she seemed very upset about something and asked if we could leave. Asked rather insistently, I might add. I apologize for our abrupt departure. It didn't have anything to do with you or the party. Actually it was a very nice party and she seemed to be enjoying herself. But then she got very upset about something and wanted to leave. I have no idea what it was."

"I do," Bob replied.

"What do you mean? What was it?"

"It was something Jennifer said when we walked past her." He told Richard about Jennifer's 'whore' comment.

"Damn that bitch! Helga thought she'd said something about a door."

"I'm really sorry, Dick. We all know how abrasive and cruel Jennifer can be, but that was inexcusable."

THIRTY-FOUR

A week later on a cold, blustery March morning Richard hurried into the stately old Norman Meyer Buildings and rushed up to the second floor, taking the steps two at a time. Breathing hard from the stairs, he pushed open the English Department door. "Is Bob in?" he asked Mona Herbert. "I need to see him right away."

"Let me see if he's busy," Mona said, giving him one of her special smiles she saved just for Richard.

"What's going on, Dick?" Bob Worley asked as Richard pushed hurriedly into the department chairman's office. "What's the big rush?"

"Helga's gone, Bob. She was out all day yesterday and she didn't come home last night. I'm worried sick. And I think something strange is going on."

"Gone? Gone where?"

"Home. Back to Germany. Heidelberg, I guess. Or it could be Prague, or . . . or . . . That's just it, I'm not sure where she is. I can't find her, Bob. I called her father in Germany this morning and he hasn't seen her either. He assumed she was still over here with me. And the strangest part of all is that she told me a few days ago her mother was very sick and she might have to fly home to be with her."

"What's so strange about that?"

"When I mentioned that to her father he told me his wife has been dead several years."

Shock showed clearly on Bob Worley's face as he sensed that something very peculiar was going on with his friend, and he immediately tried to think of something to say that might help.

Sick with worry about Helga, Richard stared out the window of Bob's office

123

overlooking the grand old quadrangle that was even now crowded with students who were laughing and happily chattering away as they hurried to their next classes. And now with this new crisis about Helga's disappearance hanging over him, he found himself more than ever envying their youthful exuberance, sensing they didn't have a care in the world. Lost in thought, he was remembering how miraculously he had found Helga that day in Prague and how now, unbelievably, it seemed that he had lost her.

"Are you sure she's gone back to Germany?" Bob Worley asked his voice quietly anxious, knowing from the intensity of Richard's words that his friend was very upset, his usually tightly controlled emotions on the ragged edge of panic. "Maybe she's just visiting friends here in New Orleans?"

"No, not likely. She's made very few friends since she came over here with me last fall. And after that damnable Jennifer Smartley was so cruel to her at the faculty Mardi gras party she's hardly wanted to get out of the house. She used to love to walk up Pine Street to St Charles Avenue and down through Audubon Park. And sometimes she walked up your way on Oak Street and over to Newcomb Hall to see what kind of pottery the students were making. And I had bought her an annual streetcar pass, and we also had an annual pass to the zoo. She seemed to be thoroughly enjoying all the new experiences of everything here. But then I noticed she'd begun to change. Even before that ugly business with Jennifer she had been having periods of sadness, almost like depression, I guess you'd say. I just passed it off as occasional bouts of homesickness. Bob, I've got to find her! Something's happened. I just know it. I can feel it. Something terrible, I'm afraid, but I don't know what."

"Are you sure she went back to Germany?" the chairman asked again, his concern for his friend obvious. "Maybe we should call the police first, or," he hesitated, almost afraid to say the word, "the hospitals?"

"No, I don't think so. I forgot to tell you she left a note. A very cryptic note I might add. She said, and I quote, 'Mother is much worse. Must leave right away.'"

124

"That's all she said?"

"Yes, and that's not at all like her. She didn't even say goodbye. Bob, something's wrong and I've got to go over there and find her."

"Yeah, yeah, okay. But not right this minute. For God sake, Dick, we're in the middle of spring semester. Can't it wait until the semester's over?" The chairman paused, thinking quickly. "No, no, wait. Forget I said that. Tell you what. Spring break starts next week. Why don't you go then? Go on and . . . and . . . What the hell leave Wednesday! No need to wait until the last minute Friday. Half the kids will already be on their way to Florida or Acapulco by then anyway. Give yourself a little extra time."

Richard listened, pleased knowing his friend was trying to help him cope with what appeared to be a disastrous turn of events. Good old Bob, trying to find some way to help. He couldn't help wondering how Bob Worley, such a kind, thoughtful man, could be the department chairman. Every chairman I've known in the past has been cold, calculating and sometimes more than a little devious, especially that woman in Virginia. If one wants to be a department chairman it doesn't hurt to be a little Machiavellian. But Bob Worley was a polite, easygoing, caring fellow and a great family man as well. Richard had been to the chairman's house on Oak Street a number of times. Bob's wife, Emily, was as clever as she was pretty. And their five boys were delightful even if a little rowdy as young boys always seem to be.

After leaving the department office and wandering aimlessly around the quadrangle for a few minutes, Richard decided to go sit on one of the benches at the entrance to Audubon Park and do some serious thinking about what seemed to be happening to his dream. He waited for one of the dark green streetcars to rumble past, its bell was clanging belligerently at a car that was trying to sneak across the tracks. 'We don't call them trams like you do in Prague and Brno,' he remembered telling her. 'They're streetcars in New Orleans.'

125

'Ja, I know of the Tennessee Williams play, *Streetcar Named Desire*,' she had told him what now suddenly seemed to have been such a long time ago.

Just when someone so perfect had come into my life that it absolutely took my breath away, this had to happen.   I had lived alone for so long I hardly knew any other way of living.   But now that I have her . . .   Had her, he corrected himself.   I don't want to be alone any more.   How could something so beautiful have gone so wrong?   And why?

That evening in the little shotgun house on Pine Street Richard slumped on his old red checked couch staring unseeing at the colorful print of Heidelberg Helga had brought with her to New Orleans.   'It will remind me of home,' she had said wistfully.   'This hot, humid city is so foreign to me.   But,' she had brightened with a smile, 'I think I will get used to it.   'And you will help me discover its wonders, yes, Richard?'   And surely, he thought with a pang of longing, she had gotten used to it.

As Helga was packing her small carry-on bag she had stopped a moment, thinking sadly about what she knew she had to do.   And she already knew she could not bear to tell him goodbye.   I know he would want to know why I have to leave, and he would try to talk me out of going.   Or go with me.   And I could never tell him the real reason, so I think it best if he believes it's because of Jennifer Smartley.   But I'm sure he will soon learn the truth about mother.

THIRTY-FIVE

This is the part of flying I hate the most, Richard thought, his hands clutching the arms of his seat, his knuckles white with tension. There's no way this thing will ever get up in the air. I just know it! Nothing this big and heavy that's made of metal can possibly get off the ground.

The huge Lufthansa Airbus roared down the Dulles runway and lifted effortlessly into the bright Virginia afternoon, leaving behind a trail of jet fumes and multiple sighs of relief.

Thank God that's over. Takeoffs are always the worst part. And first having to leave New Orleans in a blinding rainstorm to get here. Makes a guy want to take up praying. And now for ten hours of pure boredom complete with a crying baby in the back. Then when we land I'll still have to take a train from Frankfurt to Heidelberg and then there'll be another hour to her father's house. There's absolutely no way I'm going to get any sleep. But I don't believe I could sleep anyway, thinking about all the uncertainty that lies ahead. Trying to solve the mystery of where she has gone and why she left. How can I ever find her again? Helga, where have you gone, my aching heart keeps asking? If I only knew where you were and why you left. And are you safe? But no matter what else happens, please God, keep her safe.

Certainly finding her comes first, then the why questions. I guess her father's Heidelberg home is about as good a place to start as any. Maybe the old man will know something by now. I hope so. But how could he know anything about her in this confusion of unknowables that has shrouded her disappearance? How could anyone, confused and frightened as I am already, ever hope to find any answers?

He leaned back in his seat and tried to relax which, with his fear of flying, was no easy matter. Whispering her name under his breath brought a rush of memories flooding

127

back to his mind, memories of last summer and their unbelievably wonderful experiences, days of golden sunshine that seemed to smile on them wherever they went on their six weeks journey across Europe. Helga liked to say it was as if each morning we would set off trying to catch the rising sun, and always coming close by late afternoon but not quite catching it, then happily looking forward to trying again the next day.

For Richard it had been a strange, unbelievably wonderful summer. Wonderful because of glorious days filled with sunshine and new experiences and, of course, never-ending love; strangely unbelievable because at the age of fifty-five, no, fifty-six, he'd had a birthday recently, he had at last found the one true love of his life. And she loved him! That was the most unbelievable thing of all; that incredible woman loved him, too! It was the one thing he had been absolutely sure of right from the very start, her pure, sweet, undeniable love for him.

Now all that seems to have changed in the twinkling of an eye and he didn't even know why. Couldn't even imagine why. He had been asking himself that same question every day since she had left, as if by intentionally torturing himself with that question he might find an answer, and find her. But no answer ever came.

My dear sweet Helga, I never cease to be amazed at our finding each other. Two lonely people drawn together by some miracle at Wenceslas Square. What an incredible blessing that had been! And now your sudden, inexplicable disappearance tears at my heart leaving me with only pain and so many unanswered questions. I still can't bring myself to say you left me. Why Helga? Why have you gone away?

Once I had met her that day in Prague there was absolutely no way my life could have been any better. There she was, so perfect, so tuned to my every need, to my every thought, and I to hers. How could two people have been so unbelievably tuned to each other? I keep remembering a line from Daphne du Maurier's novel, *Frenchman's Creek*. 'Once in a great while a man finds a woman who is the answer to all his most searching dreams. And the two have an understanding of each other, from the lightest moment to the darkest mood.'

That was us Helga dear, it really was.   If I only knew what happened?

"Would you like something to drink, sir?" the stewardess in the tailored red dress and yellow scarf smiled down at him, apparently amused at catching him in his reverie with his eyes closed his lips moving slowly as if in prayer, the ubiquitous package of peanuts still on his tray unopened.

"Yes, ah . . .   some white wine would be nice, thank you.   Maybe a Riesling?"

Recently, in my darkest moments when I'm alone and depressed and consumed by doubts and fears about her leaving, I sometimes think could this be about something else? Could it be something I did?   Or something I didn't do but should have done?   Something I didn't understand?   Something I didn't even see?   But what could that be?   How could a man know what he had done to destroy a perfect relationship?   But no answer ever came. But the why questions keep persisting, pressing against my muddled brain demanding answers but receiving none; answers I can't find because I'm not even sure I know what the questions are.   What am I looking for that I don't see?   How can a man ever know what he doesn't see?   Doesn't understand?

When I had first met her I was fifty-five and single, and I had begun to think that life had passed me by − well, romantically anyway − when she came along and my life exploded.   Yes, it really was an explosion, but in such a wonderful way!   The feeling inside me whenever I saw her was like one of those remarkable Fourth of July fireworks displays.   The kind where there is one big, beautiful explosion of every imaginable hue and color, then all those little sparkling things flying off in all directions were like my nerves singing with excitement.   What an explosion of love and happiness!   And now this.   Where has it all gone?   Could I ever recapture it?   That elusive, inexplicable joy that warmed my heart every day?   Did she take it with her when she left?

129

Still looking for answers, I began letting those unpleasant thoughts come to my mind with their joy-killing harshness and leaving behind only misery and sadness. And a nagging question began to occur to me. Could losing her have been a symptom of my failed relationships with women? My failed marriage with Mary? Or that fiasco of an affair with Jennifer Smartley? No, don't even think that. I can't bring myself to even think of Helga and Jennifer in the same breath. Comparing Helga with Jennifer would be like comparing gold to lead. No relationship I have ever had was at all like what I had with Helga. Hey, wait a minute I didn't lose her she left me. Is there any difference between leaving and the one being left? Of course there is. But then the reality and the pain is the same whether you're the leaver or the leavee. Was there something I did that made her leave? That was the question that gnawed at me every day and night since she had left, and to which no answer ever came. There must have been something I did or said wrong. If only I knew what. But the only answer that came was more dark dismal loneliness.

My mind has been in such turmoil that I keep finding myself thinking of every possibility, every explanation for her leaving, but still with no success. But I do know if I had to give up everything my life has ever stood for in order to find her again, I would do it. Instantly, without a second thought, I would give up everything. Just to have her back. Everything!

He held the In-Flight magazine in front of his face to hide his tears. The old man in the seat next to him looked at him oddly when he sniffled behind the magazine. "Got a cold," Richard mumbled.

She had wanted me to buy a Volkswagen bug for our great summer adventure. Probably some kind of Teutonic pride thing with her, but this once I resisted. In a Prague used car lot I unexpectedly found an older Ford Fiesta convertible made in England like the one I had had when I lived for a year in the village of St Ives near Cambridge. And driving with the steering wheel on the right side nearly drove her orderly German mind crazy.

130

"How can you make a turn in this thing? The steering wheel is on the wrong side!" she shouted, her beautiful red hair blowing wildly in the wind. "You will be driving on the wrong side of the road and we will have a terrible crash and I know I will be killed before I am consumed by love," she laughed happily, but nonetheless continued to hang on, her knuckles white with tension. "We should have bought a Volkswagen, she said, pronouncing it *folksvagen,* in her terror reverting to the German pronunciation. "At least they have the steering wheel on the right side. I mean the correct side," she quickly adjusted her criticism.

Once a brilliant orange though now much faded, she nevertheless insisted on calling it our flaming chariot that was taking us to wonderful, incredible places. Magical, romantic places filled with adventure and never-ending love, she liked to say almost every day even as she desperately held on.

"Richard, all lovers should have a flaming chariot like this. But with the steering wheel on the correct side, I think."

*   *   *

The huge airliner rolled to a stop at one of the many Frankfurt loading ramps, its giant Rolls-Royce engines slowing. The same stewardess approached his seat, smiling at his tightly closed eyes. "You can open your eyes now, sir. We are on the ground."

"Ah, yes, yes, thank you. I was, ah, just resting my eyes."

"Yes, sir. Of course."

Richard paused, looking around in the Heidelberg railway station trying to decide what to do next. He had been trying to distract his mind with a copy of the *International Herald Tribune* while he sat on an uncomfortable bench next to a tiny little old lady. She had been trying without much success to daintily eat a sweet pastry, her wrinkled little fingers covered with creamy white frosting which she would not lick off unless she was sure no one was looking.

Might as well go on see what I can find out, he thought as he took a streetcar up a steep hill to the neighborhood where he remembered her father lived. He walked past the pastry shop where Helga had taken him to meet her friends the Majers on his previous visit. Frau Majer was an attractive, pleasant woman, and spoke perfect English; almost better than Helga. One afternoon while he and Helga were having tea at their shop he had asked about her excellent English. She told him that when she was much younger she had been an *au pair* girl in England, and she had fallen in love with an English boy and he didn't speak German. So, what was a girl to do? She knew she had to learn to speak English perfectly. And she did.

After asking directions from several people in his halting German he finally found the Wintermantle house, and when he recognized it he recalled she had told him it had been her childhood home. What if she's there – right now? What do I do? What do I say? Don't make it a confrontation, and certainly not an accusation. For God's sake, don't do that. No matter what she says, try to be understanding and loving. Above all be loving. Yes, that's it. Be loving. Be loving, he kept repeating over and over to himself like, 'Remember the Kiss,' he had said repeatedly that second weekend in Prague.

Herr Wintermantle answered the door, his unfashionably long gray hair disheveled and a little damp as though Richard had disturbed a nap. "Ja, vas is? Ah, professor Rouse is it you?" the old man said, changing to his rusty English. "What brings you to our little house?" he asked, unable to hide his surprise at seeing Richard standing there. "Have you found my little girl, Helga?"

"No, I'm afraid not and I don't even know where to look for her. I was hoping she might be here with you."

"Nein, I do not know where she is," the father answered with a puzzled look, his eyes already misting with tears. "Until you called I thought she was in America with you. Do you mean she just left with no explanation?   What could she be thinking?"

Yes, indeed, what could she have been thinking my aching heart asked a dozen times or more each day?

I sat quietly with the old soldier in the house where she had grown up with only the sound the slow ticking of a grandfather clock for company as if it were relentlessly clicking off the hours of my life.   I tried to imagine her as a child playing on the floor in front of the hearth, then rushing to the front door to meet the father home at last from work; then as a teenager excited about a date who had come to take her to a dance.   "She was mein baby, you know," the old man said as if an explanation were necessary.

Those thoughts only brought more tears to my eyes as I sat quietly, feeling only the slow thudding of my heart like the ticking of the old clock reminding me if only I knew where she was.   Surely that would help me deal with this terrible feeling of failure that keeps creeping over me, leaving me bewildered and lost.   And hopefully it might give me a clue to where she could be now.   But then I had to turn my head away so her father wouldn't see my tears.

Later that afternoon just at dusk Richard, at Herr Wintermantle's invitation, walked slowly through a well-kept cemetery with the old man.   The father paused at a small, carefully tended grave where delicate little blue flowers tried to bloom, nodding bravely in the chill early spring breeze.   Richard had always been fascinated with the orderliness of the German and Czech cemeteries, each gravesite seeming like a miniature garden that had been lovingly cared for as if the deceased would surely smile on the efforts of the bereaved.

"This is mein wife here," Herr Wintermantle said, pointing to the grave as he stooped to brush away a few of last year's dead leaves.

"It is her mother," he said as if he needed to explain.   "She has been dead these ten years." With a catch in his voice, tears forming in the old man's sad eyes when he thought about his long-dead wife. "So many years and I still miss her."

Like many other grave markers, it had a small picture of the deceased in a plastic holder. Bending low, Richard brushed away a few grains of rain-spattered sand from the picture, and looking closely, he could see a striking resemblance between Helga and her mother. And he smiled faintly when saw that they both had the same red hair.

"Someday I will lie here beside her," the old man said, gesturing at his wife's grave. "But I think I will not be at peace if I do not know where is my little girl Helga. I know I mustn't say it, but she was my favorite." The father wiped his eyes with the back of his hand and blew his nose in a wrinkled gray handkerchief.

Richard didn't want to think about years without Helga but he knew that might happen. And if it did, he knew he would love her and miss her forever if it came to that, and he had to turn away to hide his own tears.

Back at the house he said goodbye to Herr Wintermantle. "No, I can't spend the night. However, I do thank you. I don't have very much time so I think I must hurry and take the night train to Prague. I will keep looking. If I find out anything I will let you know."

On the train to Prague he once more fought back tears, remembering the sad old man. I'm sorry for the loss of his wife, I really am. And now with Helga missing his loss is doubled.

THIRTY-SIX

I couldn't find out anything about her in Europe on my spring break. Couldn't find any trace of her – simply nothing at all. Where could she have gone? And why? It was like she had simply disappeared in a puff of smoke, carrying all my hopes and dreams with her, tightly guarded against my ever finding them again.

I know I over-simplified this thing as I tend to do. I thought I'd go to Prague and find her in a few hours. Well, maybe a day or two. We'd sit down and talk a little, she'd tell me what was wrong and I'd fix it. How wrong could a man be? How naïve to think I could, at least figuratively, snap my fingers and everything would be fine. In retrospect that had been absurdly optimistic. Almost like a man whose boat had sunk in the middle of the ocean assuming the Coast Guard would come immediately. Five minutes, tops. The over simplified optimism of my thinking now amazes me.

I guess deep down inside I knew I probably wouldn't find her that easily, not unless she had been waiting for me there at Wenceslas Square by the Saint's statue. But I knew I had to force myself to stop that kind of ridiculously wishful thinking. Why is it when something like this happens, a person's common sense completely deserts him and he assumes one foolish, wrong-headed idea after another, thinking that surely everything will work out right away?

And there hadn't been nearly enough time. I had to get back to New Orleans in just over a week. And in spite of the short amount of time I had, I still managed to ignore the inevitable. The real problem was I was torn by so many conflicting ideas I didn't even know where to start. Prague, of course, seemed to be the logical place to start. But where in Prague? That big beautiful old city must have a million hiding places. Not just criminal or communist era spy places, but hundreds, no thousands of nooks and crannies and unknown apartments of unknown friends on unknown streets. The possibilities seemed endless, and I was immediately overwhelmed with a multitude of *unknowns*. She had lots of friends there who could help her if she really wanted to disappear. She could be anywhere. But is that what she wanted? To disappear? What I couldn't understand was why would she want to hide from me after all we'd come to mean to each other? But that's exactly what she'd done when she left New Orleans. Leaving me with no explanation was a kind of hiding from me, wasn't it? I knew I had to admit the truth of that one simple fact no matter how reluctantly, otherwise there would be no way I could ever find her if I didn't face up to that one indisputable fact. She had left me; no matter why, she had left me.

Wherever I looked, she wasn't there. I began to think she might not have been in Prague after all. And in my frantic, anxiety-driven haste I tried Brno, and even considered Paris but there simply wasn't enough time. Spring break had been such a ridiculously short amount of time, but what else could I do? I tried everything I could think of, but found nothing. Not a single clue. Nothing.

I could feel a slow, encroaching dread beginning to take possession of my thinking, and I reluctantly began asking myself, what if I never find her? And with that possibility slowly dawning on me, I began to be badly frightened. My God, I don't dare think about that – never finding her? But as hard as I tried to fight it I could already feel the beginning of despair that comes with abandonment, and it seemed to be creeping closer; every day a little closer, already knocking on my door. I have to come back and search some more. I can't let it end this way. Please, God, don't let it end like this. Please, please, I whispered with more tears

On the flight back to the States it had finally become clear to me that finding her was not going to be any simple matter like I had thought. The very fact that I couldn't find her on my spring break as easily as I had thought should have warned me. But what else could I do? Who could I have asked? I knew I should have called her former roommate Monika or even her friend Bettina, but I was embarrassed for them to know she had left me. And that was just the first in a long line of stupid mistakes.

Back in New Orleans after his fruitless search he wanted to arrange for someone to finish out his spring semester classes, but Bob Worley was adamant. "Dick you've got to finish the semester. You can't just leave me in a lurch like this."

"But Bob, can't you see what this is doing to me? It's tearing me apart. If I have to stay here and finish out the semester the trail will be completely cold. How will I ever find her again?"

"You can go back later and . . ."

"Go back later?" Richard shouted so loud Bob had to get up and close his office door.

"Yes, Dick, I really am sorry. I know how that must hurt, but you can't leave here without finishing the semester," Bob Worley repeated. "You just can't." The chairman was quiet, watching his friend's drawn face, afraid to meet his gaze as he tried to put himself in Richard's place and failed. With the security of a loving wife and five wonderful children in a snug little home and an excellent job, it was impossible for him to imagine the kind of pain that was so clearly etched on his friend's face.

"Tell you what let's do," Bob Worley continued, struggling to find a workable solution that would somehow help his friend. "The semester will be over in what, a month and a half? Then you can take off the whole summer."

"A month and a half!"

"Yes," Bob continued, trying hard to ignore Richard's outburst. "You don't really need to teach summer school. Most of us just do summer school for the extra check anyway. Yea, that's it. Take off the whole summer. That'll give you six, no, almost eight weeks to make a thorough search. Maybe even a little longer." The chairman sighed, pleased with himself for coming up with at least some semblance of a solution.

But a month and a half of sitting here alone in New Orleans, Richard thought, my heart over there and aching. How can I stand it? That's like a lifetime of waiting. She

137

could be anywhere in six weeks. But then she already was he thought with a heavy sigh. Anywhere.

"Dick, I want you to know we're all pulling for you. We want her back, too. Mona is more upset than anyone."

Yea, sure. Big deal. But then he did appreciate how much his friends were concerned. Dear, sweet Mona Herbert was beside herself with worry. And really, how much could he expect anyone to understand his feelings – his torment – his sense of loss?

THIRTY-SEVEN

Summer at last and I'm back in Prague again hoping and wishing, even dreaming a little and trying hard not to think about the dark, unanswerable questions like how had this awful thing happened? Was there some dark, unseen mystery behind her disappearance that I'm missing?

Did I really think if I came back to Wenceslas Square she would be here like she had been so many times before; like I had so fervently wished on my spring break? But, of course, finding nothing? How I wish she were sitting over there by the statue right now – this very minute. Just waiting for me like always, I thought as I stood looking at the Saint's statue and the empty wall where she had always sat. What a silly idea. Just my heart's wishful thinking, I suppose. There was no one there I wanted to see, only young, fresh-faced tourists and a McDonald's hamburger wrapper blowing in the faint breeze.

But I have to start somewhere I reminded myself, and it might as well be here at the same spot where I first met her. Maybe the symbolism of my being here and looking at the exact spot where she always sat will help me think of something. Oh, God, what I wouldn't give to see her smiling face and to hear those magical words she always said so matter-of-factly, but were always so laden with feelings. 'Ah, there you are. I wanted here.'

"Yes, my darling I am here." I murmured the words under my breath as if by saying them aloud that might help make them be true today. Then I added another dreamy whisper, "Yes, I am here for you, Helga," just as I had said once not long after we had first met here. But of course she wasn't there, only in my most fervent, wishful thinking. There was only the cold, vacant stone bench waiting to mock me.

With a heavy sigh I sat on the exact spot where she had always waited for me, thinking again about symbolism. And as I sat there alone and sad near the statue, the Saint's standard with its little flag threw an elongated shadow across my lap like some

139

long, slim exclamation mark promising . . . Promising what? Success or failure? Renewed happiness or a long dark future of loneliness? Which would it be? If only I knew. But no, I don't really want to know the answer unless it's success and happiness. I'd even be willing to take the pain and uncertainty of not knowing rather than the agony of sure defeat.

Anxious to do something I stood, and closing my eyes I imagined she was standing right there within reach, so close I could feel her breath on my cheek and her lips on mine. I remembered again how soft and sweet tasting those lips were when we had kissed on the night of our first date. And I was slowly enveloped in a warm, dreamy mist and dared not open my eyes. She's here, right now. I know she is! I'm sure of it. She was smiling that special smile she always saved just for me. And feeling her presence so close, I reached out to caress her face with my fingertips, but she slowly evaporated in the mist and I stood there alone looking foolish, my trembling hand touching nothing, only tears streaming down my cheeks. I didn't even look around to see if anyone had seen my foolish gesture. I didn't care. My heart was broken anyway.

Summer in Prague was just getting into full swing, sidewalks crowded with tourists, older American men in their shorts which European men almost never wore, and those crazy flowered Hawaiian shirts and brown dress shoes with black socks. The Prague pickpockets were busily cruising Wenceslas looking for careless victims, knowing that a few of the more naive still wore their fanny packs on their backsides as tempting as if they were written invitations.

American teenagers with their ever-present backpacks seemed to spring out of the subway ramp like some kind of lop-sided mushrooms. It was as if they had just sprung to life in the damp, semi-darkness of the subway tunnels. With a catch in my heart I was reminded of last spring when I had just met her and had thought I ought to apologize for the American college students' cheerfully exuberant behavior.

140

We had our beginning here. Right here next to this same wall where I'm standing now. And he touched the stone as if to remind himself that it and the memories were real. The mystery of that first meeting still thrills me whenever I think about the improbability of it. That one incredible moment remains firmly planted in my memory never to fade, breathtaking even now. The wonder of what her one simple inquiry about the time of day had led to is still unbelievable in its simplicity, and yet so extremely complex in the love and adventure it had unknowingly foreshadowed.

But now that same memory haunts me as it grips my heart with icy fingers that refuse to leave me. Even Wenceslas Square has lost its magic. It has become a sad, desolate place. And even the beautiful flowers overflowing their planters cannot brighten my dismal mood. If only there were some way to recapture the magic of our first meeting here, to tear down this wall of doubt and fear that has arisen in my mind as surely as if it were made of cold, dark stone. But I don't want to recapture a moment or a memory. I want to recapture what we had. I want her! My God, how I would love to meet her here again just like before. Right here! Right now! And try as I might, I could not stop the fresh tears from tricking down my face.

Sitting here in this wonderful old Square I have the eerie feeling of being completely alone even with the hundreds, no thousands of people passing by. It's as if being here without her makes me so completely alone that even in these pressing crowds I might as well be invisible.

I raised my head looking around, hoping for some ray of hope as I tried to dry my eyes. The warm summer sun that was shining so cheerfully gave the old buildings facing the Square a golden patina that spoke of quiet comfort and peace, and a profound sense of place and permanence. Yes, permanence. That was what I most long for. The kind of quiet, loving, permanent future with her I thought surely I already had, but which is now so sadly lost.

THIRTY-EIGHT

Maybe taking her to New Orleans had been a mistake? But it seemed the obvious thing to do, the logical extension of our time together here in Europe and our loving each other and wanting to be together always. And she seemed to be so happy there – at least at first. Maybe there's some kind of clue in that. Something must have happened after we had been there a while. But nothing comes to mind except for that business with Jennifer Smartley at the Mardi gras party. But as terrible as Jennifer's behavior had been, was it really awful enough to drive Helga away? Surely there must have been something more. Why do I keep having this uneasy feeling that I'm missing something? Maybe something big? Something big and dark and unknown? But what? And how can I find out?

I could sense her disappointment at our not getting married right away. And although we never discussed it, I felt sure that was what she wanted. Was that my big mistake? But I didn't want to rush into anything. Not after being divorced and all the negative background I had been carrying around all my life since childhood like some awful unseen burden. She never said anything about marriage or complained but I could see it in her eyes, and in little things she would say once in a while. Like talking about her sister with her two children. Children? Was that what she wanted? Probably. And like a fool I ignored my better instincts.

I'm beginning to think she might have been happier if we'd stayed in Europe. Maybe that was my mistake? Then why didn't we? But I had my career at Tulane and I was tenured and that would have been hard to give up. And how would we have lived over here? But I know now I would have happily given up everything for her. I really would have. Why didn't I think of it that way then? But she seemed so willing to come to America with me, and she really was happy in New Orleans. I keep coming back to that same thought. She was so happy there at first. Is there an answer somewhere in that that I'm missing? At first? There has to have been something more to her leaving – something I didn't see, something I don't understand.

Maybe if I just sit here quietly for a while on this familiar old stone wall I'll think of something. Get some idea of what to do. Try to think of where else I should be looking?

I love this big, beautiful old city. This wonderful ancient Prague where we truly fell in love. And we had our first sex at her apartment on, now what was the name of that street? Jakubska Street? Yeah, that was it. What an exquisite moment that was. It had been wonderful almost beyond belief! And now this.

This dazzling bright summer sunshine seems to be so out of place with my mood, taunting me cruelly as if it were gleefully mocking my misfortune. Of course she wasn't here at the Square like I had most fervently wished, only that group of rowdy, noisy young Americans. If I can't think of what to do here in Prague, what hope is there anywhere? Where else could I go that would help?

Walking slowly down Wenceslas toward Old Town Square, lost in the constantly moving crowds, I was attracted by the enticing aroma coming from one of the ubiquitous sausage vendors. And I thought I might as well eat now, but then realized I wasn't hungry. When I looked up I saw that it was the same stand where Helga and I had eaten that day, and I remembered the old man knew her. I approached the old vendor and tried to talk to him. But my Czech was so sketchy I couldn't even remember if *Pani* was male or female, and what was the word for Ms. and I only managed to say, "Fraulein Helga?" as I made an awkward gesture around my head trying to indicate her red hair. The old man only smiled and shrugged his shoulders.

I waited until a young woman with red hair happened to be passing nearby, and desperate for any kind of help I hurried over to her. "Excuse me, miss," I said as she shied away from me unsure of my intent. "I didn't mean to startle you. Do you speak English?" When she nodded a cautious yes I asked, "It's that I'm trying to find, ah," I stammered. "A friend of mine has red hair and the man over there knows her but I don't speak Czech. Would you please ask him if he has seen her? A woman with red hair named Helga." When she asked, pointing to me, the old man's face lit up. "*Ano* (yes*)*," he answered beaming when he remembered me being there with Helga. But when she asked if he had seen such a woman recently his face fell. *"Neh, neh.* (No, no.)"

I walked away, forgetting to thank the woman. Just when I was more aware than ever of the futility of my aimless searching, and trying hard to fight back tears I had a sudden inspiration. Helga's old phone number! Of course! Why hadn't I thought of that earlier? She couldn't possibly be there could she? But I had to try something. Try anything. Why not try that?

When I dialed her number, my heart was thumping like a big bass drum, and I had to remind myself that the Czech ring tone sounded almost exactly like the American busy signal, and when I had first come to this country I had hung up several times before friends could answer. Now all I could do was to hold my breath and wait.

"Come on, ring. Ring dammit!" I said aloud, trying to make something happen.

"Ja, hello," a woman's German-accented voice answered the phone and I thought my heart had stopped. No, this can't be. It can't possibly be this easy. Dear God, please let it be her! "Is this Helga?" I asked, holding my breath, not sure that I recognized the voice but hoping, then not daring to hope, but still hoping.

THIRTY-NINE

"Nein, this is Monika," Monika Schmitt said cautiously when she answered. "Who is this?"

"This is Richard Rouse. You remember, I was . . ." I paused in mid-sentence, unsure of what to say, not even bothering to hide the disappointment in my voice. "I was Helga's, ah . . ."

"Ja, I remember Helga talking about you Richard," Monika interrupted. "But Helga is not here. She went to America with you, yes? Isn't she with you?" her voice was confused, questioning.

"Yes, she did, but then something happened and she disappeared. I think she came back to Europe. To Prague maybe? Have you seen her?" I asked, holding my breath again. Please God, please, please let her say yes.

"Why did she leave America?" Monika asked. "Was something wrong?" Her voice was questioning again, suspicion beginning to grow.

"No, no. I mean, I don't know . . . ah . . . That's just it, I don't know what happened. Or why she left."

"But you must have some idea, Richard. She left without you?"

"Well, there was this other woman," I stammered, then realized immediately how that must sound.

"Oh?" Monika said, beginning to get an unpleasant picture.

"I know you don't understand, Monika. There was this other woman in America I had had a relationship with several years ago."

"Oh, really?"

"Please, Monika, let me explain."

"I think you had better."

"I had broken off the relationship with that other woman before I ever met Helga. This other woman, for reasons of her own, tried to make life unpleasant for Helga when we went to New Orleans. This other woman was a colleague in the English department and apparently she seemed to think she and I still had a relationship. I guess it was jealousy or something. I don't know what it was, but she sure played hell with my relationship with Helga. I had already ended the relationship with that woman before I even came to teach at the University in Brno.

"When I met Helga Wintermantle every woman I have ever known simply faded away as if they had never existed and I knew immediately she had to be the one true love of my life, and that she had always been there just waiting for me. And it was as if I had waited all my life to find her, too." I paused, catching my breath after such a long speech and trying to hold back tears. "Monika, I know I'm just a voice on the telephone. I'm not even sure we've ever met. But I want you to know that I love Helga Wintermantle more than anything in the world."

"Yes, Richard," she said, clearly relieved at my explanation, "I do believe you. Helga spoke of you very often when she lived here with me and it was always with a voice that spoke from the heart. I think she loved you very much."

"Thank you for that, Monika. Thank you for believing me." I made myself pause, tears of relief in my eyes at her answer; at her understanding my explanation. I waited a moment, fearing the answer she would give to my next question. "Please, Monika, can you tell me where she is? Do you have any idea where she might be?"

"No, Richard I don't know. I have not seen her. But if I hear from her I will certainly tell her you were looking for her and I will tell her how upset you were and . . . No, no, wait! Wait a moment! I just remembered something. Someone said they had seen her on the Charles Bridge just a few weeks ago and later at the Éclair Pastry Shop. You know that nice shop on Platnerska Street near the river? The one where many of us like to go on Sunday mornings?"

Someone had seen her! My heart took a great leap and I forgot to breathe again. "Who told you they had seen her?" I finally managed to gasp. "I mean, can you tell me who she is? What was her name?"

"I'm not sure. Let me think. It could have been, ah, yes, probably it was that other German girl who taught in the same school as Helga. I think that's likely who it was. Her name is Bettina."

"Do you know how I can get in touch with her? Bettina, I mean?"

"Nein. However you could go by the language school on Celetna Street and . . . Oh, no, today is Saturday. I think they are not open. But just a minute, I think I have an idea. Why don't you try the pastry shop tomorrow? Sunday, that's when we will all be there, but I think it would be Bettina who can help you the most. Yes, that might be the thing to do. Come tomorrow morning."

"Thank you, Monika. I will be eternally grateful to you whether I find her or not."

"And Richard?"

"Yes?"

"I hope you find her. Something must be very wrong. I think she loved you very much. She talked about you all the time."

Hearing that made my heart lurch again and tears came once more despite this faint glimmer of hope.

147

FORTY

After she hung up the phone Monika stood quietly staring into space, her mind far away thinking about Richard losing Helga and wondering about her friend's whereabouts and her unexplained disappearance. She tried to imagine Richard's feeling of loss. Could it even have been some sort of betrayal? But surely not. That would be unthinkable. Not that sweet, lovingly innocent Helga Wintermantle. Betrayal? No, that had been my experience, she thought with a painful sigh, not Richard's. I'm sure she has not betrayed him. There must be some other explanation.

Her mind turned back in time to her own lost love remembering how, even after all these years the hurt never really went away. She forced herself to move to the fridge where she poured a glass of wine and then, as if in a trance, she moved slowly to the couch and sat thinking and remembering, the wine already forgotten on the coffee table.

Thinking of Richard's dilemma, she smiled a sad, sympathetic smile, hoping he would soon find Helga. Certainly no one was more deserving of a little happiness than Helga and, of course, Richard, too.

The two women had become close friends, sharing adjoining rooms and a common bath in the old house as they had. Both of them were a good bit older than the other women teachers who lived there. Helga was the oldest by far, but even at thirty-five Monika was closer to her age than she was to any of the younger women. But they both enjoyed the companionship of the young women and they were always included in the group that went to the Éclair Pastry Shop on Sunday mornings for coffee and pastries and, of course, lots of gossip. The young women delighted them with their tales of romantic exploits from the previous week, some of them quite racy.

Monika picked up the forgotten glass of wine and took a sip, her mind already turning to Hans, fighting the tears that always came whenever she thought about him. She had met him many years ago on a Christmas skiing trip she had taken with several

148

university friends to Sennwald, a small, not very exclusive ski resort in the Swiss Alps just across the border from Germany. His name was Hans Christian, and she often teased that he should add Anderson as a third name.

Their affair had been right out of one of those racy romance novels, she thought with a wry smile. He was the handsome but poor ski instructor, and she, the very pretty young woman just out of university. And even after all these years Monika still pictured herself as a young girl whenever she remembered the experience. There were parties almost every night among the young skiers and the instructors, and Monika had quickly fallen in love with Hans. Her eyes were dazzled by new love, and she thought of her life as a never-ending fairy tale of parties and adventure and, of course, unbelievably romantic love; breathtaking, fiercely intense, all-consuming love. And she was reminded of that English expression she was sure applied to her. She was 'head over heels in love' with him and loving every minute of it.

It wasn't long before Hans had begun coming to her room every night. He was young and handsome and he said he loved her. Their lovemaking was torrid despite her inexperience, but Hans praised her for being a quick learner, reassuring her that her clumsiness and lack of experience simply made her more desirable.

One night after having made love they had come downstairs and were sitting alone in front of the fireplace in the Great Room. All the other young people had rushed off to a new pub one of them had discovered that afternoon. They were sitting very close when Hans pulled her into his embrace and kissed her tenderly. When the kiss finally ended he murmured, "Monika, I love you very much. Don't you think it's time we should talk about getting married?"

Her heart thrilled at his question, her breath coming in short gasps as she tried to answer. "Yes, Hans, my love. I do. Yes, I do!" She threw her arms around his neck and hugged him fiercely, thinking that her heart would surely burst with happiness.

They chatted excitedly about the prospect of their marriage, each of them making promises of undying love and devotion as well as grand plans for the future. Monika, especially, was carried away in the excitement of the moment. To be married to this wonderful man was almost more than she could bring herself to believe. Never in her wildest dreams had she ever expected such a thing to happen to her. He was so beautiful and virile and simply too good to be true.

A few nights later after even more special lovemaking – she was indeed a quick learner he thought, pleased – they were again in the Great Room in front of the fireplace holding hands and staring into the flames. Hans was being the attentive lover, fixing her drinks, bringing her special little hors d'ourves, even running to her room to get her sweater when she had just casually mentioned she was a little chilly. And she didn't recognize the voice of doom when it came out of the blue with no warning.

"Monika, your name is Schmitt and you are from Munich, Ja?" he began cautiously. "Your father, is he one of the Schmitts of the Schmitt Brothers petrochemicals in Munich?"

There it was. The question fell like a blow to the pit of her stomach coming as it did without warning. It was the one question she had been dreading and had no idea how answer. How would she explain her family? Her father? Of course she knew she could lie and she wanted to badly. Just say yes, he's one of those rich Schmitts. What's the harm? Trap him into marriage until it was too late? Trap him? No, she knew she could never do that.

She had thought of several different answers if the question of her father had ever come up, even practicing a few. But none of them seemed satisfactory. And Hans' not very subtle reference to the rich Schmitt Brothers Company immediately alerted her to his intent, and it showed very clearly what he was looking for. And almost like hearing the voice of doom, she knew what she feared most was surely coming next.

Monika hesitated, knowing instinctively this was a critical point in her life and that her entire future might well depend on her answer. How would she deal with it? Should she try to be evasive? Or just simply lie? Surely there was some way she could save herself from the embarrassment and heartbreak she knew was lurking just around the corner, her vision of a happy marriage already beginning to fly away. But lying had always been difficult if not impossible for her. What should she do?

"Nein, he works at Munich University," she whispered quietly, hoping he would ask nothing more. But of course he did. Hans Christian was an ambitious young man whose plans for the future did not include a lifetime as a ski instructor, but most certainly did include a wife from a well-to-do family.

"So he is a professor at the University, Ja?"

"No, he's . . ." she hesitated, desperately searching for some escape, "in the administration."

"Yes? What part?"

"The buildings and grounds division." She tried to think of some reasonable explanation that would satisfy him, but knowing how persistent Hans could be she could think of nothing more, already seeing her dream world beginning to crumble.

"So, he is an executive in the University management system?" Hans doggedly pursued his probing questions, intent on finding the pot of gold at the end of his rainbow.

"No, not exactly. He works in the buildings and grounds division," she repeated, knowing and dreading that Hans would have to know the truth.

"I see," Hans said still unsure, but beginning to see a flaw his grand scheme.

The next afternoon after his last lesson Hans sought out one of the young men in Monika's ski group.

"Monika Schmitt? Yes, of course. Nice girl. Bright girl. What? Her father?

151

Nice fellow. Everyone likes him. His job at the university? He's a janitor there."

Hans began coming to her room much less often, using the pressures of work as an excuse. They still had sex occasionally but it was far too quick and mechanical with no real display of affection. And although he still professed his love for her, she sensed that was simply a way for him to get into her bed and satisfy his sexual urges. And it seemed that his promises for the future were quickly becoming much more vague.

All too soon the Christmas holidays came to an end. And even though she dreaded having to leave, Monika, being the intelligent and intuitive young woman she was, had already guessed that her romance with Hans was coming to a rapid and unhappy end.

When her bus was ready to leave that last day, Hans bid her a coldly indifferent goodbye and walked back to the ski lodge without even a farewell wave.

She never saw Hans nor heard a word from him after that.

And now what is to become of my friend Helga? And poor Richard, too.

FORTY-ONE

His head bowed, Richard wandered aimlessly through the busy streets of Prague trying to hide his tears behind a handkerchief, hoping to make it look like he was wiping his nose. The day had turned dull and gloomy with a fine misting rain falling. To his sad eyes the dark gray cobblestones appeared like giant tears glistening in the gathering dusk. Tears? How appropriate, he thought. He kept playing over and over in his mind what Monika had said. 'I think she loved you very much, Richard.' And remembering her words, the fear and longing clutched even tighter at his heart.

He stumbled along the old cobblestones sidewalk trying not to bump into people he could hardly see through his blurred vision, repeating Monika's exact words over and over to himself. What are people going to think, seeing a grown man walking the streets of Prague crying.

A vision of their joyous adventure last summer crept into his mind, battering his wounded spirit as if intentionally torturing him with the uncertainty of what he might learn tomorrow from her young friends. But then his doubts became a new source of insecurity and pain. His spirits, raised mountaintop high at the prospect of learning where she might be, were dashed low again when it occurred to him that Bettina might not be able to help, that she might not know anything. What do I do then?

He spent a restless night waiting for Sunday. When he realized he was not going to get any sleep at all, he got up and found the half bottle of wine he had left on the nearby table. He sat on the side of the bed drinking the warm, bitter wine and feeling sorry for himself, then he was angry for drinking alone.

He went back to bed and trying not to cry, he dozed off and on, then thinking excitedly about what he hoped he might learn tomorrow. He awoke at the first faint light of dawn, quickly dressing and hurrying to the pastry shop only to find it was not yet open, realizing that in his haste he was much too early.

Walking aimlessly, he found himself near the river and the Charles Bridge. He thought about of walking the length of the bridge and finding that statue with the shiny head so he could rub it again. 'You must rub his head for good luck,' she had said, beckoning for him to join her at the statue on the bridge just last year. And he had, but where had the luck gone? He decided not to try to find the statue this morning, thinking that the sight of the bridge and the river would only remind him of her and saddened him even more.

When at last the doors of the pastry shop opened after what seemed to him to have been an eternity, he hurriedly entered and quickly looked around but then realized they couldn't possibly be here yet because he had been the first customer to come in.

He looked around, unsure of what he should do. The place soon began to fill with some of the emerging Czech middle class who were all happily chatting away, their cheerful greetings and smiles acknowledging a future brighter than any of them could have thought possible just a few short years ago under the cold, repressive eye of communism.

But then the tantalizing aroma of freshly baked pastries reminded him he had not eaten. Carrying his coffee and cinnamon roll, he found a table near one of the large windows overlooking Platnerska Street where he thought he might be able to see the group of young women when they came down the street, and where, by turning a little, he could also watch the front door. And like a general planning his strategy, he began thinking about what he would say when he met the young women.

The bright morning sun that came streaming through the window made playful little shadows on the tabletop, and he realized how nervous he was at the prospect of hearing something about Helga when he saw that he had been tearing his cinnamon roll into small pieces that were scattered all over the table, but he had eaten none of them.

When the women had not appeared right away he started to question how long he should wait, and he began to panic. What was he supposed to do, wait all day? Maybe several days, he thought, his anxiety getting the better of his reason. Had they forgotten to come? Had Monika forgotten to tell them he was waiting? But certainly not that. Monika had been very specific about Sunday mornings. And to leave Prague without a clue would be just as bad as the waiting, maybe even worse. It was unthinkable, really. And where would I go without knowing anything more?

FORTY-TWO

Almost two hours and several cups of coffee later, Richard was wondering if maybe he should give up and leave when a group of chattering young women entered the shop. There were five of them, and watching them closely he thought he recognized one of them from having visited Helga at her language school last year.

After the women had made their selections and were seated, eating very little, but talking non-stop, he hesitantly approached their table, thinking that the small one with the short hairdo might be the one he had seen with Helga and her friends at their school.

"Excuse me, aren't you Bettina? Didn't you teach at the language school on Celetna Street with Helga Wintermantle? I think I met you there once."

"Ja, ah, yes, I did."

"Have you seen her?"

"Ja, have you lost her?" the girl laughed, making a joke. But seeing his sad, pained expression, her laugh died in her throat. "Aren't you the professor she went to America with?"

"Yes, I'm Richard Rouse," he mumbled an answer, embarrassed in front of the other young women. "But she seems to have disappeared. She left New Orleans without a word and I can't find her."

"Why did she leave?" Here was another suspicious voice asking that same question.

Monika, who was sitting at the same table, had decided not to tell Bettina that Richard would be there this morning. Better to let him tell her everything in his own way.

"That's just it, I don't know. And I'm desperate to find her," and he explained as he had for Monika who nodded in silent agreement.

156

"Which one of you is Monika," he asked looking at each of the young women but thinking it was most likely the slightly older one. Monika smiled and raised her hand a little.

"Monika, I want to tell you how much I appreciate everything you have done to help me. I owe you such a debt of gratitude; a debt I could never repay. Thank you very much."

"Of course, Richard. I hope you find her," she said, hoping she was giving him some much needed encouragement.

Turning back to Bettina he asked, "Didn't you tell someone you had seen her recently? Monika said she thought you had."

"Yes, it was only a few weeks ago. I'm not exactly sure when. But yes, she was here in Prague. I chanced to meet her on the Charles Bridge. However we talked only briefly." Bettina paused, unsure if she should say more. "She seemed not to be very happy."

"What did she say? I mean, did she say where she was staying? Or where she might be going? Please, Bettina, tell me everything," he urged, his anxiety overriding his caution. "Don't leave out anything. I want so badly to find her."

"Nein, she did not say where she was staying, but she did mention the home of her father in Heidelberg."

"Yes, I have just recently visited her father, Herr Wintermantle. He has not seen her either."

"I remember her saying something a little sad," Bettina continued, smiling wistfully. "When you're forty-eight you can't stay at your parents' home for very long. They don't know how to treat you. You are no longer their child, so how can you be an adult in the home of your childhood?"

157

"Did she say where she might go when you saw her? Back to Heidelberg?"

"I'm not sure. But no, I don't think so. I do remember her saying something about going to Brno; something very mysterious about a party and a hat. I think she said something like, 'Where it all started.' Do you have any idea what she could have meant?"

"Yes, I think so. I mean, I hope so." My excitement was as brightly immediate as my gloom had been in all the sad weeks before, illuminating what only moments before had been dark and dreary. This was the first word I had heard of her since I had returned to Europe, and I was momentarily elated, but I sensed that caution still lurked nearby.

"I hope you find her, Richard" Bettina said, "I think she loved you very, very much."

"Thank you for that, Bettina."

Still standing next to their table he paused a moment longer, trying hard to keep his emotions under control. "I've got to find her, Bettina. I need her. My life has become so empty without her. Please help me find her. I love her so much."

Bettina reached out and took his hand pressing his fingers to her lips as she watched the tears roll down his cheeks. The other women at the table averted their eyes, not in embarrassment, for what woman could be embarrassed at seeing a man pouring out his profound love for a missing woman, but simply to give him a moment of privacy.

As Richard walked away, Bettina thought about Helga's love for this tall American and she tried very hard not to be jealous. She wondered if she would ever have such a wonderful romance. Just two weeks earlier she had met Monika Schmitt's handsome cousin Harkmut. As seemed to be her custom with men, Bettina had immediately fallen in love with him. But this time she warned herself she must not hurry an affair with him. After all, Monika was her friend and she, Bettina, should show some restraint. But he was so handsome, and if he would like maybe they could . . .

158

Hearing that Helga had been there in Prague, might still be near, made excitement pulse through him like an unstoppable current charging him with renewed hope.

Maybe she's in Brno. Bettina said she might go to Brno, the place where I spent two years teaching at the University there. Two wonderful years where I thought I was having an absolutely grand time until I met Helga. Then everything else just faded into nothing compared to the incredible wonder of loving her.

FORTY-THREE

Brno! That's what her friend Bettina said Helga had mentioned when the two of them had talked on the Charles Bridge a few weeks ago. Brno, where the most incredible thing in my life started. Well, maybe it had started in Prague at Wenceslas Square, but this is where my love for Helga emerged full grown; where our love for each other blossomed like some incredibly beautiful flower exquisite and tender, but born already strong and healthy. The place where we tentatively tried to express our love for each other that very first time. And like young lovers always seem to understand, there is a small constant flame they keep deep inside themselves that warms their hearts with the sure knowledge that love will come to them someday. And when it comes, that tiny flickering flame will burst into an unimaginable conflagration, enough to warm the whole world it seems.

Young lovers? Well, sure, why not? Our love for each other made us young at heart. And like young lovers everywhere throughout the ages, we began fiercely loving each other, fearing nothing, expecting only great things. Our wondrous love for each other was so much more than either of us could have possibly imagined, the thought of which still takes my breath away. We couldn't even imagine what marvelous, loving adventures lay ahead for us. Only new, limitless love.

And now, after what seems like the mere blink of an eye, I'm standing lost and alone in the ashes of this unbearable loss.

So here I am back in Brno again and sadly remembering so many wonderful things about our time here, like her marvelous personality that seemed to shine on her face all that day. And how could I ever forget Matthew's Strange Hat Party and Helga's New York Yankees baseball cap? And especially everything that happened that wonderful evening at Matthew's party at the Lektorsky dum, and how Helga seemed to fit in so smoothly, so seamlessly just as if she had always been one of the group.

160

He allowed his thoughts to drift slowly back to the intense feelings they had discovered for each other on their visit here just last year. He recalled clearly every detail of the things they had done on that memorable party weekend, and on their excursion into old Brno. And especially, he remembered how they had each hesitantly begun to express their love for each other at that little hilltop beer garden the next afternoon. And what an incredible life together that seemed to be leading to.

In everything they did that weekend Helga's innocence was so childlike, so open and trusting and, of course, that was one of her most endearing qualities and he loved her even more intensely for it. But he quickly reminded himself there had always been a very quiet strength in her. He often thought of her as having an inner core of very strong steel covered in soft, beautiful velvet, and he quickly realized it had always been there. But that didn't threaten him. He had no ego problem with her being strong and self-assured. Quite the contrary, he welcomed that as yet another facet of her marvelous personality.

And the strength of her character kept surprising and pleasing him. Like that time in New Orleans she had told him about when she and old Frau Meir were having lunch at that wonderful little French café on Robert Street in the Garden District. They had been enjoying talking to each other in German and apparently the waiter, hearing their talk and having assumed they were German tourists, had grossly over-charged them. Frau Meir loved to tell how Helga stood at their table tall and defiant, and said in her perfect English, "If you do not correct this outrageous bill immediately I shall call the manager. Or would you prefer that I call the police? And as you can see I have an excellent witness here who, by the way, also speaks perfect English." The waiter scurried away to correct his larcenous bill.

FORTY-FOUR

Now back in Brno again, I sadly watch as the tram approaches the neighborhood of the Lektorsky dum where I had lived just last year, but what now seems like a lifetime ago. My thoughts turned to the little beer garden in the park just up that hill over there where we both had begun to grope for words to express our newly emerging love for each other. Words that were spoken tentatively at first, each of us still unsure of the other's reaction, or of our own for that matter. I think we each were hoping for something to happen that day and were trying not to hold back, just hoping and wishing; but then afraid, too, thinking what if the answers were not what we wanted to hear? Even those first few tentative words we managed to say to each other that beautiful sunny afternoon had sounded as ordinary, as commonplace as seeing the children playing nearby. But for the two of us, our eyes aglitter with still unspoken love, those first few hesitant words were like the essence of the greatest Shakespearean sonnets, and even more. How wonderfully painful that moment had been! That has to be the perfect definition of bittersweet.

But the words were spoken clearly and emphatically the very next weekend in her apartment in Prague. Like two dams bursting, we each let go in a rush of emotions that now seem rather mild, but at the time were more like a massive flood. And for once in my life I didn't let caution rule my feelings. I was determined to say exactly what I had been feeling and to hold back nothing. And I reveled in the miracle of our new love even as we each groped for the perfect words we both found so difficult to say; then suddenly finding that the words didn't seem to matter at all, only the feelings. Those unbelievably wonderful feelings that were at last out in the open. And although the words we found to express ourselves were surprisingly simple, the feelings were unbelievably profound. Like all new lovers, young and not so young, we were absolutely convinced that no one in the world had ever felt this way. Not like we did!

We had been so happy here in Brno. And in Prague. Nothing could ever top Prague. It was like a birthplace. I think that's a good metaphor. It really was the place where our love for each other was truly born. It may have been conceived in Brno on that little hilltop, but it was most definitely born in Prague that night in her apartment. Without Prague there could have been no Brno, no Paris, no Venice, no Rome, no Schinoussa that perfect little Greek island. And certainly there never could have been Vernazza that amazing little Italian village clinging as it did to the cliffside on that rugged Mediterranean coast like a child's improbable clay model. Our one truly perfect place.

And now standing here in the middle of the street in front of the Lektorsky dum with tears in my eyes, I find myself thinking again how could something so wonderful have gone so wrong? If only I knew why? Helga, my darling, my life is so empty without you. My heart is aching with loneliness and visions of life without you are simply too painful to imagine. What I wouldn't give to hear her voice once again, to hear that lilting laugh of hers and see that magical smile.

I used to enjoy being alone. My friends would sometimes describe me as a loner and I didn't take offense at that. Actually, I rather enjoyed the independence and unfettered freedom of being by myself, free to come and go as I pleased and to do whatever I wanted whenever I wanted, having to seek no one's permission. But now, being alone without her near me seems like a death sentence – a death of the spirit. How can I ever enjoy another moment of my life without her? Even in my sleep she's there. Constantly in my dreams but always just out of reach. And too often I wake up sobbing, my pillow wet. How can I think about the splendid exhilaration of our love here in Brno, and in the next moment remember losing her? It's just too much to bear!

Later, when we had come back to Brno from Prague with the old Ford Fiesta at the beginning of our fantastic auto adventure our visit had been longer and very different. By then we were full-fledged lovers and were ecstatically happy about it. We took a room at a small second rate hotel around the corner from the Lektorsky dum and enjoyed our being alone in this grand old city. It seemed almost like a honeymoon of sorts.

But now, with all those wonderful memories pushed into what seems to be a dark, bottomless oblivion, I couldn't think of what to do next.   I couldn't find out anything at the Lektorsky dum.   Even Matthew Smithson had gone back to England for a holiday.

FORTY-FIVE

Bettina said Helga had mentioned she might go to Brno when they had talked briefly on the Charles Bridge, but where could she be in this city of half a million people? I'm at such a loss to know what to do, where to look. It's beginning to feel as if doubt and indecision have left me paralyzed – like I'm wandering around in a dark room, not able to find anything.

Still impatiently waiting for something to happen, my emotions in turmoil, I couldn't think of what else to do so I took a tram back to the Brno Old Town center hoping that might help. But then I found myself wandering around in a daze of memories, even ignoring familiar landmarks, my eyes threatening to fill with tears. I was hardly aware of where I was until I saw the twin spires of the St. Peter and St. Paul Cathedral pointing like two sharp fingers into the sky. It was then that I remembered my favorite café, the Kavarna u Kapuchinu that was neatly tucked into a hillside in the shadow of the cathedral as if trying to hide, but still anxiously awaiting favored customers. It had been my favorite pastry shop where I often came after work from the University for my customary afternoon cup of tea and a sweet roll. And I remembered I had taken Helga there when she was here with me for the party weekend – Matthew's rambunctious Strange Hat Party – and all my old friends who worked there liked her immediately. Maybe Pavel, my special waiter friend has seen her. He might even know where she is. That's what I should do. Go ask Pavel.

At the restaurant's outdoor terrace I took a seat at a small glass-topped table, putting on sunglasses against the glare of the bright afternoon sun. I tried to relax while I waited for Pavel to come take my order, thinking about the wonderful time I had had in Brno with Helga and how she had virtually invited herself to come that wonderful weekend. And I smiled, remembering she had wanted to know if Brno had a Romance Square or better yet a Lovers' Square and how I had been taken by surprise by her seemingly aggressive suggestion, or at least the bold hint of one. And I chuckled momentarily at what was now only a sad memory.

The hard metal chair pressed uncomfortably against my back as I watched people hurrying to and from the Cabbage Market, the nearby outdoor fresh vegetable market with its fourteenth century statue. Radim, one of my advanced English students, had told me it was called the Cabbage Market because in the winter during the communist era cabbage was about all that could be found there. Now, in the few short years since the Velvet Revolution had driven out the communist, one could find the market brimming with every imaginable kind of produce even in winter. There were even oranges from Spain and pears and apples from South Africa and much more.

Sitting at one of the café's outdoor tables had always been one of my favorite pastimes when I had lived in Brno. I liked watching the people passing by and thinking about their lives, where were they going, what could their lives be like? And sometimes, dozing in the warm sun, I fantasized about a woman who would have lived upstairs in the building across the cobbled street where lace curtains always seemed to be blowing in the breeze. I imagined her abusive lover beating her and I would rush to her aid and drive him away, and afterwards she would throw herself into my arms. Of course, she would be gorgeous.

"Dobra den (good day) my American friend. You have come back to visit us again?" Richard was startled out of his fantasy by the sound of Pavel's familiar voice and he greeted him warmly. "Yes, Pavel I have come back. But this time I come with a heavy heart."

"What does heavy heart mean, professor?"

"It means I am very sad, Pavel. Do you remember the lady who was here with me last summer?"

"Yes, and you both seemed to be very much in love. We all noticed it and were very happy for you. So why is sad?"

166

"She's gone Pavel and I can't find her. You remember she went to America with me where I thought we would live and be happy forever?   But then she left without telling me why or where she was going.   And now I am back here and I have looked everywhere for her.   But I cannot find her."

"But she was here!" Pavel said excitedly, hoping to help his American friend.

"What?   Oh, my God, Pavel.   She was here?   Are you sure?"   I blurted out, my mind already racing like a freight train.   "Is she still here?"

"I do not know.   But she comes and has tea with us for several days.   She talks with me.   Sometimes in German but mostly we talk in English like you always did."

"Tell me, Pavel," I asked excitedly, my breath coming in short, ragged gasps. "Did she say anything about me?   Please, tell me what she said.   Tell me everything.   Don't leave out anything."

"When I ask where you are she does not answer.   She has tears in her eyes and she only says, 'I am reliving a memory, Pavel, and I must be alone.'   She says it is a divinely special memory but then she does not explain.   That is what she says the last day she is here.   She was very mysterious.   What is divinely special memory, professor?"

"It means, I think, a very special memory one likes to remember always with a smile.   Like something you dream would be the best thing you could ever imagine."

I tried to think what could her memory have been about?   I hope it was about us and our time together here.   Could it have been about me?   Is that too much to hope for? But if that's true then why did she leave New Orleans?   Oh, God, I'm back to that again. Why can't I be honest with myself and say she didn't leave New Orleans, she left me.

"She didn't say anything else, Pavel?   That was all she said?"

"Yes, and then I think she goes away."

167

"Where? Did she say where she might go?"

"No, professor. She only says, 'I must go far away, Pavel.' And she says, 'To places where I can watch the sea and remember. Where I must try to forget, but the sea will always remind me. But I must try.' I think your lady is very sad."

Where I can watch the sea? Did Pavel say she said places, plural? But what places could she have been thinking about? Surely not those marvelous places we had visited on our wonderful auto trip last summer? Normandy, Venice, Nice, Vernazza, Brindisi, Athens, and Schinoussa, that special little Greek island. They were all places by the sea. But if that's what she meant, which one could she have been thinking about? All of them? And why would she be going to those places – our special places?

When Pavel brought my tea and sweet roll he quietly withdrew probably sensing my need to be alone. It was then that I noticed a man who had been sitting alone at the opposite end of the group of nearby tables. He had been reading a book for a long time but he closed his book and sat staring off into space, his hand on his chin exactly as I was doing at that same moment. About my age, too. Maybe a little older. Thin gray hair stirring in the faint breeze. A sad, lonely looking fellow sitting there all alone like that. Where were his friends? His special lady? Could that have been me? Is this some kind of omen? Is this what my life will become? The sadness of those thoughts assaulted me, making me weak with images of being always alone, an old man in a rocker with a shawl over my shoulders still dreaming of the lost Helga. Oh, God, no. Please, not that!

In the foreign language department at Masarykova University where I had taught English, no one had seen her. They were all politely concerned but I could tell they had to get on with their work and they had cares of their own. Talking with them only saddened me more and I hurriedly left.

It was while riding a tram back toward the Old Town Center that I thought I saw a familiar face a few seats in front of me. When we both got off at the same stop in front of the *Halvah Nadrazi* (main railway station) I recognized a former colleague. "Leonard? Leonard Novotny, is that you?'

"Richard, what are you doing back in Brno?"

"Looking for someone. Do you remember the woman I was here with last summer?"

"Yes, I remember her. You made a very nice looking couple. She went to America with you, I think. Did you marry her?"

"If only I had." I paused, momentarily lost in the vision Leonard had so innocently suggested, seeing us together again in the little house on Pine Street.

"She's gone, Leonard. She left America without telling me and I can't find her anywhere. And I don't even know why she left. I know she came back to Europe but I don't know where to look. Someone in Prague said they had seen her and she had mentioned Brno. And someone else told me they had talked with her here in Brno recently. By any chance have you seen her?"

"Yes, as a matter of fact I have. Just a few weeks ago, I think it was. I saw her at the Kavarna u Kapuchinu cafe. She was chatting with one of the waiters and I spoke to her. And she remembered me," he said smiling as if pleased. "We talked for a few minutes and I wondered why you were not with her. But I thought it might be impolite to ask where you were so I said nothing."

"Did she say anything about us? Or where she might be going?"

"Not specifically. But I do remember her saying she might go to Italy and try teaching in a language school there. Some place where she could watch the sea is what she said rather mysteriously. And I think she mentioned Venice."

Where she could watch the sea. That's the same thing Pavel said she had told him!

169

"But the waiter had to go back inside and we talked a little more," Leonard continued. "She also mentioned Paris. Said something about it being the City of Light and the wonders of the Eiffel tower. Do you have any idea what she could have meant?"

"Yes, I think I do. I mean, I'm sure I do!"

At least I hope so, I muttered under my breath. I was suddenly gripped by a new excitement that once more stirred my sagging spirits.

Paris? Of course! The City of Light where we had watched from the top of the Eiffel Tower as the sunlight slowly faded and the lights began to come on all over that enchanted city. Where we clung to each other in the cool breeze and promised to love each other forever and never part. But now I can't find her, and I've been the mere shell of a man ever since.

My hopes, so exquisitely heightened in Prague, slowly began to deflate and even this questionable news failed to buoy my spirits.

FORTY-SIX

Paris! The City of Light. How I do love this most wonderful place in the world. We stayed here two whole weeks on our wondrous car trip last summer. Two of the most wonderful weeks of my entire life because I love Paris so much and because I was with there with her and we were so much in love. We lived and laughed and loved here like nowhere else. But then again, maybe everywhere we went was like that. Actually, I think it was!

Looking around at this marvelous city and thinking about Helga, I was reminded of Humphrey Bogart's line to Ingrid Bergman in the movie *Casablanca* that I had once quoted to her, 'We'll always have Paris.' But now thinking about missing Helga and her not being here in Paris with me, I muttered under my breath, "And I thought we had."

Traffic in Paris is maddening: taxis honking non-stop, brakes screeching when you try to cross a street, and those wonderful buses that run on hydrogen, putting our fuel-guzzling Detroit monsters to shame. As for traffic, I had once heard they even have different car insurance rules just for traffic around the Arc de Triomphe everything there is such a madhouse. How can anyone know when to go? And who has the right-of-way? Or is there even such a thing as the right-of-way in Paris? So we had left the old Ford Fiesta in a picturesque little village not far from Paris until we could return and pick it up later on our way to Nice and the Rivera.

When we got to Paris I remembered a small, well-kept left bank hotel on rue Cler in the seventh Arrondissement not far from the Eiffel Tower. Hotel Leveque was one of those nice small hotels made popular by Rick Steves in his guidebook, *Europe through the Back Door.* I had stayed there a couple of times in the past and was pleasantly surprised when we checked in to find that at last the four-story hotel had installed an elevator, coffin-sized though it was. Our room was on the fourth floor, which in Europe means the third floor. And what we Americans, confused as I usually am, call the first floor Europeans call the ground floor and so on up.

The elevator was very helpful despite its tiny size. In fact Helga and I actually liked being crammed in so tightly there was no way for our not touching. Like sardines in a can she would say giggling as she pressed her breasts firmly against my chest. And with my hormones raging as usual who was I to complain? We laughed and giggled each time we rode up to our room, each of us trying unsuccessfully to keep our hands to ourselves. Actually we didn't try very hard. And we noticed that Candice, the ever-present desk clerk, seemed to have a knowing smile for us whenever we came down. She even gave me a very un-Parisian thumbs up sign one morning when we came down and I was grinning from ear to ear.

In front of the hotel rue Cler was a pedestrian street two blocks long where vendors sold mostly fresh vegetable and meat and some fish. Many of the shops along the street sold wine and cheese and those ubiquitous baguettes, some shop owners often moving their wares out onto the street to provide better viewing in order to tempt prospective customers. Helga was fascinated by it all, especially the man carving great hunks from the huge tuna on his outdoor table we could see from our hotel window. The sights, the sounds, the smells were uniquely a part of Paris where there seems to be a special kind of atmosphere that defies description, only that it's so magical, that it's, well, it's Paris.

*   *   *

One morning as we headed for the *Ilde de la Cite* and Notre Dame Cathedral, we were crossing the River Seine on *Pont Neuf,* which I told her means new bridge although it is the oldest bridge in Paris. Looking at her bright, smiling face as we walked along I suddenly stopped and on an impulse asked her, "You seem to be so happy here, Helga. Why is that?"

"I am happy everywhere we go."

"Yes, of course, I know. But why especially in Paris?"

"It is, I think, something about the French attitude toward living. It seems to be in the air. You can feel it everywhere you go in Paris. You can almost taste it on your tongue. It's as if I were half French and half German. Maybe I was a French baby adopted by a German family," she joked. "I feel such a kinship with them." She was thoughtful for a minute longer, all the while looking deep into my eyes as if she were recalling a special memory.

"Do you remember the first time we met in Prague?" she continued when we stopped to lean against the bridge railing. "You asked me what is it that I do? I knew you meant what kind of work, but my answer was that, I live every day to the fullest with what the French call the *joie de vivre* – the joy of living. And when one is in Paris I think that feeling is almost contagious like the flu. You cannot escape it. And it is here in this Parisian air where one can find this most wonderful feeling."

"Yes, I think you're right," I said, my arms encircling her waist and pulling her close. "Who but you could have thought of such a fascinating description for the atmosphere of Paris? But is that the only reason you are so happy to be here in Paris?" I asked in a sort of teasing tone, but still wishing to hear her usual, delightful answer; her answer that always warmed my heart.

"I am happy here in Paris and everywhere we go because I am with you Richard, my love! So very happy to be with you." And she pressed her body firmly against mine, pinning me against the bridge rail as she squirmed erotically, and we kissed quite passionately. A passing American mother grabbed the hand of her gawking little girl, quickly pulling her along saying, "That's the French for you, Eleanor. They don't know how to behave in public."

"Ah, that's more like it," I said, pleased with Helga's answer about loving Paris and loving me as I tried to catch my breath and control my rising desire that was quickly responding to her kisses. "Stop it, Helga," I urged when she continued to press herself against me and persisted in even more vigorous squirming. "Or I won't be responsible for my actions. And yes, I am madly in love with you, too," I managed to gasp as she

173

reluctantly relaxed. "I still can't believe what an incredible thing it was to have fallen in love with such a wonderful woman so late in life."

"I think we must not talk about, 'so late in life,' Richard, my love. We must live in the present; live as if we were young and carefree with a whole lifetime together ahead of us. Live every day as if we were only twenty-one. Do you remember when you were twenty-one and how you thought life would go on forever? When you were so young and carefree and you thought life was perfect and you never even thought about being hurt?"

"Yes, I actually do remember being that young."

"And we never thought about being hurt at that age, did we? The only possible hurt could come from a careless lover," she said, her voice slowly becoming serious.

Noticing how her voice had changed, I asked, "Were you ever hurt by a careless lover, Helga?" But then I hesitated to say more, afraid of dredging up what her changed expression told me might very well be an unpleasant memory. We had resumed strolling along the bridge, but then Helga stopped again and she looked into my eyes with a most unusual expression as if she were trying to work out some confusing memory in her mind. She continued to stare at me with such intensity I began to feel uncomfortable.

For a long time she said nothing trying to decide if she should tell him what she was remembering. "Yes," she finally managed to say very quietly. We were leaning on the bridge railing again watching the river and the ever-present tour boats, and we could hear the sound of the tiny waves that were lapping at the bow of the boats that seemed to be making soft, happy music. But despite the bright sunny morning and the cheerful sound of the passing boats, I sensed that Helga was about to tell me something unpleasant, maybe even sad. Finally I felt I had to say something, "You don't have to tell me if you don't want to. I didn't mean to pry."

"No, I want to tell you. You are involved and I want to tell you so you will understand."

174

"Me! How could I have been involved? Do you mean recently since we have come to know each other so much better? How have I hurt you?"

"Not you, you silly man. I have nothing but complete adoration for you. You could never hurt me – could never hurt my heart." She paused again, thinking about the past, both distant and recent. "Do you remember the first time we made love in Prague? In my flat?"

"Remember? How could I ever forget!"

"Do you remember that at first I was a little hesitant?"

"Yes, I noticed and I was afraid I might have been rushing you."

"No, not at all. Just for a moment that night I was recalling my first time. I was just a schoolgirl, only fifteen, and a boy named Boris I liked very much wanted to have sex and I agreed. I thought I was in love with him and it would be wonderful like something in a romantic film. But he was clumsy and he hurt me. And worst of all he seemed only interested in his own pleasure."

"Was that when you lost your virginity?"

"Yes, and I immediately regretted it."

"But it's supposed to hurt a little the first time, isn't it?"

"Yes, but I expected that. My sister Eska had told me how it would be. But the worst hurt was emotional. He seemed only to care about himself, about his own pleasure. And he seemed to be in such a hurry. Why was that? You are a man, why was he like that?"

"I have no idea. Perhaps he was so young and inexperienced he thought he had to rush to make sure he could complete the act. Young men, boys I should say, are notoriously self-centered when it comes to their early sexual experiences. Sometimes when I think about young boys and sex, and young men too, I swear I think their brains are in their genitals until they are thirty or forty years old. Maybe even older."

Helga said with a bright smile, "I am so thankful that at fifty-five you have outgrown that."

"I certainly hope so. I really believe my brain is finally where it's supposed to be." I was thoughtful for a moment longer wondering what she was trying to tell me and how I could have been involved. Afraid of upsetting her, I only managed to add, "But I have to admit that now that I have met you I do think about that sort of thing very, very often."

"And I am so glad."

"But I still don't understand why you say I was involved."

"Because as bad as that experience was with Boris, you made up for it that first time we made love in my flat in Prague."

"I don't understand? How could I have made up for it?"

"That experience with Boris was so crude, so awful that when I left his parents' house that afternoon I was terribly disappointed. And I kept thinking about this sex thing I had heard so much about, and I found myself wondering about what we had just done and thinking, is that all there is to it? But that first night in Prague you treated me with the most unbelievable tenderness and, most of all you treated me with love and respect. Later that night I remember saying to myself, the thrill of what we had just done still absolutely unimaginable: So *that*'s how it is supposed to be! And every time since then I have never for one moment thought you were only concerned with your own pleasure. You have completely erased that memory for me."

Richard, completely amazed at what she was telling him, said slowly and very emphatically, "I always think the most loving thing I can do with our lovemaking is first and foremost to be concerned with *your* pleasure, my love. You can't imagine how much

176

it pleases me to see your loving enjoyment of our sex. Besides, excerpt for the male orgasm which only lasts about four or five seconds, otherwise it's so intense it would probably kill a man, *Le petit mort* – the little death the French call it – my greatest sexual pleasure is giving you pleasure in any way I can. In any way you want!" In the intensity of that moment and thinking about what she had just said about our first time, I felt tears puddle in my eyes.

Helga gently brushed a tear from his cheek and clung to him as if she never wanted to let go. "And you do, Richard. Oh, my how you do!"

"I think your idea of our being forever young is perfectly wonderful," I added. "I like it very much. From now on we shall always be twenty-one. Both of us, I promise."

That night in our hotel room we made love with the most exquisite pleasure we had ever experienced, rising to unbelievable heights of ecstasy on gossamer wings like we had never known before, not even that first time.

On another night not long after that conversation on the bridge we had made love again, and I was surprised when Helga, who usually moaned softly with pleasure and moved erotically with me was, on that particular night very quiet and completely still. Afterwards, worried that I had done something wrong, I asked, "You were not your usual self with our lovemaking tonight. Was something wrong?"

"No, not at all," she beamed, holding me tightly. "It was wonderful as always. But after our talk the other day, tonight I made myself focus on how wonderful it feels and how much I love you."

"Okay. I guess I see."

"Let me try to explain. Tonight when you were inside me I wanted to concentrate on the intensity of that pleasure. I wanted to become perfectly tuned to the very essence of our lovemaking and my love for the pleasure you give me every time."

I could say nothing I was so stunned at the intensity and the depth of the feelings she was expressing so beautifully.

Later the next day after immersing themselves in the grandeur of Notre Dame, they were walking around the Square in front of the cathedral where gypsy women with babies and street urchins regularly gathered to beg from tourists, obviously trying to prey on their guilt feelings in front of the beautiful cathedral. And Richard, having no patience with their begging, said to one of them, to the amusement of several nearby tourists, "Why don't you go get a job!"

We crossed the bridge in the shadow of the cathedral where dozens of artists stood painting the view, their outlandish use of bright colors seeming to shout to passersby, 'If only someone would look and buy me, I could be the next Picasso.' But it often appeared that many of them used an abundance of color in an unsuccessful attempt to hide a lack of talent.

FORTY-SEVEN

Every day we strolled that incredible boulevard, *les Champs Elysees*, each time stopping at a different sidewalk café for wine and for people watching. I had quickly learned that Helga was just as much a student of human nature as I, and we enjoyed watching people, often comparing notes.

"Look at that huge couple!" she remarked on one occasion as a young man and woman made their way laboriously up the sidewalk.

"They must be some of our dysfunctional, obese Americans," I said, revolted by the sight of them because they were so disgusting and so obviously American. "Those two are a symptom of a terrible disorder raging in my country caused by watching television, playing video games, eating fast food and no exercise. And very shallow-minded people, I might add."

"What is that English word, obese you just said?" Helga asked.

"There it is," I said, pointing to the two grossly overweight monsters. "Look at them. I think if you looked for that word obese in a dictionary there should be a picture of those two. You can see it right there in front of you waddling up the street like two hugely overweight ducks. The word fat does not begin to describe those obscene creatures. Look at them. They are the perfect definition of obese."

"They must weigh three hundred pounds each or maybe more," Helga whispered. "How do you suppose they manage to, ah . . . you know?"

"I suppose the same way elephants do it," I whispered. "Whatever that is," and we fought unsuccessfully to stifle our giggles at the image that evoked.

"Did you enjoy the Louvre Museum, darling," I asked one afternoon after we had spent almost an entire day there.   We were making our way back to the hotel on rue Cler.

"Ja, but it is so large.   And now my feet, they hurt."

"Then tomorrow we will go to a very small museum just on the western edge of the Tuilerie Gardens.   The *Musee d'Orangerie* is in a place where hothouse oranges were formerly grown for the royal family.   There you will see dozens of those marvelous French Impressionist paintings.   And in the basement you must see Monet's huge painting of the water lilies in his garden.   The painting covers an entire wall."

"Oh, my, it must be very grand.   I can't wait to see it.   But we don't have to walk very much, do we?"

"No, it's a very small building.   Then we will find a bench by the River Seine where we can rest and have a picnic and watch the boats go by.   And you can put your feet in my lap if you wish for a loving foot massage."

"Richard, what a wonderful idea.   You are so sweet."

I just grinned.

The next morning, happily browsing the shops on the rue Cler, we gathered the ingredients for our picnic: two kinds of cheese, Brie for me, Camembert for her, a baguette, some fruit, and a bottle of our favorite Burgundy wine with some very un-French plastic cups.   She carried our picnic with her throughout the little museum, the baguette cheerfully peeking out the corner of her carrier bag that had the Eiffel Tower printed on it.

After our visit to the Musee d'Orangerie we sat on a bench by the river in the shade of several old plane trees as I had promised and had our picnic.   We drank from the unfashionable plastic cups anyway and laughed about it.   Then Helga laughed again when I spilled wine on my shirt.

"Richard, you are so clumsy.   But you are so endearingly clumsy, what will I ever do with you?"

180

"Just put up with me, I guess. Wash my shirts and," I paused pretending to be thinking very seriously, "make love with me very frequently."

"I'm not sure about washing your shirts, but the other part will be very easy," she said with her best coquettish smile, remembering that from the very beginning of their relationship he had promised never to say 'I want to make love to you.' He had always said 'I would like to make love with you.' To Helga, that minor distinction between *to you* and *with you* explained the very essence of this wonderful man. And she remembered again the intense feeling she had that day on the Pont Neuf when he had said: 'My greatest sexual pleasure is giving you pleasure in any way I can. With our lovemaking my concern always is, first and foremost about *your* pleasure.' Just at that moment he reached for her hand and another warm shiver ran through her body sending her heart spinning away with indescribable joy.

After our picnic we sat very close to each other and watched the boats go by on the river. When we leaned close so we could whisper to one other I loved the way our bodies touched lightly but enticingly.

On a nearby bench a man held a CD player that was playing a lively Latin tune. After a while Helga stood, still watching the river boats as she began swaying gracefully with the music. I stood behind her and put my arms around her waist and pulled her close, her delightful buttocks swaying provocatively against me, and each of us had visions of what the coming night would surely bring, each thinking in his or her own way what it would be like, and what each would do to please the other.

Later that same afternoon Richard suggested they visit the Eiffel Tower. "Have you ever been there?" he asked.

"Nein, I have only been to Paris one time before and it was a very hurried visit. But never have I been to that most remarkable landmark."

"Then we must go. And we should go just at dusk and go all the way to the top."

181

"We can go all the way up to the very top?"

"Yes, and we can stay as long as we like. It's very much like sitting at a café. The French never hurry you to leave."

"Why should we wait until dusk?"

"Because just at dusk when we are at the top we can watch the lights come on all over the city. And then you will see why Paris is called the City of Light. It is a beautiful sight and very romantic."

"Romantic? Very romantic? Then we should go, Ja?"

While waiting for dusk we sat on the grass in the *parc du Champ de Mar,* that delightfully long grassy expanse where lots of tourists like to sit while waiting to go up on the Eiffel Tower. And we were entertained by three young American girls frolicking about like excited young colts, chattering non-stop and taking pictures of each other, barely able to restrain their enthusiasm and joy at being in such a magical place. And they happily agreed when Richard offered to take a picture of three of them together with their camera.

A little later just at dusk Richard was standing behind Helga on the top observation deck, his hands on her shoulders like that time on the Charles Bridge in Prague, and they both were awed by the spectacle of the lights coming on all over Paris. And he tried to absorb the intensity of the moment, smelling the faint lavender perfume of her hair and drinking in the soft, sweet feeling as she pressed her marvelous hips against him. He wanted to devour her there on the spot as if she were a delectable morsel of the sweetest kind. And at that moment each of them, without the other knowing, silently pledged their undying love for the other. And Richard felt Helga's body shudder and he thought he knew why and he was glad. Surely it was a shudder of delight and happiness.

FORTY-EIGHT

One evening near the end of our stay in Paris we were looking for a different experience, hoping perhaps to find a small intimate place in which to have a glass of wine as a farewell salute to Paris.

*   *   *

"I think it would be nice if we could find a small, cozy place," Helga said as we strolled across the Parc du Champ de Mars with its wonderful view of the Eiffel Tower, and on into the Fifteenth Arrondissement and the Montparnasse neighborhoods. "Do you think we can, Richard?"

"Yes, I hope so. But first we have to get away from all these tourists."

"But we are tourists, too, Ja?"

"Yea, of course you're right. But we're different, don't you think?"

"Yes, I like to think we are very different indeed," she smiled her agreement as she took my arm and gave me that Mona Lisa smile I loved, and I thought I was pretty sure what later this night would hold for us. Another, but a very different kind of farewell salute to Paris, I hoped. But, after a moment's though and looking again at her beautiful smile and that particular gleam in her eye, I didn't hope – I knew. Because knowing the kind of open, loving, giving woman she was I was more than sure we would have our very own personal, remarkably loving farewell to Paris.

"And I think I know how to find such a place," I encouraged, forcing my mind back to finding just the right café.

Crossing the Boulevard de Grenelle we began looking for a café in a quiet residential neighborhood, moving on disappointed whenever we saw any group of people, hoping that for this special night we could get completely away from the cloying

183

atmosphere of crowds.

"I've often wondered," I said, pretending to be very thoughtful for a minute as we wandered small side streets, looking at café signs, "Why a small French restaurant is called a *brasserie*, which seems to be almost the same word for a woman's undergarment."

"Ja, and I know which you prefer. I know where your hands like to go," she teased. "And I love it. Please don't ever stop."

Remembering something from my distant past, I laughed aloud and told her, "Once on a date when I was still in high school the girl I was with said I was a foreigner. What do you mean? I asked her completely mystified. She had said I had roaming hands and rushing fingers."

"Knowing you I think she was probably right."

"Yes, I'm pretty sure you and she both were right."

I had forgotten how intriguing the 'other' Paris could be away from all the crowds. Tourists always seemed to be on the Champs Elysees or at the Eiffel Tower or wandering lost and weary in the Louvre Museum trying to remember where they had seen a McDonalds. But I passionately loved the other side of Paris; those small out of the way neighborhoods with tiny little streets that seemed to beckon one to come and explore, perhaps even to spend some time and relax. Streets crowded with small shops that all seemed to be run by little old men in black pants and sleeve garters; shops that sold everything imaginable at sometimes ridiculously low prices, away from the tourists as they were. And always there were those wonderful, ever-present bistros where the local people met to drink dark, hearty wine and gossip about their neighbors. That was the kind of place we were looking for, and just then out of the curling early evening mist there it was, on a street so small I wasn't sure it even had a name. The bistro had a small, faded sign that had been tacked to a gnarled old chestnut tree that stood resolutely immovable as if standing guard near the front door that announced itself simply as, *Chez Reynaud.*

The street with its quiet shops and the bistro and the old chestnut tree created such a marvelous atmosphere I expected any minute to see Gene Kelley to come dancing by. Of course he would be *Singing in the Rain* complete with umbrella and splashing in the puddles.

Shading our eyes against the glare of the streetlight, we peered in the dusty plate glass window. "I think we've found it," Helga whispered as she squeezed my hand.

"Yeah, I think you're right," I said looking through the smoke darkened window at several men and one slightly bedraggled old woman sitting at the zinc bar, each carefully nursing a glass of red wine.

We entered hesitantly, hoping not to be disappointed as we stood awkwardly at the door looking for a place to sit until Helga spotted a small round table that was unoccupied near the back of the room. The place was so small there were no waiters, only the owner who was tending bar, and Richard had to go to the bar to order their bottle of wine.

Past their table in the very back of the room, shrouded in a blue cloud of cigarette smoke, a very old man sat on a rickety stool playing an ancient accordion that looked to be older as he was. The music immediately made Richard think of old movies about Paris from the nineteen-fifties when there always seemed to be accordion music in the background.

The entire experience in this quaint little neighborhood bistro was so wonderful we even tolerated the cigarette smoke and the sweat of old men because we loved the atmosphere of the place, and knowing that this last adventure was our farewell to Paris.

Just as the old man stopped playing, Richard, who was so moved by his playing and the atmosphere of the place, leaned over and kissed Helga lightly on the lips. The accordion player looked at them, his wrinkled old face wreathed in smiles. "*Mes Amie* (my friends)," he said to the people at the bar. Helga, realizing he was looking their way and talking about them, quickly began to translate. "Paris is always the city of love, and I can see we have two lovers here with us tonight," he said beaming at them. "It is, I think, a very special night for them so I will sing for them a love song."

He began to play and sing in a soft, quiet voice that was more like a whisper as if he were talking only to them, and it quickly became apparent he was making up the words as he played. Thankfully the old fellow sang slowly so Helga could translate every word. She began:

Two lovers gaze into each other's eyes as their lips meet.

Here in this moment nothing else matters, time stands still.

Wishing for the moment to last forever, they listen only to the voice of love.

Love is not always for the very young.

Love is for all whose hearts are warm with thoughts of love.

It knows no age. Love is forever.

In this moment they are alone with only their love to warm their hearts.

The people disappear, the café disappears, only the two of them remain lost in this moment of love they hope will never end.

Moonlight shines on their faces and they smile.

The moon is always full when there is love.

Let it always be so for them.

To you we wish love forever and happiness beyond belief.

As Richard and Helga listened to his words, their two hearts sang together in perfect harmony; a duet to the unquenchable love that even now dazzled their eyes, bringing fresh tears to them both.

When the old man had finished, they both stood with tears still in their eyes and Richard bowed gravely and she curtseyed demurely. As they stood there a moment longer thinking about leaving, a man at the bar called out in halting English, "Non, non. You must no leave. We buy un ..." But then his English deserted him. *"Un verre du vin pour vous (*a glass of wine for you.) And we toast to your love and happiness," Helga translated.

The old accordion player put away his instrument and walked over to their table where he said something Richard didn't understand. Helga translated: "He asks if he could buy us a glass of wine also?" And when she asked him to join them the old man pulled his stool over to their table and Richard, not understanding their conversation, nevertheless loved sitting quietly and listening to the lyrical French the old man and Helga were speaking.

When their glasses were empty, the owner came to their table with three more glasses of wine. When he said something in French Helga said, "He means something like, 'This is on the house. You must not pay.'" Richard managed a quiet, but very heartfelt, *Merci.*

A few minutes later Richard went to the bar and ordered three more bottles of wine, two of which he handed to the man who had toasted them earlier, gesturing that they were to be shared with the others at the bar. And not wanting the evening to end, everyone was quietly excited with what they were sure had become a special moment for them all. Even the old woman at the bar smiled and grinned at Richard and raised her glass in salute.

When it finally came time to leave, the people at the bar all stood and clapped their hands and said *Au revoir* (goodbye) and wished them well as if they were old friends. And the accordion player left with them, carrying his cumbersome instrument by a tattered handle. He explained to Helga that his home was only a few blocks away and so they walked together in a silvery, companionable silence, watching the moonlight spangle the ancient cobblestones with fairy dust. At the next street corner the old man said goodbye and kissed Helga lightly on both cheeks, his white, unshaven chin whiskers glistening silver in the streetlight. She didn't seem to mind and flashed one of her fantastic smiles at him and he stood on the corner as they walked away, his hand raised in what seemed to be a sad farewell gesture. "*Au revoir*," he called quietly to them.

The two very tipsy lovers walked slowly back to their hotel, their eyes still brimming with tears, their hearts overflowing with love for their new friends and for each other.

Holding Helga's hand tightly in his as they wandered back to the hotel, Richard repeated Humphrey Bogart's 'We'll always have Paris,' line. "I think that was written for us, too, my love." Helga smiled as she felt a fresh shiver of joy, and she clung even more tightly to his arm.

*   *   *

Now the gaiety of this fantastic city and that special night seem only to mock me. Every street corner, every sidewalk cafe where we sipped that wonderful French wine reminds me of our time together here which only heightens my pain at losing her. Paris, the City of Light. But without her the light has gone out of my life and I stand in this beautiful old city shrouded in darkness. A darkness of the spirit. Where can she be? Sometimes I think I might be getting close, but then she evaporates like a summer morning's mist on the River Seine.

I had asked a few people we knew here if they had seen her; the wonderful lady in the cheese shop and the man in the bakery where we bought baguettes. No one had seen her. Even Candice the clerk at the hotel said she had not seen her. I even went to Chez Reynaud, that marvelous little bistro. Nothing.

FORTY-NINE

It was while I was in Paris fruitlessly searching and it had seemed so hopeless that I would ever find her that I finally realized my search for Helga was going to take much longer. Weeks more, probably even months.

It had slowly begun to dawn to me that apparently she was retracing the route of our last summer's adventure city by city, place by place just as I was doing now trying to find her by following the few hints I had gleaned from friends. But for what reason she was doing that I couldn't imagine. And there seemed to be no end to the places where we had been and where I knew I should look, hoping by some miracle that I might find her, or at least more about her in one of those faraway idyllic places. And that made me realize more than ever that I must not allow myself to miss a single place no matter how brief our stay had been there or how insignificant it may have seemed. My heart despaired at the thought of looking in all those wonderful places and not finding her, each one filled with poignant memories that were now only painful reminders of what I had lost. But I could not, would not stop looking.

But then there really were no insignificant places on our magical summer adventure, only beautiful, unbelievably wonderful places filled with sunshine and happiness and love; sweet, perfect, never-ending love.

Why do I keep saying never-ending love now that it has surely ended? Or has it really ended? Could there be some odd, irrational explanation for her disappearing but still loving me? Oh, God how I hope there might be. If only I could find her maybe, just maybe I could . . . Do what? Find some answer? But finding her would be the final answer – the only answer I wanted.

I dreaded making the phone call I knew I had to make, knowing full well how upset Bob Worley would be at my request. But I knew I had to do it. I simply had to make the call even as I stood hesitating at a little call box on a quiet Paris side street waiting to pour out my heart to my friend.   There was simply no other way.

"Bob, I hate to pull this on you, but I've got to stay over here longer.   I can't come back now.   Not yet.   I've looked in so many places, but there are so many more places where I need to look."

"Now, wait a minute . . ." Bob Worley tried to interrupt.

"But now I can see that I'm going need more time," Richard continued relentlessly.   "Probably a lot more time.   With summer ending and still not finding out anything, I know I'm not going to be able to come back for the fall semester."

"Now, look Dick, I realize summer school wasn't long enough for you to look thoroughly, but you've got obligations here.   You can't just and up and not come back."

"Dammit, Bob, you don't understand what I'm up against.   And I guess I should have realized you wouldn't understand, what with you having a marvelous wife like Emily and those wonderful boys.   But let me say this just as plainly as I know how.   I'm staying over here whether you or the dean or anyone else likes it or not.   I just don't give a damn. I'm staying.   I mean it, Bob.   This is far too important for me to just drop.   I truly wish I could make you understand.   You've always been such a special friend and I would do anything in the world to help you out.   But this is my future.   This is about rest of my life, Bob."

"Has it ever occurred to you," Bob Worley began hesitantly, not wanting to hurt his friend, "that she might not want you to find her?"

"Yes, I've thought of that – many times.   But even if I knew that was true I'd still keep looking."

"Okay, Dick, just hold on," Bob Worley said, sensing the desperation in Richard's voice, and knowing he would do anything possible to help this special friend.   "I'll fix it with the dean somehow. I guess I can get a visiting professor from somewhere. Had an inquiry from some guy up in Virginia just the other day. He'd just retired from Old Dominion University in Norfolk and he's already getting antsy to get back to teaching. But you're going to owe me for this one, ole buddy. Owe me big time."

"Thanks, Bob you truly are a good friend."

"Yea, yea. Right. Hey, hold on a minute, Dick. Mona is making frantic motions at me. I think she wants to talk to you."

"Dick, have you found her yet?" Mona Herbert asked, coming on the line, the intensity of her worry clear in her voice.

"No, and I'm going crazy trying. I don't even know where to look, Mona. I think I might have a better idea if I only knew what happened to her; if I knew what made her leave. What drove her to leave? Other than Jennifer Smartley's unspeakable behavior at the Mardi gras party, I don't have a clue. Did anything else happen back there in New Orleans just before she left that I don't know about? Something that might help me understand all this? Might help me find her?"

"That's just what I wanted to talk to you about, Dick. The day before she left Helga and I had a date for lunch. And when she finally got here more than an hour late she was so upset she could hardly talk. She was actually hyperventilating. After I calmed her down and gave her a little of that brandy Bob keeps in his desk drawer he thinks none of us knows about, she told me a positively horrible story."

"What in the world about?"

"Apparently Jennifer Smartley went to your house and caused a big scene with Helga. It wasn't exactly a fight. Probably would have been better if it had been. I expect Helga would have kicked her ass. No, it was more like Jennifer was giving her an ultimatum; reading the riot act to her about you. As if she had any right. To hear Helga tell it, and I don't doubt her for a moment, apparently Jennifer said some really awful things to her. You know what a bitch she can be. Hey, look, if anybody hears me talking about this I'll swear I was talking about my mother-in-law whose name is Jennifer. I don't want to get fired over you-know-who.

"Anyway, as I was saying. Of course you weren't there to defend Helga. Your Wednesday afternoon class, remember?"

"For God sake, Mona, what did that bitch say to her?"

"Helga didn't want to tell me. I really had to drag it out of her. It was like she couldn't bring herself to repeat the awful things Jennifer had said. Just something about Jennifer saying that your relationship with her was still very much alive and well."

"What?"

"That's not the worst part, Dick. Jennifer said the best thing Helga could do was to go on back to Germany and forget about you."

"Damn that woman!"

"Yea, tell me about it."

*   *   *

There was a knock on the front door of the little house on Pine Street. Inside, Helga wondered who could that possibly be. She was not expecting anyone and hardly anyone ever came visiting, at least not in the middle of the afternoon. She hesitantly opened the door and found Jennifer Smartley standing on the little porch. "Yes?" was all she could manage to say.

"May I come in," Jennifer asked politely, "I would like to talk to you for a few minutes."

"Yes, of course. Come in," Helga said trying to sound cheerful, but feeling very wary as she immediately remembered Jennifer from the Mardi gras party.

192

Wisely, Richard had not told her about Jennifer's 'whore' comment. He would not have dared hurt her any more than she had already been hurt by the other incidents at the party. But Helga did remember clearly the other vicious, hurtful things Jennifer had said there.

After closing the door Helga watched as Jennifer walked confidently into the den as if she were at home.

Helga began to feel very uncomfortable. She didn't know what to say, but finally managed, "You have been here before?"

"Yes, of course," Jennifer announced smugly. "Very often in fact," she lied.

There was a long pause as the two women eyed each other suspiciously. In order to break the awkward impasse, Helga asked, "May I get you something? A drink, perhaps?"

"No, thanks," Jennifer said. After another pause she continued, "You must be wondering why I've come."

"Well, yes."

"About the Mardi gras party. I'm sure it was awkward for you."

Jennifer had planned to be disarmingly pleasant – at first. "But surely you must have heard," she continued smoothly, "that Richard and I have had a longstanding relationship and, to put it mildly, his bringing you here was quite a shock to a lot of people, and especially to me."

Jennifer crossed her long legs, the very tight sheath dress more than half way up her thighs, its plunging neckline leaving little to the imagination. She had worn it as a reminder of the dress she had worn at the party. She had decided to show this German broad just how much more she had to offer.

"I see," Helga managed to mumble without really understanding. She had no idea where this conversation was headed, but she already didn't like the tone of it, or the direction she thought it was taking.

"To put it another way, I wonder if you really feel comfortable living here," Jennifer said with a smug look as she waved her well-manicured hand at the room. She had decided it was time to take off the gloves. "To be brutally frank, I don't think you belong here. Wouldn't it be better for Richard and for you, and for me as well, if you went back home?"

Helga gasped, "Better for you? But I don't see what . . ." Jennifer interrupted, all pretense at civility gone. "If you're so damned concerned about him and his career the best thing you could do for him is to go the hell back to Germany, and let us get on with our lives over here."

Helga, shocked into silence, could only stare in disbelief. Finally, gathering her wits about her, she managed to ask, "Do you mean that you and Richard still have a relationship?"

"Yes, of course, I mean Richard and me. Who did you think I was talking about?"

"But Richard told me you and he had only a brief affair two years ago. Before he ever knew me."

"Is that what he told you? Well, let me tell you, honey," Jennifer said, relishing her lie with a cruel smile, "there was a whole lot more to it than that. And there still is."

"Still is? But he said . . ." Helga's voice trailed off, her thoughts thoroughly confused.

"It's still a lot more than that. A whole lot more. And not just two years ago," Jennifer repeated her lie, enjoying the look of shock on Helga's face.

"You mean . . . you mean recently? Now?"

"Damn right, baby. You don't think those faculty meetings last all afternoon, do you?"

"But . . . But . . . what . . ." Helga broke down in tears, sobbing uncontrollably. Gasping for breath and hiccupping hysterically, she finally managed to shout at Jennifer, "I want you to leave. Please, leave this house right now."

"There's another thing . . ."

"No! I want you to leave, now!" Helga took Jennifer's arm and roughly pushed her out the front door and screamed at her as she violently slammed the door behind her, but not before she had shouted a few choice German words at Jennifer's retreating back.

*   *   *

If only I had known, Richard thought when Mona had finished her story, the phone in his hand momentarily forgotten. Or if only Mona could have somehow overheard what Jennifer had said and told me about it while we were all still in New Orleans. But apparently Jennifer was too smart for that. She had chosen her time and place very carefully. In her graduate years at Georgetown University in D.C. Jennifer had had a brief internship with the CIA. And she had learned one of their mottoes: Leave no witnesses. And she had learned it very well.

Richard sadly realized after hearing Mona's horrible story, he might never know the full extent of the incredible damage Jennifer Smartley had tried to inflict on his relationship with Helga. Nor would Jennifer ever have any understanding of, or care about, the one pure, unbelievably wonderful love of his life she had so recklessly tried to destroy.

Back in Paris, Richard was still holding the phone in his hand, muttering to himself, "I don't know how long this is going to take, but now that I have the whole fall semester I'm going to keep searching, no matter what."

And thus began his autumn odyssey.

FIFTY

I can recall clearly every detail of our train ride when we left Paris last year; can see every moment of it in my mind's eye as we headed back to the tiny village of Chambord, intending to pick up the car where we had left it and be on our way.

We had decided to take a slow moving local train so we would have a better chance of seeing some of the French countryside. As the train slowly rumbled along we could see farmers cutting hay, their haystacks standing fat and happy like rows of dumpy old men sitting contentedly in the warm sun. The countryside was breathtakingly beautiful and so soothingly peaceful one wished for nothing more than to curl up next to one of the haystacks and take a nap. Everything about the scene was the clear, precise definition of bucolic.

When we arrived back in that delightful little village both of us were immediately struck by its charm and quaintness, enchanted once again with its picturesque uniqueness. The little village looked exactly like a page out of a beautiful picture book. It was as if someone had said, this is what a perfectly beautiful little French village should look like, and there it was. A tree-shaded main street of only three blocks was lined with delightful little shops, each seeming to beckon us to come in and explore. There was a butcher and a green grocer, and another shop that sold wine and cheese and, of course, a bakery with those wonderfully, crunchy baguettes.

*   *   *

"Richard, isn't this little village the most picturesque place you have ever seen? And the local inn is in that old millhouse. Don't you remember we saw it when we were here before when we left the car? Couldn't we stay a few nights? We are in no hurry, are we? After all, we have no specific destination."

"What about our romantic Greek island?" I reminded her.

"Yes, but it will still be there, won't it?"

"Yea, I think you're right. Let's do stay a while. This place really is something, isn't it?"

We wound up staying an entire week and loved every minute of it. We quickly became accustomed to hearing the mill's slowly turning old waterwheel with its perpetual creaking and groaning, the sounds of which we soon accepted as restful background music. And with our window open on soft summer nights we began looking forward to its nightly lullaby as it gently soothed us to sleep.

At the inn Monsieur Bonet was the consummate host. He and his wife Bridget did everything in the inn except that his cousin Jacques did most of the cooking, but with Monsieur Bonet's insistence on helping much to Jacques' frequent dismay. We soon learned from Madame Bonet that Jacques, who was middle aged and a bachelor, was very much a fussy old maid. And typically for a French chef he was quite temperamental. On one occasion I saw him shouting and throwing eggs at Monsieur Bonet. Luckily, they were hard boiled eggs. But still, they made quite a mess.

It must have been our ages and the fact that we were a couple very much in love that appealed to Madame Bonet's romantic French nature. And on a whim I signed the guest register as Doctor and Mrs. Richard Rouse, and I noticed that Helga seemed especially pleased by that.

Madame Bonet insisted on calling Helga, Madame Rouse. And despite Helga's very German name and accent, they would have long womanly talks in a mixture of French and German with an occasional English word creeping in. They usually sat at the kitchen table with a glass of wine, but if Jacques was in one of his moods they would move to one of the outdoor tables on the terrace near the waterwheel.

The tiny village of Chambord was endlessly fascinating and we loved to walk the one short street, investigating each little shop. And Helga, missing nothing, seemed intent on buying something in each one of them. "Something to help us remember this marvelous adventure in our old age," she explained when he had asked.

But then she felt uneasy at mentioning their being together for years to come, hoping he would not think she was being presumptuous, maybe thinking about marriage and children. Which, indeed was exactly what was on her mind.

In the evenings just as a breathtaking sunset painted the old village buildings a warm, tawny gold, we liked to sit at a small table on the terrace by the mill where we enjoyed a glass of the local red wine. The creaking of the millwheel and the cheerful splashing of the water as it turned on its never-ending cycles created the perfect setting for a quiet, romantic evening.

On several occasions we would buy a baguette and some cheese and a small bottle of wine and have our lunch on a bench next to the village fountain. Madame Bonet insisted on our using some of her best wine glasses and, of course, I spilled wine on myself. But miraculously I managed not to break any of her glasses.

The little man who ran the wine shop across from the fountain introduced himself to us the first time we went there. His name was so long and unpronounceable he told us with smile, "You must call me Monsieur Alfred. And I know who you are," he had said that first day in his best English as if knowing a secret. "Madame Bonet has told me all about you," he whispered with a twinkle in his eye and a conspiratorial smile, proving once again the French fondness for romantic secrets. He was dressed in black trousers and sleeve garters like the shopkeepers we had seen in Paris, and I smiled, wondering if perhaps there might be some kind of dress code for French merchants.

At the tiny square in the middle of the village where we sometimes ate our lunch, the soothing sound of the splashing fountain and the peaceful atmosphere made an afternoon nap hard to resist. Leaning against each other on our favorite bench by the fountain, we dozed happily like two well-fed old crows unable to hold up our heads, and I thought what a nice way to spend the two hours the French insisted on for lunch; although

199

I had always suspected there were other things they might have had in mind for one of those hours.

One day after our fountain-side lunch we decided to walk to the end of the village street where the countryside began. Looking at the pastoral scene spread out before us we both grew quiet, trying to absorb the peaceful vista of farms and tree-lined lanes leading, we imagined, to ancient chateaux and, of course, to excitingly romantic places. And nearby a small stream was making happy chuckling sounds as it hurried over rocks making its way, most probably, to the River Seine.

"You know, it never ceases to amaze me," I said in a thoughtful mood as we stood looking at the countryside, "that in a world with places like New York and Paris and London and Prague and Chicago, all teeming with millions of people, that something as quiet and peaceful as this even exists on the same planet."

"Ja, it is so remarkably peaceful and quiet, isn't?" Helga murmured. "So restful one could easily sit beneath that tree over there and go to sleep and, I expect, dream very happy dreams."

"And what would your happy dreams be about, Helga?"

"I'm not sure. But I know that first they would be about being with you and loving you so much as I do. And perhaps later they would be about our happy lives together." She paused, searching for the end of her dream. "Our lives together as very old people still loving each other and our children." She was immediately sorry she had mentioned children, afraid Richard would think she was hinting in some subtle way, but pressuring him nonetheless. Children were still very much a part of her dream, but she kept that part to herself because she was still not sure if Richard's dreams included them. Maybe they could talk about it once they were settled in New Orleans.

They loved the village and the countryside and the tranquility of this special place so much that it seemed to intensify their feelings for each other like some kind of tonic.

200

And they were immensely happy there. It was as if all their cares had simply vanished.

One day as they were finishing their wine by the fountain, Helga asked very quietly, "Richard, when we go to America we will live together, Ja?"

"Yes, of course. That's the whole idea." He thought for a moment, trying to understand the intent of her question. "Why do you ask?"

She was quiet for a long time but finally answered, "I was just thinking maybe we might . . . that is, if we both agreed, we might want to get . . . Oh, never mind, it was nothing."

But of course it was something. Something very important to a forty-eight year old still single woman. The question of marriage kept intruding on her consciousness, and although she tried to ignore it, it would never entirely go away. But she sensed that Richard was not ready to discuss the idea and she instinctively realized she should not pursue the issue now, and maybe never, although her heart still longed for marriage and for children of her own.

Sometimes in quiet moments when she was alone she tried to imagine what it would be like to be married to Richard, and she enjoyed having daydreams about how happy they would be together. And, of course, there would be children. Her fantasy grew, expanded, and took wings of its own. Maybe they would have two children or, she thought wistfully, perhaps even three. She could see herself very clearly preparing dinner, the oldest two helping while the youngest snuggling contentedly in the lap of a very happy father. Should they all be girls? No, probably at least one boy for him, discussing football – soccer, the Americans called it.

She had been taking the birth control pills Richard had suggested she use, but she was not at all happy about it and she pondered her future with vague misgivings.

Occasionally, in the midst of her daydreams, the reality of their differences would intrude and leave her troubled. She thought about their different backgrounds, like their language differences although she knew she was very proficient in English. But more importantly, what small but incalculable differences were there in their personalities, in their feelings and how they expressed them, in their attitudes about so many little things? Surely his being seven years older couldn't make that much difference? But did these small things really matter that much? No, she reprimanded herself. Do not give in to negative thinking. I must focus on the positive. It will happen. I know it will! Just give him time.

For his part, Richard remained quiet whenever he suspected what some of her vague comments were about. But why couldn't he discuss them with her, he asked himself often. I love her dearly. This is the most unbelievably wonderful woman I have ever known; could ever hope to know. And I want to be with her always. So why could there possibly be this hesitation about marriage? Could there be some lingering guilt about his divorce from Mary? Surely not that? Should I have tried harder to make that marriage work? But what else could I have done? And Mary had always been so inflexible. He found no clear answer to these and other imponderable questions.

FIFTY-ONE

One day soon after we had come to that beautiful little French village we had a most memorable picnic.

"Richard, Madame Bonet says she and her husband own a small farm just outside of town, and she says it would be a wonderful place for a picnic. It had been part of her dowry when they married. And she was born in a little farmhouse nearby."

"That sounds nice. Shall we?"

"Yes, I think I would like that very much. And she told me where there is a small stream," Helga hurried on enthusiastically, "and very old trees and a lovely meadow."

Richard drove slowly, hesitant about driving the old car on such a narrow bumpy road, and when it was time to stop he decided to park by the side of the road. Summer was in full bloom and even the tall rangy weeds were beautiful with their purple and yellow flowers that were nodding in a faint breeze. Helga didn't know the names of them, but she stopped to pick a few anyway before she jumped the small roadside ditch. Richard followed close behind, struggling with the picnic basket and hoping not to hear the crashing of Madame Bonet's wine glasses.

In the distance they could see the meadow and its one very large, very old oak tree that towered above the countryside like some ancient sentinel standing watch over the idyllic meadow; perhaps as if keeping away prying eyes and even intrusive noises, its gray-green canopy seeming to cast a shady oasis just for them. And they could hear the happy gurgling of a nearby stream that would be like a special musical accompaniment for their dining pleasure. Our own private dinner music, he thought, smiling at the image.

"This looks like a wonderful spot," Helga said, pointing. "That old tree and the stream nearby and the beautiful green grass as soft as . . ." she shrugged impishly.

"As a bed?" he teased.

"Ja, and we do have the picnic blanket."

"I think we ought to eat first. I don't think I want to, ah, you know," nodding toward the blanket, "on an empty stomach."

"But if we eat first you might fall asleep."

Richard, looking at this adorable woman standing so very close, her amazing figure no longer hidden by that drab green coat, answered with a sly smile, "I think I'll chance it."

They were ravenously hungry and made short work of the bread and cheese Madame Bonet had packed along with a bit of veal left over from dinner the previous night. The small bottle of wine she had packed was the perfect complement to their wonderful picnic. The little nearby stream was chuckling merrily over rocks as it whispered seductively to them. And birds singing in the big tree were like more distant music.

After we had eaten and had settled ourselves on the picnic blanket – Helga, her head on my chest, my arm warmly against her breasts – we were staring at the clouds in the perfect blue sky and we began playing a game of seeing shapes in the clouds like children everywhere seem to do. And Helga was much better at the game than I. And every image she described seemed to be a romantic one.

With the wine and full stomachs our eyes began to grow heavy. But when I leaned over and kissed her all thoughts of a nap disappeared. I began to undress her very slowly, kissing each bare patch of skin I uncovered.

"Richard, someone might see us," she said, but not really protesting.

"I don't think we have to worry. We're a long way off the road. And besides, the French expect this sort of thing," I explained as we continued to remove each other's clothes. "Why do you think they have two hours for lunch? You don't think they eat for two hours, do you?"

204

"Now that you mention it, I think they are very smart."

As I pulled her wonderful naked body close to me, I thought of a question I had been meaning to ask her for some time. "Helga, why don't you ever call me Dick like some of my friends do?"

"How can I call you Dick? It will always remind me of the American obscenity for the penis. So I shall always call you Richard. Even in moments of greatest passion I shall call you Richard! But it will be a very passionate: Yes, Richard, yes!"

I kissed her again and began to explore her body with my lips and tongue, kissing her breasts, her amazingly flat belly down to her beautiful red pubic hair, and she cried out, "Yes, Richard, there! There! There!" And she felt herself transported into unbelievable heights of erotic pleasure, her every nerve tingling with the sheer physical pleasure of his lips caressing her.

"I cannot stand it! The pure, unrelenting joy I feel with you is beyond belief. You are a Greek god sent to devour my poor defenseless body. And I love it!" Gasping for breath, she managed to say, "Oh, Richard, how I do love you and what you do to me! For me! she corrected herself. How can a woman be expected to endure the intensity of this kind of pleasure?"

Afterwards they lay together happily exhausted. And Helga, still on top of him panting, murmured her love for him, her passion not yet spent. Her hair brushed his face with soft, delicate strokes like tiny angel wings as she kissed him again and again.

But Richard, like all men, once he had had his orgasm was finished with the whole business in two minutes, ready to go out and play golf or shoot some basketball.

Gradually their eyelids began to droop and Helga sighed heavily as she rolled off him, halfway intending to sleep, but waiting just in case there might be more to come.

Later, while I propped up on an elbow and was looking down at her as she lay dozing I seemed to sense in that single moment the entire essence of this amazing woman. Her plain simple goodness was completely unaffected, yet it was supremely complex in its seeming simplicity. This incredible woman was completely without guile which, added to her red hair and freckled nose and that infectious laugh made the sum total of her personality that of a bright, happy young schoolgirl. But, oh yes, she was a woman, too! And what a women! In that one special moment my love for her was so intense it made my heart catch with that odd little skip I had first experienced in Prague. And amazingly, I finally and fully understood the exquisite intensity of my love for her that knew no bounds – would never know any.

But a moment later as I lay back, looking at the sky again my thoughts turned to her question by the fountain yesterday; the question she had hesitated over and had finally left unasked. I'm sure she was thinking about our getting married when we go to New Orleans. Why was my answer so vague it was almost unkind? Why can't I be sure? What's so hard about saying yes? Why can't I just go on and say it? There's no reason that I know of to hold back, but I still do. And I don't even know why.

Later, after napping briefly Helga, seeing that it was now Richard who was asleep, rose very quietly so as not to wake him and slipped into her clothes. She walked toward the giant oak tree, the tall grass swishing against her legs. The afternoon sun spangled the sky with amazing brilliance as large dollops of bright sunlight fell through the branches of the tree, leaving quivering patches of gold on the grass. She reached down to touch one as if she could feel its warm golden glow with her fingers.

When she reached the tree she was surprised at how large it was and she gently stroked its rough bark as she tried to guess its age, and she wondered about the scenes it had witnessed. Wars, of course, and families living out their lives nearby. And perhaps, she thought, smiling, other couples making love beneath its wide shady branches as she and Richard had just done. But then she hoped not. I would like to think that our lovemaking here made this our own special place. Just ours alone. Even with no way of knowing, I shall always think of it that way. Our special place in this lovely little French meadow.

Only ours where we can share our very special love.

She thought again of Richard and their love for each other, and in a burst of joyous exuberance she hugged the old tree then swung around and around, dancing in a flurry of happiness, lifting her arms as if in prayer while she whispered her love to the heavens. How could a woman feel any happier; could want anything more than the love she felt for him, knowing how intensely she loved him and how he loved her?   The vision was unbelievably vivid, and with her heart near to bursting she threw herself on the grass and closed her eyes drinking in the heady wine of her love for him.

FIFTY-TWO

On another day they had made love again in the same meadow, and it was just as breathtakingly wonderful as before in that beautiful place. Afterwards, when they had put their clothes back on and were lying close together quietly drowsing for an hour or so, Helga propped up on an elbow and looked at him with an odd questioning expression. She touched his face with her fingertips and asked, "Why did you divorce your wife? Or did she divorce you?"

"My heavens, what brought that on?"

"I've been thinking about it a lot lately. But I don't want to know just out of morbid curiosity. Is morbid curiosity a correct English term?" I nodded, yes.

"I just thought if I knew about her; about you and her, I might understand you better."

"Do you want to understand me better?"

"Ja, of course. I want to know everything about you. I want to know what you think. What you feel. What you dream."

"Mostly I dream about you, my darling."

"But you know what I mean, Richard." After a pause, she added softly, "I want you to know everything about me, too."

"And I do. At least I hope I do."

"So, tell me about your wife."

Richard was quiet, apparently thinking about the question for such a long time she began to wonder if maybe he was not going to answer. Maybe there was something in their past he didn't want her to know.

208

Finally he sighed heavily and began, "I married her because she was safe – at least safe in a marital sense. I know that sounds crazy but let me try to explain. A therapist friend of mine once told me I had married her because she was like my mother. Can you imagine that? What an awful idea. But he wasn't trying to be complimentary. In fact, the way he explained it was very negative. What he meant was, from the things I had told him about our marriage, that like my mother, Mary was very safe and non-threatening in all her personal relationships.

My mother never made any kind of demands on my father or any display of affection that I ever saw. And never in all my years of growing up did I see my mother and father so much as touch each other. Not once! And worst of all, at least from my point of view, she never showed any affection for her children, either.

"When we were in our forties my older brother and I discussed this one day when I was visiting in his home. And we were both surprised that each of us had exactly the same memory. Neither of us ever remembered our mother tucking us in bed at night, never reading us a story, never kissing us goodnight. Later, when I was alone and thinking more about it, I realized I had no memory of my mother ever hugging me or kissing me, and not just at bedtime, either. Never once! Never saying 'I love you.' Not once in all my first eighteen years of life at home! Never! I didn't even know that other mothers hugged their children or kissed them goodnight and said, 'I love you.' As an adult I've always thought back on my childhood as having been completely barren. A Sahara devoid of love of any kind. Dry, barren, and loveless. I was well into maturity before I came to realize that not all mothers were like her.

"And, of course, with the kind of home life I grew up in where my father and mother never expressed any affection for each other, there were no role models for how a man and a woman should relate to one another. Consequently I spent my entire boyhood being uncertain about girls. No, it was more than uncertain. I was actually afraid of girls. Not physically afraid like they were going to beat me up or something. It was the fear of not knowing how to deal with girls. How to act. What to say. How to behave. And, of course, after puberty it got worse. I never had the self-confidence to ask a girl for a date, although my hormones were in turmoil like any teenage boy's. Consequently I was painfully shy. With girls, that is. Otherwise I was the life of the party. The class clown. Everyone's friend.

"So I guess it was inevitable that I was attracted to a woman who was like that – like my mother. Of course that turned out to be my wife, Mary. And just like my therapist friend had suggested, she was almost a carbon copy of my mother. But, of course, I didn't realize that until it was too late – much too late.

Helga raised an eyebrow in shocked surprise at this revelation, but she chose to say nothing. Let him finish. Let him say whatever he wants. But she couldn't help thinking how awful that must have been for him. Then another terrible thought popped into her mind. How could a mother be like that? If I ever have a child he will know he is loved. I will cuddle him and kiss him and hold him so much he will have to ask me to stop. I will tell him every day how much I love him. And more importantly, I will *show* him that I love him. Poor Richard, how awful that must have been for him.

Then another even more amazing thought occurred to her. How could Richard have learned to love as well as he does with me, giving unselfishly of himself and his love when he had come from such a barren, loveless family? She shuddered again at the thought of the mother he had described, so cold, so hard, so unloving.

"You don't seem to have any problem with women now," she whispered encouragingly.

"That's because of you," I said.

And Helga felt a small, happy smile.

"As a child," Richard continued without prompting, "you have no idea it's okay not to love your mother, that you didn't have to pretend to love her. It's simply not allowed. I was nearly forty years old before I finally came to understand that I didn't have to love my mother that I didn't even have to like her." He paused again thinking about what he considered his unpleasant past. "She's dead now and I can say out loud how I really felt about her for all those years. My God, how I do loathe the thought of how she treated me. Or more accurately, what she didn't do. How could she have been like that? And I find myself frequently wishing I had said some of these things to her while she was still alive, mean-spirited and bitter though they would have been. And, of course, had I done so she would have been horribly shocked. How could I say such a thing to her? That's what the surprised, unrepentant parent always says, isn't it? *After all I've done for you?* And there's the rub. Her friends would have said she was a good mother. She bought us clothes, poor though we were, she cooked our meals, sent us to school, did all the obligatory things a mother was supposed to do, except for one. There was no love. None – what – so – ever!

"I would have gladly given up all the fried chicken dinners, all the not so fancy but sturdy clothes and shoes, even the Sunday school lessons that always sounded so hollow when I thought about how she treated me. I would have given up all of them for just one hug, one goodnight kiss, one 'I love you, Richard my son.'"

Richard felt drained after his long stressful confession. Or was it an accusation? Or maybe more like the reading of an indictment against the accused? Her actions might as well been crimes, he thought. Not real criminal acts, but in my mind they were like crimes nonetheless. Crimes of omission against two small helpless boys who surely couldn't understand or appreciate the difference between acts of commission and acts of omission. And once again he felt that vague, sad longing he had known as a child that he hadn't understood. But somehow he had always known something was missing. Something important.

FIFTY-THREE

Helga, trying to hide her shock and growing distaste for a woman she had never known, asked very quietly, "Does saying it aloud now help ease the pain of those memories, knowing it's all right to feel about her the way you do? Does that help make them go away?"

"No. To tell you the truth I still feel that same way. In fact, it's worse now that I understand how important loving one's child can be. Should be. Must be! And I still long for what I know I missed.

"It's almost like someone has stolen something that was very important to you and you knew they had destroyed the thing, and no matter how much you wished it, you knew there was no way you could ever get it back. You don't forget something like that. That intense resentment of having been robbed of the most important feeling a human could ever hope for, the feeling of being loved. The hurt is always there. And almost every day something I see or think or feel reminds me of that pain, and it only intensify the resentment. Like that mother walking through the village yesterday holding her little boy's hand and smiling at something he had said. Such a simple, wonderful, loving thing to do.

But as a young child you don't know what it is you are being robbed of. You just know it's something. And you feel it every day. Day by day, every day."

Thinking about Richard's feelings for his mother, Helga found herself wondering if these could be the seeds of problems that might come between them, may have already begun to come between them. Could this be why he never mentions marriage and children, why he seems to always shy away from the idea?

But she continued, "What does all this have to do with your marriage to Mary, I think her name was?"

"I'm coming to that." He paused, grappling with yet another unpleasant memory. "By the time I graduated from college I had convinced myself, with a lot of help from an old maid aunt, that it was time I was married. And so I did. I know that sounds terrible, and I'm not proud of it, but that's exactly what I did. It's almost like I walked out on a crowed street corner and called out, 'Okay, I'm ready to marry somebody now.' There's an old song, *Falling in Love with Love is Falling for Make-believe*. But that's exactly what I did. I convinced myself I was in love with Mary and it was time I should marry. But it became clear to me from the very beginning I didn't really love her. She was almost a carbon copy of my mother.

"Mary and I were married for eleven years. We lived together, worked in the same profession, teaching. And yet almost immediately we were virtual strangers in our private lives. Thank heavens there were no children. Remember I told you how Mary was non-threatening? And she was even less demonstrative with affection than my mother, if you can believe that."

"Perhaps she grew up in a home similar to yours?"

"Perhaps. But as far as I'm concerned that's still no excuse. And certainly no excuse for my mother's actions either. Or her lack of actions, to be more precise. Anyway, Mary wanted to stay there in Raleigh, stuck in her safe, comfortable rut. She never seemed to grow at all. Church became more important, her beliefs more dogmatic, her outlook on life even more restrictive at the same time I was finally beginning to learn to spread my wings, anxious to embrace new ideas and adventures. To live life more fully, more adventurously. I guess you'd say I was trying to find happiness where it had never been before. But with my background, can you imagine what a daunting task that was going to be?

"And, as if in a carefully planned counter-attack, when Mary undoubtedly sensed the changes in me, she became even more domineering, more restrictive. Not domineering in an abusive sense. She never said much. Never attacked me head on.

She was smarter than that. But she had a consistently negative way of approaching things. And she always had such a subtle, oblique way of having her own way, and conversely, denying me mine. And for years I knuckled under and I don't really know why I did. I know I'm a strong person now, but I guess a lifetime in a loveless home had conditioned me to accept that sort of thing. And, of course, being married to Mary just made it worse. She was without a doubt the most negative, the most manipulative person I have ever known. I suppose the ghost of my mother played a part in how I responded to that, too. Maybe a large part. Before we were even married, I could see that my mother didn't like her. I suspect she saw her as competition.

"And to make matters worse, or at least inevitable as often happens with two people, one grows and the other doesn't. Or sometimes they grow in different directions. I began to grow emotionally and intellectually. But Mary simply drew herself tighter into her already self-absorbed shell and didn't grow at all. Except that she retreated more and more into religion. Rigid, dogmatic, unforgiving religion.

"Beginning to find myself at last and to know what I really wanted from life for the first time, I made a conscious effort to reject the unrelenting negativism of the past. And more importantly, I was gaining a fuller appreciation for the uniqueness of life and the terribly short amount of time we all have. I wanted to be *someone*. Someone new.

"But finally I had had enough. I knew I had to make a clean break or be doomed forever to a life of dull, loveless mediocrity with no hope of escape. I wanted my spirit to fly, to go on to new adventures, new experiences. I once read that if person doesn't reinvent himself every ten years he will die of boredom. And I didn't want that."

"What did you want to become?" Helga asked quietly.

"I didn't know then and I'm still not sure I know even now. But that's okay, too, because to me growing is an ever-changing process not an end in itself, and the answers are never very clear-cut. All I knew was that I wanted to grow, to become something more and better than what I had been. To spread my wings and fly. To live life! Really live it to the fullest! Not hopelessly trapped in a cage with the unbreakable bars of a loveless marriage.

"Even now I'm not sure if I know how to say it. It was, and still is, just an urgent feeling of wanting to become something more than I was. To keep growing. I sometimes think of my years married to Mary as a time that has left no memories, just a long dark place where I once lived. Isn't that a terribly sad way to think about a large part of one's life?"

He lapsed into quiet thoughtfulness for a long while, and Helga was so struck by how profound the moment had become she was determined not to interrupt.

Finally he took her face in his two hands and very gently kissed her lips. "But no matter what I wanted my life to become, I always knew you were there just waiting. Not as Helga Wintermantle because I didn't know you then. But I sensed it as clearly as if you were already there with me. I just knew it. I could feel it. I was sure that somewhere there was a woman as wonderful as you just waiting for me. The only thing missing was I didn't know her name yet. And then all of a sudden there you were sitting beside the statue on Wenceslas Square. And suddenly my life was complete. I suppose I must be saying all this rather badly."

"No, Richard, my love, you are saying it beautifully. What you just said to me, about me, would make any woman cry for joy. When you said, 'And suddenly my life was complete,' shivers ran up my back. What an incredibly wonderful thing for a man to say to a woman. And you just said it to me!" Her eyes filled with tears at the thought of the love he was expressing for her. Both of them were very quiet, overwhelmed by the magnitude of what they each had been saying; this new expression of the love they had for each other, now more profound, even deeper.

"Richard, you said your mother died, but what about your father?"

"My father is eighty-seven years old now. He still lives in the same town in

215

eastern North Carolina where I grew up. It's a small town and the people there were very nice and friendly, and they always kept a watchful eye out for young children to make sure they were safe and happy. It was quite simply a wonderful place for a young boy to grow up carefree and safe and happy. And loved, if only I could have felt that way," he added with a wistful sigh, thinking about the need for a child to be loved.

Helga waited, again sensing he could not be rushed.

"You have to understand," he hesitantly began again. "My parents were basically Victorian in their approach to life. And my father was far from blameless, but I always felt it was the mother who was the primary caregiver; the one who should give her love most generously to her children.

"I had so much negative background to overcome I was in my mid-thirties before I really became comfortable being with a woman. But now, being with you and loving you has changed all that and has made up for all the regrets I ever had."

Helga felt anew the immensely of her love for him as it seemed to fill her heart to overflowing. She knew she could never make up for his mother's neglect, but she wanted to hold him and cuddle him against her breast and smother him with love and kisses every day. And she promised herself that was exactly what she would do.

FIFTY-FOUR

"Mona, by any chance have you heard from Helga? Have you had any word at all?" Richard had called New Orleans again like he had done recently in Paris, desperate for news of any kind. But no, on second thought, he hoped to hear only good news, or at least encouraging news. The little French village had only one ancient pay phone, but it worked and he was grateful for that.

"I'm glad you called, Dick. Helga called here last week and asked to speak with me, so we chatted a while. I think she just wanted to keep in touch with us. I've wanted to call and tell you but we didn't know how to get in touch with you."

"Did she give you any idea where she might be? I'm at such a loss to know where to look next. Do you have any idea at all where she was?"

"No, not really, Dick."

"How was she, Mona? I mean, how did she seem?"

"Really subdued. Actually rather sad, I'd say. What happened to you two, Dick? We all liked her so much. That is, everyone except Jennifer."

Richard resisted the urge to lash out at Jennifer Smartley's unforgivable treatment of Helga. "I don't have any idea what happened, Mona, that's the problem. Did she say anything that might give you some idea where she was," he repeated, anxious for some clue. Any clue?

"No, not a word. In fact she was very evasive when I tried to find out. I knew you would want to know if I could possibly find out where she was and I even asked quite casually about the weather there, hoping she might give me some sort of clue. But I guess she caught on right away and she just said the weather was fine. It seemed obvious to me she didn't want any of us to know where she was. And I got the clear impression that included you. Especially you," Mona said quietly, knowing how devastated Richard

217

already was.

"Did you tell her I was trying to find her?"

"No. I started to, but then I thought maybe I shouldn't. That might make her even more difficult to find."

"Yea, I think you were right not to say anything about my searching. Did she give you any idea where she might go next?"

"No, not really. I guess she was being very cautious. But after we talked a while she seemed to relax a little. She sounded really tired and sad, too. Actually she sounded very sad. I could almost hear the tears in her voice. It was like she wanted to keep me on the line and tell me about lots of little things just to hear a friendly voice, I guess you'd say. And she just sorta began rambling. And after a while one of the things she mentioned was something about Omaha, but we had a bad connection and it wasn't very clear. And I thought at the time that was kinda odd. That's a city in Nebraska, isn't it? What could that have to do with anything? You don't suppose she's still here in America, do you?"

"No, I'm pretty sure she's still over here in Europe. Some of her friends told me they had seen her recently. But the question is, where is she now."

Omaha, Richard thought. Now what could she have meant by that?

"Then I think she said something about going to the beach. They don't have any beaches in Nebraska, do they? The connection was really bad and I wasn't sure what she had said. Maybe it was just a lake or something."

He paused trying to think, trying to remember. Why would she say something about an American city? About a beach? What could that be about? Normandy! Of course, the D-Day beaches at Normandy! Omaha Beach. We had been there!

Mona went on, unaware of his idea. "But then she mentioned something about Italy. I don't think it was Rome or Florence or any of those famous places but it was

218

definitely Italy. Some place where she could sit and watch the sea was what she said."

That's what she'd told Pavel and Leonard Novotny in Brno. But where could that be?

"It had two names but I can't remember what they were," Mona continued.

"Two names?" Richard's heart began racing again. "Would you recognize it if you heard it, Mona? Was it Cinque Terre?"

"I'm not sure. But yea, I think that might have been it. It sounded something like that. She sounded almost dreamy when she said it. But then I guess she sensed she was saying too much and she wouldn't say any more, and she hung up after a quick goodbye."

He said goodbye to Mona and stood there unaware he was still holding the old phone, his mind in a quandary over what to do next. And like always, he was dreaming about Helga and where she might be and how he could find her. Slowly he walked back to the village fountain where he sat, sad and weary and thinking about her and all that had been, and what might never be again. Even the soothing sound of the splashing fountain couldn't ease his sadness.

He played over and over in his mind what Mona had said about Italy when suddenly it became clear to him. Of course, it hadn't been Florence or Rome at all! Could it have been Nice? Not likely, we spent so little time there. And after all, Nice is a French city. But I have to look there anyway. Most probably it was Vernazza in the Cinque Terre. One of the five little Italian villages clinging to the cliffs overlooking the Mediterranean, our most favorite place of all. It had turned out to be even more special than our dreamed-of romantic Greek Island.

But still, I should check the hotel where we stayed in Nice just in case. I hope I can remember where it was. I do remember it was very close to the beach, and across the street from the hotel on a modern building there were two huge statues of shapely women who seemed to be peeking out at us. I have to go. Right now!

219

Please God, please let her be . . . Hold on a minute, I'm about to forget Normandy! Mona said she mentioned something about Omaha and now I remember! After we left Chambord last summer we decided on the spur of the moment to visit the D-Day beaches on the Normandy coast. I remember specifically we went to Omaha Beach. I had better look there before I go to Nice. I can't afford to overlook any possibility.

Why would she be there? But why anywhere?

FIFTY-FIVE

Richard had stopped overnight at a small hotel in Rouen on his way to Normandy and he was surprised when his new mobile phone vibrated and then chirped anxiously. "Dick? This is Bob Worley."

"Yea, Bob, good to hear from you. What's up?"

"Man, am I'm glad I found you? Thank goodness I talked you into buying one of those new satellite phones with international access. Dick, something really strange is going on here, something I think you ought to know about."

"What is it, Bob? You sound very mysterious."

"It's Jennifer Smartley. Now *she's* disappeared."

"What do you mean, disappeared?"

"Let me tell you the whole story then you can draw your own conclusions. Jennifer came to me a few weeks back and said she had been invited to chair a panel at a conference at Harvard University. A conference on Modern American Literature – you know, that's her specialty."

"What's wrong with that? We know she is tops in her field even though we both hate her guts. This should be a feather in the cap for the University's, right?"

"Yea. But just wait until you hear the rest of it. Mona went to her office a couple of days ago to pick up some standardized test results, and she noticed Jennifer's laptop was on her desk. You know how she is about that laptop. Even gives her lectures using it instead of written notes."

"So?"

"I thought she might have forgotten it. Might need it at the conference so I called

Harvard and a very mystified chairman of their English department told me there was no conference scheduled there.

"What? That sure sounds crazy."

"Yea, it sure does. And, of course, I immediately thought, where could she be? She hasn't been in a class herself in over two weeks, although she did have the decency to have a young graduate student meet her classes."

"Did you find out where she's been?"

"Just hang on to your hat my friend, and let me tell you the rest of it. It gets even more peculiar. Yesterday I went to the New Orleans airport to meet my in-laws who were coming for a few days visit. The thing is, while I was waiting for their flight to arrive I saw one of my former students who works at the American Airlines check-in counter and we chatted for a few minutes and then she asked, 'Did Professor Smartley enjoy her trip?' And she went on to tell me that Jennifer had left a week ago on a flight to, guess where? Prague."

"Damn! What can that bitch be up to now?" After a pause, Richard added, "As if we don't know? But what can she hope to gain by coming over here? Even if she does find me?"

"She probably thinks she has a chance with you now that Helga has disappeared. Maybe she thought if she could find you over there she could, ah, what would you say she was thinking? Get you back? You know how Jennifer hates to lose. In anything."

"How would she have known about me being back over here in Europe?"

"You know how gossip gets around the University. And that blog you've been posting on the Internet? Everyone back here has enjoyed reading about your adventures. But, of course, Jennifer had access to it, too. In fact, Mona told me that before Jennifer left she had her download the whole thing and print it out for her. It's like you gave her your entire itinerary."

"Damn! I never thought about that. So, do you have any idea what I should do now? Just try to avoid her, I guess. But how?"

"I'm not sure, Dick, but I expect she thinks you're fair game now. You better watch yourself, old buddy you know how dangerous the Black Widow can be. And you know how persistent she can be. And after that Mardi gras party incident I expect she's out for blood. By the way, Mona told me about her going to your house and confronting Helga. What a crappy thing to do." Bob Worley, thinking more about Jennifer and the unpleasant situation added, "You know how domineering and bossy she can be."

Richard stood in front of the small hotel where he was staying in Rouen, the mobile phone momentarily forgotten in his hand as his mind was carried swiftly back to memories of his relationship with Jennifer Smartley. In spite of her beauty and the sometimes wonderful sex – that is, when she decided to put her mind to it – Bob's remarks made him remember just how bossy and even domineering she could be.

"Thanks for calling, Bob. Please call me again if there are any more developments. And Bob, of course I still haven't found her."

"I hope you do, Dick. We're all hoping you will."

Bob Worley and Richard both knowing Jennifer Smartley so well, immediately assumed the same thing. It wasn't that she wanted Richard back in a relationship so much as it galled her that he had found someone else. And that Helga being German and older just made it worse which Jennifer probably took as a personal insult like a slap in the face. Like Bob said, Jennifer hated losing.

FIFTY-SIX

After a restless night of wondering what Jennifer Smartley was up to, I left the little village near Rouen and headed for the Normandy coast as I had planned. I was glad that with Mona Herbert's help I had figured out what Helga had meant when she had mentioned Omaha. But I tried not to build up my expectations for finding her although it was difficult not to keep wishing while my heart insisted on pounding out its persistently sad song of forlorn hope.

When we had left the little village of Chambord on our wonderful summer auto trip, we drove through the Normandy countryside to the World War Two D-Day beaches. Along the way we passed mile after mile of vineyards, the vines rich to overflowing with plump, dark grapes ready for picking, a rose bush planted at the end of each row to attract bugs away from the vines.

In addition to local farm laborers, many young people were already gathering in campgrounds or pitching tents haphazardly anywhere, ready to help with the grape harvest, many of them young American or Brits seeing Europe on a lark and earning a little eating money.

*　　　　　*　　　　　*

"I've always wanted to do that," I said to Helga, pointing to the young people already hard at work in the vineyards as we drove by, and thinking how nice it would be if only one could roll back the years and be that young again. We could just jump out of the car and offer to help pick the grape. And in the evenings we would join the other young people singing around their bright campfires as they enjoyed liters of new wine.

When I mentioned what fun it might be to stop and help with the harvest Helga immediately wanted to try it. "Let's do, Richard. I think it would be great fun." But I mentioned our next destination and made an oblique reference to our ages. Actually, trying to be diplomatic, I only mentioned my age and she had reluctantly agreed we probably shouldn't stop, accepting that we would most likely be out of our element.

As we neared the Normandy coast, and knowing what had happened there in the spring of 1944, I had a feeling that going to the D-Day beaches might be a very emotional experience for us both.   And I was afraid our different nationalities might be a problem on this historic coast; that it might pull us apart emotionally.   But instead, I was surprised that our visit there seemed to pull us closer to each other, each of us acknowledging the sacrifices the men in each army had made for their country.   And Helga took pains to remind me that less than one percent of the German troops were members of the Nazi party, and most of those were officers.   The others were just ordinary everyday working men, very often frightfully young men simply doing what their countries' asked them to do.

As we stood together on that rocky shore overlooking the English Channel I thought about those horrible days on that beach in 1944, and images of what had happened there became starkly clear and cold like the thousands of graves that seemed to be everywhere.   But sad and painful though it was, I made myself remember that the road to victory against Hitler's evil scheme also had begun here.   But thoughts of victory seemed somehow inadequate, overshadowed by so many visions of suffering and death.   I had to keep reminding myself that those who died here were literally saving Western Civilization from Adolph Hitler and his evil cronies as they were busily trying to make a totalitarian dictatorship out of all Europe and even beyond.

And I had to remind myself that we owed an unbelievable debt of gratitude to those brave young men who had died here, the enormity of which we could never repay.   The seemingly endless row after row of grave markers stood in mute testimony to their unselfish sacrifices.   The allied forces had suffered more than four thousand killed that first invasion day.   That one-day number still staggers the imagination.   And one can understand why General Eisenhower considered for a while withdrawing the invasion forces the German resistance was so unexpectedly stubborn.

Helga and I each had some special connection to these terribly beautiful beaches. My father's older brother Fred had been killed at Omaha Beach the second day. And being here where it actually happened I could close my eyes and imagine the troops coming ashore like I had seen in TV documentaries. Frightened young men so recently away from home, some for the first time, dying by the thousands, many of them before they even reached the sandy beach.

And although neither Helga nor Herr Wintermantle ever talked about the war, I still had the distinct feeling there was something about this place that she kept to herself. Something she kept very, very private. She had once mentioned her father's younger brother, a favorite uncle Rudolf I think the name was who had died during the war. She never said where or when and she would never say any more about it. But I sensed that maybe it could have been at this place, and that our being here held a special meaning for her, too. And I chose not to intrude.

I could see how preoccupied and sad she seemed to be while we wandered through the German Cemetery at *La Cambe*. I tried to imagine what must have been going through her mind as she walked past row after row of the German dead, the graves uniquely clustered in groups of five. I had learned earlier that there had been twenty-one thousand Germans killed in those first invasion days, five times as many as the allies.

And my being here with her and knowing that she and old Herr Wintermantle were German and were such good decent people made me think very differently about what happened here. It was no longer like a John Wayne movie fighting a faceless Nazi scourge. The German troops who died here were also young men and very human, and like the allied troops who died here they, too, were far from home. Walking hand in hand with my German lover and feeling tears in my eyes, and seeing tears in her eyes as well, made my perspective change quite dramatically.

Later, at the American Cemetery at *Courville sur Mer* overlooking Omaha Beach, it was my turn to walk slowly past row after row of grave markers, lost in thought while I

226

read the names and home states of those who had died here those first few days. There was something about their youthfulness that tugged at my heart like an unspoken prayer, and I thought of the wonderful years of young adulthood and beyond they never had.

I had once heard there was a disproportionate number of officers buried here. It was said that when the French government offered to ship home any the American bodies, many of the officers' families thought they would have preferred to remain here with the courageous men they had led into battle.

And the French government had placed all the American graves facing westward, toward home, knowing their young souls would be yearning to be free and home again and wishing to be forever young. And when I closed my eyes I imagined I could see their ghosts hovering nearby, flinging themselves hither and yon in agitation as if in a fierce struggle to find something they desperately wanted and needed; and not finding whatever it was, their agitation increased. And this sad, poignant image moved me to tears.

Although neither of us was of that generation, nevertheless we were strongly affected by what we saw and experienced here the day of our visit.

FIFTY-SEVEN

Everywhere we walked the day we were here at Omaha beach I kept thinking what a tragedy it was that these dead would never see home again or taste mom's apple pie. And when I thought how young most of them had been I was especially saddened by the thought that many of them, no, probably most of them, never had the chance to know the love of a woman or feel her warm body in bed next to his, and I was humbled by my own inadequate understanding of their sacrifice. They had given so much. They had literally given everything. And I was reminded of the line in Lincoln's Gettysburg Address when he had said that those who had died there had given *the last full measure of devotion.* And so had these, here on this French coast.

I found myself standing among the American graves with tear-streaked cheeks without really knowing why, except that I understood that they had given so much and I so little. And the point kept coming back to me time and time again that most of them had been so very, very young; that they had had their entire lives ahead of them only to have them snuffed out like so many expendable candles.

How could we ever forget they had literally saved Western Civilization, these brave young men from Phoenix and Paducah and Chicago and Providence and Norfolk and LA and Muncie, and so many other towns and villages, some so small they had no names. And, of course there were the thousands from London and Manchester and St. Ives, and from Quebec and Ottawa and Bombay and Sydney and Cape Town and hundreds of other Dominion towns and villages. The list goes tragically on and on seemingly endless. Troops from the British Empire struggled through the war far longer than any others. Yes, they all had saved us from the darkest forces of evil the modern world has ever known.

Then I remembered the concentration camps and the Jews. A friend named Kozak, himself a Jew, once told me how he was in the US Army unit that liberated Dachau, and with tears in his eyes, gave tetanus shots to arms that were only skin and bone. And tears clouded my eyes again.

As I walked between the rows of grave markers I was so lost in my own thoughts that it hadn't occurred to me that Helga was not there by my side. Looking around, I saw her far off in the distance over near one of the cliffs. She was standing very close to one of the German bunkers the French had left intact as a sort of memorial, or perhaps as a reminder of what never should have been, what must never be allowed to happen again.

I stood silently watching her, unwilling to intrude on her privacy. After a while she walked over to another of the remaining German fortifications and stood there quietly alone for a very long time. Her head was bowed in what must surely have been a prayerful attitude, one hand reaching out to touch the cold, wet concrete. She was probably thinking about her father or her long dead uncle. She had told me that Herr Wintermantle never talked about his war experiences, but I felt sure that at this moment she must have been imagining his having been here, and if so, how could he have possibly survived this unspeakable horror?

When at last she slowly and very deliberately walked back to where I was standing I took her hand in mine and stood quietly with her for a long time, choosing again to say nothing. When she finally released my hand to put her arms around my neck, I gathered her into my arms and held her tightly, gently rubbing her back, my lips against her hair but still not wanting to say anything.

But at last I reluctantly asked, "What have you been thinking, Helga?" She was silent for such a long time I thought maybe she didn't want to answer. But finally she whispered against my chest, her voice hoarsely quiet, "So many young men had to die here, your countrymen and mine. And for what? And who could ever say how this terrible thing happened? Why did it have to happen? Why was it not possible for someone to stop it? Better yet, prevent it? Who was more to blame, Hitler or Chamberlain? Or someone else we do not even know about? And that evil monster Stalin lurking somewhere nearby ready to pick up the broken pieces.

"And was it ever about right or wrong? Or did right or wrong make any difference? You certainly like think so, especially you Americans and British and French and so many others who helped stamp out the evil menace of Nazism. But did that make any difference to a grieving mother or wife or sweetheart? I suppose that surely a German mother mourns the death of her son just as much as an American mother, or a British mother, or a French mother, or a Canadian mother or . . . ." her voice trailed off. "The list of mothers suffering is too horribly long. They were also casualties of that horrible war."

For a long time I didn't try to answer her imponderable question. And knowing there was no answer, I simply held her tightly. But at last I managed to say, "Yes, you're quite right. Who could possibly have the answer for so much death and destruction and heartache? The word unthinkable applies here more than any other place I could ever think of. Yet one of the reasons I love you so much Helga Wintermantle, is how acutely you are sensitive to the feelings of others. In this case friend and foe alike."

At her mention of a German mother mourning I recalled a walk I had taken several years before when I had lived in Heidelberg, Germany. I had been walking through a hillside vineyard in the small nearby village of Schriesheim where grapes were ripening in the warm September sun, and I was trying to figure out how to get to a castle ruin I could see on the nearby hilltop where someone had told me there was an excellent restaurant with a terrace overlooking the beautiful Neckar Valley. I finally had to stop an old gentleman who was coming my way and ask directions. The old fellow, struggling in his halting English, answered hesitantly, "If you valk through vineyard in that direction," he had said pointing, "you vill come to top vhere is castle."

Just as I was nearing the top, I happened to glimpse a granite marker nearly hidden in some nearby bushes. Although unable to read the German inscription very well, I managed to make out that four young German soldiers were buried there who had been killed nearby in 1945. And that reminded me of a similar site I had come across in the French countryside a few years before. There were markers in a small grove of trees beside a rural road for five young Americans killed nearby that same year, most likely having been buried there by grateful Frenchmen who, in all probability, had lost sons of their own.

The somber mood that hung over the D-Day beaches followed us that night. It was very late and we were looking for a bed and breakfast when finally, well after dark, we happened on a stark, what could even be called a bleak house. The overall impression of the Normandy coastal villages was of ugly, box-like houses apparently made of concrete. And it finally dawned on me that in all probability every house there had been destroyed in the furious invasion fighting, and it was most likely these ugly replacements had been hastily thrown up following the end of the war. The house where we stayed that night was one of those box-like creations. A very old man and his wife who spoke not a word of English were happy to have us and our money.

Our room was clean but dark and dismal and for some unknown reason all the lights went out at ten o'clock. And trying to find an unfamiliar bathroom in the dark was like groping one's way in a pitch black cave at midnight. We were glad to be on our way to Nice early the next morning.

*   *   *

Just like the time when we had been here before, the Normandy beaches today were again dark and gloomy, blanketed by a slow, steady rain that seemed intent on depressing me and reminding me of my futile search.

I chanced a glimpse at one of the concrete fortifications on the cliff and was instantly carried back in time to when we had been here together. And I was struck by an aching realization that my chances of finding Helga might be as dead as those brave men who were buried under this beautifully manicured French grass, where delicate little purple flowers were trying to hold up their heads in the cold rain. And once again I felt terribly lost and alone.

FIFTY-EIGHT

Jennifer Smartley was just leaving the McDonalds on the corner at Wenceslas Square trying to decide what to do next. Where the hell do I start? If it hadn't been for that damn German woman I wouldn't have had to come over here at all. The more I think about it the more it really pissess me that Richard took up with that damn kraut slut. Why would he do that? What did she have I didn't have? Nothing, of course, the old bitch.

But I'll find him, dammit. And just let him get a little horny and I'll wrap him around my little finger just like before. I'll screw brains out and then get rid of him. If I don't want a man, I just dump him. It's just that simple. The crazy thing is I'm not at all sure I even want to get back in a relationship with him. But no foreign whore or any other woman for that matter is going to take a man away from me even if I don't really want him back. It's just the principle of the thing.

He kept mentioning this place in his blog, she remembered, looking around the Square, thinking her narrow, myopic thoughts, completely unaware of the beauty of the old city of Prague, oblivious to the wonders of being in this marvelous place in the heart of Europe where she had never been. Jennifer was so completely ethnocentric she might as well have been in Atlanta or Los Angeles or even Baton Rouge.

He wrote something about some king or saint or something like that on a horse. I guess that must be it over there where all those college kids are sitting. Thank goodness Bob Worley let it slip in a faculty meeting that Dick had gone back to Prague. At least that gave me an idea where to start. I'm glad I had that grumpy old Mona download all his stuff and print it so I could bring it over here with me. And I'm glad I didn't bring my laptop. One of these damn gypsies or whatever these weird-looking people are might have stolen it.

He mentioned something about some other German woman named Betty or some strange German name, she thought looking again at Mona Herbert's printout of Richard's blog. Yea, here it is. Bettina, that's what it was. Another funny damn Kraut name. Apparently she was a friend to that damn Helga. I guess the first thing for me to do is to find her and ask if she knows where he is. But how the hell can I ever find her in this strange city?

Unsure what to do or even where to go Jennifer suddenly remembered. Hey, wait a minute I think he mentioned meeting that Bettina woman at a pastry shop with some other women. I don't see any pastry shop around here. I wonder what one looks like. You would think at least they'd put up a sign a person could read.

She searched angrily through the papers, all the time muttering about 'that damn German bitch.' Ah, yes, here it is. The Éclair Pastry Shop somewhere near the river not far from the Charles Bridge. I don't see any river. Where the hell is it? I guess I'll just have to ask someone. From the looks of it on the map it might be a long way from here. Guess I better take a taxi. I hope some of these people can speak English.

"Hey, you there. Do you speak English?" she called out to the young man she encountered on the Charles Bridge.

"Yes, of course, may I help you?"

Humm, '*may I* help you?' Good grammar, too. Doesn't seem like such a backward communist country to me. "Could you tell me where I can find the Éclair Pastry Shop?"

"Yes, of course. Turn left at the end of the bridge," he said pointing, "and go two streets past a very large, very old building and then turn right on Platnerska Street."

"Hey, wait a minute. What do you mean, go two streets?"

"Oh, yes, my English teacher at the university told us you Americans call them blocks. Go two blocks past that big building and then turn right. The pastry shop will be on your left in just a short distance. You should see the sign."

"Yea, okay. And, ah, thanks."

Jennifer walked away, studying her map of Prague, still hardly noticing the beauty of the old city. Its marvelous stone buildings, some of them eight or nine hundred years old, made no impression on her at all. She had read somewhere that Prague was the only major European city that had not been bombed in the Second World War. So what the hell do I care? Jennifer may have been young, beautiful and well educated, but for all practical purposes culturally she was as shallow as a very small dish. She was the epitome of the 'ugly American' in every sense of that term. Her myopic vision saw only things American. For Jennifer everything worthwhile began in New York and ended in New Orleans. Well, maybe a little in L.A. And as if to verify that point, she had had breakfast that morning at the McDonalds on Wenceslas, although the sausage and egg biscuit was not to her liking.

Now what was that street name that guy mentioned? Sounded like Plat, Platner-something. Should have asked him to spell it for me. Oh, yes, here it is on the map, Platnerska Street. Funny name for a street.

I think today is Saturday. At least I hope so, she thought, looking at her watch that said four-thirty although it was mid-morning. I better change the time on this thing. I wonder what time zone we're in anyway?

I guess I should try that pastry shop. No, she corrected herself remembering it was Saturday. Might as well wait until tomorrow. Sunday morning was when he said that group of women meets there. Well, hell! What am I going to do for the rest of the day and tonight? I guess I'll have to find a bar and have a few drinks. Maybe a place where there might be some dancing later on. Might as well show these Czechs how we Americans can 'shake it, baby.' And that's exactly what she did that night, leaving quite a few young Czech men gasping for breath, and most of the older one scandalized.

FIFTY-NINE

When Jennifer entered the pastry shop Sunday at mid-morning the smell of fresh cinnamon rolls immediately reminded she had not eaten. They were very tempting but she told herself she had to resist. Got to watch my figure. My best asset – definitely my best asset. She had dressed in black slacks and a white blouse. No need to put on something provocative they'll just be a bunch of old maid school teachers. Might as well keep the tight tee shirts and low cut tops for the guys in case they're needed.

On entering the shop she noticed several groups of people sitting around small tables busily talking and laughing. She finally decided to approach a likely looking group of several young women, all of them cheerfully chattering away at a nearby table. They're dressed rather nicely, she thought, surprised. I guess what I was expecting a bunch of plain Jane frumpy old maids. Or something like that. Could this be the right group? That one with the short blonde hair looks like the one Richard described in his blog. Leave it to him to pick out one of the good-looking babes.

When she approached their table she asked the one she thought she needed, "Would you happen to be," she paused, referring to her printout, "would you be Bettina?"

"Ja, may I help you?"

"Yes, I'm a friend of the American professor Richard Rouse. Have you seen him?"

"And who might you be?" Bettina asked giving the beautiful Jennifer a quick look, her suspicions immediately aroused.

"Dr. Smartley. Professor Jennifer Smartley. I'm a colleague of Dick's at Tulane University."

Bettina remembered Helga mentioning that name in a letter, and it had been in a most unflattering way that she had reluctantly described the unpleasant scene at the Mardi

235

gras party. And why was this beautiful American woman looking for Richard? With Helga still missing this certainly seemed like a further complication. And why was she using the American informal form of Richard's name?

"No, I have not seen him. Are you a relative?"

At that point Jennifer, in her haste and arrogance, made a crucial mistake. Instead of saying something reasonable like, 'Yes, I'm his sister and we are so worried about his being missing.' Instead she answered in her most haughty voice, "No, not a relative, but a good friend. A *very* good friend," she said with a meaningful smile that came across more like a smirk. And her arrogantly condescending attitude ruined any chance of her getting any information from these young women.

Helga's former roommate Monika Schmitt was in the group but she said nothing only quietly seething at the arrogance of this insensitive woman. In stony silence she stared at Jennifer, remembering that this was the awful American woman who had caused Helga so much heartache and grief in New Orleans. And the no-nonsense Monika, older than the other women, solid, astute, and very intuitive, was watching Jennifer like a hawk ready to pounce and desperately wanting to. If she speaks to me or even looks at me, I will tell her what I think of her, and I will not be nice. But it will most definitely be in English. As shallow and self-centered as this one seems to be I'm sure she doesn't speak any foreign language, and I would want to make sure she understood every word I said.

"I really have no idea where he is," Bettina said again and turned away in a dismissive gesture, hoping to end the conversation.

"Well, hell," Jennifer muttered as she turned and stalked out of the shop. "You people don't know shit, do you?"

When Jennifer was out of hearing, Bettina said to the others, "Can you imagine? How did she expect to get any information with that attitude? It was like we were peasants or something and we should do her bidding. I was tempted to speak only

German, pretending not to understand English." And the group laughed at her idea. The Belgian girl said, "I wish you had."

"That was the American bitch Helga wrote to Monika and me about," Bettina continued. "Do you remember, Monika? She was the one who was determined to break up Helga's relationship with Richard. The one who suggested at a faculty party at Richard's university that he had probably found her in a Frankfurt brothel. Can you imagine! Our dear sweet, innocent Helga? Why can't all Americans be as nice as Richard?"

"And why was she over here looking for Richard, anyway?" Monika added suspiciously.

SIXTY

From Normandy I took a train to the city of Nice on the French Riviera where I found out nothing. Absolutely nothing at all! We had stayed there only a very short time last summer. I seem to remember it was just one night, so I really didn't expect to learn anything. And I wasn't disappointed – disappointed at not finding out anything, that is. Actually I was very disappointed. I hated myself for the feeling that I was beginning to accept the inevitability of not finding her. Was this a shadowy glimpse at the lonely darkness that was to be my future? Was this to be my ultimate fate? Where I would wander forever lost and forlorn – always looking for Helga?

I find myself thinking more and more often these days, do I keep looking? It's beginning to feel like I might as well give up. No one could go on looking forever, could they? How do I keep going, feeling as hopeless as I do? But I can't let this end not knowing what has become of her; at least I have to know that she's safe. I know I can't just give up and quit. I have to know what happened. At least know something; feel something other than this dull, dismal ache. But what if I did find out what made her leave, would the ache go away? Or, more likely, would it get worse?

I already know what would happen if I did give up no matter how reluctantly. Wherever I went for the rest of my life someone or some little thing will give me one more scrap of information, one more tiny clue. And that's all it would take to start me looking again. And the pain, which hopefully would have subsided by then would come rushing back as if it had never left. If only I could . . . My life seems to have become a constant succession of, 'if onlys.' Like a drowning man, I'll clutch at any straw. I can't help myself. I have to keep trying!

Maybe I really should just give up and go home. Why not? But the mere thought of home makes me think of our little house on Pine Street and the short time we had there together. She was so happy there. If only we could be happy there again.

But then an unwanted thought intruded. Was she really happy? How can I be sure? Did I drive her away in some inexplicable way I don't understand? Didn't even see? Oh, my God, how I do love that woman! If only I could . . .

*   *   *

On our one and only bright sunny morning in Nice we were sitting on a bench overlooking the pebbly beach, watching several young men on their sailboards skimming over the waves, pulled by some kind of kite arrangement. And young people lay sprawled about on the pebbly beach which looked to be terribly inhospitable, the multicolored pebbles winking softly in the morning sun. It seemed as if perfectly suntanned bodies and conformity with their peers was more important than comfort. I had just made a silly joke that 'Nice is nice.' But then I had to explain the identical spelling.

Helga, her mind elsewhere, had commented on the topless young women sunbathers nearby. "How can they lie there on those awful rocks? Do you think when they get up they will have little round marks all over their beautiful bodies?"

"Yes, I guess you're right," I said, visualizing how odd even their perfect young bodies would look.

"I guess they will do anything to look beautiful," she said.

"Yes, but . . . Ah, Helga, I want you to look again at those young women lying there topless on the beach you were talking about. Those beautiful young women with their perfect bodies."

"Ja, I see them, Richard. And I am jealous."

"But you mustn't be. It's time I told you something I've been thinking for a long time." I paused, trying to decide how I wanted to say it.

"I want you to know that no matter how young, how topless, how sexy, how beautiful those women are, to me you are younger, sexier, and far more beautiful than any of them could ever be."

"What, me beautiful?"

"Yes, you."

"Richard, I think you have very poor eyesight. But I love it! And I love you for saying it. But how could I look in the mirror every morning for forty-eight years and not know that I am not pretty?"

"You may not be the prettiest girl in the world, but you are beautiful."

"How can I be beautiful if I'm not even pretty?"

"To me you are the most beautiful woman in the world because your beauty shines in your face. It comes from inside you. It is a deep inner beauty that comes from within the very center of your being – from deep in your soul. It shines in everything you say or do. It's the spirit of a most wonderful, loving person. There is in you a loveliness far deeper and more lasting than beauty or even prettiness. You are a woman who not only loves me but who loves other people and who loves to be with people. It's your open-armed spirit of love for others that shines in your face, and especially in your eyes that makes you so incredibly beautiful. And I am so very thankful that those eyes are looking at me most of the time. You are truly beautiful in such a very special way. And most importantly, that kind of beauty that will never fade – will never grow old. And I love you a thousand times over for it."

Helga stared at him, her mouth agape. "Richard, you are the most incredible man I have ever known. No, more than that. The most incredible man in the world."

I started to protest but she put a finger on my lips to silence me.

"You, too, have such a wonderful sensitivity for others," she said with a loving smile. "I have seen it often when you did not know I was watching. And the most wonderful thing of all is your sensitivity to me, to my feelings. And when I think of you and how much you love me, my love for you just keeps growing. And growing. And growing!" she said, each phrase more emphatic than the last.

They both grew quiet and Helga looked back out to sea apparently daydreaming, but she was quietly thoughtful, her heart near to bursting from the joy of loving him. How can I find the perfect words to tell him just how incredibly wonderful I think he is? If he only knew how he fills my being with his loving me. It is such a wonderful thing to feel him inside of me. Not sexually. But yes, that too, of course, she thought with her Mona Lisa smile. His love for me fills my mind, my body, my soul and I know I can never get enough of it. Does he know this? Should I try to explain it to him? I have heard other women say one should never tell her man everything. And I am sure I understand their feelings. But with Richard I want to tell him everything about how I love him. Everything! To hold back nothing.

*   *   *

There was nothing I could find out about her in Nice. No one there knew anything about her. Absolutely nothing. Not even the young man at the desk of the *Hotel sur la Mer* who had been so helpful last summer. He had not seen her. Not even the arrogant waiter at the *Café Emile* we had asked to take our picture. No one I asked had seen her. There was absolutely no sign of her anywhere.

SIXTY-ONE

We both loved Vernazza, this incredible little Italian village clinging precariously to a stony cliff-side, overlooking as it did the blue Mediterranean that every day seemed to sparkle with diamonds. We had been so very happy here. More than any other place we went. The sights, the sounds, even the smells were enchanting. And always there was the sea with its ever-changing face, murmuring quietly one day with wavelets only a few inches high, the next day with huge waves crashing over the breakwater driven by the capricious winds from out of North Africa. Pavel and Leonard Novotny both said Helga had mentioned that she had wanted to be in places where she could watch the sea, and I knew she had always been fascinated by it. And here in this enchanted place there was always the sea. We both loved being here where we could be near it, and each day the ever changing sea showed a different mood.

Everything about this wonderful place was magical. And just like the sea, the magic was always changing; a new adventure, a new dream, a new experience every day, each one better than the last. Being so near the sea just made it even more magical for two young lovers completely lost in the euphoria of newfound love.

Did I say young lovers again like we'd said that time in Paris? But yes, of course, we were most definitely young at heart, and that certainly should count, right? And how amazing that had been. I wish some poet would write about how ageless love can be; how love can come to the not so young as well as the very young. But now that I think about it, the song the old accordion player in Paris sang for us was, we both had hoped, a poem to the agelessness of our love. Maybe like a fine wine, love mellows with age I thought, remembering how my love for Helga had never stopped growing. Even now with all the craziness that's happening and with her not being here with me, my love for her just keeps growing, and I wonder at the unbelievable miracle of that. And that makes my need to find her keeps driving me relentlessly.

I remember that here in Vernazza we rented a room high up on the top floor of a very old building of almond colored stone that faced the sea. And on the ground floor there was a harbor-side restaurant we liked where the owner Giorgio seemed to be always smiling and laughing and sometime singing. Almost immediately he took to us as if we were long-lost family, joyously hugging us and beaming at us like some sort of overgrown teddy bear. I think he must have sensed there was something special about us, something intangible that glowed like a shining light just beneath the surface of our faces. Something that was strong and vibrant, hearty and flavorful like a very old, very fine wine. I mentioned that idea to Helga one day when we were having a glass of wine on his terrace and she had whispered, 'Of course, I think he can see that we are very special lovers.'

The view from our room – we had number eleven on the top floor – was spectacular overlooking the sea as it did with the incredibly blue Mediterranean just outside our window. Seagulls woke us every morning with their raucous quarreling as they flew past our window. And lying in bed next to the open window I could almost feel as if I were up there flying along with them. And kissing Helga and caressing her beautiful body I felt like I, too, was flying, but in a different, far more heavenly sort of way.

Looking around at this special place today and missing her terribly, my mind gently eases back to one of my most favorite memories of our being here; those special waking moments each morning in the big old brass bed with Helga still asleep, warm and delectable beside me, her woman scent sweet and provocative. I liked to wake her with the lightest of kisses and if she didn't stir I would very gently unbutton her pajama top and kiss her nipples, and invariably she would wake with a start and immediately throw herself on top of me, pinning me to the bed with her wonderful body and smothering me with kisses. "Helga, stop, I can't breathe like this," I would gasp laughing and resisting, but only feebly. I wondered if sometimes she had not been pretending to be asleep, only waiting for my advance so she could retaliate. And, of course, I found myself anxiously waiting, and I was wonderfully excited whenever it came.

Later, exhausted from our lovemaking but immensely happy, we would watch the morning sunlight that seemed to peek at us from over the mountains on the east as it came slanting through the window on the other side of the room. And on the shadowy western side the sea seemed to be waiting; patiently waiting until later when the afternoon sun eased around, seeming in no hurry, stronger, more vibrant than the morning sun as if drawing strength from the mountains and the sea. And finally those incredible sunsets, each one better than the last, their dazzling colors breathtaking as only a Mediterranean sunset can be and, of course, different every day. There's nothing like a sunset to remind one of that familiar expression: The only thing constant in life is change.

We had stayed here two, or was it three weeks? We both loved it. Vernazza was truly incredible. Everything had been so perfect here. New love in a spectacular, spellbinding new place. And certainly no man could have ever asked for a more wonderful woman to share such an extraordinary adventure with. It was as if she knew my every need and I hers. And we each unconsciously made a competition of trying to please the other. Not a competition really, we simply loved and shared and reveled in the pure joy of each other. And the giving to the other was so spontaneous, so totally unselfish, that each of us was sure we were the winner in this amazing, never-ending non-competition.

But those are just memories now. Only fuzzy, out-of-focus views of better times as I stand here looking at the little harbor. And the pictures they bring to mind only intensify my pain and my sense of irretrievable loss. No matter how wonderful the memories, they could never blot out this terrible feeling of losing her, or the intensity of this gut-wrenching pain. The more wonderful the memories, the more intense the feeling of loss.

*   *   *

One day we were sitting at a café terrace watching the sparkling sea, the sting of salt spray strong and pungent in our noses. Helga had been quietly gazing out to sea, and I noticed her fingers were working in her lap as if she were writing a story, her lips moving as if perhaps reciting a favorite poem or telling herself a story. She had been thoughtfully quiet for a long time, a faintly mysterious smile playing about her lips as her imagination was beginning to build a far-away dream.

"Richard, this is the most fascinating place I have ever seen! It's so incredibly beautiful! And just look, the sea is right at our feet. And the quay. And the fishing boats. It's so beautifully quaint I cannot take it all in! And the villagers are so nice, so friendly. All this seems to fill my heart with some special kind of joy."

She reached across the table touching my face in an exquisitely tender gesture of love. She continued gently caressing my face with her fingertips, and I was thrilled beyond what mere words could possibly express as I always was by her loving touch.

SIXTY-TWO

After having been in the little village of Vernazza more than a week, we were sitting on the breakwater very early one morning as had become our custom. We were enjoying steaming cups of cappuccino from a harbor-front café while the morning sun gently began to warm our backs. We had been watching the brightly painted fishing boats putting out to sea, the fishermen shouting good-naturedly at one another as they departed.

Helga had been quietly leaning against my shoulder for a long time, apparently lost in thought while she watched the boats moving out to their fishing grounds. She turned to look back at the village with a quizzical expression and then out to sea again as if working out a puzzle. And I could tell that her mind was busy as usual.

When the chug, chug, chug of the boat's motors died away and the only sound was the gentle lapping of waves on the rocks and the cry of gulls, she said, "Richard, I know this is not America or Germany, but I could stay here forever!" The wistfulness in her voice surprised me every bit as much as the simple idea she was suggesting.

"Yes, and I feel the very same way. It really is a remarkable place, isn't it? I have never seen anything like it. And now with you being here with me it has become a perfect place. A perfect place for lovers, I think." She beamed happily at my comment and pressed her lips to the back of my hand where I could feel their warmth that exceeded even the warmth of her words.

I smiled a sort of quiet inner smile, trying to see a picture of the vision she had suggested. What would it be like? Staying here? Maybe even living here?

"Then why shouldn't we stay? What is there to prevent us?" she said with even more wistfulness in her voice this time.

I didn't answer right away but in my mind's eye I could easily visualize our living here years later, two very old, very happy people tottering down the stone street to the quay

246

holding tightly to each other for safety. Then sitting on the seawall holding hands, enjoying the tangy sea air and dozing in the warm sun. The local people would have come to know us well, and they would say to one another, 'They have lived here for a very long time and they still act like young lovers. Really quite remarkable, don't you think?'

But then my vision of that dream was blown away by the capricious winds of harsh reality. "But we've made so many plans, haven't we?" I said quietly cautious, not wishing to shatter her dream. "Going to Venice and the Greek islands and then to America to live in New Orleans." I caught the disappointed expression on her face and quickly resumed, "And I have to think about my work and planning for retirement and so many other practical things." But even as I said those things I felt an unaccustomed hesitation because I wanted more than anything in the world for her to be happy; for the two of us to be happy together. And I forced myself to look away, trying not to see her saddened expression.

"Practical things?" she said, the disappointment already clear in her voice. "But plans are made to be changed, Ja? Couldn't we be impractical just this once? We could spend the rest of our lives in this little paradise." But she said nothing more only closing her eyes, still dreaming of how it would be and seeing precisely the same vision Richard had seen. And although hers was more real, more detailed, it was still very romantic. They would be living in one of the quaint little stone houses, she preparing dinner in a tiny little kitchen, and Richard . . . Now, where would Richard be? Talking to some of the fishermen who had become his friends? Perhaps bringing home a fish or a lobster one of them had given him for their supper? Maybe later he would be smoking a pipe in front of the fireplace with one of the children on his lap.

"We don't speak Italian," I said feebly, knowing what a weak excuse that was.

"We could learn."

I said nothing more. But later, alone on the quay that afternoon, watching the sunset with only the soft lapping of tiny waves on the rocks for company, I was enjoying the soothing quiet and thinking about our conversation earlier in the day. With no wind there were hardly any swells on the nearly flat sea, and I was reminded how the slow rhythms of the sea were very much like life itself as it pulsed in and out with a rhythmic certainty like the unalterable tides, but holding no clear plan of what was to come day after day, bright sun or storm. Only the colors of the sunset were constant in their perpetual variety. For hours I sat there alone pondering her idea, fighting with myself, trying to decide how I should answer her.

And Helga, casually browsing in a nearby gift shop, could see him and thought: I think it would be best if I leave him alone over there. He needs to think about this place and our plans and the idea I have suggested. What will his answer be? But I do wish that he would say . . . She made herself leave the thought unfinished.

Richard also thought about her idea for a very long time. What did he really think? Feel? A part of him liked the idea immediately. He had always dreamed of living in a picturesque place like this or maybe in the south of France. But he also remembered being vaguely uncomfortable when she had suggested the idea and not knowing exactly why, or how to reply. How would his answer affect his future? Their future? How would they live? Would it even be possible? Where would their money come from? Always there was the question of money, that hard, undeniable reality that has changed and dampened many a dream. He thought long and hard but found no easy answer.

But then a happy memory chased away his confused thoughts. One day last week there were huge white-capped waves rising far out to sea pushed by the Sirocco, that dry, dusty winds out of North Africa that drove them thundering ashore, crashing violently on the rocks making the quay look like the prow of a ship plunging through the rough sea. Helga had insisted on standing far out on the quay, her knees awash in the foaming waves as they rushed ashore. And I laughed at her when she tried to run from a very big wave that caught her and knocked her down and she got soaking wet, her thin dress clinging provocatively to her delightful body. Even then she refused to leave. "No, Richard, come out here with me!" she called when I had urged her to come back from there. "It's too wonderful!"

And she insisted on standing there facing the sea with the waves crashing about her, arms outstretched like some ancient sea goddess in a gesture of exuberant joy. And when I had gone out on the quay to try and persuade her to come in, I got soaked as well. And she laughed so hard I couldn't tell if her eyes were full of seawater or laughter tears. She grabbed me and we held tightly to each other so we wouldn't fall, and we stood there in the wild ocean spray laughing and kissing and being totally amazed at our love for each other.

SIXTY-THREE

Almost every day we climbed many of the narrow twisting stone steps that served as miniature streets in this enchanted place just as if we were characters in some fairy tale that had gone exploring with no bread crumbs to mark our way back home, and we didn't care. We wandered around in this special place, exploring small, out-of-the-way nooks and crannies as if we were children looking for perfect hide-and-go-seek places. And we found many and reserved them in our minds in case we actually did play some day, careful not to let the other know of the special ones we each had found. But knew we finally would share.

One day we climbed all the way to the top of the highest place in the village where there was a stone watchtower that was part of the remains of an ancient castle. It was from there the town's people had kept watch for invading Turkish pirates centuries ago.

We sat for a long time on a low stone wall near the tower, looking down at the lemon and orange trees on the back terraces of local people, listening as the wind rattled dry palm fronds that made us think of nomads and desert oases far away. And we told each other fanciful stories of beautiful young women who had been carried away from their homes by evil men, and of the brave young Bedouins who risked everything to rescue them. And she was much better at making up the stories than I. And, of course, hers were far more romantic than mine.

One day we decided to climb all the way to the very top of the watchtower where we enjoyed the incredible view of Corsica set in the amazing blue sea just on the horizon. And on clear days we pretended we could even catch a glimpse of North Africa far beyond, each of us describing it in meticulous detail as if we really could see it.

On another day we sat on the wall near the watchtower enjoying the ever-changing moods of the sea, and the warm Mediterranean breeze touched our faces with whispered tales of long-ago pirates and ill-fated lovers. And it brushed Helga's beautiful red hair against her face, sending her imagination spinning off into flights of romantic fantasy, dreaming of how very much she loved him, would always love him, and still dreaming, too, of a life they could have together in this magical place.

For a few nights we had gone to a rooftop restaurant that was almost as high up as the old watchtower. We would have dinner at one of the small round tables under the restaurant's colorful green canvas awning. I always ordered a bottle of our favorite local white wine to go with the wonderful seafood dishes; wine that came from the nearby vineyards high up on the steep mountainside just beyond the railroad tracks.

On one special night we watched a full moon rise in the east from over those same nearby mountains, flooding the village with a silvery glow like the dust from angel wings. We stayed there a long time that night with a second bottle of wine and much talk, both foolish and intimate. And we lingered long enough to watch the moon slowly glide across the sky until it slid over the edge of the dark sea and disappeared, leaving behind only a brief silvery afterglow and then finally, the dark, mysterious sea once more.

Our waiter was silently nodding nearby in a hard-backed chair, and quite unexpectedly we realized that it was almost dawn.

On another night, taking pity on our sleepy waiter, we agreed to leave the restaurant early, and carrying a bottle of wine we had walked down the uncountable stone steps toward the quay. The warm, comforting glow of lamplight from small medieval windows in the stone houses greatly intrigued us, and we wondered what stories could lie behind their doors, each of us making up stories in our minds about the people within and their lives. And we didn't share every detail of our stories, wishing to keep some in the secret places in our hearts, hoping that someday they might come true. Especially Helga.

We made our way down to the steep central street and out onto the quay, and the sea was very quiet as if waiting for lovers to come. We chose to sit on the breakwater rocks and Helga took off her sandals and let the small waves splash her feet. We sat very close together with our arms around each other as we watched the moon slide slowly down the western sky, making a silvery pathway to our feet. "Wasn't there a song many years ago," I whispered hesitantly, fearing the sound of my voice might break the spell. "Something about a stairway to the stars? That's what this looks like, doesn't it," I said, pointing to the shimmering streak of moonlight at our feet.

Helga wanted to tell him she was not old enough to remember the song but then, not wishing to break the magic of the moment she made a happy murmuring answer and lay her head on his shoulder.

Neither of us spoke again, instead enjoying the quiet intimacy of the moment, spellbound by the beauty of the village and the mystery of the sinking moon shining on our feet and our incredible love for each other. A love we vowed would never end.

But climbing to the restaurant high up the steep steps was a bit arduous, and by our second week we had begun having dinner at Giorgio's ground level restaurant at the edge of the harbor. The restaurant was named *Chez Giorgio sul Mare* and our room was upstairs on the top floor of the same building. We liked to eat at an outdoor table on the restaurant terrace that overlooked the sturdy breakwater while the colorful fishing boats rocked gently where they were safely anchored; fishing boats I thought looked like so many bright, sparkling Christmas ornaments. And as always, there was the ever-changing sea just beyond. The image of Christmas lights made me wonder where we would spend Christmas that year. New Orleans? Some other place? Who knows? But surely it would be New Orleans, wouldn't it?

The taste of seafood and good wine, the salty smells of boats and fishing nets and dried sardines was a unique medley of all that was wonderfully special about Vernazza.

The restaurant, *Chez Giorgio sul Mare* was wonderful, and the combination of the French and Italian names intrigued and amused us. From our terrace table the view of the harbor and the sea was breathtaking, the atmosphere perfect and the food delicious. We quickly learned to love our genial host and landlord Giorgio who, with his pencil thin mustache he thought made him look like an Italian movie star, began to take a special interest in us and often served us himself. It seemed that every night he insisted we each try a different seafood dish prepared especially for us under his close supervision. And he frequently served us himself.

Richard, who had always dreamed of living in Maine where lobsters were so plentiful, could never get enough of the delectable shellfish. The smaller Mediterranean lobsters that Giorgio served in a mysterious but delicious cream sauce were heavenly and Richard ordered them almost every night.

From somewhere inside the restaurant – the kitchen we thought most likely – we could often hear a rich baritone voice singing, somewhat off key but still hauntingly beautiful in what we took to be an Italian folk song.

One night after we had finished dinner and were starting on a second bottle of wine, a new moon appeared in the western sky over the sea like a curved eyelash of silver, and it threw its gentle radiance on the flashing water as we held hands and gazed into each other's eyes like love-struck teenagers.

Late one afternoon we were having coffee on Giorgio's terrace and watching ominously dark clouds from over the sea that were getting closer. It was obvious a storm was coming as many of the local men joined together and began pulling the fishing boats onto the little sandy beach out of harm's way. And I took off my shoes and waded into the stormy water and tried to help. And Helga, too, came to help but I told her that maybe this was something just the men would do. And she understood with one of her bright smiles. But she continued to stand nearby with her knees awash in the foaming water wanting badly to jump in and help, still shouting encouragement to me as her words were torn from her mouth by the now howling wind. And we were happily wet again.

SIXTY-FOUR

On another occasion we had taken a day trip to one of the nearby villages in the Cinque Terre. Corniglia was charmingly quaint and high up on a cliff with no sandy beach, but with a spectacular view out to sea. Quite by chance we had happened on the villagers that day at their annual winemaking festival. It seemed that each village of the Cinque Terre had vineyards high up on the stony hillsides across the railroad tracks.

We stood on the fringe of the crowd enjoying the festivities, hesitant but wanting to join in, especially Helga who was immediately caught up in the crowd's carefree mood. And when a portly old gentleman invited her to join a group of women in the traditional pressing of the grapes with their feet, she happily pulled up her skirt and tied it between her legs like she had once seen in an Italian movie, and she quickly joined in the lusty singing with the locals just as if she knew the Italian words to the songs, laughing all the while. A young woman stomping grapes next to Helga helped her in hesitant English, translating some of the words for her. Later when a middle aged man pinched her bottom she chose to ignore him, instead she just smiled and kept on singing and laughing. And the bright magic of her smile dazzled everyone. And her feet were stained for days afterwards.

Even as the afternoon shadows grew longer we still wanted to stay and enjoy every moment of the festival, but the magic of Vernazza kept calling to us and we reluctantly made our way back on an early evening train, a little sad at having to leave our new friends.

On our last day in Vernazza we had tried walking north to the next village along the narrow pathway that was literally carved into the seaside cliffs. We had been told that the path that connected the five villages of the Cinque Terre had recently been made a national park. I watched in fascination where far below the sea was crashing on the rocky shore, each marching wave seemingly tipped with flashing diamonds like beacons that warned, 'Beware, there is beauty here, but also danger.' And with the village of Vernazza in the background, its pink and salmon and cream colored buildings overlooking the seawall, the view begged to be photographed.

The dizzying heights frightened Helga and she clung tightly to my arm the entire way. But knowing what a brave and adventurous woman she was I suspected that was simply an excuse to hold onto me and press herself firmly against my arm. And who was I to complain?

Later, on a last souvenir gathering trip she found a perfectly beautiful color photograph of our adopted village taken from the same dizzying height where we had been earlier that same afternoon. And she had to have it.

*   *   *

On my first dreary day back in Vernazza while searching for her, I went to the harbor-side restaurant, *Chez Giorgio sul Mare* we had visited so often. Giorgio, the affable owner, said in answer to my question after I had told him my sad story, "Si, she has been here. She asked for your old room. You remember, Signore, it was number eleven? The one on the top floor with the view of the harbor and the sea?" I nodded sadly, remembering.

"She stays here for many days. And she goes to the harbor every day and sits on the breakwater where you used to try fishing. And watching her sitting there I remembered how she would laugh when you caught something but you could not get it off your hook."

Listening to Giorgio talking about her and looking at the gray, cheerless sea on this cloudy autumn day, I thought that today Vernazza was very much like the fog-shrouded coast of Normandy where the sea had also been gray and moody as if in keeping with the solemnity of that place and my mission. And now here, where the Mediterranean had always seemed to be so gay and cheerful, so brightly splashed with ever-changing shades of blue, radiating happy warmth, it too, had turned cold and somber as if to match my mood.

"But now she does not laugh so much," Giorgio continued, "She only stares out to sea and I think she is very sad. One day she says to me, 'Giorgio, my life she takes a strange turn and I think I must hurry and get on with the rest of my living.' I think Signorina Helga speaks in riddles, no?"

Later that evening after my solitary dinner – I had refused to order the lobsters I liked so much, for to have eaten them would have only reminded me of better times – I sat alone at one of the small terrace tables we had often shared at Giorgio's, sipping a third glass of the same local white wine we both had liked so much. And as the sun began to set with flashing arrows of red and gold I could feel the last of the late afternoon rush of wind out of North Africa carrying with it the smell of dry deserts and lost hopes.

Giorgio discreetly left me alone with my sadness and dreams, while my thoughts wandered over the pathways of my increasingly futile search. The sun sank slowly beyond the hazy gray Mediterranean, disappearing quietly with the certainty of millennia of never ending cycles. But for me it was disappearing like my hope of ever finding her.

A light evening breeze began blowing in from the sea, and the wine and the pleasant coolness of the night air made me forget for a few moments the hard reality of my searching. And looking around I felt myself almost smiling at the familiar sights of places and things we had enjoyed here. But seeing them now, I was struck once again with the realization that my simple, unfettered longing for her was, in part, an unconscious yearning centered in the dark recesses of my being. And even in its simplicity it was becoming a hopelessly crushing burden.

For the short time I was there – even though Giorgio had told me she had left – I was determined to search everywhere in Vernazza for any sign of her. It was almost as if I expected to find some memento of her having been there, a forgotten note perhaps. I looked in all the romantic haunts we had enjoyed together, had secretly explored as if there were no other people in the world, only the two of us free forever to do whatever we wished. But when I found those places there empty and forlorn I strangled on a cry of pain and longing.

Everywhere I went I found nothing of her, only memories that were already beginning to fade, bringing with them a sharp sense of urgency and a new panic. And I realized once again how it was that the exquisite joy of my memories of her made my failure to find her so much more painful.

SIXTY-FIVE

I took a mid-morning train from Vernazza across the Italian peninsula to Venice, and even as depressed as I was I vowed to keep looking no matter what. I was glad I didn't have to make the decision about booking a sleeper. A couple of years before I had taken a sleeper from Rome to Venice, and even then the noisy train rumbling over tracks and crossings made sleeping difficult. And with the pretty young Czech student who was traveling with me undressing in the upper berth, sleep was the last thing I was thinking about. Unfortunately, or maybe fortunately, thinking was all I did.

The train arrived just at dusk at the garish railway station in Venice that Mussolini had had ordered built for the tourist trade, its Art Deco facade glaringly out of place among the beautiful old palazzos and houses that lined the Grand Canal. The attractive young woman in the blue uniform dress was about to close the information desk but she said she would be glad to stay if she could help. But I told her she should go on home as I already knew which hotel I wanted. I told her it was the same one where Helga and I had stayed last summer, and she looked at me confused, trying to figure out where this absent person named Helga could be, much as the American Airlines clerk in Athens had done. There was no one standing near me, so with a shrug the young woman took her purse and left.

With the setting sun flashing streaks of red and orange and gold that danced their way across the famous Venetian lagoon, the waterbus ride down the Grand Canal brought back bittersweet memories of our time together here in Venice, and even the beauty of the old Rialto Bridge could not stir my heart like before. It seems that everywhere I go I find myself vacillating between the wonderful memories of our time together in so many magical places, often on the verge of tears of nostalgia, then alternately having daily to strengthen my resolve to keep looking, but then once again having to fight back the bitter tears of failure.

By the time I reached St. Mark's Square the hustle and bustle of the daytime boat traffic had subsided and a cool early evening quiet had descended. Couples were strolling arm in arm around the Square even as the tide was beginning to push its way up through the storm drain grates, gradually covering much of the Square. I remembered that all around the Square were stacked temporary wooden boardwalks on legs that at times of exceptional high water were laid end to end to create raised walkways through the high water; a feature apparently unique to Venice, and which the Venetians seemed to take in stride as a normal part of life in their incredible city.

And tonight as usual the local people seemed not to notice the rising water at all as they simply continued about their business as if it were nothing out of the ordinary. Many strolled about St. Mark Square quite leisurely, simply skirting the rising water and stopping at cafe terraces for an evening of wine and conversation with friends. And I was bitterly jealous. My heart wanted to cry out at them: Why are you having such a pleasant, carefree evening here with loved ones when I am so alone and miserable? It's not fair! But I knew that fairness had nothing to do with it, only that mysterious force called fate – always unknown and unknowable.

I managed to get a room at the Venetian Hotel where Helga and I had stayed last summer. The young desk clerk was very helpful but he told me someone else had already booked the room that we had had last year. However, another third floor room was available overlooking the same small canal and the Bridge of Tears where the Doge's prisoners were transported to meet their inevitable fate; as if I needed a reminder of the hopelessness of their plight, or mine.

In answer to my question the clerk said no, he had not seen Helga lately. Not since we had been there together last summer, which to me now seemed to have been ages ago. "And where is the Signorina?" he asked innocently. "Perhaps she has mistakenly gone to meet you at a different hotel?" But when he saw my face already screwed up with the beginning of tears he said no more, probably afraid his question had offended me, and he said nothing more.

It was becoming increasingly difficult having to explain to virtual strangers why I was looking for her and didn't know where she was. Especially since many of them, like this young man, remembered us from last summer as lovers who had made no secret of our being deliriously happy together and being so very much in love. But I couldn't think of any other way for getting information about her no matter how painful and embarrassing the asking was for me. And the longer my search dragged on, the more it seemed as if some of the people we had come to know along the way would give me hostile looks as if they assumed I had done something wrong; as if my not knowing where she was could imply something mysterious, perhaps even sinister. And even though explaining my increasingly desperate search was a painfully necessary way of trying to find out where she had been, I willingly endured the hostile stares in hopes of getting some new scrap of information.

I have to keep telling myself I will continue my quest whether I find her or not. But the finality of not finding her keeps pushing its ugly face into my consciousness, and inevitably a black mood of hopelessness clutches at my heart more and more tightly and refuses to let go.

Venice had been such a wonderful experience for us. On our first afternoon there last summer we had visited St. Mark's Square and the Cathedral, and later we took the elevator to the top of the bell tower. We were enchanted by the view overlooking the red tile rooftops of this unusual city, and turning in the other direction we watched the sun sparkling on the Venetian lagoon and, in the distance, the Adriatic Sea. We stood there quietly holding hands and making plans about forever as lovers always seem to do.

We loved finding those quaint little sidewalk cafes in Venice everywhere that seemed to beckon to us to come and relax and have a glass of wine. Why hurry, they seemed to ask?

And we were fascinated by all those crazy little streets that weren't really streets at all, but were stone walkways bordering the ever-present canals that seemed to wander aimlessly through this amazing city without apparent rhyme or reason. And in each one we could see reflected images of boats tied to black iron railing and brightly painted posts as if waiting for something. Or someone?

*   *   *

One of our great pleasures in Venice was going to one of the many small restaurants, cafes really, where one passed down a line very much like an American cafeteria, ordering from the man behind the counter whatever pasta one wished and to choose from among the many cheeses. And I always insisted on having the large black olives in oil and garlic, and Helga would tease, "Richard, your breath makes you smell like an Italian."

"Do you know why Italians have so few colds?" I teased.

"No, but I have a feeling you are going to tell me."

"Because they eat so much garlic no one wants to get close to them. Certainly not close enough to catch their germs."

"Richard, you are so silly," she said, then adding a teasing afterthought, "But I adore you anyway."

On our second day in Venice we took a waterbus over to Murano Island and watched the wonderful Venetian glass being blown by puff-cheeked craftsmen whose red faces glistened with sweat in front of the furnaces, oblivious to gawking tourists who stared in amazement.

Afterwards a guide showed us into the most expensive gallery of chandelier and elaborate ornamental fixtures and, when we showed no interest in them, she skillfully guided us into another gallery of slightly less expensive fixtures and so on until we were in the gallery of the least expensive, mostly touristy items. Here Helga bought a small pair of angels that appeared to be suspended in midair hovering very close to each other.

"They will be our guardian angels and will protect us from harm and

261

disappointment," she said as she smiled her incredibly loving smile at me that continued to melt my heart no matter how often I saw it.

SIXTY-SIX

Our visit to Venice was an amazing mix of wonderful experiences that were enchantingly romantic, except for one episode where Helga scared me half to death. We were in St. Mark's square looking up at the bell tower thinking about riding to the top again for another glimpse of the breathtaking view when a voice called out, "Richard? Richard Rouse, is that you? What in heaven's name are you doing here in Venice?"

I looked around and saw striding across the Square to meet me, an old friend from my graduate school days at the University of Virginia. "Ralph Cooper, I could ask you the same thing?"

"Just being typical American tourists, I guess."

We exchanged pleasantries and immediately began to catch up on University gossip, and we were so intent on who had done what in Charlottesville that I almost forgot to introduce Helga.

When I finally did Ralph said, "My wife Helen is off shopping somewhere. Goodness knows what she might wind up buying."

As Ralph and I resumed talking nonstop I couldn't help but notice the bored look on Helga's face, and I began to feel guilty about ignoring her. I know there is nothing quite so boring as having to listen to people talk about other people you don't know or care about. She tried to mask her impatience but with only partial success. Finally she said, "Richard, if you and your friend don't mind, I think I will go back to that little shop where we were looking at those beautiful wine glasses."

"Yea, great. We might take some of those with us when we head for New Orleans. I'll be right here."

"You might even find Rebecca," Ralph suggested, trying to be helpful. "She's a tall woman in a bright yellow dress. But don't tell her I said that about her being tall. She

263

hates how tall she is.   But personally I think it's rather becoming, even if I do have to look up at her."

Helga walked away trying hard not to hurry or show how relieved she was to get away from their boring talk, and looking forward to a little carefree shopping.

There was a nearby café terrace with little tables covered with white lacy cloths and I suggested, "Ralph, "Why don't we have a glass of wine over there?"

"Sure, great idea."

We had talked for almost an hour when Rebecca at last returned laden with a number of ominous looking shopping bags, and I grinned when I heard Ralph groan. After a few more moments of idle chatter, she and Ralph said goodbye and left, and I began to wonder what had become of Helga.   It had been more than an hour since she had gone looking for the wine glasses.

I decided to head down the narrow stone walk past the Cathedral and find the shop she had mentioned.   She was probably still there.   The wine glasses were, but she was not.   Oh, well, I thought, she must have gone on to another shop.   So I strolled down the same walkway to another shop where we had been window-shopping earlier.   She was not there either.   And then another shop.   And another.   And another.   By then I was beginning to get worried.   Where could she be?   Don't panic, I kept telling myself. She's just wandering around looking in all these wonderful little shops.   And who could blame her?   But I panicked anyway.

Seized with increasing anxiety, I began hurrying along any walkway I came to, sometimes in my haste even bumping into strolling tourists.   There really are no streets in Venice and thankfully no cars, only those mysterious canals and the sometimes not so wide stone walkways next to the canals.   I knew my haphazard, panicky searching was not the right thing to do but I couldn't stop myself, my fear of losing her defying all reason, and I kept running into those ever-present canals that seemed to spring up everywhere and block my way. Occasionally there were those pretty little footbridges that were arched so gondolas and other boats could pass underneath them, but they never seemed to be where I thought I should cross. The narrow walkways that often turned unannounced at right angles or even worse, reminded me of a recent fad among North Carolina farmers who would cut a maze of paths through their corn fields and then charge admission for those hardy enough to enter the maze and try to find their way out.

Of course Helga's disappearing like this immediately made me realize how much I loved her, and my fear of losing her only intensified my feelings tenfold or more. What if I don't ever find her? And I immediately thought of dozens of things I had not yet told her and now desperately wanted her to know, especially how much she brightened my life and how much I loved her. What if I never saw that wonderful smiling face again? And I let one negative thought after another push its way into my mind frightening me even more.

Panic kept coursing through my mind was like an out of control freight train, pushing and shoving me in odd directions, the fear of not finding her overriding any sense of caution or restraint. Fear simply consumed me. Rational thought was gone, obliterated by blind, irrational panic. Where could she be? Why can't I find her? My panic grew and my irrational searching continued unabated, and it seemed to become even more haphazard. Could something awful have happened to her? I realized again how my reaction to thoughts of losing her immediately intensified my feeling of love for her. This woman had become such an intimate part of my life so quickly and so easily that the intensity of my feelings for her still surprised me.

Finally, I knew I had to make myself stop. This is crazy, I thought. Running around like a chicken with its head chopped off. Maybe I should call the police. But how does one call them? I don't speak Italian, and anyway they would probably dismiss my panic as if I were just another crazy tourist. What can I do? Think! Think! I've got to find her! But how? Where? If these blasted canals weren't so wide I could jump across some of 'em.

265

In my panicky, erratic running around I found myself at the Grand Canal with no idea of how I had gotten there. Hurrying along the wide walkway next to the big canal I kept watching the waterbuses as they rumbled past in case she was on one. But why would she be on one of those? And the thought kept recurring to me, what if I never see her again? What if something really awful has happened to her? My crazy questions were as haphazard as my running around and immediately of all kinds of terrible, irrational scenarios popped into my mind: murder, rape, kidnapping. Could she have fallen in a canal and drowned? I unconsciously began watching the dark water for a body. Her body? What am I going to do?

"Richard."

I couldn't be sure but I thought I heard a voice faintly calling my name. Then it came again a little louder. "Richard!" And there she was calmly waving to me. But she was on the other side of the Grand Canal!

"Helga, what are you doing over there?" I shouted but then realized how stupid that question was. What earthly difference did it make why she was over there? The important thing was that I had found her at last!

She called out something and waved her arms pointing to the water but I couldn't understand over the roar of the ever-present boats. I was beginning to panic again when I caught sight of the beautiful Rialto Bridge just a short distance away. I remembered the famous old bridge lined with shops from when we had passed under it on the waterbus when we had first arrived. I tried again to call out to her, but with the noise of the water taxis and other boats I knew she would never hear me.

When I thought again about the Rialto Bridge I had an idea. With frantic waving of arms and gesturing I hoped she would understand, I tried to tell her to stay where she was and I would cross the bridge and come to her. She made a sign that she understood and I hurried across the bridge.

Once on the other side of the Grand Canal I began to race toward where I thought she was, and almost at once I came to one of those little cross canal that barred my way. After much confusion and a little cussing, I finally approached a well-dressed man whom I hoped was a local resident and he politely told me in excellent English how to get to where she was, and he even showed me the way. With profuse thanks I rushed to where she stood patiently waiting.

When at last I reached her I gathered her into my arms. "Helga, here you are! I thought I had lost you! What would I have done if I couldn't find you?"

"I'm here, Richard. I waited like you said. But you were rather funny," she smiled, "waving your arms about so."

"I'm not even going to ask where you have been. It doesn't matter just so long as I've found you."

Explaining anyway, she said, "I looked for the wine glasses and it seemed that every shop had different ones, and so I kept looking and looking but I couldn't make up my mind. Then I saw one of those funny little boats where everyone stands while crossing the big canal. I had to try it and maybe find more shops, and a very nice businessman helped me not to fall but first he had to pinch my bottom. And here I am."

I took her in my arms again and held her so tightly she finally had to say, "Richard, you are hurting me. But I do love you for caring so much"

"After this I will never let you out of my sight, Helga. Never again." And I held her hand tightly all the way back to the hotel.

*   *   *

If only I had known how prophetically wrong those words would turn out be.

SIXTY-SEVEN

I left Venice after another day of fruitless searching and took a train to Rome because I remembered that the night before our departure from Venice last summer we had changed our minds and decided to make a brief stopover in the Eternal City. After all, it would have been hard to resist the many spectacular sights in what had been the heart of the Roman Empire. And just as we had done while visiting Paris, we decided to find a little nearby village where we could leave the now dusty and, I feared, nearly exhausted car.

La Storta was a pleasant little place with friendly people who always seemed to be busily going somewhere. And being located on the ring road around Rome I figured it would be easy to get a bus or local train into the city center. But we found no hotel with parking to our liking in the town, and I had about decided to try driving into Rome and take our chances with its notorious traffic when we found a garage that was operated by a very old man who spoke no English. But his kindly, wrinkled old face seemed to smile all the time, especially at Helga. His son, who also worked there, assured us the car would be safe, and we gladly promised to pay him a few Euros for his trouble when we returned.

On our auto trip from Venice to Rome I had convinced Helga we could make an easy visit into the city if we took a local train, and that I knew where there was a bed and breakfast near the main railway station. And I knew how to get around in the city on the subway and by walking. The bed and breakfast was only two blocks from the train station and I had stayed there before with that same young Czech student. I had wisely decided not to bother Helga with the details of that or some of my previous adventures, innocent though they had turned out to be. What's that saying? Don't wake a sleeping tiger?

I really didn't expect to discover anything about her in Rome because I remembered she had not liked the city on a previous visit some years ago, and having been disappointed with the traffic and noise and congestion, and I didn't think she would have returned there now.

That first evening last summer when we had come back to our room in Rome, the landlady asked if we would like the two beds in our room pushed together to make one large bed. But Helga had answered with her telling grin, "No, we will only need one of the small beds." And the landlady gave her a knowing smile and quietly left us to make our own arrangements, she now understanding precisely what they would be.

The next day we toured the Coliseum and Helga immediately expressed her sympathy for the Christians rather than the lions naturally enough, except when the gladiators fought the animals to the death, then her sympathy shifted to the lions.

I was in a silly mood that afternoon after we had just left the Forum, and standing near a statue of the Emperor Caesar Augustus on a nearby street, I raised my arms as if issuing a royal decree and flexed my biceps to show my awesome power, and Helga laughed hysterically at my silly antics. "Richard, you would have been a wonderful emperor. But I think you make an even better lover," she shouted from across the street where she was waiting, and several tourists stopped to look at her, and some laughed.

At the Trevi Fountain I showed her how to throw a coin in the water. "You must turn your back and throw it over your shoulder."

"But why?"

"I don't know. It's just a tradition, I guess. I remember the Trevi Fountain from a nineteen fifties movie I had seen long ago on TV. The one where the name of the film was also the title of the song, *Three Coins in the Fountain*. I think it's supposed to bring good luck to the one who throws the coin, if the back is turned."

"Do we still need good luck?" she asked.

"As wonderful as things are now I don't think so," I suggested. "But why tempt fate?" And we looked at each other with smug, self-satisfied smiles, but just the same we each tossed a coin over our shoulder.

We had planned a quick trip, hoping to see only the Coliseum and the Forum and the Pantheon with its hole in the roof and, of course, the Spanish steps and the Trevi Fountain. But purely by accident we wound up seeing something else that was delightfully special.

SIXTY-EIGHT

We had been wandering around the streets of Rome happily lost in a maze of small streets when Helga grabbed my arm and whispered, "Richard, look. Just ahead in that piazza with the fountain. Do you see them?"

A wedding couple was posing for a photographer, and the bride in her beautiful white gown had put one foot on the rim of the fountain, showing lots of thigh and her probably borrowed fancy lace garter. Her smile was radiant as only a bride's would be, and Helga loved her for it. The sun glittering on the splashing fountain was like a unique stage setting, the perfect accompaniment to the picture and to the bride's happiness. Helga wondered about the couple's honeymoon and the months and years to come when they would be together, and she was jealous; very jealous, and a little sad.

The groom was standing nearby, hardly more than a spectator. I think he was holding her purse.

"That's typical, isn't it?" I had commented when I pointed to him.

"What do you mean?"

"The groom really isn't very important is he? After all, weddings are for the women, you know."

"Now Richard, don't be cross."

"I'm not being cross I'm just stating a fact. I have always said that someone could hire the town drunk, dress him in a tuxedo, make him stand in for the groom at the ceremony and no one would even notice, especially not the bride or her mother. They probably wouldn't ever notice until the wedding photographs came back from the photographer. Well, the bride might finally notice on their wedding night."

"Richard, you are awful," she chuckled. "Delightfully funny but still awful."

A moment later, sensing a subtle change in her, I noticed that Helga was watching the bride with a wistful, almost pained expression. After a long pause, she whispered quietly under her breath, probably thinking that I wouldn't hear, "I wonder if I will ever have a lovely wedding gown like that?" But she immediately regretted having said anything. Had he heard her? And if so would it upset him? Would he think she was trying to hint, perhaps seeking to pressure him into something he might not be ready for? She didn't want to let herself think those kinds of thoughts, but they always came unbidden to her mind just the same, and to her heart as well. Would he ever be ready? But with his frequent declarations of love for me how could he not be ready? What is stopping him? Still, it must be that he doesn't want to . . . She left the thought hanging, afraid to finish it, afraid of what it might foreshadow.

And as they looked at the wedding couple again, each of them had a mental image, each delightful, but each very different.

Why can't I just go on and ask her to marry me? Richard prodded himself. I love her dearly. She is the most wonderful woman like I have ever known. So why this hesitation? What's wrong with me?

Will he ever want to marry? Helga asked herself looking at his confused expression. I had hoped I might marry a few times all those years ago when I was much younger. After all it is every girl's dream. I had wished for it often, dreamed of it almost every day. And of course there had been Helmut Brimmer in Heidelberg. He had been young and handsome and I loved him desperately, and he said he, too, loved me very much. But for some reason I didn't seem to measure up to his mother's expectations for her son's wife and after that Helmut just seemed to fade away. Why did he do that? Why couldn't he stand up to his mother? Why couldn't he say it was he who knew what it was he wanted? Maybe with that kind of weak character it had been better that we didn't marry, she thought with a sad shrug.

As the years went by nothing much seemed to happen with other men as well, not that there had been all that many. Was there something wrong with me? she had asked herself often. Something awful that I am not aware of? But if there is, how am I to know? Who could I ask? And who would be willing to give me an honest answer? Certainly not a man. But who, then?

And as more years passed it seemed that for whatever reason I didn't understand, the attention of men came along less and less often. And those few who did try to pursue me seemed to lack very much passion. Not just sexual passion, but passion of any kind. Not even passion for love or for life. They all seemed to be so humdrum without that magic spark that would lift a woman's heart out of the ordinary into incredible dreams. None of them. Why was that?

But then Richard burst into my life like a flaming meteor and it was as if I had been reborn. Suddenly life was wonderful again like when I was twenty-one and everything was beautiful; the sky blissfully blue, the sun always shining, and my skin seemed to tingle with excitement whenever he was near.

But then her thoughts of his hesitation about marriage came creeping back again. Could his having grown up in such a loveless home as he has described made him fear the commitment of marriage, compounded by the equally loveless marriage with his first wife Mary? A loveless marriage? She shuddered at the horrible thought, thinking about how loving she knew he could be, and how loving he was with her now every day.

His first wife? Am I already expecting to be his second wife? I know I shouldn't be thinking that way just now. Surely that's rushing things? What had the grandmother with the crooked nose said about counting chickens before they hatched? But how I do long to be his wife. And to have his children. Oh, my, yes what a joy that would be!

But could I expect anything like this now? she asked herself, looking again at the beautiful young bride in her white wedding dress. A wedding at last? And in a gown like that? At my age? But my heart does long for it just the same. My sister Eska is married with two beautiful children, and I do adore them. But they are not mine. Will I ever have

273

any of my own? At my age? And why do I keep thinking about my age? I suppose it's because I know that my – now, what's that expression, I've heard? Oh, yes my biological clock is running. Desperately running ahead of me and I am powerless to stop it. Could Richard and I ever have children? But he has never mentioned marriage and certainly not children. He told me that he and his ex-wife Mary never had children. And although that had made the divorce easier, did that mean Richard might never want children? Or could it be he is biologically unable to father children? What a terrible thought. That has never occurred to me. But how would he know? Maybe his ex-wife never having had a child is a sign. But maybe it was she who was barren. But how could I know. How could we ever know? I do wish he would talk with me about it but I am afraid to bring up the subject, afraid he might resent it. I would not like for him to think I was pressuring him. Still, I wish he would talk about it. At least say something. How I would love to have a child of my own to love. A child by Richard. Maybe two or three. She smiled wistfully at the thought, delicate little tears beginning to form in her eyes as she looked again at the young bride.

They were to live together when they went to New Orleans, this much she knew. But then what? It all seemed to sound so impermanent, so meandery. What must I do? Remain silent, of course, and say nothing, she reminded herself. What else can I do? But her heart hammered out a sad measured song she couldn't ignore.

*   *   *

I remember that the next morning after our brief visit to Rome we went to the train station early and left to pick up the car in the little village where we had left it. We decided to skip Bari where we could have taken a ferry to Athens. Instead we drove all the way to Brindisi on the heel of the Italian boot, hoping to see some of southern Italy. From there we were to take a ferry to Athens and the beautiful Greek islands beyond.

SIXTY-NINE

Jennifer Smartley was looking around in the main Brno railway station thoroughly confused. Not only did she have no idea what to do or where to go, but the abundance of signs in the Czech language and a few leftovers in Russian added to her confusion. And her cold, calculating eyes did not even notice the beautiful old buildings of honey-toned stone, nor did she see the spectacular early autumn flowers that were blooming profusely in large urns on a nearby street corner.

I remember in his blog he said something about where he stayed at some place called a . . . Now, what was that crazy Czech word? Lekor something or other? Whatever in the hell that is? Hold on a minute! Now I remember something that might help. He said there was an Englishman living there. He might know where they are — Richard and that damn German woman. If I can ever find the place maybe that guy can help. At least he should be able to speak English. If need be I can use a little charm on him. Men are such pushovers for a smile and maybe an accidental bumping with a boob. They are all so damn shallow and transparent.

A few nights before while she was still in Prague, and aided by several glasses of Czech beer, she had had a quiet talk with herself and it had at last become clear that she wasn't really over there to try to reestablish a relationship with Richard. Far from it, she had finally decided in her cold, calculating way. I wouldn't have the bastard back on a silver platter. Not after he took up with that damn German slut. But then, why have I come over here?

The second part of her reasoning was not nearly so clear. It seemed to be very much like something she remembered from her childhood. She had taken a doll that belonged to the little girl who lived next door, and she wanted it for herself but her mother had insisted that she return it. And, in her rapidly developing self-absorbed thinking, Jennifer decided that if she couldn't have the doll then no one else should have it. She had taken the doll out in the neighbor's back yard and destroyed it, viciously smashing it into pieces with a hammer she had stolen from their garage, and then burying the pieces in the neighbor's back garden. "If I can't have it, then no one else can," she kept repeating to herself in her strange, childlike mantra.

Later she realized quite clearly that she had not really wanted the doll at all, she just didn't want anyone else to have it. And it had finally become clear to her just last night the same reasoning now applied to Richard. She no longer wanted him for her lover she just didn't want Helga to have him. Or any other woman for that matter. Dammit, if I can't have him, no one else is going to. I'll get him back, use him a little. Screw his brains out and then dump him. That'll serve him right.

The tram rattled to a stop at the end of Line Number 3. When she saw everyone getting off she thought, now what? But when she saw another tram ahead of them loop around and presently head back the way they had just come, she realized that this must be the end of the line. What should she do now? She was nearly exhausted after her trip from Prague and the frustration of trying to get directions from old men who hadn't bathed in who knows how many weeks and dowdy old women with their net shopping bags, and none of whom spoke English. And to make matters worse she had gotten on the tram without a ticket and the man who checked tickets caught her without one. Son-of-a-bitch acted like he was going to put me in jail or something. I didn't know what in the hell he was so upset about. Thank goodness that high school boy spoke some English and paid the fare for me. I guess I should have offered to repay him, but all he could do was to listen to me speaking English and stare at my boobs. Anticipating having to deal with the Englishman, Jennifer had changed in the railway station toilet and put on one of her new low cut tops that showed lots of cleavage. And it had unexpectedly come in handy with that high school boy. That was probably payment enough for the kid. Men, ha!

After asking half a dozen people, none of whom spoke English and getting almost as many different answers, she finally managed to find the Lektorsky dum purely by accident. The door was locked and it seemed to take forever for a very old security man to answer the bell. His face was a mask of incomprehension in response to her questions. At last she remembered the Englishman's name. "Matthew?" she asked. "Is there a Matthew here?" she said, pointing to the building. The old man's face brightened and he nodded and showed her inside and led her to a room on the second floor and even knocked for her.

"It's open," a male voice called from inside the room. Jennifer pushed open the door and found Matthew Smithson sitting up in bed reading.

"Well, well, well, come into my parlor, said the spider to the fly," Matthew quipped, sitting up a little straighter. "And who might you be?" he asked. Jennifer introduced herself as she strode confidently into the room. Smiling to herself she thought this one will be a pushover. He sure has that horny look, and he can't take his eyes off my boobs.

Matthew Smithson was thirty-two years old and a handsome young man with a devil may care look in his eye. A raffish young rogue might have been a better description of his outward appearance. But Jennifer did not notice the sadness lurking behind those eyes that Helga had immediately seen at Matthew's party.

He watched Jennifer closely as she began explaining about looking for Richard. Mostly he was admiring her beauty, especially her marvelous figure. He found himself hoping she would hurry and shut up so he could make his move. After all, she had come uninvited into his room. And, my God, look at those boobs! She's half naked! What was he supposed to think?

However, as she began to explain her mission a subtle change began to come over Matthew's face and she thought, now what? Seems like every time I explain to these people over here what I'm trying to find out they all clam up. Like those women in Prague. It's like they're all trying to protect Richard. But protect him from what? From me? Or are they covering for that German bitch of his?

Jennifer decided it was time for a change of tactics. She had an old maid aunt who liked to say, 'You can catch more flies with honey than with vinegar.' But if that was true, Jennifer thought, then why was she still an old amid?

But forgetting the old aunt, Jennifer started turning on the charm and, of course, Matthew was readily susceptible. She sidled over and sat on the edge of his bed, and leaning over, she made a pretense of trying to see what he was reading, making sure he could see deep into her blouse. She was immediately glad she had changed into the new low-cut top as Matthew's breathing quickened, and she smiled when he licked his lips several times. She looked at the open book and whispered in her softest, most seductive voice, "What are you reading, Matthew?"

"*Lady Chatterley's Lover*," he answered with a sly grin. But in spite of himself his voice croaked.

"Isn't there a lot of sex in that?"

"Ah, yes, quite a lot," Matthew managed to croak again. But then regaining some composure he said, "I haven't finished it yet. Maybe you could tell me how it ends."

Jennifer put a hand against his chest, and leaning over, she pretended to look at the book again, and said in her best breathless voice, "Maybe it would be best if I showed you." Matthew gulped audibly when she pressed her breast against his arm and whispered in his ear, "Matthew, do you know where I can find Richard Rouse?"

"No, but if we keep working on it I think I might remember."

But after more compliments and several more bits of not very subtle touching that seemed to promise there could be more to follow, Matthew managed to regain his composure and offered no information, although with great reluctance.

While Matthew continued to remain seated on the bed, probably in order to hide his arousal, Jennifer saw that her seduction was not going to work although a fine sheen of sweat glistened on his brow.

After a few more minutes of her attempts at persuasion she sat back and said, "You don't know shit, do you?"

"Jennifer," Matthew said very slowly, "Richard Rouse is the kindest, most decent man I have ever known. I have heard about you. We all have, and I wouldn't tell you anything about him for a piece of your beautiful ass every day for a month." Matthew picked up his book and pretended to resume reading not even looking at Jennifer as she straightened her skirt and stalked out of the room muttering, "Well, hell! Outsmarted by a damn Limey."

Matthew's remarks about Richard made her realize that all the people over here had somehow heard about her and had no intention of helping her, and she couldn't imagine why.

SEVENTY

I've got to try some different approach, Jennifer thought as the tram trundled past Brno's new opera house. When the tram stopped at the pedestrian street Ceska, she decided that maybe a slow walk through Namesti Svobody might help clear her mind and help her to decide what she should do next.   Unfortunately, her high heels were more appropriate for a cocktail lounge than for walking on cobblestones.   Might as well stop at that McDonalds over there and get some real food, she thought.   When she had finished eating, she tossed her cheeseburger wrapper at an outdoor trash receptacle but ignored it when it missed and rolled on the ground.   It was then that she remembered reading in his blog about Richard's favorite sweet shop.

The twin spires of St. Peter and St. Paul Cathedral loomed high above the Kavna u Kapuchinu café, seeming to pierce the startling blue sky.   She asked for the waiter by the name of Pavel who, upon seeing her, was immediately captivated by this beautiful American woman.   However, after hearing her story he, too, seemed to forget virtually any knowledge of Richard or Helga.   And when his boss flashed an angry look at him for spending too much time at her table, he hurried away to get her Cappuccino.

Matthew Smithson's refusal to help her and now Pavel's reluctance to help made Jennifer realize that all the people over here had somehow heard about her and had no intention helping.   And she was completely mystified by that kind of loyalty.

She remembered with a grimace her biggest failure when, hoping to get a promotion and probably a big raise, she had tried to seduce Bob Worley, the department chairman, and she had been summarily rejected.   Afterwards she had seethed for days, raging at herself for her failure, but all the time trying to find some way to blame him.   She had tried for weeks to think of a way to get back at Bob.   After all, to her revenge was almost as sweet as a sexual conquest.   But she finally had to give up when she realized the chairman was such a dedicated family man with a beautiful, loving wife, he was admired by all his colleagues, and as far as vices were concerned, he was Mr. Clean.   And now, here in Europe, some of that still pent up anger at Bob Worley was compounded by her failure at finding Richard. And she made a decision that when she found him she would, at least emotionally, castrate the bastard.

Maybe I'll do better in another city where he's been. I know I haven't been very subtle, so I guess it's time to try a different approach. How about, let's see, maybe a relative bringing news of grandma's death? Or something like that? Maybe with a few tears thrown in for good measure?

Or better yet, she thought with sudden inspiration, maybe it's time to call in some reinforcements.

"Hello, Otto? This is Jennifer Smartley. Remember we attended that language seminar in Paris last year? You represented that University in Munich, right?

"Ja, I remember you very well, Jennifer. I am glad you asked for my phone number." Jennifer had long made a habit of keeping the phone numbers of every man she met no matter what his station in life or age, just in case.

"You do remember the part in my room *after* the evening session, don't you?"

"Ja, of course I remember quite well. How could I forget?" Otto seemed to be having difficulty breathing.

"Otto, I need some help. A friend of mine has found himself a German girlfriend over here and I need to find out where they are."

"Yes, I understand, Jennifer" Otto Housmann said, switching to his best English.

"If I give you the girlfriend's name and some addresses in Prague do you think you could find out from some of her friends where my friend and the German girl might be?"

"I don't know, Jennifer. I am quite busy right now trying to finish work on my dissertation.   You remember it is on modern American literature?"

"Yes, Otto, I understand, but I would be ever so grateful if you could help me. And," she added slowly and a little breathlessly for effect, "You do remember how grateful I can be, don't you, Otto?"

"Yes, of course, Jennifer," he stammered, still trying to catch his breath as he remembered an extraordinary night in Paris last year, "I will see what I can do.   In Prague you say?"

"Yes, and Otto, maybe you should make up some sort of story like my friend's mother has died and no one seems to know how to get in touch with him over here in Europe and they desperately need to find him."

Jennifer gave Otto the names he would need in Prague and her contact information, and she hung up with a satisfied smile.   This was a good idea.   And after all, she remembered, Otto wasn't all that bad in bed, either.

SEVENTY-ONE

In the town of Brindisi, far down on the heel of the Italian boot, we had stayed in a harbor-side hotel with a beautiful view of the Adriatic Sea. It was from there we expected to take the ferry to Athens and on to the fabled Greek Islands.

The next morning Helga and I were up very early. She quickly made coffee in our room which we took out to the hotel terrace where we could enjoy the sunrise. Just as we were taking our seats, out of the womb of early morning the sun rose gently from over of the sea, taking its time, spreading the sky with a comforting golden glow, warming the cool morning with its pleasant rays. We savored the delightful taste of the strong Italian coffee that was the perfect accompaniment to the blazing display that heralded the birth of a new day.

Watching the sunrise together was an unusual experience for us, and we both commented on how special it was to see the sun rise out of the sea. Everywhere else we had been we had only seen the afternoon sun setting in the sea like at Venice and our most favorite place of all, Vernazza on the Italian Riviera. Well, maybe Normandy, too, but only if one wanted to see the sun setting over uncounted numbers of headstones. Somehow it didn't seem right to enjoy the sunset there.

*   *   *

On our second morning in Brindisi as we were preparing to get up from our breakfast table on the terrace, but not really wanting to leave the magical view, a very old man hesitantly approached our table. He was dressed in a drab, much-worn suit with a stained tie, and he was wearing a very old hat that showed many years of wear, and the morning sun reflected brightly off the greasy headband. But he swept off the hat and bowed in a very courtly, old country manner, his long gray hair sweeping over his face. He began speaking hesitantly in Italian, which neither of us understood. His tone was very quiet, seemingly apologetic.

283

"Richard," Helga whispered, "He keeps looking at our coffee cups and the last of our rolls. I think he's hungry. She tried speaking to him in German and French but with no success. Finally using hand sign and some pantomime, she managed to make him understand that he should sit down and they would buy him coffee and a roll. When he began to devour the roll ravenously but with as much mannerly grace as he could muster, Helga summoned the still sleepy waiter and ordered a complete breakfast for the man. The waiter glared menacingly at the old fellow but nevertheless brought the breakfast, then stood nearby as if guarding against some kind of anticipated wrongdoing.

Afterwards as they walked back to their hotel room, Richard remarked, "It seems that some of our most memorable experiences have been with newly met strangers like that accordion player in Paris. And now this old fellow."

"I just wish we could have done more for him," Helga said with a note of sadness in her voice.

"Well, I did slip a fifty Euro note to him."

"Richard, you are so kind," she smiled and gave him a resounding kiss on the cheek.

SEVENTY-TWO

How could I ever forget the ferry ride to Greece, and the unbelievable adventure we didn't know was awaiting us? Helga and I had been standing close together at the rail holding hands and dreaming of the special little Greek island we hoped we would soon find, and we watched the sea and the passing offshore islands where the trees and bushes seemed to be cloaked in every imaginable shade of green.

Now here I am on that very same ferry remembering and dreaming, and wishing so fervently I could find her. Of course, she wasn't at the hotel where we had stayed the two nights in Brindisi and where she had helped that old man at breakfast.

I had decided to stay close by the Brindisi ferry terminal and watch every ferry that came and went for two days until I was sure of getting on the same one we had taken last summer. It seemed important for me to take the exact same ferry, although I wasn't quite sure why. But I did it anyway. And it turned out that even though all the deck hands clearly recalled our adventure, none of them had seen her recently. But they did remember every detail of our daring rescue, and one of the crewmen even spoke excitedly of Helga's bravery.

Oh, well, I guess I'll head on to Athens and look for . . . My God, I'm getting so tired of saying, *look for*. But what else can I do?

*　　　　　　*　　　　　　*

The sun was shining brightly as the ferry pulled out of the harbor at Brindisi into the Adriatic leaving Italy behind. The white-capped waves sparkled like millions of miniature diamonds dancing over the water.

"The sea is so beautiful," Helga said as she leaned close against me at the rail. "I don't think I could ever get tired of looking at it and dreaming happy dreams. And, of course, they would be dreams about you, Richard, my love," she said as she let her eyes

285

move slowly up and down his hard, lean body liking him in his tight jeans. He's such a sexy man she thought, as she let her gaze stop for a moment midway at her favorite spot. Behave yourself, Helga Wintermantle, she whispered under her breath.

The dull throbbing of the diesel engine could not disturb the beauty of this spectacular day. And even though there was a strong breeze, the sun was bright and warm on our faces, but our minds were far away, dreaming of romantic little Greek islands and looking forward to new adventures and endless love.

Dozens of white gulls were screaming and circling the stern of the boat, their wingtips a stark black as if each had been dipped in an old fashioned inkwell. Probably some kid throwing pieces of bread to them, I thought. I hope none of them fly up front where we are and poop on us like they sometimes do on the Cape Hatteras ferry back home.

Hours later after a brief stop at the town of Kerkira on the Greek island of Corfu, the ferry continued southward following a narrow twisting channel between Corfu and the mainland side which was dotted with numerous small islands. It seemed as if the same squawking gulls were circling the stern again, probably looking for another free handout. Must be the same kid, I thought.

So far the ferry ride had been so uneventful as to seem almost boring except for the glorious scenery. The small offshore islands – one after another like delicate green emeralds threaded on a silvery necklace – seemed to be competing with one another with their display of vivid shades of green, each one trying to outdo the others. And the mountains on the mainland looked like they were brushing the incredibly blue sky with a special paintbrush as if they were trying to keep the entire scene quiet and peaceful, trying to make a perfect picture for a guidebook. And I remembered that somewhere over there just out of sight was Mount Olympus, the legendary home of the Greek gods.

We were standing by the port rail watching the tiny coastal islands slide peacefully by and we had been talking quietly, dreaming of our upcoming stay at one of the small, sparsely inhabited island in the Small Cyclades, the fabled Greek islands far out in the

Aegean; one we hoped would be quietly peaceful and not overrun with tourist. And, of course, we hoped it would be a very romantic place as well.

Suddenly there was a lot of shouting and screaming from the rear of the ferry and we could see people running in that direction and waving their arm, some excitedly pointing at the water. We hurried to the stern to see what the commotion was about and I had a sudden, terrible thought: I hope we're not sinking.

SEVENTY-THREE

One particular middle-aged woman who seemed to be the center of attention was pointing at the water and screaming hysterically louder than any of the others. Of course, neither of us understood Greek, and we had no idea what the fuss was about so I asked a man we had heard speaking English earlier in the day what was going on. "That woman's child has fallen into the water," the man said, pointing to the small head and thrashing arms that were receding behind the ferry at an alarming rate.

"Someone should do something," Helga cried, terrified for the child's life. "Why do they all stand and scream and do nothing?"

I watched as the child's head bobbed in the rough water, getting smaller and smaller as the ferry moved away. Just then I heard a splash near the side of the boat and I looked and saw Helga swimming toward he child. "Helga, what are you doing?"

"Someone has to do something," she called matter-of-factly.

Hesitating only a second, I vaulted over the rail and into the water and began swimming furiously to catch up with her.

"Damn," I muttered aloud, "My passport and money belt are going to be soaked. Won't that be a mess?"

As I continued swimming toward her, Helga's head suddenly went under and when she didn't immediately reappear I swam harder, desperately trying to get to her, panicky at the thought of losing her. The clear, cold hand of imminent death gripped my heart, seeming to pull me under with her. I've got to get to her! "Hang on Helga, I'm coming!" I was horrified by the images of her drowning that passed before my eyes in a kind of deadly slow motion; her lifeless body sinking to the bottom, her beautiful red hair gently waving in the water like seaweed. Could this be how it ends? All our dreams gone in a flash? What would I do if I couldn't get to her? I have to save her. I have to!

288

Swimming like a madman, oblivious to everything else, I kept choking on seawater when I tried to call out to the empty sea. "Hang on, Helga, I'm coming!"

Then, just as suddenly as she had disappeared, Helga popped back to the surface just as I reached where I thought she had gone under. "I am sorry, Richard," she said as I grabbed her hand, "I had a cramp for just a minute. I went under to massage my leg."

"My God Helga, you scared me to death! I thought you were gone," I sputtered, still trying to catch my breath in the choppy water. "I thought I had lost you forever."

"I am not so easily lost Richard, my darling," she said, sputtering while she tried to wipe the seawater from her eyes, "now that I have you." I released her hand, knowing we would need both our hands if we were to get out of this predicament.

Together we swam as fast as we could and soon caught up with the child that turned out to be a little girl. Each of us held one of the child's arms, supporting her in an awkward way. She gave a halfhearted smile and said something in Greek.

"It's okay," I said, trying to sound braver than I really felt, "We'll help you."

"You are Americans," the girl said in very good English as she smiled brightly. "Or British?"

"Americans," Helga said, apparently deciding not to confuse the issue of our different nationalities in this crisis.

The ferry was rapidly moving away, and although some of the deck crew threw life preservers into the water, the increasing wind blew them in the wrong direction like vain, elusive hopes.

"Richard, why don't they come back and rescue us?"

"I don't know, but I imagine it's because that ferry boat is very large and I guess it will take a long time for it to turn around. And the channel here seems to be especially narrow so I'm not at all sure they'll be able to turn around just yet."

The little girl spoke again. "I am sorry for the trouble I am causing. I was trying to get one to eat the seagulls to out of my hand and I leaned over too far," she said matter-of-factly.

"So you were the one feeding the gulls?" I said with a hint of irritation in my voice that I immediately regretted.

"Yes, I am sorry I have caused so much trouble."

"How old are you?" I asked, hoping to take her mind off the seriousness of our situation and maybe lessen her feelings of guilt for having caused this crisis.

"I have ten years," she said proudly.

"Quite a precocious little thing, isn't she?" Helga said, smiling at the small child then adding, "You seem to be a very good swimmer. We promise we will stay with you until help arrives." The girl grinned happily at having found not one but two rescuers.

I was hoping the child would begin to feel a little safer if Helga and I both reassured her that everything would be okay, and hopefully reassure ourselves as well with this new, unexpected responsibility and our precarious situation.

All three of us continued to tread water and ponder our plight, each of us probably thinking the same thing: How do we get out of this predicament? And having no flotation device to hang onto, treading water was quickly becoming tiring.

"What should we do, Richard?" Helga asked seeming to read my mind as the three of us watched the rapidly disappearing ferry.

In spite of her instant reaction to the child's plight, Helga was very glad to have him there to help share the responsibility for what looked increasingly like a very important decision; possibly a life or death decision.

As if in answer to Helga's question the little girl turned her head and pointed to the western sky where that the sun was just now dipping behind some ominously dark clouds. "It will be dark soon and I think it might storm tonight," she said, trying with little success to hide the fear in her voice. She looked longingly at the receding ferry for a moment then said in a small, frightened voice, "I do not think they will come back for us, do you?"

"I'm not sure. Maybe they can't turn around just yet," I suggested again, trying to downplay the seriousness of what I was beginning to realize was our very dangerous situation with no flotation devices and, apparently, no rescuers.

Studying the shoreline, the child said, "That little island over there seems to be quite close. Perhaps we should try to swim ashore," she suggested, her small arms splashing when she tried to point, "and wait for rescue?"

As that seemed to be to best alternative, we all agreed, and the three of us began to swim in the increasingly choppy wind-driven water. Actually, when I thought about it, this was clearly our only alternative.

I soon realized that the little island looked deceptively close, and no matter how hard we swam it seemed almost as if it were receding. I kept trying to help the little girl but it soon became apparent she was probably the best swimmer of the three of us and I gave up trying to help her, although even she was beginning to show signs of fatigue. Occasionally I tried to help Helga but it soon appeared that she was also a better swimmer than I, and it wasn't long before I began to lag behind thinking, I'm not going to be macho about this and try to keep up with them. I'm just going to plod along and get there when I can. Can one plod along while swimming? I wondered with a half-hearted chuckle, but then I choked on a mouthful of sea water. That certainly feels like what I'm doing. But maybe slogging along is a better description.

After more than an hour the three of us finally managed to drag ourselves onto a rocky little beach, exhausted but safe with me bringing up the rear. Actually I was a distant third. Each of us flopped on the pebbly sand, thankful to be on land again wet though it was. We were so tired that for several minutes we all simply lay where we were, our feet still awash in the waves from the increasing wind and the passing of small boats, none of which seemed to be coming to our rescue. "I wonder if the ferry managed to launch a boat to come get us," I thought aloud. Helga and the little girl both of whom were too tired to answer, frowned and said nothing.

"That was a lot further to swim than it looked," I gasped, still trying to catch my breath. A few minutes later the three of us managed to crawl out of the water and up among some large boulders where we sat wet and cold, trying our best to keep out of the wind. Dressed only in shorts and a polo shirt I tried manfully not to shiver, but I couldn't help but notice the goose bumps on my arms and Helga's, and the little girl was shivering violently. I suggested that Helga and I move, putting the child between us and we snuggled very tightly together trying to share our body heat.

"I imagine we make a sad, bedraggled sight," Helga said, trying to inject a little humor into our situation. "Is bedraggled a good word, Richard?"

"Yes," I said, forcing a smile I didn't really feel, "and I think it fits us perfectly right now." No one laughed.

Darkness was rapidly falling and still no boat came. And with the sun almost gone the air was becoming increasingly chilly, more like an early autumn evening and not like summer at all. All three of us were shivering in our wet clothes, and although there was only a slight chance of hypothermia, nevertheless we were all very cold and uncomfortable.

"Maybe we could find a village or something," I ventured, trying to sound brave and in command of our situation, something I didn't really feel.

"These small islands are not usually inhabited," the child said. "But maybe there could be a fisherman's cottage or something like that. Or a goatherd."

All three of us shivered and looked around hopefully as if we were sure we would

292

see something.   Of course there was nothing to see.

SEVENTY-FOUR

After a while the little girl, still shivering and shaking, asked permission to go relieve herself. When she went behind some nearby bushes I said to Helga, "You are too kindhearted for your own good. You could have drowned."

"Nein, I am a very good swimmer, Richard. And you, too, are very kindhearted, my love. You jumped in also."

"I was trying to save you."

"And?"

"Well, yes, I thought she might need a little more help."

Just then the child came hurrying back to where we sat, smiling hugely and clapping her hands in excitement. Breathlessly she told us, "There is a path of some sort behind those bushes where I went to wee wee? You know, to make a water. It looks as if goats and people, too, may have used it. Maybe we should see where it goes. Perhaps we will find a house." But seeing my exhausted look of disbelief she quickly added, "Or something."

Helga smiled encouragingly at the child, "Of course we should look. Don't you think so, Richard?"

"Yea, sure. It's worth a try. It's certainly better than sitting here freezing. And walking will get our blood flowing and help keep us warm."

After walking along the faint trail for a long while, scratched by unknown thorns and stumbling over unseen rocks, the girl suddenly exclaimed, running ahead and pointing, "Look, there! A cottage, I think!"

The little whitewashed cottage had a thatched roof and a small door painted blue and one tiny window. And most importantly, there was the reassuring sign of smoke coming from the stone chimney that seemed to beckon to us with a comforting finger as if encouraging us to come get dry and warm ourselves.

When we approached the cottage a dog ran from around the corner of the house and began barking, and an old man opened the door and stared at us curiously. Seeing our wet clothes he began waving his arms about and talking excitedly. He was very old, probably eighty or more, his slightly longish hair was snow white and he had a stubble of white on his chin as if he had not shaved for several days. He had an old man's eyes, but they were brilliantly blue and very clear. And they began to twinkle merrily when the dog and the little girl immediately made friends.

"I think I must translate," the girl said as the man began talking again, his tone clearly indicating that he was asking questions. "He wants to know what happened to us and how did we get here. And he makes a joke and asks if we had to swim."

Richard and Helga both chuckled and grinned in spite of their discomfort and answered together, gesturing at their still set clothes, "Yes, we did indeed have to swim." When the dog, an odd looking mixed breed, saw his master welcome the wet visitors, he began romping around and licking their hands, especially the little girl's. They were invited into the cottage and were told with signs and gestures that they should come warm themselves by the fire.

Later, standing in front of the small fireplace with our hands outstretched to the warmth, the girl described our watery misadventure to the old man who listened, occasionally nodding as if remembering something sad. After a few minutes he quietly began talking as he gestured at the room. The girl explained, "This is his cottage and he lives here with his son and the son's wife." She was interrupted by the old man who repeatedly pointed to the dog and said something in Greek with an impish grin, and she quickly added, "And the dog lives here, too.

"He and the son make their living fishing. And the son and his wife have gone to a village on the mainland to sell their fish and to buy supplies. They go in their boat with, ah, what do you call the motor outside at the back end of the boat?"

"An outboard motor," Richard explained. "Ask him if the son can take us to the mainland when he returns."

She asked and they watched in disappointment as the old man said something with a negative shaking of his head while pointing toward the west. "He says a storm is coming and we will have to wait until tomorrow. The son and his wife probably will stay with the wife's mother and not get back tonight because of the weather." All three of them tried with considerable difficulty not to show their disappointment.

"But," she continued, "He says we are welcome to stay here tonight and enjoy his hos, hospi . . . . What is that English word that means you are welcome to stay in my house?"

"Hospitality is what I think you mean," Richard said.

"Yes, I must remember that word. I shall tell all my school friends and they will be impressed with my new English word and my new American friends."

Later the old fisherman dragged from behind a curtain what appeared to be a large old-fashioned seaman's chest, and after rummaging through it for a few minutes he finally came up with two of the traditional blue striped Greek fisherman's sweaters for Richard and Helga. He gave the little girl a puzzled look, and finally digging deep to the bottom of the chest he brought out what must have been one of his very old flannel nightshirts. Then all three of us took turns going behind the curtain to change out of our wet clothes.

"I think I must roll this up very much," the child said laughing as she struck what she thought might be a fashion model pose, then she began an impromptu whirling dance. And we all clapped and joined in her laughter and the dog decided he would dance as well and he began running around and around barking excitedly. At last the dance ended when

296

the little girl and the dog fell in a giggling heap with the dog happily licking her face.

With their wet clothes steaming near the fire on a rack made from the tangled branches of a driftwood tree, the three of them began to feel more comfortable in their borrowed dry clothes. Helga's not very large sweater barely covered her buttocks and she grinned mischievously while trying to sit down. "Richard, I must not bend over wearing this," she said.

"Go on," I teased. "What's the harm?"

"I don't know about our host, but I do know what the harm would be from you. Don't forget, I know about your roaming hands and rushing fingers." And we both laughed heartedly at her suggestion. And now that I was warm and comfortable, it was much easier to let my mind wander to thoughts of her delightful body.

"We have not even asked you," Helga said to the little girl, thinking to change the subject before Richard got any more ideas. "What is your name?"

"Athene."

"Is that like Athena the Greek goddess?"

"Yes, my mother named me for the Greek Goddess of Wisdom."

"I think she named you quite appropriately."

"I hope so. I do try to live up to it."

"I have been meaning to ask you," Helga continued as they all began to get comfortable in front of the fire. "Where did you learn such good English?"

"We start to learn English when we are only five years old in what you call, ah, kindergarten, I think is the word."

297

"Ja, das ist correct," Helga said with a bit of Teutonic pride at the German word.

A little while later the old man provided a meager supper of cold fish and flat bread with a small communal bowl of olive oil in which we each could dip small pieces of bread. Helga and I watched the other two closely to see how it was done so we would not make a social mistake. Later the old man produced a goatskin of wine, which I immediately managed to squirt on my face and the borrowed sweater much to the amusement of them all.

After a while Richard spoke quietly to Athene. "Ask the old man if he ever leaves this island. If you think he would not mind. He looks like he has been here forever." Athene nodded and translated the question.

The old man thought for a while and then began talking quietly in a very subdued voice, his eyes filling with tears. "He says he only leaves this place one time each year. It is at the time of Easter and his son takes him to the mainland in his boat to visit the grave of his wife." The old fellow stopped talking to wipe away his tears with the back of his hand and they thought he would say no more, but then unexpectedly, he began again. "He says," Athene began translating once more, "his wife has been dead for many years. She died in a terrible accident when a ferryboat sank. Many people drowned that awful day. Now he says he has no one except for this old dog who is his very best friend." The dog, knowing he was being talked about, looked at the man while he happily thumped his tail on the floor.

Soon after they had eaten, the old man put blankets on the floor for them in front of the fire. Richard and Helga lay there for a few minutes whispering to each other, the glow from the fire softening the planes of their faces, each of them stifling yawns as their eyes began to feel heavy with exhaustion and the wine. "All that swimming was more exercise than I've had in years," Richard said, already half asleep.

The old man said something to the dog and pointed and the dog obediently walked over and lay down close to Athene with a big doggie smile. The little girl fell asleep almost immediately with the dog snuggled close against her back. Richard and Helga held each other tightly for a few minutes longer, happy that they had survived the harrowing experience of the afternoon and thankful once again for the love they had for each other. With full stomachs and the warm fire it wasn't long before all three of the exhausted mariners were asleep.

All night a fierce storm raged with thunder and lightning and rain so heavy it sometimes rattled against the window so loud it might have been hail. The storm woke Helga and Richard, and they lay whispering to each other for a few minutes, happily content in front of the dying fire and trying to explain their actions in the water that afternoon while they clung lovingly to each other, each pledging silently never to let anything part them.

Later, Helga turned over trying find sleep again, but the memory of the harrowing experience with Athene in the water kept her awake. Why had she jumped in? Was it as if the little girl were her own child? And just as she knew a frantic mother would have done, she had not hesitated a moment to try to save the child. But Athene was not her child. Was this a silent cry to show Richard how much she wanted a child of her own? But he had jumped in also? To save her and their imaginary child, she thought with a happy smile?

Remembering the experience that was slowly turning into a fantasy, she imagined Richard leaping into the water to save his beloved family. The courageous husband risking everything for the love of them both. The fantasy kept playing itself over and over in her mind like an endless tape, each time embellished a little more. As sleep at last crept closer, she snuggled against Richard's back and closed her eyes and smiled at the warm comforting feeling the fantasy gave her, and she fell asleep thinking about what she still wished could be.

SEVENTY-FIVE

By morning the sky had cleared and the sun was shining brightly, the stormy night already just a memory. The old fisherman's son and his wife, both apparently in their early thirties but looking more than their years from the hard life of fisher folk, had come in at dawn and were just now listening to the old man relate the story of their adventure, ably assisted by Athene. The young wife smiled shyly as she looked admiringly at Helga who was now wearing her dry clothes. She said something and touched her own hair, and Athene translated, "She thinks your red hair is very beautiful."

"Tell her I said thank you very much." Athene did so and the woman beamed.

They all had breakfast of coffee and coarse bread and a little goat cheese, and afterwards there was a long discussion, complete with Athene's usual translations. It was decided that the young man would take the three of them back to Corfu in his boat where they could arrange with the ferry company to resume their interrupted trip to Athens.

Richard had asked Athene if he should offer to pay the old man for staying the night but she said to do so would probably be an insult to his hospitality, and she beamed using her new English word. But Richard and Helga both thanked him profusely with *kala*, the Greek words for thanks Athene had taught them.

Their parting was a little sad, and with no grandchildren of his own the old man had quickly become very fond of Athene, tears glistening in his eyes when he kissed the top of her head and said goodbye. Even the dog seemed reluctant to let her go. He kept trying to get in the boat and the old man had to call him back several times.

The trip back to Corfu was uneventful except that the sea was still a little rough after the storm, and with the spray from the bow of the little motorboat their clothes were soon wet again. But none of them seemed to mind. They were only too glad to be back on land. "Back to civilization," Richard whispered to Helga at the sight of the ferry terminal.

After a lengthy discussion and profuse apologies from the ferry officials who, probably fearing issues of liability, went out of their way to be very helpful, and they made sure that the three of them were on the very next ferry to Piraeus, the Athens seaport southwest of the city. The ferry she could not turn around they were told in at least four languages, three times of which were in English.

When at last they arrived in Piraeus they found that the ferry officials had called ahead and Athene's mother was waiting on the quay with frantic waving of arms and hugs and kisses for them all. She hugged Helga most of all. After all, the mother, who had relentlessly questioned the ferry officials, explained with Athene's translation it was Helga who had initiated the rescue. The girl had to translate again and again while they received her mother's profuse thanks for saving her daughter.

Richard heaped abundant praise on Athene, saying, "She is such a good swimmer and such a smart child she probably could have saved us." When Athene translated, the mother beamed with pride and hugged them all again. Then there was a sad parting when Richard and Helga had to say goodbye to Athene. Helga, especially, was very distressed as if she were saying goodbye to her own daughter, and she and Athene both cried as if their hearts would break.

To round off their adventure, the ferry company had found and held their luggage. They stayed one night in a beautiful Athens hotel, compliments of the ferry company with still more profuse thanks. Helga and Richard both wanted to see some of the sights in Athens and the ferry officials happily provided them with a complimentary guide. He took the two of them on a hurried tour with the obligatory visits to the Parthenon, the Agora which was the ancient marketplace, and the outdoor theater where the plays of Euripides had once been performed.

"Helga, I read somewhere that Athens has the most polluted air in the world." And after a few hours of bus and auto fumes, they both could believe it.

"Ja, it really is awful," she said, her eyes red and tearing.

So they cut short their tour, anxious to get to the idyllic Greek island they knew was waiting.

SEVENTY-SIX

The very next Sunday morning after having talked with Jennifer on the phone and getting explicit instructions, Otto Housmann took a train from Munich to Prague and easily found the pastry shop that was frequented by the young women language teachers. Using a carefully rehearsed ruse, he managed to get a good deal information about Helga and Richard from the unsuspecting women, especially from Bettina who was easily captivated by his good looks and charm. She immediately decided that he was much more handsome than Monika's cousin Harkmut.

His story was that he was a private investigator hired by Richard's American family that was frantic to find him because his mother had died. It seemed a plausible enough story with just the right element of family tragedy that touched the not usually gullible young women, all of whom were anxious to help, especially Bettina and Monika. They thought this young man's story was a welcome change from the abrasive American woman, Jennifer Smartley. Little did they know he was there on Jennifer's orders.

"Helga kept mentioning an Italian village called Vernazza," Bettina told him. "Some place on the Italian Rivera," Monika added, trying to be helpful. "She was most emphatic about it. It seemed to have been a place they both liked very much when they were on their summer trip."

"Thank you very much," Otto said, the model of good manners and propriety. "I think this will be very helpful."

"We certainly hope you find him," Bettina said. "When you find him please give him our condolences," Monika added.

Jennifer was pacing her hotel room in Paris, glad she had finally heard from Otto. He had telephoned that he was in Prague and had what he thought would be some useful information.   She had tried to get him to give her the information over the phone, but Otto was too smart for that.   "I think it would be best for me to meet with you in person.   There is quite a lot to explain," he lied.

I might as well let him come to me, she thought.   Looks like he hasn't forgotten about that little romp in the sack I promised him.

Later that same afternoon there was a knock on Jennifer's hotel room door and she hurried to answer it.   "Come in, Otto.   It's good to see you again."   Jennifer, who was in no mood for small talk, came straight to the point.   "Tell me what you found out.   And it better be something useful."

"Ja, it is," Otto answered and he proceeded to tell her everything he had learned about Richard's recent travels and especially about his fondness for the little village on the Italian Riviera.   When he had finished, Jennifer got up from the sofa and headed for the door to show him out.   But Otto was a young man with a very good memory, and a beautiful woman like Jennifer was not easy to forget.   "Ah, Jennifer," he said, intent on refreshing her memory, "I believe you mentioned how grateful you would be for my assistance.   Like that other time here in Paris."

"Yea, I forgot.   Okay," she said as she headed for the bedroom, already unbuttoning her blouse.   "But come on Otto.   I'm in kind of a hurry."

SEVENTY-SEVEN

When I stepped off the ferry I had taken from Piraeus, footsore and weary from searching, my heart aching, I had to remind myself that this wonderful little Greek island was the last stop on our incredible journey last summer. But instead of a joyous welcome, the screaming gulls and the bright sunshine seemed only to mock my sadness and loss. This was the end of the line. If she hadn't come here, what could I do? There would be nowhere else to look.

The tiny island of Schinoussa was exactly what we had hoped a romantic Greek island would be. And it was much more than we could have ever hoped for. The perfect breathtaking scenery filled the eyes and calmed the soul. There were those quaint little houses that all looked like miniature wedding cakes glistening so white in the sun that the light hurt your eyes, and then quite unexpectedly, the cool grayness of their shadows were like wished-for sighs of relief.

And most important of all, we were immediately struck by the leisurely pace of life here. The local people never seemed to be in a hurry, and yet they managed to get things done. Fish were caught, wonderful meals were cooked, rooms were cleaned and drinks were poured all without any hint of the frantic lifestyle in what now seemed such faraway places we had known, especially in America.

The pace of life on the island was such a delightful, unhurried calm that it immediately seemed to cast its spell over us, making us feel as if we were in another more remote time and place. We noticed that almost everyone seemed always to be smiling, except for one grumpy old fisherman who, nevertheless, always seemed to have the best fish and lobsters to sell. It was as if the attitude of the people toward each other was very much like that I had pointed out to Helga about the mothers and daughters in Brno; laughing, smiling, cheerfully talking to one another as if they were good friends. Which they probably were. Laughter was commonplace here, and we were surprised and very pleased at how everything about the island seemed to exceed our expectations.

The island's only village of any size was called Iraklia, and there were only a few small taverns on the entire island that had upstairs rooms to rent. The one where we stayed was just up this street a little ways from the harbor where I am standing now, only a short walk from the ferry dock. I remembered that the tavern keeper's name was Minos, a rotund, cheerful little man who was also an excellent cook. We quickly learned that like our Italian friend Giorgio in Vernazza, Minos loved to prepare all kinds of seafood dishes which, after all were the island specialty, and which I have always liked. And Helga was learning to enjoy them as well, although her growing up in the Black Forest region of Germany didn't present so many opportunities for seafood dining. But she was enjoying learning about the abundance and variety of food from the sea that was so plentiful here.

I remember that one afternoon one of Minos kitchen helpers was chatting with us in his broken English, and he told us, in hushed conspiratorial tones, that the lamb kebabs on the menu were actually goat kebabs. He explained that Minos had originally put goat kebabs on his menu but their few tourist customers didn't seem to like the idea of eating goat. But once he changed the menu to lamb kebabs sales had increased.

Minos' wife Eleni was a large, buxom woman and such a sweetheart and she took to Helga right away. It seemed that everyone who met her liked her instantly. Like Madame Bonet in Chambord, that little French village, and Giorgio in Vernazza with his restaurant with the mixed French and Italian name. And, of course, Mona Herbert and Bob Worley in New Orleans. It seemed as if there was some special magnetism about her that attracted people. Of course, it was just her wonderfully cheerful personality that immediately put people at their ease. Needless to say it had certainly attracted me.

And now all that's lost.

In a few more minutes I'll have to force myself to go to the inn and ask Minos if Helga has been here. I really don't want to ask because I'm afraid of what his answer will be. I keep trying to think of some excuse for putting it off because this is the last place I can think to look, and if he says no she has not been here then what will I do? There's nothing more I can do – nowhere else I can look. She will be totally, irretrievably lost to me.

My heart's already pounding, dreading what he might say. I'm afraid it will be the same that I keep finding everywhere I go; that she has been in all our other special places just ahead of me, but has already gone on before I get there. It's like we've been following the same route but on different schedules. I keep wondering why she's been going to all the same places we visited last summer. At first I didn't realize that was what she was doing. But by the time I got to Paris, and even more so later it became apparent she was following our summer route and, of course, that made it even more mysterious. But I hope with all my heart she came here, too. This will be my last chance because if I can't find out something more about her here, then what else can I do? Where else can I look? It's like coming at last to the end of a seemingly endless tunnel only instead of finding a light at the end there is only more darkness; cold, impenetrable darkness. After this heart-wrenching search, what if it doesn't end here? I don't know what I'll do. And in every place I've looked and she wasn't there, I could feel the dream slipping further away. And now, this is what, the end of the dream?

But what if I have somehow managed to get ahead of her? Damn, I hadn't thought of that. And if I have, then what do I do? This whole business just seems to keep getting more and more complicated. And more painful, too.

We had sold the old Ford in Brindisi last summer before we took the ferry to Greece. After our unbelievably wonderful week's stay here on the island we took the ferry back to the Greek mainland. I'm glad we had flown to America from Athens. After all the wonderful places we had seen, this last beautiful place had to be the icing on the cake. To try and continue any more of the trip would have been anticlimactic. From Athens we flew to New York and on to New Orleans where we settled in to live together. Sounds so simple, so wonderful. But what happened? I've asked myself that a hundred times – or maybe it's a thousand times. But always finding no answer.

307

When we were here before on this wonderful little island and talking about going to the states, I was so pleased at how enthusiastic she was about coming to America with me. She kept asking me questions about New Orleans and the people and the Mississippi River and everything she could think of. And her excitement was contagious. Her attitude about going there and our being together thrilled me beyond belief. I didn't realize until later how much her coming to New Orleans had pleased me.

We had been so happy there in New Orleans. And I was so much in love with her, and she with me that sometimes I had to pinch myself to make sure it was really true. I still found it hard to believe I had finally found the one true love of my life. And so late in life. In my mid-fifties, no less. And I think our being older made the love, the intimacy better, even sweeter.

Everything was going beautifully in New Orleans. At least I thought so. And then, just when I thought nothing could possibly get any better, out of nowhere everything fell apart. And I still don't know why except for that horrible scene Jennifer Smartley caused at the faculty Mardi gras party. And there was that story Mona told me about how Jennifer had gone to our house on Pine Street and caused such a terrible scene with Helga. What a cruel, heartless thing to do. What did Jennifer think she would gain from that kind of behavior? But surely there must have been more to Helga's disappearance than that? And now, according to Bob Worley, Jennifer's over here in Europe trying to do heavens knows what. It's certainly clear to me she's up to no good. Of that I'm very sure.

Well, no need to put this off any longer. Standing here staring at the tavern door isn't going to change anything. I might as well go in and talk to Minos and get a room and ask him the dreaded question.

SEVENTY-EIGHT

When we had finally arrived here last summer, late but happy, this beautiful Greek island was even more wonderful than we had imagined. The sea, the quaint little houses, the inn. Everything. Even the old dog we had to step over that always seemed to be sleeping on the front steps of the tavern. Everything here was so special.

*   *   *

"Richard, I think this place is almost better than Vernazza, if anything could possibly be better," Helga said soon after we had first arrived. "I never thought I would hear myself say that. The sea here is incredible! I have never seen water such an unbelievable shade of blue. And the tavern is perfect. It's so quaint, and our room overlooking the sea just makes it perfect with its unbelievable view of the beautiful blue sea right outside our window," she said with a sweep of her arm that seemed to take in everything beautiful about the island.

I only managed to nod in agreement. She was so excited, her little girl-like enthusiasm kept bubbling over as usual.

"Minos is wonderful," she continued. "He is such a perfect host. And his wife, Eleni. It's as if she just stepped out of a story book like she was someone's fairy godmother. She reminds me of Madame Bonet in that wonderful little French village. They are so charmingly alike. I know I'm babbling like a child with a new toy but it is all too wonderful for words. And being here with you and loving you so much just makes it utterly perfect. I like that English expression, utterly perfect. Especially when it applies to you. You really are, Richard. Utterly perfect for me!"

I could only grin foolishly and hope for more.

"There couldn't possibly be anything or anyone more perfect for me than you. And I love you so much," she said again, putting her arms around my neck and pulling me close. Whenever we hugged she always pressed her breasts firmly against my chest because she knew how much I liked it; and how much she liked it, too, she had finally confided to me one night recently as if divulging a special secret.

"This place really is something, isn't it?" I said, embarrassed at her compliments, but like always, wanting to hear more. "I don't think I have ever experienced any place or anything so incredibly wonderful!"

"The island or me?" she grinned impishly, her freckles dancing in that funny way.

"Both. But especially you."

"Ah, that's more like it," she said with a special smile. "Our dinner last night was delicious, wasn't it? Did you enjoy your squid?

"Yes, it was very good. I just wish I hadn't seen that fisherman smashing it on that big rock before it was cooked. I guess he must have been tenderizing it."

"Yes," she said a sad pout, "poor squid."

The delicious taste of the local seafood reminded me of the fried Croakers and crab cakes I had often eaten at a friend's cottage on the remote island of Ocracoke on the North Carolina Outer Banks. The Outer Banks are wonderful, but they are nothing like this. Nothing could possibly compare with these wonderful islands set in this unbelievably blue sea.

In our room the first morning we were there Helga asked, "Do you think that sometime this morning we can go down to the sea and have a swim?" She asked the question rather demurely, trying not to smile and hiding the two very small parts of a bikini behind her back. Then she dramatically brought them out into the open with a triumphant "ta-da, and wearing this," she said with them dangling from her hands. I could tell she was enjoying watching my shocked expression. "I bought it – or do I say them – at a shop near the shore in Brindisi. I could wear it when we go for a swim today. I will wear your blue shirt over it until we get to the shore."

"Yes, that's probably best. We don't want Minos to have a stroke when he sees you."

"But you would like for me to wear it, Ja?"

"Yes, I'd like that. Like that very much," I said eyeing the bikini closely, trying to imagine how much, or more accurately, how little material was in it – or in them. But for some reason I seemed to be having trouble swallowing. "You could just swim without it, you know. I wouldn't mind. We could pretend you were a mermaid."

"I know you wouldn't mind. But I know you so well I am sure there would be no swimming at all. Or if we did swim we both might forget to breathe and drown."

"You're probably right," I replied, trying to slow my breathing. "It might be better not to go skinny dipping.

"After breakfast this morning I asked Minos where there was a good place we could go for a swim. He told me about a special secluded little cove at the south end of the island not far from here. Quite a romantic spot he said. You should have seen his mischievous smile when he told me about it. When he mentioned how romantic it is."

"It sounds wonderful, and I promise not to jump in and try to rescue anyone. Unless perhaps it's a very handsome young man."

"If you do, it had better be me."

"Of course, my darling."

"Minos' wife has promised to pack a picnic lunch for us," I reminded her. "Some sandwiches and a bottle of wine."

"That sounds wonderful. I'm so excited I can hardly wait."

Minos had given Richard careful directions to the cove, and as he stood at the kitchen window watching as the two of them walk away hand in hand, he recalled one special time when he had been much younger and had just moved to the island. The memory came rushing back and with a wistful sigh he remembered how he and Eleni had gone on just such a picnic. However, they never reached the cove and there had been no swimming. Among the ancient olive trees they had found a sheltered spot out of the sun. And like Helga in the French meadow, Eleni quietly mentioned the picnic blanket and the day had dissolved in an afternoon of wondrous lovemaking.

Later, Minos was telling Eleni's father how, in the hot afternoon, they had forgotten the time because they had been so busy collecting ripe olives off the ground. 'And where are these olives now?' the father had asked sternly, trying to hide a grin.

'A thousand pardons, sir' Minos remembered stammering, 'but I managed to tip over the basket in a muddy place.' And the father, remembering when he had been a young man, had said, 'Yes, I imagine you did.'

As we strolled along the rustic path toward the cove, Helga paused under a twisted old olive tree, her expression growing quite serious. "Richard, everything this summer has been so perfect. I mean, loving you has been the most incredible thing I could ever imagine. No, no, that's not right. No one could possibly *imagine* something so lovely, so breathtakingly wonderful. One could only hope for it to come true. And I have found it with you. My innermost wish for an incredible love was so completely fulfilled when you came into my life. And it still takes my breath away to think about it."

I took her in my arms and pulled her tight against my chest, loving the feel of her warm body against mine as she clung to me, her head cupped beneath my chin, her breath warm against my throat. How could a woman be so unbelievably wonderful; could say such amazingly special things; things that always felt as if they were gifts from the gods? It was simply too good to be true. And miracle of miracle, just such a woman was in my

312

arms right now in this perfect and place loving me.

"And the places where we have been together," she whispered, her lips against my skin, "and the things we have done have been, ah, what is that American expression? 'The icing on the cake,' I think it is. Each place we go, every new thing we do seems to be better than the last."

"*Everything* gets better?" I asked with a teasing grin.

"Ja, especially that! Can you believe how wonderful it is? I don't know how it can keep getting better, but it does."

"This whole experience really has been that way hasn't it, my darling?" I whispered my lips against her hair. "Truly beyond belief. And I agree with you, everything just keeps getting better and better."

"How can that be? Each place better than the last?" she wondered aloud.

"I guess we've made it that way, you and I. And the newness of each place seems so special. Maybe it's because our loving each other has become more intense, more profound with each passing day. And we are seeing everything through the eyes of young lovers like you said that day in Paris."

"Yes, seeing everything anew through the eyes of young lovers," she agreed. "I like the way you describe it. I think that must be it."

The path to the cove was narrow and very stony and Helga held tightly to my arm, and I liked the way she was holding on to me. It gave me a warm feeling as if I were her protector as well as her lover.

We walked out of the bright sunlight into a shady avenue of cypress trees and then passed another grove of ancient olive trees, their gnarled trunks like so many hunchbacked old men who had been standing forever in the same place. Then there was a field of poppies nodding gently in the breeze looking like a red carpet. And suddenly there was the sea.

When we reached the cove the quiet solitude and soft murmuring of the sea made the moment even more enchanting than we had expected. We could feel the warm sun gently reflecting off the white sand, making dreams of pure gold and silver, and Helga continued to hold onto my arm even when there was no longer any need for it. And we stood there fascinated by the beauty of the scene. Minos had been right. It was indeed a very beautiful, very romantic place.

We ate our sparse lunch and enjoyed all the wine, sipping it slowly trying to make each drop last as long as possible, hoping that would also make the day last longer. And for once I didn't spill any wine on my shirt.

"Richard," Helga asked, leaning against my shoulder, "Do you think it would be wrong, perhaps a sin, to wish that something could go on forever? Like this moment. In this place and my being with you?"

"No, I don't think it would be wrong. I do it all the time now that I have found you. I cannot imagine that God or any person would think we were wrong for wishing such a thing if we both wanted it and we were not hurting anyone. But we know it can't be that way, so I guess we have to keep on living – and loving. I think what we should do is to keep looking forward to every new day and each new experience with happy anticipation. Always looking ahead, never back. And always acting as if we are only twenty-one like we said that day in Paris."

Later after our swim, Helga was sunning topless on the sandy beach, and she turned and smiled her special smile at me that seemed as bright as the Mediterranean sun, quite capable of melting my heart all over again as if it could stand more of her loving gaze. And lying next to her and looking at her face, I realized that even her complexion had improved over the weeks we had been together. It had taken on a warm, creamy look as if being in love had improved it, and I couldn't resist putting my arms around her, and my lips found hers and we held each other very tightly and began to kiss passionately. When I moved down to let my tongue brush a nipple I was surprised and pleased at the salty seawater taste, and she gasped, "Should we here?"

"I'd love to but we don't know if anyone is around. And these Greek fishermen might not be as broadminded as the French."

"Yes, I suppose you're right. So, I suppose we must hurry back to the inn, to our own little room. But please, hold me tightly for a moment longer Richard, my darling. I never want to be away from you. Never."

"And I will never let you go, Helga. Never! I promise! You are mine forever."

Later that evening at one of the outdoor tables in front of Minos' tavern we quietly began making plans for our trip to New Orleans and our new life together there.

"You'll love it Helga, my darling."

"Yes, I know I will. If I am there with you."

               *   *   *

No need to stand here any longer staring at the tavern door. I guess I'd better go on in and talk to Minos. Maybe he has seen her. Or at least get myself a room.

SEVENTY-NINE

"Greetings, Minos. I have returned to your wonderful establishment. Do you remember when my friend Helga and I stayed here with you last summer? Do you have a room for me?"

Minos looked mystified. "Of course. But don't you want to share the room with Madame Helga?"

"What do you mean? What are you talking about?"

"Yes, Professor Rouse, she is here."

"What! You mean here? Now? Here?"

"I was wondering why the two of you were not together."

"But I have been looking all over Europe trying to find her. She's here? Right now? Here?" Richard realized he was shouting his words over and over, unable to grasp this new reality, but he couldn't stop himself.

"Yes, she is here. She does not know you are coming? Then she will be much surprised to see you. She has just now gone down to the little cove the two of you liked so much for swimming and . . ." He smiled with a knowing shrug.

"How could this happen? I mean when did she come? Minos, this is not a prank, is it? I don't think I could stand it."

"No, professor. Is no prank. She has been here a week. But she says she will leave today. And a word of warning, though. There is a sadness in her eyes I do not like. And she seems not to be feeling very well. But perhaps it is only the sadness. Seeing you here should cheer her up, yes?"

Ignoring the rock-strewn path, Richard hurried toward the spot where they had picnicked and gone swimming so often last summer; past the cypresses, past the olive trees, ignoring the last of the poppies in bloom, he rushed headlong down the path, hurrying recklessly, oblivious to everything, his mind only on finding her, seeing her again at last.   She's here!

In his haste he stumbled and fell on the rocky path skinning his knee.   He picked himself up and hurried on, glancing briefly at his knee, ignoring the blood on his khakis, oblivious to the poppies and the beauty of the sea and the wheeling birds.   He had only one thought; to get there as quickly as possible.   She's here!   Right now!   I can't believe I've finally found her!   How can this be?

But then a dark thought intruded.   Minos said she was leaving today.   What if she leaves before I get there?   But there's only one ferry a day here, and the one I came on just a little while ago waits half an hour before it makes the return trip.   Surely I'll find her before if leaves.   But looking at his watch he realized he didn't have a lot of time to spare. And the sooner he found her and held her in his arms the better.   Only then could he relax and breathe easier, and say a little prayer of thanks.

He reached the cove they had loved so much and there she was sitting on the same big rock where they had sat together so often.   Seeing her there made a sharp ache in his heart.   Her beautiful red hair sparkled in the bright sunlight, blown softly against her cheek by a gentle ocean breeze, her long arms dark from days in the sun.   The only sound was the soft lapping of the little waves and the singing of a solitary meadowlark somewhere off in the olive grove.

She had thrown off her sweater and was leaning back against the big rock looking out to sea.   She absently reached below where she sat and lightly brushed the delicate little blue flowers that grew there with her fingers.   She smelled their fragrance on her fingertips like that time on Wenceslas Square.   Then she sighed and smiled a sad, wistful smile.

Something about her body language stopped me.   There was an overwhelming

317

sadness in her posture and her head was bowed, evoking a heart-wrenching image like that day on the Normandy beach.   And as I watched, she lifted a finger and wiped away a tear. Tears for what, I tried to imagine?   For me?   Surely not that.   After all, it was *she* who had left *me* in New Orleans.   But if not that, what then?   Isn't that what she wanted?   No, I still don't think so.   Even after all this time, after all this searching, I still don't think that was what she really wanted.   There has to have been something else.   Was there something unknown to me that drove her away?   Could that be it?   I thought for a minute, worrying with the puzzle I had already tried to solve a thousand times, fearful of finding an answer I didn't want to know.   Are those tears for herself?   For being back here and remembering?   And being alone?

Oh, my God, how I wish I knew those tears were for me.

Seeing the tears made me want to fly to her and take her in my arms and hold her close.   To comfort her.   To crush her in my arms like I had done hundreds of times before. To hold her so tightly neither of us could catch our breath.   But then maybe she wouldn't want that.   And what would I be comforting her for?   If only I knew what to say.   My arms ached to hold her, my lips longed to kiss away those tears and whisper in her ear the loving things she always liked for me to say.   I could sit there and say them over and over all day long if only I knew what . . .

Could it be she just wanted to be left alone?   Then why is she here on this island? At the cove?   At our special place?   The place we loved almost as much as Vernazza. She could have been alone in Prague or in Heidelberg.   Anywhere.   Why here?   And why has she visited all the other places where we had been?   The mystery only deepened, leaving me even more confused.

Looking around at the cove and the beach and the unbelievably beautiful sea, I could feel my heart struggling to reach out to her, wanting to enfold her in its most fervent embrace.

I have searched for three months and finally, like a miracle, here she is!   But I'm afraid to approach her. What should I say? What would she say? Did she hate me for taking her to New Orleans and for what happened there? Surely not. She seemed to have been so happy there. Would she ever explain why she had left so abruptly? Was it something so unusual, maybe even inexplicable that she couldn't tell me? Some mystery? But what? What could it have been?

Could it have been another man? Surely not that? There hadn't been enough time for that to happen in New Orleans had there? But then how long does it take to find a new ... My God, I can't finish that sentence. It really doesn't take all that long to find someone, does it? Look how long it took us in Prague. What was it two, maybe three weeks? But if it was another man he would be here with her, wouldn't he? And why bring him to this special place? The mystery continues to deepen, only adding to my fear and trembling.

Then a horrible new thought pushed its way into my mind. Would she say she no longer loves me? She couldn't have changed her mind that quickly, could she? Surely not. And what should I do now, standing here longing to hold her in my arms at this very moment, my heart pounding so I can hardly catch my breath I want to reach out to her so badly.

All these frightening thoughts flashed through my mind in a blur of seconds. What should I do?

Nature decided for him. He shifted his weight and his foot slipped on some loose rocks and he almost fell. She heard the noise and turned.

319

EIGHTY

"You are here?" she said, surprised. It was almost the same greeting she had always used when I approached her at Wenceslas Square in Prague. 'Ah, there you are,' she would say. It was the simplest of greetings given in such a matter-of-fact way, and yet it was so laden with love and excitement and expectation that it always took me by surprise no matter how often I heard it. And my breath had always caught in a confusion of emotions, all of them wonderful and laden with promise. Then she would add, 'I waited here.' And that always made the moment perfect.

And being here today and seeing her again like this made it feel as if only a day had passed since we had last been together, and I was suddenly caught up in the bittersweet memory of our meetings at that lovely old square in Prague. My eyes were stinging with tears as I vividly recalled her words of greeting and the wonderful feeling I always had whenever I heard them. And now, just when I was afraid I would never hear her voice again, here she was saying almost the same thing to me again. I still couldn't believe she was here; could hardly believe my luck at finding her at last.

"Yes, Helga, I am here. I have found you. Found you at last." My eyes were brimming with tears as I stood there looking at her, and I realized I had been holding my breath.

"You have been searching for me? But why?"

"Because I love you, why else?" I decided this was not the time for adding my usual joking, 'Because you silly woman.' "Because I thought I had lost you forever. But now that I have found you again Helga, my darling, I find myself loving you even more. Just seeing you again takes my breath away."

"And I love you, too, Richard. More than I can ever say," she whispered as she stood and moved slowly into his arms, tears streaming down her face. At first their embrace was unsure, tentative even, but then their love for each other erupted in a firestorm

320

of joy, and they clung together laughing and crying, each desperately afraid that if they dared let go the other might disappear.

After a few minutes they moved to the big rock where they sat close together holding hands and talking very little. Helga's head rested lightly on his shoulder as she stroked his arm, ruffling the thick masculine hair just as she had done so often, remembering the night of their first lovemaking in her apartment in Prague. Richard enjoyed the sensuousness of it but said nothing, afraid that one wrong word would break the wondrous spell of this special place and the memory of their time here together. And most importantly, the spell of her being here now and in his arms again. He knew he shouldn't talk, but he couldn't stop himself from putting his lips against her ear and whispering ever so softly, "I love you." Her only answer was a pleased "umm, yes," said a deep sigh.

He desperately wanted to ask why she had left New Orleans, had fled so abruptly, but he knew this was not the time or the place. Not yet. And he hesitated, unsure of himself, unsure of what to say or how to say it. He didn't want anything he said to sound like an accusation. But what could he say? And what might her answer be? Would it be something he didn't want to hear after the incredible love they had found together? But then why was she holding him so tightly?

"Richard, you searched for me?" she repeated, amazed.

"Yes, of course."

"How did you know I was here?"

"I didn't. I started in Prague and when I realized what you were doing and where you were going I retraced every stop we had made together on our incredible journey last summer, always hoping to find you."

"You went to every one of the places where we had been?" she asked, surprised and pleased. "Prague and Brno?"

"Yes."

"Paris?"

"Yes."

"Venice?   And did you go to Normandy, also?"

"Yes."

"And Nice and Vernazza?"

"Yes, yes."

"Rome?"

"Yes."

"Everywhere we had been?"

"Yes, everywhere.   I even took the same ferry from Brindisi."

"But that's what I have been doing," she said with a sad sigh.   "Going to every one of those wonderful places we had shared.   Even the sad one, the Normandy beaches."

"Yes, I know, I was there.   And everywhere I went you seemed to have been there ahead of me.   In each place I asked people we had known and they always said, 'Yes, she has been here.   But then she left.'"

"You asked them all?

"Yes.   Bettina and Monika, and your father, and Matthew, and Pavel, and Monsieur Bonet, and Giorgio.   Everyone!"

"Even my father?"

"Yes, especially your dear old father.   I went to Heidelberg looking for you, and he is very worried about you and misses you terribly. Like me, he was afraid something awful might have happened to you. He didn't say much, but I could tell by the tears in his eyes whenever he mentioned your name."

She smiled sadly when she thought of her father and more tears trickled down her cheeks.

"Tell me Helga, my love," he asked hesitantly, still afraid of what her answer might be. "Why have you traveled to all the same places? To our special places. To all the places we loved?"

"I have been retracing our wonderful trip of last summer."

"Yes, I know. But why?"

"I wanted to revisit each place where we had been together. To savor the wonderful memories of our time together in each one. To see them again and to plant them firmly in my mind so I would never forget them. To store up those incredible memories of our time together. To remember every moment of loving you in each of those enchanted places. To save them in my memory for the difficult days that lie ahead. But my journey was a lonely one without you. Every day I have wished you were with me, loving me, holding me close just as if we were at the top of the Eiffel Tower again. And in so many, many other places."

Why did she say, *for the difficult days that lie ahead*? What could she mean by that? But he was afraid to ask.

"Yes, my darling, I understand," he said. "I felt myself thinking, even feeling that exact same way wherever I went looking for you. And while I looked I was afraid I would never find you again, and my heart began to break without you. And in each place where I looked it broke a little more when you were not there."

"But why did you look for me?"

"I had to find you. Don't you know how much I love you? How could I have gone on living without you? I would have searched to the ends of the earth to find you, Helga."

"But I left New Orleans. I left you. How could you ever forgive that?"

"Sitting here beside you now and holding you close the word forgive doesn't even enter my mind. I can only think of how very, very fortunate I am to have found you again. And how unbelievably happy that makes me! And how much I love you. Now more than ever."

"Richard, you are such a wonderful man. I don't deserve anyone as wonderful as you."

"No. It is I who doesn't deserve a woman as wonderful as you. You are quite simply too incredibly wonderful for words. I love you beyond what any human being could ever expect to feel for another."

"I do love you, too, Richard, with all my heart," she whispered softly, pressing herself hard against him, her eyes brimming with more tears. He could feel her body trembling against his, and he worried.

For a long time they sat in silence, just holding each other, saying nothing and staring out to sea. One of them thinking wonderful, the other unspeakable, thoughts.

EIGHTY-ONE

Cautiously Richard decided at last to ask, "Do you think maybe we should talk about making some plans now that I've found you? When should we think about going back to New Orleans?"

"Richard, my darling, that's the one last terrible thing you must try to forgive."

"Forgive what? I don't understand."

"I could never go back to America with you. To New Orleans, knowing that woman was there. I just couldn't bear it."

"Yes, of course, darling, I can understand you feeling that way, and I don't blame you in the least. We will probably never see Jennifer Smartley again. I will see to it. I will make absolutely sure we never see her. That is my solemn promise to you. We can be happy there like before. I know we can. I promise you."

"But as terrible as what Jennifer did, that's still not the worst part." She paused, gathering the strength to say what she knew she must tell him. "Richard, my love, there's another reason why I cannot go back to America with you. Why I cannot be with you ever again."

"What! What do you mean not be together? Ever again? Did you say, *ever again*? What are you talking about? What kind of thing is that to say now that I have finally found you?"

"I cannot go back with you, Richard. But what is even worse, I can no longer live with you anywhere."

"What! What are you saying? What do you mean we can't live together? How can you say such a thing? You're not making sense, Helga. What are you talking about? Please, for God sake, don't say that. You're breaking my heart. What is this?"

"Yes, I know. And it's breaking my heart, too. Don't you think I want to go with you? To be with you wherever you go? For the rest of my life? You have become my whole life, Richard. I was never a complete woman until I met you. And I fell in love with the most wonderful man in the world. And like a miracle too good to be true, you fell in love with me, too. Me, Helga Wintermantle, the plain German girl in the drab green coat. I would go to the ends of the earth with you, too, and love you forever but . . ."

"But what? Helga, what in God's name are you talking about? Is it something I've done? Tell me! You know you can tell me anything. Haven't we always been honest with each other?"

"Yes, my darling that's very true. However, this one last, final thing is something so very terrible I could not bear for you to know. I cannot even bring myself to say what it is. I don't dare let myself even think about it. Richard, you couldn't bear it either. I know you couldn't. This is something I must bear alone. I must! If you knew and we stayed together, it would spoil all those wonderful memories we have made together. The most divinely wonderful memories any woman could ever wish for. Our lives would become a tragedy and a misery."

"What thing? For God sake, Helga, what are you talking about? You're talking in riddles. What could possibly separate us now? Don't you have any idea how much I love you? Helga, talk to me!"

"I have written to Bob Worley asking him to tell you when you get back to New Orleans."

"Tell me what?"

"The one last, terrible thing I cannot bring myself to tell you. Not here. Not now. Not in this special place," she said, waving her hand at the cove and the sea. "I could not bear to see the look that would come into your eyes. I just could not bear it."

"Is there someone else? Have you found someone new?"

326

"How could you think that? I love you. Only you, my darling Richard."

"You sure have a funny way of showing it. You left me in New Orleans. And now you're running away again. What am I supposed to think?"

"It's for the best."

"How can your leaving me be for the best? Leaving me again?"

"You will see. When Bob Worley tells you"

Just then the ferry blew a warning blast on its whistle, announcing its approaching departure and Helga picked up the sweater she had dropped on the rock. "I must go Richard. I must take the afternoon ferry. I think you Americans say 'catch the ferry' as if it were running away." She tried to smile at her little joke but failed, tears coming instead.

"Do you remember that quotation I read to you one evening in Prague last year, Richard? *Whoever you love is alive as long as you are.* The memory of that person will always be with you; is alive inside you as long as you live and hold to that memory. Their image is always in your mind and in your heart. And as long as you are alive, Richard, I will be there with you. In your mind, inside your very soul. I promise. You have become a part of me. A part of the very essence of who I am and what I am. I was never a whole woman until you came into my life. Always remember that, my love. And when you do remember, think of me as we were. Please think of me, my darling Richard. Always remember me *as we were.*"

She was wracked by sobs so violent they seemed to burst from somewhere deep within her body. She tried to wipe her eyes with the back of her hand but failed. The tears poured down her cheeks unchecked. She tried to blot them with a small lace handkerchief she pulled from somewhere inside her blouse, but still with little success.

Richard stood dumbfounded, his heart in his throat, his mind in a whirl of confused thoughts, his breath coming in short gasps as she started to move away. He grabbed for her hand to stop her but she pulled away, leaving only the tear-soaked handkerchief in his hand.

He could already feel his heart flying away on the wings of despair and he was powerless to stop it. He ran after her, nearly catching up with her on the stony path when she stopped and waved him back. "No, Richard! Please don't! Please don't come any further."

He stopped, his mind in a whirl, his hands still reaching for her.

She waved him away again. "No, Richard. Please, no! For my sake don't come any further. I must go. Please don't come! Don't make it any harder for me. Bob Worley will tell you."

With one last longing look she turned and fled for the ferry, running, stumbling from blinding tears, almost falling. She had already taken her suitcase to the ferry landing and she grabbed it and hurried aboard.

Richard followed, calling her name. "Helga, no! Wait! Don't go. Please don't leave me like this! Don't leave me here alone. Can't you tell me what's happening? Bob Worley can tell me what? Helga, stop! Please, Helga!"

He could hardly see her as she began to blur in a hazy, out of focus image barely seen through his blinding tears. With a final blast of its whistle the ferry pulled away, churning the beautiful blue water into frothy ugliness, and he had a sudden memory of the Vltava River in Prague tumbling headlong across the weir. And like that swiftly flowing river, he saw the ferry carrying away all his hopes and dreams. His future. His life.

Can a man really die of a broken heart? A heart attack, yes. But a broken heart? Already the loss was a sharp a pain that centered itself clearly and unmistakably in his heart; at the very center of his being and he was helpless to stop it.

"Helga, please come back! Please come back." I found myself whimpering like a brokenhearted child. "Helga, please come back."

The day fell silent and empty as he stood rooted to the spot, too stunned to do anything. Even the gulls seemed to sense his anguish as they flew silently away, following the departing ferry.

His heart broken, tears streaming down his face, he watched the ferry disappearing, the little lace handkerchief forgotten in his hand. Unconsciously he clung to it, squeezing it with all his strength as if trying to press something of her into himself, the veins on the back of his hand standing out rigidly. Finally, as the ferry was disappearing, he looked down and slowly unclenched his fist, seeing for the first time the little handkerchief. And seeing it there in his hand he realized she was truly gone, and that this tiny white thing in his hand was the only part of her he would ever have again; a painful symbol of the finality of this moment. But he realized immediately that the handkerchief would become a talisman he would never let out of his sight for the rest of his life. The only part of her he would ever have again. But he would not wear it on his wrist like an amulet. No, I'll always carry it in my shirt pocket where it can be close to my heart.

Helga leaned against the railing of the ferry, refusing to allow herself to look back. She had intentionally chosen the port side but didn't know why. Maybe it was a reminder of how we had stood together on the ferry when we left Brindisi. When we stood there by the railing holding each other tightly, and my loving him so intensely I thought my heart would burst.

He must be standing back there now watching as I go, she thought, her face flooded with tears. If I look back I know I will jump into the water like I did on the Brindisi ferry. But at least I will be swimming back to him. But I cannot. I must not look. I - must - not - look - back!

The doctor in New Orleans had told her that the cancer was already well advanced. She could remember his exact, horrifying words. 'It's melanoma, I'm afraid. Someday it will erupt and attack your face. I'm sorry, I don't know any easier way to explain it to you. To tell you what to expect.'

She gripped the railing, her hands white with unbearable tension, steeling herself not to look back. I must not look back!

I want him to always remember me as we were in Prague. And Brno. And in Paris. And Venice. And Vernazza. Yes, especially in Vernazza, our most special place of all. Goodbye, Richard my love. My heart will always be with you wherever you go. I will think of you every day. A hundred, no, a thousand times each day. I love you so much. You have been the one, unbelievable happiness in my life. Goodbye, my love.

EIGHTY-TWO

With tears streaming down his face Richard watched as the ferry slowly receded to a mere speck on the horizon and disappeared, carrying all his hopes and dreams with it. That forlorn ghost of emptiness and loss that had followed him everywhere now reached out and squeezed his heart once again, making him breathless with despair and rage; despair at the idea of ever finding her again, rage at what she had just done by leaving him a second time. He stood very still, rooted to the spot as if paralyzed, unable to move, not knowing what to do next or where to go.

He tried to force himself not to think about what had just happened, to not think about this very moment because he knew that was all he could stand; anything else and he would crumble into pieces. How much can a man be expected to endure before it crushes himself and his dreams into dust? Now I'm lost again.

Why did she have to leave like that? Why didn't I run grab her? Force her to stay. At least make her explain her strange behavior. Explain those mysterious words that made no sense – her storing up memories for the difficult days that lie ahead? What could she have possibly meant by that? Now that I had miraculously found her again I knew we truly had a love beyond belief, a lifetime of happiness that was just waiting for us. And now this. She's left me again. The new intensified pain centered itself in his heart like a knife twisting – slowly twisting, never stopping.

His conflicting feelings of sadness and anger slowly subsided, replaced by a gnawing awareness of his complete and utter defeat. How could she have done that to me? No, not just to me – to us? Yes, she had done it to us both. Even at the very last she still professed a deep love for me. And even while she was telling me her terrible decision, I still believed she loved me. But she left anyway, and I'm not even sure what happened just now? There were those incredible moments of reunion at the cove by the sea, and I thought our love had been reborn better than ever. There was no way I could have been more excited, any happier.

And now this. Again. That *word* again keeps mocking me. But this time it mocks me with what I feel is a painful finality.

With some kind of unknowable symbolism he refused to wipe away his tears as they dropped off his chin onto the front of his shirt. He reached down and touched one dark, wet spot with a finger wondering why it was so large and prominent. Was there some symbolism in that, too?

He looked around as if wishing to find someone who could explain to him what had just happened. Of course there was no one, and he only managed a deep painful moan knowing it was the forlorn sound of his final defeat.

He continued to stand in the same spot, still unable to move, not knowing what to do until people around the waterfront began staring at him, some whispering about the grown man standing there with tears streaming down his face, muttering what must have been someone's name. Probably a woman they guessed.

Finally, mustering all his strength from some unknown reservoir, he turned back toward the tavern. Might as well get my things and check out. There's nothing to stay around here for any longer.

Trudging slowly back toward the tavern, his head bowed in pain and misery, he remembered his marriage with Mary ending, feeling that somehow it was his fault and being responsible as if he had failed. But that feeling of failure was never like this. Nothing had ever felt like this. Had he failed again? Now I really am lost. Lost just as surely as if I'd been dropped in the middle of the Sahara with no water. And just as helpless. Oh, God, please help me! If I only knew what to do! Is there any way I can get her back? Again? Please God help me find a way. Then he smiled struck by an odd, baffling thought; why it is that men instinctively turn to prayer when something unspeakable happens? Even the unbelieving?

Walking slowly, his head still bowed in agonizing thought, he suddenly realized he was on the path back to the cove, not the tavern. When he reached the edge of the sea he glanced around, confused by where he was as if this were some alien place, for now it had suddenly become a cold, lonely place without love. He sat on the same big rock where he and Helga had been sitting only minutes earlier hoping desperately for a way to recapture what had been, already dreading what surely would never be again. And he found himself staring out to sea just as she had done when she had sat there alone. And he, too, had to wipe away tears.

He reached down and gently caressed with a finger one of the same little blue flowers just as she had done. And he picked one and smelled it hoping that maybe her scent might have mingled with its fragrance. And very slowly as if performing some sort of ritual, he touched his lips to the flower petals, and then without even thinking what he was doing he gently brushed his cheeks with the innocent little flower as if it could stop his tears. But still they came.

What could she have been thinking when she sat here? What could have caused her tears? Even before she knew I was standing nearby I saw her wipe away tears. Were those tears for me? Or for herself? Or for whatever that thing was she couldn't bring herself to tell me? Or could there still be some other thing she wasn't telling me? Maybe that was it. But what? How could I ever know? What could she have been thinking that made her leave like that? If I only knew why she thought she had to leave? Why couldn't she tell me? How could she do that to me? No, she did it to us, he thought again.

Should I catch the next ferry and hurry after her? Find her again? And then do what? Force her to come with me? Of course that would never work. How could I force her to do anything, the woman I love? So what do I do? I need to think of something now or she'll soon be so far away I'll never find her again. But what could I do that would make any difference?

He hesitated, saying aloud to the darkening sea with fresh tears, "Why did she have to leave me? Again?" But, of course, that was exactly what she had just done – left him a second time. And that made the pain so much worse. Of course there was no answer, only the quiet murmuring of the sea which, as always, kept its own counsel.

That business with Jennifer Smartley obviously hurt her very deeply; apparently much more than I realized. But I still can't help thinking there's something else she wasn't telling me. And what was that about a letter to Bob? What in the world could that be about? And why did she say she was storing up memories for the difficult days that lay ahead? That's the way she put it. But what did that mean?

EIGHTY-THREE

"Minos, I have to go back to America. I can catch a plane from Athens, right?"

"Yes, of course, professor. But where is Madame Helga? Does she not go with you?"

"She had to leave, ah, right away on the ferry. Something about her father being ill back in Germany," I said, realizing I was telling a lie just as Helga had done when she had left New Orleans, telling me her mother was ill.

"But you said you would fly back to America?"

"Ah, yes, I did didn't, I?" I stumbled, recalling the old adage that one lie always leads to another and then another, *ad infinitum*. "I meant she will join me there later."

"Ah, I see," Minos said without conviction.

"When is the next ferry, Minos?"

"Not until tomorrow afternoon. You remember there is only one ferry here each day?"

"Then I guess I'll have to stay one more night."

Later, I was sitting at one of the outdoor tables just at twilight staring at my plate, the food cold, the wine bottle empty and forgotten. Lost in sad, bitter thought I was trying unsuccessfully not to think about her. Why, Helga, why? Why did you have to break my heart again? Again? Yes, of course, it was again. First leaving New Orleans and now this second time. Saying we could never be together again. Never? I don't think I can bear the thought of that. Never again? What have I done to deserve this? I thought our love for each other was stronger than that. Stronger than . . . Stronger than what?

Unbreakable? But no, apparently not.

I know we could have gotten through this some way, surely we could have. But it was obvious she had made up her mind. She had been adamant about it when I tried to follow her to the ferry.

I've been sitting here all afternoon trying to think of some explanation for her behavior, but I keep coming up with nothing. Maybe it was me after all. Maybe she had found something about me she couldn't live with. But what could that be? And why couldn't she tell me?

Or could it be another man? Oh, God, here I go thinking that again. I hope that wasn't it. And she had said most emphatically it wasn't that. But if not that, what then? I paused, groping helplessly for some kind of answer, but my mind was blank. And after all, there's no way I could know what was in her mind.

That now all too familiar devil of uncertainty kept pushing relentlessly through his shattered grief, torturing him with more questions he couldn't answer.

The old fisherman who delivered the fish and lobsters to the tavern every day passed my table and said a cheery hello. At least it was as cheerful as the grumpy old fellow could manage. I guess he's wondering where she is, too?

She said she still loved me. Even there at the very end, she said it most emphatically. And she clung to me and cried as if her heart were breaking. I had always believed her when she said she loved me. Always! Never for one moment have I ever doubted her love for me. That is until now. God, please help me! Help me to understand! Help me to get through this! But after a pause that quiet inner voice whispered in his ear, 'You know there's no way you are ever going to get over this.'

"No, never," I said aloud, ignoring the old lady tourist at the next table who glanced my way.

The next morning when he came down late for breakfast after a sleepless night he thought he might like to eat outside to be alone, but he saw it was raining.

"I am afraid there will be no ferry today professor," Minos said sadly as if sensing his mood. "This rain is part of a big storm that is coming our way. On our radio to the ferry terminal they said probably there will be no ferry for several days"

Well, damn, Richard muttered to himself. I'll have to sit around here all day and think about her. Probably analyze the thing to death like I'm already doing. Come up with a hundred ideas, scenarios and explanations, all of them wrong. Oh, well, I'd be doing the same thing if I were on the ferry or at the Athens airport. Or even in New Orleans. Especially if I was in New Orleans. I don't think I can ever live there again. Certainly not in the house on Pine Street. It had become our home so quickly. Our home together. Just the two of us and our new love. And now this! Ignoring that old lady who was watching him again, he held his face in his hands as more tears dripped on the table. I might as well be miserable here as anywhere else. At least the scenery is better. And the wine.

And so it happened that he spent even more time on the island, vowing each day to leave and always changing his mind at the last minute and never quite understanding why, even after the storm had passed. Did he think that putting off leaving here was a subconscious grasping at straws? Thinking, hoping and wishing that she might come back? Waiting for her? But no, surely not that. That's just too much to hope for, isn't it?

He dreaded being alone in his room at night. Even when he stayed up late and drank too much wine he would try manfully not to cry, but each morning his pillow was wet. He felt as if his heart had been cut in half like a melon. One half mourning his

337

inconsolable loss, fighting tears all day; the other half recalling every wonderful thing about her and all the incredible things they had done together, and then crying again.

After a few more days he made up his mind. I'd better catch the afternoon ferry and head on back home. The word home that had once evoked such warm comforting feelings, a haven against the storms of life made infinitely more wonderful when her presence had filled it, now sounded empty and meaningless. They say home is where the heart is. But my heart only wants to be with her. And I don't even know where she is.

EIGHTY-FOUR

Richard approached the American Airlines ticket counter in Athens International Airport, his mind still seething with doubts and unanswered questions about all that had happened. But he'd resigned himself to do what he knew he had to do. There was no alternative. He had lost again. He knew he might as well go home. What other choice did he have? What else could a man do who had lost the best thing in is life? Twice.

"I think I'd like to book a flight to New York. And I guess on to New Orleans," he said hesitantly as if still unsure of what he should do.

"Yes, sir," the pretty young woman in the blue uniform said smoothly in her perfect English, giving him her most engaging smile. "Just the one seat, sir?" she asked, looking behind him as if a handsome man like this should not be traveling alone. There should be a beautiful woman with him. Of that she was sure. "First class or coach?"

Her innocent question about just one seat struck him a cruel blow. The words stung him with a sharp pain and his heart lurched. It was not the happy little Prague skipping he remembered so well, and he had to turn away so she wouldn't see his tears.

"I've changed my mind," he mumbled without turning his head. "Maybe I'll come back later."

Late in the afternoon, sitting at an outdoor café sipping a glass of the famous Greek Ouzo and watching a hazy sunset, he decided to change his plans. I still have a few weeks left before fall semester is over and I have to get back to the Tulane. There's certainly no need to go back just yet and face the stares and questions, even those from well-meaning friend. Sometimes their concerns and condolences are the worst. Their good intentions would just dredge up every detail of the hurt.

And what would I do when I saw Jennifer? I'd love to create a huge scene. Scream and shout at her and call her every vile name I could think of. But that would only

339

show her she'd won. Better just to ignore her. Don't let her know how much she has contributed to my unhappiness. And for all I know she might still be over here in Europe.

I might as well stay over here until Christmas break and have a look around. He remembered the cheerful and pleasantly comforting atmosphere of the Heidelberg Christmas Fair from when he was there before. May be I'll take that in again.

I think I'll just wander around for a while longer before I have to head back home. Maybe take a train to . . . Humm, I guess maybe Nice. Then I could take that super-fast TRV directly to Paris. See Paris one last time. I've always loved Paris. But then again, I'm not sure I can take being there without her. Please God, don't let me keep dwelling on losing her. But the tears started anyway and he couldn't help himself so he simply gave in and let them come, taking a sip of the Ouzo and hiding his face behind the *International Herald Tribune.*

He crossed over from Greece back to Brindisi on the same ferry, remembering their incredible adventure with that charming little girl and later, the old fisherman. Then on to Rome the next day where he spent one fitful night at the same bed and breakfast place, trying unsuccessfully to sleep in the same bed they had shared there.

Why am I doing this, he thought, as he tossed and turned all night? Choosing the same ferry, and now this same room in Rome, even the same bed where we had slept together before? Must be some kind of neurotic self-flagellation. Punishing myself by dredging up old memories of what can never be again. Wallowing in self-pity. Loving it. Then hating it.

EIGHTY-FIVE

Helga looked around in the Prague railway station trying to think what to do, but everything seemed to be out of focus, blurred by her confused state of mind and her bitter tears. She tried to think of where she could go, what she should do, but her mind was in such turmoil she couldn't think clearly. There must be something I can do, somewhere I can go. I would love to go back to Heidelberg and see my old father. But my sorrow would only make him sad, and he already grieves so much for mother.

Thinking about the shock of the past few days and leaving Richard again, she kept asking herself over and over, what have I done? Every moment of the day he was in her thoughts reminding her of his incredible love for her she had so recklessly thrown away. Again. I miss him so much, she thought, new tears blurring her eyes. Why does life insist on playing such cruel tricks on us? But she knew there was no answer to that kind of question. Only more heartbreak.

Monika Schmitt wasn't sure she had heard a knock on her door it had been so quiet, timid-like. But she finally opened it thinking probably there was no one there, just her imagination. "Helga. What are you doing here? Didn't Richard find you?"

"I had no other place to go and I thought . . ." she couldn't finish the sentence as she burst into tears.

"Helga dear," Monika said as she gathered her friend into her arms and pulled her inside, closing the door and holding her close. "What is it? What's happened?" Helga burst into fresh sobbing as the question opened a new floodgate of tears, and Monika quickly realized it might be best to say nothing more just yet. She held her sobbing friend tightly as she gently rubbed her back hoping to give her some comfort, but for what she, Monika, wasn't sure. She could feel Helga's trembling body as it was racked with spasms of unbearable grief and pain.

341

"Monika, it's so terrible. He found me on our favorite Greek island, but then I left him again, and now my heart is breaking once more." She continued snuffling, her upper body convulsed in little jerks, the desolate expression of pain and sadness shining through her tears making her face look years older.

"There, there dear sweet Helga. Try not to talk. I think what you need is to lie down for a while. We can talk later when you are feeling a little better. Just lie down here on the couch and try to rest."

Later, while she sipped the glass of wine Monika had brought her, the sweet taste on her lips reminded her of his kiss and she broke down again, sobbing quietly. After only half a glass of wine Helga lay back on the couch and quickly fell into an exhausted sleep. Later that evening Monika made her take a long, hot soaking bath and then put her to bed in their old room. "We will talk tomorrow, Helga dear. You need to rest. You are not to worry. I will be in the next room. If you need anything just call me."

Alone in her old familiar bed, Helga fell into a fitful sleep as tiny little dreams flitted behind her eyes, relentlessly pushing her memory back toward him. But then the dreams abruptly ended and the sadness came rushing back stark and cruel.

The next morning after breakfast they were seated on the couch with a second cup of coffee when Monika gently encouraged Helga to tell her what had happened.

At first her eyes filled with tears, her look faraway and forlorn. But then she hesitantly began to tell her story. She told about their wonderful auto trip last summer, each memory bringing fresh tears. Monika, sensing how difficult those memories were for her, asked about their going to America. Helga began talking about New Orleans and a slight hint of excitement crept into her voice, but even then the tears were never far away. When she told about Jennifer Smartley's behavior at the Mardi gras party Monika's eyes grew flinty with anger. "What kind of evil person would say such things? But," she said after a pause, "that woman was here in Prague so we know about her." Helga shuddered at the thought that Jennifer Smartley might be nearby, but she said nothing.

342

She became quiet for a long time while she wrestled with the horrible, unspeakable part of her story. Finally gathering her courage while she tried to dry her eyes, she began to tell Monika about her visit to the New Orleans doctor. Her voice was quietly subdued but determined as she told about his diagnosis and about how she had left New Orleans without telling Richard why. And how he had come back to Europe looking for her and their reunion on that special little Greek island.

"When he found me on what had been our island paradise, I told him everything except about the doctor. But my courage failed me and I couldn't tell him about the horror that was to come. I didn't want him to have to suffer through all that with me, and so I left him, thinking it was for the best. Best to spare him. Best for me to face it alone. But every night I have cried myself to sleep. And now I am not so sure."

Monika sat very close to Helga while she talked, gently rubbing her friend's hand as she listened quietly, her heart reaching out to her, feeling her pain and hating Jennifer Smartley.

"Monika, what must I do?" Helga implored, trying unsuccessfully to stifle more tears. "I love him so much I don't think I can live without him. What must I do?"

"I am not sure, Helga dear. Why not sleep on it another night? You must still be exhausted from traveling and your ordeal. Yes, I'm sure the rest would do you a world of good. And I think I have an idea," Monika added, trying hard to sound upbeat. "Tomorrow is Sunday and we could meet with the others at the pastry shop. I think they would like to know what has happened. They all have been very worried about you. Maybe some of them can offer some advice."

The usual group of young women teachers gathered around their favorite table, ignoring their pastries their untouched coffee cooling as they listened quietly while Helga told her story. There was no idle chatter and no racy stories this morning. Bettina, especially, was quietly sobbing as Helga's story unfolded. When she had finished, the other women looked at one another and at Monika and Bettina. "That damnable woman came here," Bettina said. "Trying to find out where Richard might be. But we told her nothing. If we had only known the entire story I, for one, would have scratched her eyes out." The others nodded in grim-faced agreement.

"But what must I do *now*?" Helga pleaded, fighting back more tears. "I love him so much. What should I do? Help me, please. Monika, Bettina, everyone, please help me decide what to do."

The group talked on for more than an hour, each of them taking turns trying to think of a workable suggestion, each wishing she could soothe Helga's broken heart. And each of them thinking what they would do if they had found a wonderful man like Richard Rouse. Finally Bettina summed up all their arguments. "Go back to him, Helga. Tell him everything. Tell him how it is likely to be. I think he will understand. I am sure he will stay with you as long as you both live. I have never seen a man who loves a woman as Richard loves you. Go back to him, Helga. Before it's too late."

EIGHTY-SIX

The next morning after a sleepless night in Rome, Richard was on the fast non-stop train that followed the northern route through Italy close to the Mediterranean coast, headed toward Genoa and Nice and probably Paris. He had been trying unsuccessfully to read a paperback novel he had bought at the railway station in Rome, but his eyes kept blurring with tears so often he couldn't make out the words on the page. So far about all he had done was to stare at the cover. And even though the book was in English, his mind was a world away from reading. When the train whizzed by a small village station he glanced up from the unopened book. He barely had time to read the sign above the station window, Corniglia.

Hey, this is that little town where Helga helped press the grapes and her feet were stained for days after. I smiled at the memory then had to fight back more tears. But a moment later I remembered that the village of Vernazza we loved so much was just up the tracks a little ways. We had come from there that day to explore the village of Corniglia where we discovered, quite by chance, that the people were having their annual wine festival. I wonder if I should stop there? In Vernazza? Well, how about that? I haven't even thought about Vernazza. Not lately.

He thought for a few moments more and suddenly decided, why not? It really was our favorite place. It might be heartbreaking with all the memories flitting about and reminding me of being there with her, but my heart would be breaking anyway no matter where I go. But I do remember how the little coastal village had always been so quiet and peaceful. I think the slow pace of life there might just suit my present emotional state. And that's certainly what I need right now – some kind of healing. It's late fall now and the tourists will be gone. It might even be nice, and I wouldn't mind seeing Giorgio again.

The train sped past the Vernazza station before he could make up his mind, and he remembered he had to go almost all the way to Nice before the train stopped again. He finally managed to get off at Genoa and made sure he got a local train back to Vernazza.

He finally arrived back at the village in late afternoon.   When he got off the train he stood on the familiar station platform soaking in the atmosphere and breathing the fresh sea air, and remembering better times.   He looked longingly at the little village as he watched the few late-season tourists who were cautiously walking down the steep street toward the harbor.   But most of the local people were headed up the street to their hill-side homes.   Some of the women were laden with packages and plastic carrier bags that indicated a day of shopping in Genoa, and some even in Nice.

As the crowd began to disperse he remembered when they had first arrived here there had been an American woman on the station platform who had been screaming hysterically that someone had stolen her purse.   Stupid tourists, why didn't they keep their valuables in a money belt?

The same young man from last year was working the new arrivals, hustling for rooms. "Find you a room, sir?   Nice clean room with an ocean view," he said in perfect Brooklyn English that carried only a hint of an Italian accent.

"No, thanks, I know where to find a room," I answered him without even thinking. "I'll go to Giorgio's.   But thanks anyway, you helped us last year."   The young man looked around, puzzled at Richard's implying there was another person.   A wife or a girlfriend, perhaps?   But where was she?

I walked slowly down the steep, gently curving street toward the harbor.   It was the only true street in Vernazza but even then no cars were allowed except a select few on market day.   As I walked I found myself looking in familiar shop windows as I passed, recalling all sorts of things.   That restaurant over there on the left, that's where we had dinner our first night here.   I remember Helga had grilled swordfish but I can't remember what I had.   I guess I was just too much in love to notice.   And there's that shop where she bought that beautiful picture of Vernazza that had been taken from high up on the cliff-side trail; the picture that's still hanging in our Pine Street house in New Orleans.   Our house, he thought with a catch in his heart.

When I reached the harbor I stopped and looked at the brightly painted fishing boats that were anchored just where they had been that day during the storm when I had helped pull some of them ashore. Nothing much seems to have changed. Not the village, not the boats, not the quay, they're all the same. Only I've changed. Only my life has changed. Please, please if only something would happen. But what could possibly happen now? And here of all places? It's all too late now. The only things left here are wonderful memories now made unbelievably sad by her leaving. Helga, how I do miss you and love you still.

One or two tourists and a few local families sat or stood on the breakwater rocks. Some were fishing but most were just enjoying the sea view. And with no wind there were hardly any breaking waves.

I stood there for a long time looking out to sea and I remembered Helga sitting on the nearby rocks watching the colorful boats and me fishing without success, and Giorgio standing in front of his restaurant nearby trying hard not to laugh at my awkward efforts. Later Giorgio had taken pity on me and brought over a chilled pitcher of the local white wine and three glasses, and we sat on the breakwater drinking wine and enjoying the beginning of a new friendship. One American, one German, one Italian.

When I slowly walked toward Giorgio's restaurant he was standing in the doorway as if he sensed I had come, and he welcomed me with open arms. "Ah, professor. It is so nice to see you again. But where is Signorina Helga? You have not found her?"

"I found her but then she had to go back to Germany, Giorgio. Her father was ill." There's another lie. That same lie again. I wonder if it counts as another lie if you tell the same lie to a different person. Probably does.

"I hope she returns soon. You were so perfect together. I like very much for the two of you to stay at my establishment. And Signorina Helga is so charming."

"Oh, yes, don't I know it," I whispered to myself like a small prayer.

His comment about Helga brought a searing ache of grief, but it was a pain I knew I had to endure like all the others, and all those I knew were yet to come. And I looked out to sea so he wouldn't see the tears in my eyes.

I engaged one of Giorgio's upstairs rooms for several nights. And in spite of the memories and ghosts, I took number eleven on the top floor; the same one with the sea view Helga and I had shared. I thought about asking for a different room but any room would be sad and forlorn. And being in our old room would be just as bad with only sad, lonely ghosts flitting about. But at least they would be familiar ghosts. Might as well stay here a few days and . . . And do what? Recall every moment of what has been? Dreaming of what could have been? Dreaming of what can never be again? Torturing myself with loneliness and remembering? Probably.

The next day I was sitting on the seawall dreaming of what surely could never be again. And hoping to distract my mind from the pain and agony of what now seemed my irretrievable loss I tried to remember our physical relationship. I tried to call up macho, testosterone-driven images of her face, her beautiful red hair, her delectable body. But those kinds of memories were immediately driven away by the sweet, blinding love I still felt for her. The love I knew I would always feel. And the silent, aching loneliness that was always lurking just below the surface ready to consume me came rushing back.

After three days in Vernazza and trying to deal with unforgiving ghosts, I had about decided to take a train to Nice and maybe on to Paris. But an odd feeling kept nagging at me and I thought again how much I liked this little village; how much *we* had liked it. Loved it, really. Why not just stay here a couple more days? What's the hurry? Maybe I should just avoid Paris all together. There'd be too many special memories there that would just break my heart again. Those special romantic memories it seems one can only find in Paris. Oh, yea, that kind.

A couple of days later I had definitely decided to give up the idea of going to Paris and had reluctantly begun thinking about booking a flight to New York. But for some reason I didn't feel right about leaving this remarkable little village we had enjoyed together more than any other place. It had been so special for us. And to leave here would be like closing a book. The final chapter finished. Irretrievably gone. Almost like being at a movie when *THE END* appears in bold unmistakable letters.

Why not just enjoy Vernazza a day or two more? Don't try to resist remembering her, just immerse yourself in this wonderful little place. Bury yourself in it. Bury? Damn, what a metaphor.

Maybe just a night or two more. What can it hurt? But how can I possibly enjoy it? This whole thing about losing Helga again has made me begin to doubt myself, to doubt all sorts of things. My life – my ideals – my purpose. My lost youth? No, it's not lost youth. You know what it really is, don't you? It's lost love. Yes, my love for her that is now irretrievably lost. I looked out the window of our room at the sea and my eyes clouded with tears again. Why did I keep thinking of it as *our* room?

After a few more days in Vernazza I had finally made up my mind. I had definitely given up the idea of going to Paris and had decided to take a train back to Rome and catch a Friday morning flight to New York and on to New Orleans. Giorgio kindly offered me the use of his restaurant phone to help me with the reservations.

Late Wednesday afternoon as had become my daily custom during my week in the village, I climbed the steep steps all the way to the old watchtower. I sat on the nearby stone wall looking out to sea and dreaming, wishing, trying not to hope, and trying hard not to cry. The sun was going down, the dozen shades of red and violet and gold were breathtaking as always. Every time I see a beautiful sight like this I wish I could share it with her, and today I whispered aloud just as if she were here, "Look at that sunset, Helga. Isn't it fantastic?" But she wasn't here and the tears came instead.

After a few more minutes of my reverie I dried my eyes and tried make myself

349

think of something else. It was then that I remembered something that had happened a few days earlier that made me chuckle again.

EIGHTY-SEVEN

Late one afternoon a couple of days after I had arrived in Vernazza I had gone to Giorgio's restaurant for a glass of wine. I was about to sit at my usual outdoor table when Giorgio rushed out and whispered loudly, "No, professor, not there. No, no! Come inside, please! Quick, quick!"

"What? What is it, Giorgio?"

Once inside Giorgio whispered, "She is here!"

"Who, Helga?"

"No, no. That woman you do not wish to see. The American woman. The, ah, how do you say, the Smartley Jen'fer, I think it is. The one you told me about last summer."

"She's here? Here, now? I knew she was in Europe but how did she know to come here?"

"I do not know professor. But she is here. She is ... what is that English word that means very demanding to know about you."

"Insistent?"

"Yes, she is very insistent. Very demanding."

"She's here? Are you sure?"

"Si." I speak with her this morning. She is very beautiful and very mysterious, and she uses her eyes very well. She is very . . ." Giorgio gave an exaggerated shrug and kissed his fingertips in a salute that could mean only one thing to an Italian man.

I felt a cold chill creep up my back knowing that damnable woman was here in this place, our special place. And, of course, it was obvious that she would be up to no good.

351

I was immediately consumed by a wave of hot anger when I remembered how much hurt she had caused Helga.

"I think no one could mistake her," Giorgio continued, unaware of what Richard was thinking. "No man could, I am sure. She comes to my restaurant this morning. She seems to know you are here in village. How could that be? And she seems to know much about you and Signorina Helga."

"What did she say?"

"She asks about you. Are you here? Have I seen you? Are you here with Signorina Helga?"

"What did you say, Giorgio? You didn't tell her I was here, did you?"

"No, no, professor. Giorgio is very smart," he winked, tapping the side of his nose with a finger. "I remember you do not want to see her. But I do not understand why. She is very beautiful."

"Yes, she is. And a deadly snake can be very beautiful, also."

"Si. And you have Signorina Helga, yes?"

If only I did, I thought with a heavy sigh. "And I wouldn't trade her for ten like Jennifer." Lost in thought for a moment, I was comparing Jennifer with Helga. But, of course, there was no contest. And now here's another problem to deal with – a new mystery. "So, what did you tell her?"

"I am very, what is that English word that means I avoid to say much?"

"Evasive?"

Si, I am very evasive. But she says she will be come again this evening. She is very beautiful," he kept repeating. "But there is something about the eyes I do not trust."

"Yes, I know exactly what you mean. What do you think I should do, Giorgio?"

"Come in the back where there is small store room where we can talk."

The storeroom was dark and musty with discarded food boxes and plastic trash bins full of empty wine bottles, and cobwebs were everywhere. Giorgio was quietly thoughtful for a long time. "Ah," he said suddenly. "Leave it to me. You must go away very soon. Right now. Just for a little while. Take the evening train to Genoa. Yes, that is a good idea. You must stay in Genoa until I call you. Give me the number for that funny little telephone you carry in your pocket and I will call when, what is that American expression? When the coast is clear? Here, you must take my old raincoat and hat. She must not see you. I will show you a way to the station by what you call the back alley. But you must hurry. I think she comes back soon. Come!" Giorgio was grinning as he led the way through the back door and into an alley, thinking that in the raincoat and slouch hat Richard looked like a secret agent he had once seen in a James Bond film, and his jolly little belly was bouncing as he tried to hurry.

Giorgio was frantically busy all the next day. Twice he ran to the shop of his friend Carolos who sold tourist items like mugs and posters and ceramic ashtrays. Later that afternoon he saw Jennifer headed toward the restaurant and he ducked into the kitchen and told the staff that if she came they were to say he was out of town. He knew Carlos was not finished.

The next morning Jennifer appeared again very early at the restaurant dressed in a tight black skirt and a revealing blouse which she hoped might help loosen Giorgio's tongue. But it was clear she was very upset with the delay. "Gregory, or whatever your name is, have you been avoiding me?"

"No, Signorina. I want to wait to tell you this very special news when the time is right, like beautiful morning," he said sweeping his hand at the clear blue sky. "And you must see newspaper."

"What?   Is something wrong?"

"Nothing wrong, Signorina.   Very happy news.   But I fear you might not want to hear this news if it is professor Rouse you look for.   A beautiful young woman like yourself."

"Tell me.   What is it?   Quit beating around the bush.   Has something happened to Richard, ah, professor Rouse?"

"See for yourself," Giorgio said as he handed her the local newspaper he had already opened to page four.

"He didn't?" she said as she looked at the small item in the paper, but after a minute she gave up trying to read it, and only stared intently at the accompanying photograph. "Read it for me, Gregory."

Giorgio read the short article, translating it into his best English, and trying his best to hide his mischievous smile.

"Damn her to hell!   And him, too."   Jennifer stalked off without another word.

"Is okay for you to come back to Vernazza now, Professor Rouse," Giorgio said on the phone, barely able to hide his glee.   "She goes back to America.   The Smartley Jen'fer is not very happy, but she is gone."

Richard arrived on the late afternoon train and hurried to the restaurant.   "What happened, Giorgio?   How did you get rid of her?"

"See for yourself," he said with a broad grin as he handed Richard the same copy of the local newspaper Jennifer had seen.   There on what must have been the society page among several engagement announcements there was a picture of Richard and Helga.   But not just any picture. It was a wedding picture with Helga wearing a lovely white gown with a long train and Richard in a smartly tailored tux.

Richard was flabbergasted. "But how, I mean where, who?"

"Ah, yes, you like? At first I think I might have newspaper say you had been killed in terrible auto accident. But then I fear there might be questions about police reports and where is body and when was funeral. So I think wedding would be much better. And simpler, too. Take care of everything."

"But how? I mean, how did you get a picture like this?"

"My friend Carlos he has the shop where he sells posters and many tourist things. He can copy our local newspaper and with his computer he can change the picture of anyone in it. He once had me in newspaper as a very bad bank robber. He changes the picture of the people he wants to make look different."

"That's wonderful, but how did he get our pictures?"

"You know when you check in hotel we must keep your passports for security. So, I give Carlos your passport and Signorina Helga's picture was in your room, and with his computer he makes copies of pictures and then he changes wedding couple so it is you and Signorina Helga. And he prints them in newspaper tourists like to take home for joke. With my help I tell Carlos what to write. But Signorina Jen'fer no read Italian and does not know is joke so I must read it for her. It says that wedding was last week and the couple they are having long honeymoon trip to Lake Como, and they will come back to live here in Vernazza. I think Signorina Jen'fer she is not very happy. She says words I never hear even when American sailors come here."

"Damn, Giorgio, you are a wonder! I don't know how to thank you."

Later, in his room, still holding the altered newspaper, Richard thought of Giorgio's trick and smiled. But this doesn't solve anything. It gets Jennifer off my back, but it doesn't help me know what to do now. I guess I'll call the Rome airport tomorrow.

EIGHTY-EIGHT

Richard was still sitting on the low stone wall next to the ancient watchtower, trying not to think about going to Rome and the flight home. He was looking out to sea and watching the sunset and thinking about what had so completely shattered his life, destroying his dream and everything he had ever hoped for. His entire future, really. And sadly he knew he no longer had any reason for hope. Not anymore. What was there to hope for now? He was going home admitting defeat, wasn't he? Complete, irreversible defeat. He had lost her again. That word 'again' twisted in his heart like a knife.

The pastel shades of approaching evening gathered in changing colors far out beyond the edge of the sea. The sunset was beginning to fade, its glorious shades of rose and gold and violet had been a dazzling display of nature at her very best as the sun slowly sank into the sea, vanishing like all his hopes. In spite of the incredible beauty all around him, his spirits were at their lowest. He had reached the end of his quest without success. Now he was all alone with no hope. How could he ever find her again? Again? Yes, of course, if he did find her one last time it would be again. By some miracle he had found her a second time on their little Greek island, only to lose her. Again.

How could I ever find her a third time? I'm not sure I would have the heart to try. When she disappeared from New Orleans I had no idea why she had left or where she had gone, so a search was the logical thing to do. Finally, after looking everywhere, I had miraculously found her just a few days ago on our little Greek island. But then she left me again. She said very clearly that we could never be together again. Those words *never again* seemed to hang over my head and tear at my heart, large and indisputable. I have to admit that I've been fooling himself all along, pretending there was still a chance of finding her again.

I know that once I leave Europe Saturday it will all be over. There can be no more searching, no more looking in quaint little villages or big cities. There's nowhere else to

357

look.

Defeat has always been hard for me to accept under any circumstances. But now I have to admit defeat in what has surely been the most important experience of my entire life. There's no way I can ever find her again. So what do I do now? Go home, what else?

He hung his head in despair, trying to force himself not to think about losing her. He didn't even bother trying to stop more tears he felt coming. I guess heading back home is the only thing left to do. There's nothing else I can think of. He stirred in the gathering dusk willing himself to get up and leave.

It was very quiet there high above the village with only the murmuring of the waves on the rocks far below. Even the gulls were quiet. For a moment he thought he'd heard someone calling but he wasn't sure. Probably nothing. Just some mother calling a child home, I guess.

Then it came again. A voice timidly calling, "Richard?"

What was that? Is that . . . ? No, that can't be. Must have been a dream. But it sure sounded like . . . No, probably just a dream. I think I was dozing just now, lost in that same sad daydream. Maybe Giorgio has sent one of his waitresses with a message. But why would she use his first name?

"Richard?" the voice called again in the gathering dusk.

That voice! It's her. It has to be her! I'd know that voice anywhere. But here?

"Richard, is that you?"

It was her! There was no mistaking her voice and that German accent. But how could this be?

He wanted to jump to his feet and rush to find her but he stopped himself, afraid even to look around. Maybe it really was a dream. Probably still is. He didn't dare look. God, please don't play a cruel joke like this on me.

"Richard?"

The forlorn timidity in her voice reached out and squeezed his heart taking his breath away. But this time it was breathlessness with hope. There was surely no mistaking that voice and his heart began its odd little 'Prague skipping' as he had always called it. And he thought he would never be able to call it that again.

He turned, dreading to see what he still wasn't sure he believed, that it was some kind of mistake, but hoping with all his heart the sound of that voice was true. And it was. There she stood at the top of the steps hesitant and apparently afraid to approach any closer, her trembling hand clutching the iron railing. She looked just as he always remembered her. Tall, willowy, beautiful in her understated simplicity, her red hair faintly stirring in the evening breeze.

When he had finally turned toward her and she could see his face in the waning light and she was sure she had found him, she said very quietly, "There you are" just as she had always said in Prague when he had come to her at Wenceslas Square so many times.

And without even thinking, he said exactly what he had said to her that time in Prague. "Yes, here I am. Here for you, Helga."

But still she made no move to rush into his arms and he, hesitating with the unreality of the moment, sat rooted to the spot thinking like he had once before afraid that if he moved she might disappear.

"How did you know where I was?"

"Giorgio told me he thought this is where you might be."

Richard finally stood, but his legs didn't seem to want to work and he couldn't make them move. He had a crazy idea. It was a game he used to play as a child, trying to guess how many steps it would be to where she was standing. The unreality of the moment had not yet passed. It felt like one of those artsy films where the action takes place in slow motion. Finally, he asked what he later realized was a supremely foolish question. But it was the right question. "Why have you come?"

"I've been looking for you."

"But why?" he asked in a trembling voice, still confused by the unreality of the moment.

"I could never forget loving you," she said, her voice hardly more than a whisper. "I had to come back and try to find you."

In the fading light he could see that her hands were shaking, her lips trembling. "I love you so much I could never forgive myself for leaving you, Richard. I have been following you just as you had followed me. I went back to the island and you were not there. Minos said you had left and were going back to America and my heart broke again. And I immediately hated myself more than ever for leaving you." She stopped, afraid to say more.

EIGHTY-NINE

Richard wanted to say something, but everything he thought of sounded macho, foolish and even heartless. And he chose to remain silent.

"Somehow I knew you had not gone back to America," her sad voice was hardly more than a whisper. "At least not yet. I don't know how I knew it, but I just knew. I felt it here in my heart in the same place where my love for you has always been.

"But I didn't know where to look. So at first I went back to Prague but I couldn't find you there. Then I thought of Paris because I remembered how much you loved it. So I went to Vienna planning to change to a train for Paris. But suddenly it came to me. It's not far to Vernazza from here! Why not try there first? It was our most favorite place in all Europe. And here you are. It is so utterly, fantastically unbelievable. And I still cannot believe that at this very moment you are here, and my heart is about to explode with joy. That is," she added quietly, her voice quickly dropping with a pitiable question, "if you want me back?"

He said nothing, breaking her heart with his silence. But the silence was awe mixed with disbelief, not rejection.

"When I saw Giorgio he was so glad to see me," she hurried on, "and he hugged me and he told me you had asked for our old room, number eleven on the top floor. The one with the sea view we loved so much, and that gave me hope. Do I have reason for hope, Richard?" she asked as timidly as a schoolgirl asking for a favor, "After what I have done to you? After leaving you a second time? Do I have any reason for hope?"

He stood motionless, still rooted to the spot, saying nothing, still afraid like before that if he moved any closer she might disappear. Could this be another dream? With his mind in a whirl, his heart skipping crazily, he finally managed to say very slowly, "Yes, Helga, you do have reason for hope. My love for you that is still here," he touched his chest over his heart, "tells me you have reason for hope."

He took a step toward her and opened his arms and she flew into his embrace, her face aglow with love. And his aching heart, speechless with wonder, drew her in and absorbed her into himself where she would always be; where they would always be together as one. Each of them was crying, sobbing their hearts out. But their sobbing was unbelievably joyous. And now, at this very moment, holding her in his arms, his feelings of exhilaration were as high and intense as his feelings of loss and defeat had been earlier. Only hours ago. Just minutes ago, really. And he knew with a certainty as clear as a wish miraculously granted, his search was at an end.

"My handkerchief!" she exclaimed when he tried to dry her tears with it. "Where did you get it?"

"I've kept it ever since the day you left the island. It became a part of you and I have never let it out of my sight. It has been with me wherever I have gone."

She smiled a shy, grateful smile but her heart was already singing a new song she had never heard before; a song of thankfulness for a new gift of love even greater than that which she had known before.

For a long time they sat very close together on the stone wall holding hands and watching the sea even after the sun had gone down, each clinging to the other as if still afraid to let go. The sky was streaked with afterglow leaving happy memories on the clouds as if not wishing for the day to end for this loving couple. Darkness crept closer, no longer fearfully, but now on the wings of hope, and the light from the fading sunset danced little miracles in their eyes.

"Helga," he finally managed to say, putting his arm around her and pulling her closer, "I love you so much. My world ended when you left the island."

"Before the ferry even got to Piraeus," she answered sadly, "I knew I had made a terrible mistake. But I made myself go on back to Prague to think and to decide what I must tell you if I could ever find you again. And how to tell you. And to beg your forgiveness."

Richard said nothing, sensing this was a crucial moment when she wanted to tell him something very important. Once again he wisely remained silent.

"Do you remember when we were talking at the cove on the island just before I left? And I told you there was something I didn't think I could bear? That I wanted to spare your feelings?"

"Yes, and I didn't understand. And you said you had written a letter to Bob Worley, and I didn't understand that either."

She told him about her visit to the doctor in New Orleans and his horrifying diagnosis. "I wanted to spare you the terrible experience of living through that with me. I love you so much I could not bear for you to have to see me that way."

"I'm not sure what to say," Richard whispered after a long pause. Then he said slowly and very deliberately, "The first thing to say is that I love you more than anything on this earth. And even as terrible as what you have just told me will be, it would be ten times more terrible for me if I were not with you."

"Richard, you are so wonderful!"

"No, I'm not at all. I'm just a man who loves a special woman very, very much. I would never dream of leaving you."

"But the doctor says it might get very bad. It's possible I will become quite repulsive to look at."

"When that happens," he said quietly and very carefully again. "When it gets really bad I know it will be hard for me to take. I have to admit that. To see what it is doing to you and not being able to do anything about it. But whenever I think of how bad it might make me feel I will always remind myself how much more terrible is will be for

363

you. And I will gather you in my arms and hold you very tightly. And I will kiss your beautiful hair and make myself remember how much more difficult it is for you. And I will remind myself every day that you are still the wonderful woman I love. And I pray with all my heart I can be a comfort to you. Someone you can lean on without hesitation. Always. That is my solemn promise to you now and forever. I will always be there for you. You must lean on me, Helga. Promise me that. No matter what. No matter how bad it gets, I will always be there for you. Because I love you!"

"Yes, I promise," she said so quietly it was only a whisper and he believed her.

"But maybe there will be a cure," he said. "Or maybe it will go into remission."

After a long thoughtful pause, Helga said, "And maybe we will just learn to live with it."

"Yes, and that, too."

They were still holding each other very tightly, both their bodies trembling, both still afraid to let go.

"When you were about to leave the island Helga, you quoted something to me about loving someone. Something you had told me once before in Prague. I think it went something like this: *Whomever you love is alive as long as you are.* That person will always be alive in your mind, in your memory so long as you live. And I find that an incredibly beautiful sentiment and I have thought about it every day since you first quoted it to me.

"And now, I have one for you: *The people we love are the ones we can't live without.* I simply don't want to live without you, Helga. Ever. No matter what. I'm so glad you came back; that we have found each other again. And what a miracle that has been. I don't ever want to be alone again. Being alone was beginning to make me very nervous." They both chuckled with relief.

364

"Richard, you are so wonderful. I promise you will never have to be alone ever again. That I promise you with all my heart and soul."

"I thank you for that. But no, Helga, I am not wonderful. I think it was Helen Reddy who had a song a few years ago, *'I'm just a woman in love.'* Helga, my darling, I'm just a man in love."

After they had sat quietly for a long time saying nothing still holding each other very tightly in the gently approaching night, Richard finally said, "Tell me again where you went when you left our little Greek island."

"I went back to Prague and stayed there a week. Monika was so wonderful to me. She was such a pillar of strength for me to lean on. And I talked with my friends at the pastry shop. They all understood the horror I was facing and how I wanted to spare you. But they all said the same thing. That I was being unfair to you. They said I should tell you and let you decide what it was you would want to do. That it was not fair for me to decide for you. Bettina and Monika both understood. And Bettina said it best. 'Go back to him and explain. Tell him how it is likely to be. I think he will understand. I have never seen a man who loves a woman as Richard loves you. Go find him Helga before it is too late.' And she was right."

Richard pulled her close, feeling the happy thudding of her heart against his chest. Paradise has returned to me in this golden sunset, he whispered to himself. Without my earning anything at all it has returned to me in the form of a red-haired angel, and I am breathless with wonder. Could this be a spirit, an apparition sent to tease me, to confuse me? But no, it really is her!

NINETY

The next day after lunch on Giorgio's terrace they cautiously began talking about the future. Helga broached the subject first. "When do you think we should plan to go back to New Orleans?"

"Never."

"What?"

"I called Bob Worley late yesterday evening. He told me about your letter. He was devastated for you but I told him you were back and that I already knew. And he was very happy that we had found each other again." He paused, wanting his news to be clear and unmistakable.

"I told him I was resigning my position at Tulane."

"What! But how will you live? How will we live?"

"I have been at Tulane long enough to have a small retirement pension. And I have quite a bit of money saved up and I have the house on Pine Street, and also I own a rather valuable piece of property in Raleigh, and I can sell them both. Maybe after a while we can head back to Prague and see if I could get a job teaching at Charles University. Or maybe at some language school there."

"Or," Helga said, looking around at their favorite little Italian village, "maybe we could open our own language school here?"

"Yes, I think I would like that even better. And Helga, there is something else," he said, pulling her in his arms.

"Yes, Richard, darling?"

"Will you marry me? Now? Here in Vernazza?"

"But what about my . . ." she couldn't finish her sentence. "My future?" she tried again. "What if *it* happens soon?"

"What is that quotation we hear sometimes? *One crowded hour of glory is worth an age without a name.* We'll live as if we were only twenty-one like we said that time in Paris. We'll embrace life to the fullest and never look back. We'll live every day as if it were our last. And I will be there with you. That's my solemn promise to you. Now and forever."

And taking her hands in his he repeated firmly but with remarkable love and tenderness: "Helga, my darling. Will you marry me?"

Helga, tears streaming down her face answered breathlessly, "Yes, my darling Richard, I will."

"There's one more thing, Helga. Will you have my child? Our child?"

"Oh, yes, yes, yes!" she said, her heart near to bursting with joy.

367

Made in the USA
Charleston, SC
07 August 2014